Praise for

Sunshine Nails

"A phenomenal debut. This page-turning story about the Tran family's desperate attempts to keep their nail salon in business will have you rooting for them as often as you shake your head. A delightful romp, with keen social commentary and writing that simply sparkles."

Carley Fortune, *New York Times*
bestselling author of *Every Summer After*

"Full of zany, hilarious fun . . . *Sunshine Nails* made me laugh, cry, and think deeply about culture, family, and the ties that bind. What a witty and engaging debut—I was thoroughly charmed!"

Marissa Stapley, *New York Times* bestselling
author of the Reese's Book Club pick *Lucky*

"Filled with heart and humour, *Sunshine Nails* is an insightful, moving story with striking depth, taking on gentrification, family expectations, and generational differences. You will be rooting for the Tran family through every risk and sacrifice they make to save their salon and, ultimately, themselves. Mai Nguyen has proven herself to be a real standout."

Taylor Jenkins Reid, *New York Times*
bestselling author of *Carrie Soto Is Back*

"A whip-smart and hilarious David-versus-Goliath romp. The Tran family will have you biting your nails as they claw at their competition and each other. Will they survive? Or will they lie forever in the proverbial nail bed that they made? But the Vietnamese diaspora will always find their way back home—even if they lose an eyelash or two along the way."

Carolyn Huynh, author of Good Morning
America Book Club pick *The Fortunes of Jaded Women*

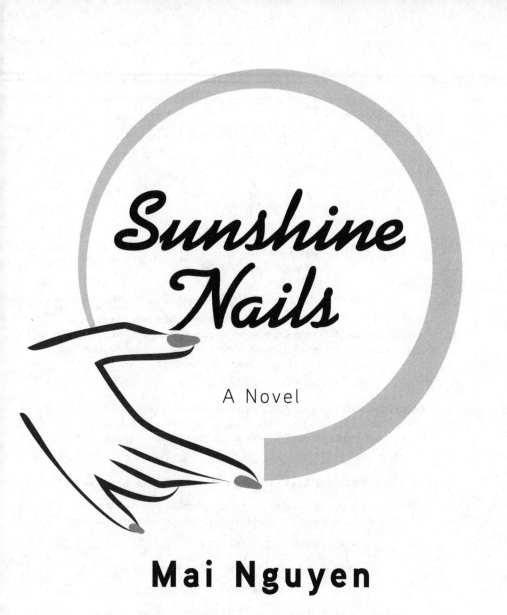

Sunshine Nails

A Novel

Mai Nguyen

Published by Simon & Schuster
New York • London • Toronto • Sydney • New Delhi

SIMON &
SCHUSTER
CANADA

Simon & Schuster Canada
A Division of Simon & Schuster, Inc.
166 King Street East, Suite 300
Toronto, Ontario M5A 1J3

This Simon & Schuster Canada edition July 2023

SIMON & SCHUSTER CANADA and colophon are trademarks of Simon & Schuster, Inc.

For information about special discounts for bulk purchases, please contact Simon & Schuster Special Sales at 1-800-268-3216 or CustomerService@simonandschuster.ca.

Interior design by Dana Sloan

Manufactured in the United States of America

1 3 5 7 9 10 8 6 4 2

Library and Archives Canada Cataloguing in Publication

Title: Sunshine nails / Mai Nguyen.
Names: Nguyen, Mai (Journalist), author.
Description: Simon & Schuster Canada edition.
Identifiers: Canadiana (print) 20220454205 | Canadiana (ebook) 20220454213 |
ISBN 9781668011256 (softcover) | ISBN 9781668011263 (EPUB)
Classification: LCC PS8627.G88 S86 2023 | DDC C813/.6—dc23

ISBN 978-1-6680-1125-6
ISBN 978-1-6680-1126-3 (ebook)

For Gemma,

my little sunshine

CHAPTER ONE

Debbie

I f Debbie Tran could go back in time, she would stop herself from reading that damn Yelp review.

It had been such a lovely day up until that point. She'd made offerings of mandarins and daffodils to the altar, cooked all her family's favorites, and cleaned the entire house. In a few hours, her eldest child would be coming home for good. Nobody in the family knew exactly why, but it didn't take a genius to figure it out. Eight years ago, Jessica moved to Los Angeles for love and a job, and now she had neither. Whatever the reason, Debbie didn't care. She was so thrilled Jessica was returning that she happily paid for the flight.

Debbie pulled out her tablet and did what she always did whenever her children got on a plane: tracked the path of the flight. As she watched that little green plane inch closer and closer to Toronto, that's when that stupid notification popped up at the top of the screen.

You've received a new review.

Without thinking, Debbie clicked on it and a big fat one-star review appeared on the screen.

I came to the salon for a manicure and pedicure on the weekend. The
lady who was working on me was SO rude and she had disgusting
black gunk underneath her fingernails. They were so long and unkempt.
It was gross. She also cut my nails too short when I specifically told
her "not too short." She doesn't speak English that well so she probably
didn't understand me. Still, SO UNPROFESSIONAL. I'm never going
back again!!! Can't wait till that new salon opens nearby. Bet it's light
years better than this one!

Debbie looked at her nails. Okay, so they were a little dry and her cuticles
a little overgrown, but by no means was there any "disgusting black gunk"
underneath her nails. She washed her hands so often that cracks had formed
on her fingertips. Besides, in her twenty years of running the salon, not one
single person had ever complained about this.

And what was this about a new salon? There was no other nail salon in the
area for miles. This person had to have been mistaken. Debbie checked their
overall rating. The review dropped Sunshine Nails from four stars to three stars.

That bitch.

She checked the flight status again. Jessica's plane was going to land any
minute now. It would take her another hour or so to get through customs,
baggage claim, and traffic on the highway. Phil and Thuy were still at the salon.
Dustin would be home from work soon. She needed to fix herself up. Wash
her hair, put on some makeup, pick an outfit that—

Not too short? How dare that person assume she didn't know English.
She'd lived in Toronto for over thirty years, took ESL for those first two, and
aced all the tests. In fact, she did so well she was invited to come back as a guest
speaker to show the new cohort what a success story she was. Too short? Next
time that woman came into the salon Debbie would show her what too short
really looked like.

It wasn't like Sunshine Nails had never gotten negative feedback. They'd
been slammed on everything from the decor ("A bit tacky but in a charming
kind of way") to the lack of air-conditioning ("Felt like I was stranded in the
Arabian Desert!") to the service ("The staff was impersonal and abrupt").

But there was a difference between constructive criticism and personal attack. And this latest review was clearly an attack on their livelihood.

Debbie was just glad her husband didn't see it. Phil got even more worked up over these things than she did. Once, he stayed up until three in the morning responding to every single negative review he could find. They were not professional or eloquent responses by any measure, but they had worked too hard, sacrificed too much, to let some ungrateful people get away with saying nasty things about their salon.

Debbie looked at herself in the mirror. She couldn't greet her daughter like this, all angry and a mess.

A bath. That's how she would calm down. She wasn't going to let this review suck all the joy out of this special day. She didn't even remember working on someone named Erin. Maybe it was one of those internet phenomena Dustin had warned her about. What was it again? A troll. Yes, that must be it. It had to be a troll.

While soaking in the tub, she thought about all the times she felt wronged in her life. There were too many to count. Bloodthirsty communists forcing her out of Vietnam was one. Being thrown onto a perilously overcrowded boat on the South China Sea was another. This one-star review? It was up there, too.

As she sank a little deeper into the warm bath, she turned her white jade ring round and round on her finger. That ring was as much a part of her body as her organs. It never left her hand, not since that treacherous voyage of 1983. When those pirates ransacked the boat and abducted the prettiest girls, Debbie instinctively tucked the ring underneath her upper lip and prayed the pirates would see her simple, undecorated body and leave her alone. They took one look at her, spat on her face, then moved along. To this day, Debbie swore the ring saved her life all those years ago. Tonight, she prayed it would bring her the peace she needed in time for her daughter's homecoming.

As her calluses began to soften in the warm water, so did her resolve to punish whoever this person was. She closed her eyes and focused on her breath. In and out. In and out. She tried very hard to let nothing and nobody penetrate her thoughts now.

But Erin's words were like a hangnail that wouldn't go away. She couldn't let it go. How could she when it felt like someone had just shit on everything she'd worked so hard for? Debbie sat up straight in the tub, reached for the tablet, and typed up a response.

> I have never met you before in my life. This review is a complete fabrication. Furthermore, we have never once had a complaint about our staff's hygiene. We take very good care of our customers and take their concerns seriously. You, however, are a liar and you should be ashamed of yourself. P.S. How is my English now?

As soon as she hit that publish button, she felt euphoric. Then came the notification. Jessica's flight had landed.

CHAPTER TWO

Jessica

According to her phone, Jessica was sixteen minutes away from her parents' house. She shifted in the back of the cab, praying for road closures or heavy traffic, anything that would stretch those sixteen minutes to infinity. She knew the moment she got home she'd be blasted with questions: Why are you home? Why did you and Brett break up? Why did you lose your job? Why is your hair like that? Actually, she could handle that last question. In fact, if all they grilled her about was her new blond hair, she would consider the night saved.

She peered over at the meter. Fifty-six dollars and counting. Her parents insisted on picking her up at the airport, but she insisted harder on getting a cab. She probably should've said yes to the free ride, given there was a little under two hundred dollars in her bank account.

The money started dwindling four months ago, when she found her fiancé fucking a woman against their brand-new marble countertop. She froze. She didn't know what to do. What was the right course of action when the person you loved for eight years, the person you were supposed to marry in six months, was cheating on you? The only thing she could think to do was turn around, drive to the parking lot of a Trader Joe's, and cry and cry until the sun went down. She felt so stupid for spending thousands of dollars on that kitchen renovation. You don't get marble in a home you don't plan to die in.

In the following months, Jessica slept on a series of couches belonging to sympathetic friends and estranged cousins who felt obligated to host her. Brett didn't even beg her to come back. Didn't even beg for forgiveness. The last thing he said to her was that he'd take care of canceling the wedding, that she need not worry about a thing. And like an idiot, all she said in return was thanks, as if *he* was the one doing *her* a favor. That was the part that hurt the most.

How easily he had let go of her.

Jessica tried to pour all her energy into her job, but she couldn't even will herself to care about the casting career she admittedly prioritized over everything else. One morning, she went into the casting agency high on weed, hoping it would make the day go by faster. It didn't. It only made her brain foggy. When the casting director asked her to read a scene with an Oscar-winning actor, all she had to do was throw an apple across the room. Except she missed and threw the apple right in the actor's face. His glasses fell to the floor as he clutched his face hard, trying to keep the blood from gushing out of his nose. Jessica was fired before she could even say sorry.

That night, she drank an entire bottle of wine and stripped her hair from black to blond because she wanted to look as ridiculous as she felt.

"We're here," said the driver. "We got lucky. Hardly any traffic."

"Great," Jessica muttered. She took a quick glance at herself in the rearview mirror. The stale plane air made her hair stick up. She matted down the static, applied some lip gloss, and sprayed some rose water on her face before getting out of the car.

The two-story semidetached house looked exactly the same. Faded brick exterior. Peeling porch railing. Sagging wired fence. Everything around it, on the other hand, had changed. The newly renovated house next door looked out of place. With large black-framed glass windows that stretched all the way to the top, it looked like it could lift off and fly into outer space at any moment. The only sign of life was a flickering orange glow that spilled out of the windows, but she could see nobody inside.

Her father was the one who answered the door.

"You made it! How was your flight? How was your drive? Did he bother you? I saw on the news the other day that some drivers will take passengers on long roundabout routes to bring up their final fare. Did that happen to you? I told you I should've picked you up."

Her father looked the same, too. At five feet five, he was a soft man with droopy, mournful eyes and a gappy smile that reminded her of the fence slats in the backyard. His straight black hair was parted to one side, showing roots that were sparingly peppered with vermicelli-like hairs. He was sixty-two, but the years he spent working as a wood chopper in Nha Trang left his face a sprinkle of sunspots and a complex river network of sunken lines, which was why many people thought he was closer to seventy.

"You haven't changed a bit, Ba. And no, my driver did not scam me."

"Everyone's in the kitchen. Come inside."

"I'm just going to use the bathroom first."

It had been eight years since she'd stepped foot in her childhood home. And yet it took no time for that muscle memory to kick in. Her legs knew how to get to the bathroom. Her hand knew to hold the flush lever down for three seconds. Her ears knew to brace for that awful foghorn sound that happened every time the toilet flushed. It was comforting how so little had changed.

After greeting her mother and brother—both of whom stroked her hair like it was a new puppy—she took a seat at the dining table. Her head was pounding; she only had a glass of merlot and some overpriced Pringles all day. Fortunately, her mother made a feast: crab legs with ginger and scallions, barbecue pork fried rice, turmeric noodles with toasted sesame rice crackers, spring rolls, minced beef congee, crispy bánh xèo, and her favorite, bánh bột lọc, tapioca dumplings drenched in spicy fish sauce. Her mother need never say the words *I love you* because the proof was on the table.

"Who wants a drink?" said Dustin, his face already flushed. "Ba? Whiskey? How about you, Jess? Wine?"

Jessica probed her mother's face first, searching for a sigh, a scrunch of the nose, any sign of disapproval. Then she remembered she was not twenty-two anymore. She was thirty, a grown woman who didn't need to hide her drinking from her parents anymore.

"Give me a Corona," Jessica said. "Extra cold, please."

She caught her mother shifting her eyes down to the new tattoo on her thigh. It looked as if she was having a series of mini heart attacks. The tattoo was of the famous Trưng sisters wielding swords atop a pair of elephants. The two Vietnamese warriors used their skills in martial arts and swordsmanship to rebel against the Chinese overlords and become queens of the land. Jessica thought they were the most badass duo east of the Mekong. It wasn't until a week later, when the scabs began to fall off her skin, that she found out the Trưng sisters eventually accepted defeat and drowned themselves in a river.

Her father stood up and raised his glass. "Welcome home, my daughter! My heart feels full now that both of my children are home."

Everyone raised their glass, even her mother lifted a cup of tepid water. She ladled the congee into four small bowls, giving Jessica a little more than everyone else, and sprinkled scallions over the top. "Ăn, ăn. I bet you haven't had a proper home-cooked meal in months," she said.

Jessica slurped the rice porridge, being careful not to burn the tip of her tongue in the haste of hunger. The carbs and salt were already easing her headache.

"Thanks for cooking all this, Má."

"More, more. Look at those skinny arms. I could practically break them. Ăn cho no, Bích."

Bích? Jessica hadn't heard her real name in years. She changed it when she was eight after kids kept taunting her and calling her a bitch. "It's pronounced *bick*!" she would routinely shout on the playground.

Her mother was against the change because she named her after her lucky jade ring, but Jessica didn't care. All she wanted was a normal name. Ashley, Emily, and Jennifer were all contenders—names of likable white girls she knew in real life or on TV. But when the *Sweet Valley High* series debuted in the fall of 1994, introducing the world to those beautiful twins, she decided to go with the name of her favorite Wakefield.

Besides, her parents were ones to talk. They, too, went by English names to make it easier on their customers. Tuyết and Xuân were now Debbie and Phil, named after their favorite eighties singers, Debbie Harry and Phil Collins.

After five more helpings, Jessica's headache was gone, replaced by indigestion. "Seriously, there's too much for the four of us," she said, rubbing her stomach.

"Thuy was supposed to be here," Debbie said, pushing the plate of dumplings towards her. "She wanted me to tell you sorry that she couldn't be home for dinner."

"Thuy?" It completely slipped Jessica's mind that her cousin from Vietnam was now living here.

"You don't remember? Trời ơi, didn't we tell you? Our sponsorship application was approved and she has been living with us for the last ten months. It was such a painful process, all that paperwork and waiting, but now that it's all over with, it was the best decision we ever made. She's been a huge help at the salon. Isn't that right, Phil?"

Her father nodded gently. "We only trained her for a month, and she picked it up just like that," he said, snapping his fingers. "I don't want to brag or anything, but her work is the best in the city. The best! Look at these pictures."

He took out his phone. "Your uncle told me she was artistic, but I didn't believe it until I saw it with my own eyes."

For the next thirty minutes her parents raved about Thuy. How she could transform blank nail beds into mini-paintings worthy of their own spot in an art gallery. How she became the most requested nail technician in the salon. One of her designs—a supposedly mesmerizing speckle of stars set against a galaxy backdrop—was featured in a national fashion magazine one time. Jessica couldn't help but notice her mother repeat this fact three times during dinner.

"That's nice." Jessica wiped her mouth. "Where is she anyway?"

"She had to work late at the salon," said Phil. "A customer wanted 3D bows attached to her nails at the last minute. You wouldn't believe how happy I was to hear that! I've had a set of acrylic bows sitting in the back for months, just waiting for someone to request them one day."

Jessica peered over at the clock. It was almost nine o'clock. "Does she always work this late?"

"You think that's late? Just wait until prom season. In a few weeks, we'll be lucky if we get home before eleven," Phil said, stretching his neck.

"She's been working really hard these days. Why don't we give her the day off tomorrow, Phil?" Debbie said. "Jessica, you should spend some time with her, get to know her better. She's shy and doesn't have any friends here."

Jessica quickly tried to think of an excuse, but none came to mind. "Fine."

The following hour went as Jessica had hoped with the conversation staying exactly where she wanted, on the surface. They gossiped about the neighbors. Ate. Talked about Dustin's job. Ate again. Complained about the rising cost of food. Ate some more. They moved between two languages like it was one. She tried to keep up, but her Vietnamese had gotten so rusty she had to constantly fetch translations on her phone.

Then it happened.

"How is Brett?" Debbie asked in English.

Everyone stopped chewing, or in Dustin's case, sucking the juice from his crab leg. Judging by the intensity of everyone's stares, it was clear they were heavily invested in this change of topic.

"I wouldn't know. We don't speak anymore," Jessica said, keeping her head down. What was she supposed to say? It was close to six in Los Angeles. He was probably picking his new girlfriend up from work, taking her home to *their* house, making her dinner in *their* twenty-thousand-dollar kitchen, pouring her a drink in one of *their* Williams Sonoma wineglasses.

Ugh.

She hated him. For cheating on her, yes, but mostly for the impudence to live his life just the way it was. Why did he get to keep everything while she had to upend her whole life? Every time she thought about that question, she felt hot with rage, but deep down she knew the answer. At the end of the day, it was easier for her to run away than fight to keep what was hers.

"What a shame to throw away so many years together," Debbie carried on. "You two made such a lovely couple, and so many people were looking forward to that wedding—"

"Má, stop."

"Are you sure you can't get back together?" Her eyes glimmered with sparks of hope. "He's such a sweet boy. I'm sure whatever it is you two fought about was simply a misunderstanding."

"Má! It's over. We're done!" Jessica snapped.

There it was. The worst kind of look a mother could give. Pity.

Jessica changed the subject. "Dustin, what about you, huh? You dating anyone?"

"Actually, I—"

"You know what, Jessica?" Debbie interrupted. A bulging vein suddenly appeared on her temple. "We are your parents. We gave you your life, so it's only fair that you let us know what is happening in it. One minute we were going to have a son-in-law and now we don't? Something is odd here. We have a right to know what happened. Will we ever get to see him again? Can't we talk to him one more time? Maybe we can change his mind!"

"Can we drop it? Please?" cried Jessica. "Ask me anything else. Anything!"

She regretted it the moment it came out of her mouth.

"Okay," said Phil. "What will you do for work?"

Jessica stabbed her dumpling with her chopsticks. "I'm still figuring that out."

"Why don't you come work at the salon?" he offered.

"Are you kidding me? Nope. No way. Absolutely not!" They may as well have asked her if she would like to jump off a cliff or eat a tarantula.

"I'm not saying you have to work there forever," he said in Vietnamese, slowing down his words so that she could understand what he was saying. "You could come in a few times a week. We'll teach you the basics and little by little you'll learn enough to start doing manicures and pedicures. Just like your cousin. Summer is a very busy time for pedicures. You can make a couple hundred bucks a day. And your English is so much better than ours. I bet you would make really good tips. You know how these customers are, always so chatty and wanting to talk all the time." He paused to bite on a sesame cracker. "Besides, what else will you do?"

"I'm going to find something," said Jessica. "It's Toronto. It shouldn't be too hard to find a casting job here."

Everyone went silent. They were all betting against her; she was certain of it. Could she blame them? She hadn't exactly given them many reasons to believe she was the type to commit to something. After graduating with an economics degree, she worked a series of jobs that had nothing to do with mathematics or statistical theory. First it was interior designer, then wedding photographer, art gallery sales associate, floral designer, public relations account manager, and finally casting associate. This last one, she was sure, was going to stick.

No one had said anything for a while. Only the sound of spoons clattering against bowls and mouths slurping up soup offered some reprieve.

"You should take Thuy to the Islands," Dustin finally said. "It's been so cold that we haven't had a chance to take her there but now that it's getting warmer, why don't you two go? She's always talking about how she misses the beaches and greenery of Vietnam."

Jessica swallowed her beer and mouthed the words *thank you* to her brother. "Good idea. I'll do that."

Phil cleared his throat. "Like I mentioned," he said, "if you can't find work, you can always work at the nail salon."

Jessica rolled her eyes. She didn't have the heart to tell him the truth. To her, hunching over the hands and feet of strangers was the type of work relegated to immigrants who had scant education and abysmal English—people who saw the service industry as their only ticket to financial salvation. No offense to them, but she was above that.

"Just promise me you'll consider it," Phil asked.

"Fine, I will," Jessica lied.

Just as the night was ending, her mother announced there would be a party at their house in a couple of weeks. It was the Trans' quarterly gambling night, an event where dozens of people would descend upon their house for a night of risk and reward. Jessica could feel the contents of her stomach gurgling as she realized that every person who showed up would see what a loser she had become. The eldest Tran child—who once brushed shoulders with A-list celebrities and was about to get married against a jaw-dropping view of the Pacific Ocean—was now broke and broken up with. It was too much to bear.

She lifted the lid from the pot of rice and allowed the mushroom cloud of hot steam to engulf her entire face.

CHAPTER THREE

Dustin

Y ou do realize everyone could smell this shit on you all night, right?"
Dustin scolded his sister as he lit up a day-old blunt covered in lint. After their parents went to bed, they snuck out to the front porch and kept the lights off, relying on what little illumination they could get from the street-lights.

"Fuck. Was it that bad?" Jessica exclaimed, taking the blunt from him and inhaling deeply.

"Quiet! You'll wake them up," Dustin hissed. "Ba was oblivious, as always. But you can't get anything past Má." He leaned over to take back his joint. "Especially not that huge tattoo on your leg! Was getting *murdered* part of your plan tonight?"

Jessica scoffed and crossed her arms. "What are they going to do? Get a scouring pad and scrub it off me? Come on, don't tell me you're still living by their rules."

"I'm not."

"Then why are you whispering?" She snickered and blew smoke directly in his face.

The familiar fuzziness washed through him as he looked straight ahead at the street. The fact that he was different from his sister was the most basic truth of his existence. Jessica always gave in to every instinct without any thought to how other people felt, whereas he mulled over all the possible consequences of his actions. Being the one no one had to worry about was something he used to pride himself on. Now that Jessica was home, he wondered if his dutiful nature would suddenly seem like a lack of selfhood in his parents' eyes.

"So," Dustin continued, "are you waiting for me to ask or are you gonna tell me?"

"Tell you what?"

"Tell me the meaning of life."

"What?"

"You idiot! Tell me why the hell you're suddenly home! I thought you had a whole ass life in L.A. What the hell happened?"

His sister waited a while before opening her mouth. "Asshole."

"Excuse me?" Dustin wrinkled his nose.

"Not you. Brett. He's an asshole."

"You just realized that now? The dude has an oversized spoiler on his car." They both burst out laughing before quieting to a soft rumble.

"You were right," Jessica said under her breath. "I should never have gone to L.A. I'm a mess. I have no job, no money. I've been gone so long I barely understand them when they're speaking Vietnamese." She pointed her finger towards their parents' bedroom. A single tear streamed down her face.

Dustin said nothing. What could he say? That he told her so? That wouldn't be fair. After all, the most advantageous thing about being the second child was getting to watch your sibling make dumb mistakes so that you knew exactly what not to do.

This was why he still lived at home, stockpiling his savings until he had enough to buy his own place. Why he was still single, having ended every potential relationship at the first sign of trouble. Why he was still working at the same tech company after five years, knowing the job market was too volatile. Call him boring, but at least he wasn't the one crying in the dark on a sad little porch.

"It will pass," Dustin offered. He knew it was a weak sentiment, but it wasn't like he could've said anything to make her sadness go away. If there was anything he knew for sure, it was that feelings were temporary. He tucked the roach away in a baggie, and the two retreated back to the house, where they sprawled out on the sectional as the late-night news roared to life.

"At least there's that big party to look forward to, right?" Dustin half joked, knowing it was the last thing his sister wanted to think about. Having your life and looks scrutinized by obliviously rude aunties was bad enough, but he'd been to enough of these parties to know no matter how bad it was for him, it was ten times worse if you were a girl.

"Maybe you'll get lucky and they'll set you up with a good Buddhist boy, someone who can finally teach you how to keep a man."

Jessica kicked him so hard in the shin that he yelped in pain. Guess he should've seen that coming.

"You never answered my question from earlier," said Jessica.

"About what?"

"Your dating life."

He shrugged. "Still as single as a single bed."

"Come on, really? You're smart, nice, and you smell somewhat decent."

Dustin laughed with her. He had been told he was attractive, what with his thick, floppy hair, chiseled jawline, and lips that always seemed to be half-puckered. But he never could see what everyone else saw.

"Well, actually . . ."

"I knew you had a girlfriend! Who is she?"

"She's not a girlfriend. She's a . . . crush."

"A crush? What are you, twelve? Ask her out, dimwit!"

"It's not that easy! She just started at the company and . . ."

"And what?"

"I've literally said two words to her. I bet she doesn't even know my name."

"Oh for fuck's sake! You are twenty-eight! Pick up your balls and ask her out!"

Dustin sighed. He was never the spontaneous type. Every move he made had to be carefully calculated and well executed. But he knew she was right. God how he hated her for it.

Dustin sat up straight and increased the volume on the TV. "Hold on, hold on. They're *still* protesting this shit?" On the screen were aerial shots of protesters in front of the *New York Times* office. The crowd was made up of mostly Asian women holding pink and green posters up to the sky.

NEW YORK TIMES COST OUR JOBS!
IMMIGRANTS WHERE CAN WE GO?
SWEEPING GENERALIZATION = BAD JOURNALISM.
SHAME ON YOUR NEW YORK TIMES, YOUR LIES KILL OUR SHOPS.

It had been a year since the two-part exposé on worker abuse at nail salons was published. Everyone in the community was talking about it. It was the first time mainstream media had paid this much attention to the nail salon industry. It wasn't the good kind of attention they were hoping for. The oppressively low wages. The exploitation of undocumented workers. The cancer risks! All of it was horrific. But the promise of legal protections appeared to be the one good thing to come out of it. Too bad it angered some nail techs, who said it unfairly painted the entire industry in a bad light.

"This protest is ridiculous," exclaimed Dustin. "If it weren't for that article, those poor workers would still be making thirty-five dollars a day under the table."

"But they have a point, don't they?" Jessica retorted. "What about the salons that did nothing wrong? It's not fair they got lumped in with all the bad apples."

"If they did nothing wrong, then what are they so worried about?"

"Um, their reputation? Their livelihood? I personally think the story went too far. How can you say the vast majority of nail salons is exploiting its workers? I was at a restaurant in L.A. and overheard two women talking about it. You know what one of them said? She said she puts the tips directly in her manicurist's pockets now because she doesn't want the manager to steal it. She thinks every immigrant-owned salon is run by crooks!"

Dustin could talk about this for hours. For someone who didn't even work in the industry, he had a lot of opinions. A reckoning was afoot. Public opinion was shifting. Nail salons had to pivot to survive. For years he'd been pushing his parents to renovate their salon, switch to cashless payments, and ramp up their social media. Anything to barrel it towards the future. But they kept resisting change. To them, nothing was broken if everything was working. Every time he brought it up, he was told to back off.

He couldn't help it. Maybe it was because he worked for a large tech company. Moodstr was constantly being optimized and always getting bigger. It was drilled into the ethos of the company. There was even a massive quote on the wall: "If you're not growing, you're dying." In Dustin's world, standing still wasn't an option. And it seemed as if Sunshine Nails had been standing still for a while. He didn't want to see his parents lose something that meant so much to them. Growing up, it was very much understood that the salon was like their third child. He felt an obligation to protect it like it was his baby sibling.

Maybe he was worrying for nothing. They'd been doing just fine for the last twenty years. What could possibly go wrong now?

Dustin looked over at his sister. She had fallen asleep with her mouth wide open. He shut off the TV, turned off the lights, and headed upstairs to bed.

CHAPTER FOUR

Phil

Phil blasted the air conditioner in the car, even though the drive to the salon was only fourteen minutes. As May stepped into June, summer was revealing itself to be like all the others in the past: hot and relentless. People of the city were swapping their cottons for linens, their thick creams for lightweight gels, their slacks for anything (anything!) that would catch the momentary relief of a breeze. It was the kind of hot day when public libraries became cooling centers first and havens of literature second.

Sunshine Nails was not one such place where one could go to cool off in the city. Sure, there were humming, oscillating fans in every corner of the salon, but all they really did was move dust-filled air into more dust-filled air.

Phil had been meaning to install an air conditioner since the salon first opened in the Junction in 1997, but there was always something that needed the money more: The motors in the pedicure chairs had to be rewired; the leather chairs were starting to crack; the ventilation system needed an upgrade; and so on and so on until it was now 2016 and the salon still had no air conditioner.

That's not to say that things had never changed at Sunshine Nails. The faded beige carpet had been ripped up and replaced with porcelain tile, which made sweeping loose nail clippings a breeze. The Sony boom box that could only play one station—soft rock with the occasional hour of jazz—was replaced with a flat-screen television that could play a total of twenty-seven channels.

Though it was far from perfect, the salon was Phil's pride and joy. He was protective of it in the same way a bear was protective of her cub. He never felt this way about any of his previous jobs: dishwasher at a suburban Chinese restaurant, delivery driver for Swiss Chalet, janitor at a bank. Those jobs did not carry the respect and nobility attached to being an *entrepreneur*.

The first time he heard that word was during an overnight shift at the bank. It came from another janitor, Eamon Harsanyi, a fellow immigrant who liked to swear a lot. To this day, Phil still remembered what he said that night, which reframed everything he ever thought to be true about what kind of future he could have: "Why are we busting our ass making some rich guy richer when we can make ourselves rich?"

Since then, Phil promised himself he would no longer bend over for bad bosses. He became his own boss and opened his own nail salon. They grew their customer base slowly but steadily and eventually saw their profits go up and up. It was true what everyone said. There was no end to how much women were willing to spend to look good. Beauty, as it turned out, was recession-proof. For an immigrant with broken English, running Sunshine Nails was the best job he'd ever had and he was hell-bent on making sure no one pissed on his dream.

As expected, Allegra Jones sauntered into the salon at exactly ten o'clock. She was a Black woman in her forties with shiny braids that swept her shoulders. Ever since the salon opened, Allegra had a permanent appointment every other Thursday. She was Phil's favorite. Not because she consistently dropped at least eighty dollars on every visit—though that didn't hurt—but because she wasn't afraid to play with outrageous designs.

Once, she asked for a silver foil effect that made her nails look like tiny little mirrors. Some people thought it was too flashy. Phil thought it was perfect. Didn't they know that the highest class of China's Zhou dynasty wore elaborate nails dusted with gold and silver to symbolize their superiority? Or that Florence Griffith Joyner became the fastest woman in the world even with four-inch, tiger-striped acrylics stretching out from her fingers?

As Allegra plopped down on the swivel chair, Phil gasped. Three of her nails were broken and the polish was so chipped they looked like they'd been picked at by scavengers.

"Jesus, Allegra! Why are you always so rough on your nails?" Phil caressed her fingers as if they were little dead birds.

"I know, I know, but I had to help my boy with a science project. There was mud and iron oxide powder and vegetable oil everywhere! Can you believe the kinds of homework they expect us to help out with? Oh, it was a mess!"

Phil put on his glasses to further inspect the damage.

"How bad are they?"

"These all have to be removed. They are starting to yellow. See?" Phil turned on the lamp. "I can soak all these off and give you a whole new set. Only twenty extra dollars."

"*What?* It's not that bad. Can't you just replace the broken ones? They're going to be painted over anyway."

"Need to start from scratch. Won't look even. I can do for fifteen." Allegra might have been his favorite, but he was still a businessman.

Kiera, a part-time employee and student at the University of Toronto, overheard the conversation and peeked over at Allegra's nails. "It's going to look so much better if you get a new set," she confirmed.

Now Debbie had come over, laying a cup of freshly brewed coffee on Phil's table. "I agree. You'll be glad you got the full set."

Even Thuy chipped in. "No better feeling than fresh new acrylics."

Allegra chuckled. "I see what you're all doing. Just take care of the broken nails for now. I'll get a brand-new set next time."

"How about a strengthening base coat?" Phil asked, putting on his mask. "It's like vitamins for your nails."

"No thanks. You guys are too much."

One could not blame Phil for trying. Sure, a salon was supposed to be a sanctuary that left customers feeling relaxed, not emotionally abused and gouged of their money. Phil was aware that some salons operated on this philosophy, but he preferred to run his salon like a car dealership. The more you sold, the more you made. After all, business was business and you had to fight for every dollar you earned.

Still, he knew when to back off, especially with Allegra. She had a lot going on in her life. Her husband recently lost his construction job. Her mother had suffered a stroke and lost her ability to balance. If anybody needed to de-stress, it was her. And Phil was happy to give her that.

"How's your mother?" Phil asked as he drilled off the acrylics on her broken nails.

"Better," said Allegra. "I'm just so thankful she can still walk. She's still independent, but she's so stubborn. The other day I caught her trying to reach for a heavy bowl on a high shelf. I nearly screamed at her. *Momma, will it kill you to ask for help?*" She paused. "Could you drill those down shorter please?"

Phil stepped on the drill and the whole table began to vibrate. Nail dust danced off the table.

"That's good," said Phil. "You did the right thing, moving her back into your house. If only all children had that same sense of duty." He sighed, thinking about Jessica's aversion to working at the salon. "Kids these days. They think once they move out and have a life of their own they can forget about the parents that raised them. You ask them to do one little thing and they act like you just asked them to build a rocket ship. Who do they think gave them the life they have?"

"Kids are different nowadays," said Allegra. "They live in their own little individualistic world. They grew up with that 'put yourself first' mentality, you know? All the while paying no mind to what people around them want and need. Makes me worried for the future, frankly."

"Is your son like that?"

"God help me, he better not be! No way am I letting him turn into a selfish brat. I have to deal with bratty people at my job all the time. Imagine having to come home to that."

Phil didn't respond as he concentrated on laying down a coat of finely milled acrylic.

"You know," she said, lowering her voice so no one else could hear, "I think Lawrence is up to his sketchy tricks again."

"Sketchy?" Phil was unfamiliar with that word.

"It means shady, strange, things like that."

"Oh-oh. How so?"

"Last night, I tried to check his call history but he keeps his phone on him everywhere he goes. I mean, *everywhere*," she said, emphasizing each syllable. "He even takes it with him when he showers. I asked him, 'Why do you take your phone in there? Aren't you afraid of it getting water damaged?' and then he takes this Ziploc bag out of the drawer, plops his phone in it, and tells me 'Best invention ever, ain't it, babe?' I'm telling you, he's up to something. When I find out, I'm going to shove that plastic bag up his—"

Phil lived for this. These were the kinds of intimate details reserved for best friends and therapists yet *he* got to be privy to all of it. What was it about getting beautified that made women want to spill all their salacious stories? Over time he came to appreciate how incredibly lucky he was to be born a man. Being a woman came with so many burdens. It was no wonder they went to great lengths for beauty, for being beautiful was perhaps the only upper hand they were born with.

After the top coat had dried, Phil rubbed chamomile-scented shea butter on her hands, being careful not to smudge her incredibly iridescent talons.

"Wait, I meant to give this to you." Allegra reached into her purse and pulled out a rolled-up newspaper. "You know that store across the street that's been sitting empty? It's going to be a salon."

Phil's eyes widened. "A what?"

"A nail salon!"

Phil grabbed the newspaper from her. The article was buried on page L8 of the *Globe and Mail*: "Meet Toronto's Most Instagrammable Nail Salon."

"Keep the newspaper. I've gotta run." Allegra put on her sunglasses and rushed out the door. "See you in two weeks," she shouted from outside.

Phil looked down at the article. Above the fold was a photo of a salon with calm, Scandinavian sparseness: white walls, hardwood floors, hanging rope lights, rows and rows of succulents, and a light pink wall that served as a backdrop for photo shoots. Leaning against a slender table was a tall, white woman named Savannah Shaw, head of global expansion for Take Ten. Her wavy bob was as white as her jumpsuit. Her lips as red as blood.

Founded in 2014, Take Ten has gained cult status in New York City, where it launched before expanding to 24 locations, including Los Angeles, San Francisco, Miami, and Boston. This next-generation salon has won New York *magazine's "Best of Beauty" awards for the last two years, thanks to its chic decor, toxin-free products, and an overzealous obsession with hygiene that puts hospitals to shame. This fall, it will open its first-ever location outside the U.S. with a new 1,400-square-foot space in Toronto.*

If the beloved nail salon chain Take Ten continues to grow at the rate it's going, conventional nail salons might soon be put on the endangered list. The company received $12 million in funding in its first year, convincing venture capitalists to go all-in on its expansion.

Debbie came out from the back room and Phil quickly shoved the newspaper in the drawer. Phil did not tell Debbie about any of this. He simply put his head down and worked on the next customer, the whole time thinking, *This is not good.*

CHAPTER FIVE

Thuy

For someone who was nineteen years old, Thuy looked more like thirteen. It had its pros and cons. Con: The salon was accused of child labor on multiple occasions. Pro: She saved four dollars paying junior fare at the ferry terminal.

When the ferry docked at the island, Thuy and Jessica got off and walked towards Hanlan's Point Beach.

"Today would be ten months since I came to Canada," Thuy said.

"That's it?" Jessica said. "It feels like you've been here for much longer."

Thuy could never forget the night Phil called with news that her immigration application was approved. She was so excited she dug up her passport and fell asleep with it clutched between her hands. She called Phil and Debbie the next morning to tell them how grateful she was for the opportunity to start a new life in Canada, how she couldn't wait to see snow for the first time, how she always wanted to walk through a giant mall, how she was so excited to go to school and become a nurse, how she—

"Hold on, hold on, child," Phil had interrupted during their transatlantic phone call. "We only have enough money to feed you and keep a roof over your head. Maybe down the road we'll save up enough money for you to go to school, but in the meantime, you'll be working with us at the nail salon."

Thuy did not protest. How could she when her aunt and uncle had spent so much time and money helping her come to Canada?

Now that she was here, it was nothing like she imagined. She did not like the snow, because it came with crippling cold temperatures that hurt her cheeks and chapped her lips. She rarely got to go to the mall, because she was too busy working at the nail salon or doing her English homework.

At least she was good at nails. It was a small relief to have one justification for all the trouble she'd put everyone through to come here. Even *she* was surprised how easy it came to her. She could draw everything under the sun with the right paintbrushes and some imagination.

These days, everybody was obsessed with marble nail art. All it required was a light-as-air touch, just a simple glide of the black-dipped brush along the surface of the nail to create realistic hairline cracks. And yet, neither Debbie, Phil, nor Kiera could do it the way Thuy did it. One customer had the highest praise to offer: "You are the Monet of nails."

It was just too bad she wasn't making enough money to relieve her family back home of all their burdens, what with the three little sisters and four little brothers and Father's asthma problems and Grandma's dementia and the house that still had a hole-in-the-ground toilet. She could barely even afford the ferry ride, discount and all.

"Here we are," said Jessica. "This is my favorite beach in the entire city. Before I moved, this was where I spent all my free time, sunbathing with my friends, playing Frisbee, drinking homemade sangria." She spread down a blanket. "You don't mind the nudity, do you?"

The beach was clothing optional. Thuy had never seen so many naked people in her life. In fact, she had never seen a naked body, period. As Thuy rubbed sunscreen on her arms, she wanted to giggle and gasp at the same time. She couldn't help but stare at all the body parts. A pair of pendulous breasts mesmerized her for a good minute.

"Oh my god, stop staring!" Jessica hissed quietly.

"Sorry, sorry. I've never been to a place like this before!" Thuy put on her knockoff Fendi sunglasses. "There's no beach like this back home. It's practically a crime to wear a two-piece bikini unless you are a tourist."

"You're telling me there's no subculture of nudists in Vietnam? No way. I'll bet you fifty dollars there's an underground nudist community somewhere in that country." Jessica took a sip of the sangria she had quickly whipped up that morning. Thuy took a swig. She was no expert in alcoholic beverages, but she was pretty sure this was all wine.

"Maybe," said Thuy. "Attitudes are changing but very slowly. The government has finally allowed some nude photography to be displayed at museums, but many authorities still think it's pornographic." Thuy whispered the last word and cupped her mouth.

"It's okay." Jessica laughed. "There's no undercover communist spy eavesdropping on us."

"My mother would have a heart attack if she were here right now."

"I bet she would." Jessica tucked her hair back in a bun. "Pass me that magazine."

Thuy pulled out a thick glossy magazine from one of the tote bags and placed it in front of Jessica. There were many words printed in big bold letters on the cover. She was only able to make out one headline: "Feel Better about Your Body Right Now."

She badly wanted to ask Jessica if she could read the story for her. For as long as Thuy could remember, she never liked her body, never sought pleasure in its image. It was always too bony, too lanky, too skinny, too something. She'd gained twenty pounds since coming to Canada, but she still felt like a stick.

Her skin was another insecurity. She suffered an unrelenting bout of acne that left her forehead peppered with dark spots. Realizing she couldn't find Pond's Flawless White lightening cream anywhere in the city, she cried on the phone to her mother, begging her to ship a few jars to Canada. She said no; the shipping fees were equivalent to her monthly income.

Thuy peeked over at her cousin. So this was *the* Jessica, the daughter who lived in Los Angeles and had a glamorous job and a glamorous house and a glamorous fiancé. Thuy had heard so much about her since she moved here. It was all Phil and Debbie could talk about. Jessica met Tom Cruise! Jessica's house has a double shower! Jessica's engagement ring is the size of Jupiter! With all the hype, Thuy thought Jessica was a goddess, but the sight of her in the flesh was underwhelming. She had barely any makeup on, her hair was tied up in a messy bun, her thighs were mottled with cellulite, and one nipple was pointing east while the other went south. So why did she look so confident in her body? Could Thuy learn to be this confident, too?

Jessica looked up from her magazine. "You can't be serious," she said. "Aren't you boiling in there?"

Thuy was blanketed in towels. From her milk-white toes to her long black hair, every inch of her body was shaded by Egyptian cotton.

"You look like a pile of laundry," said Jessica, attempting to yank one off.

"I don't want to get dark," she said.

"You can't hide from the sun forever."

"I don't want to show my skin."

"No one is even looking at you. Did you see those men over there with their half-erect Coke cans? They're all more interested in their own bodies than they are in yours."

"Maybe it's a natural thing for you to do, to show off your body like that. But it's not really who I am."

"Sweet pea, you're in Canada now. You're free to be whoever you want to be."

That's easy for you to say, she wanted to tell her cousin. Instead, she watched silently as Jessica rubbed coconut-scented oil over every nook and cranny of her body.

You're free to be whoever you want to be.

Thuy wondered if she could be like Jessica. The kind of daughter who drank beer, got giant tattoos down her leg, and vehemently said no when her parents asked her to work at the salon. Where she came from, this behavior would have warranted a public spanking in front of the entire village. And yet, a part of her wished she had a bit of that boldness.

"Fuck, I think I'm burning," Jessica cried out. She pressed her finger on her breast and watched as the white mark faded slowly back to pink. "Shit," she hissed as she put her shirt back on. "Do you think it'll fade in time for the party?"

Thuy snickered quietly. Her cousin had a nasty sunburn on the bridge of her nose and all over her chest. There was no way it would heal in time. "You look great."

She lay down on her towel and placed a hat over her face. It was her first lie in a very long time. And it felt good.

CHAPTER SIX

Dustin

ustin sat at the front of the streetcar like he always did on his way to work. He liked the front. It was peaceful and predictable, filled with harmless, curmudgeonly types who kept to themselves. Today was his five-year performance review and he needed to rehearse what he was going to say. *I'd like to bring up the topic of my salary . . . align my compensation with my value. . . . There hasn't been an adjustment since I started. . . .* By the time he reached his stop at Queen and Spadina, he'd gone over the spiel three times in his head.

The whole office was eerily quiet when he got in, save for a phone call going unanswered and an electric kettle bubbling to a stop. The entire staff of Moodstr was crammed inside the Sunset room. Half the staff looked irritated, the other half looked terrified.

"What's going on?" he asked a colleague.

"Emergency meeting. Didn't you get Chase's email?"

Dustin checked his phone. Nothing.

Chase Wakeman walked in. No hellos, no good mornings. Just got right to it. "It's come to my attention that some people have been abusing our after-hours open doors policy and using the office as a, um, shall I say, R-rated playpen? Now I don't need to delve deeper into why this is severely inappropriate on so many levels, but I'll say it once. If you see any suspicious activity taking place at work, please let me or Cindy know. If I find out this is still happening, there will be cause for immediate termination," Chase said firmly, to which everyone could offer no more than muffled laughs and shifty eyes.

Everybody was calling his bluff. The man wasn't the least bit concerned about his employees fooling around in the office. If Cindy from HR wasn't standing right beside him, he'd probably be high-fiving the offenders right now.

Dustin looked around. He bet it was Zoe Taylor and Miles Byrne. The other day he caught Zoe coming out of the men's bathroom pretending to have mistaken it for the women's. She would have been convincing had Dustin not walked in on Miles with his wrinkled slacks scrunched around his ankles, wiping his penis with a crumpled wad of brown paper towel. "Get out of here, man!" he said to a blushing Dustin.

As bodies flowed out of the room and the hushed speculations began, Dustin felt a hand on his shoulder.

"Hey! I need to bump up our meeting," said Chase. "Can you come to my office now?"

"Right, yes, of course. I'll be right there."

Crap. He wanted to go over his talking points one more time before the meeting. He only had one shot and he didn't want to screw it up. This was Chase fucking Wakeman after all. People paid five hundred dollars a pop to see this six-foot-five white Australian import get onstage and talk about the secret to finding happiness.

Dustin first heard of him six years ago when news reports leaked that Chase Wakeman was slowing down his speaking tour to start up a mystery company in Toronto. Dustin, along with hundreds of other people, sent in his thrice-proofed résumé, cover letter, and reference letters. But that didn't matter. Chase didn't care if someone changed majors three times or that they had never held down a job for more than six months. What he was looking for was not something that could be put on a list of accumulated experiences. What he was looking for was fit—and the only way to measure whether someone exuded the ethos of a yet-to-exist company was to meet every single candidate in person.

Of all of Dustin's most vivid memories—his first kiss, his first time driving a car, his first hangover—none were as clear as the first time he met Chase. He was in a lobby with at least thirty other people, all waiting to do their job interview. The room smelled of sweat, hair spray, and Davidoff Cool Water cologne. When a bespectacled assistant came out of the interview room, everyone sat up a little bit straighter. "It's your turn," the assistant had said. No one in the room was quite sure who she meant. "Mr. Wakeman would like to see *all* of you now."

Being interviewed in tandem with thirty other people was the last thing he expected. As soon as he sat down, the first thing Chase did was pull out an oblong item from his drawer, holding it from its stem. It was beet red with charred edges. Its exterior was shiny, like it was a papier-mâché model that had just been freshly glazed. "I want you to all take that paper pad underneath your seat and write down what this is."

Dustin looked around. Everyone looked dumbfounded. Was that a trick question or a signature Chase Wakeman icebreaker? They quickly scribbled their guesses on the notepad and revealed their answers. "To the ones who correctly answered that this is a cacao pod, the Amazonian fruit that I procured during my retreat in Peru, something that you would have known if you read my book, you've moved on to the next round. The rest of you can leave." Dustin was relieved. He'd read that book twice.

In the following years, Dustin rose up the ranks to become Moodstr's lead product developer. The mystery company, as it turned out, manufactured biosensors that tracked a user's electrodermal activity to monitor their happiness levels throughout the day. When the media got ahold of this news, Moodstr was simultaneously slammed and heralded. In the end, it didn't matter what the critics thought. Sales of the biosensors kept going up and up, and the staff ballooned from ten, to twenty, to ninety. This was yet more proof that Chase Wakeman was a genius and always had been.

Like everyone else who worked for Chase, Dustin succumbed to his magnetism and sheer brilliance. He admired him more than anyone else, so much so that he'd sometimes catch himself saying things that would never come out of his mouth. Chaseisms, as everyone called them. When a friend needed cheering up, he found himself saying these words verbatim: "It's up to you to harness the power that's within you."

Dustin was now standing in Chase's office. On the wall behind his desk were portraits of white men, living and dead, who Chase repeatedly name-dropped as the sources of his inspirations: Jack Welch, Richard Branson, Steve Jobs, Warren Buffett, Isadore Sharp.

"Have a seat," Chase said as he leaned against his spotless desk. "I'm going to keep this meeting short. You're an absolute fucking rockstar. You've been killing it here. Not much else to say. Just keep doing what you've been doing."

Dustin beamed. Now was his chance. He opened his notebook: . . . *took on more than has been expected of me . . . positive feedback from colleagues . . . researched my market value . . .*

"Listen, I think I know what you're going to ask," Chase said, "and I want you to know you're completely deserving of a raise, but now is not the right time. We've got something big in the works, I can't tell you what it is yet, but as a result there's barely any wiggle room in our budget right now. Trust me, if I could give you a raise, I would. You're one of my best guys. The absolute cream of the crop. No doubt about it. But when you find out why I can't right now, you'll understand."

Dustin was listening but he was distracted by a small nick under Chase's left nostril. That became all he could think about while Chase continued to explain why he wasn't going to get a raise.

"I want you to still feel like a valued employee here. Hang in there. You're doing such tremendous work. Truly tremendous. We wouldn't be where we are without you, mate."

Suddenly, Chase's cell phone rang and he launched off his desk to take the call.

Was the meeting over? Should he leave? Should he stay until the phone call was over? Dustin peered down at his notes. He was so embarrassed, embarrassed that he had jotted down three pages' worth of accomplishments, embarrassed that he ever thought he'd get what he wanted. This was the third time he'd asked for a raise and the answer was always the same: not right now.

He thought about quitting just then and there, but that damn practical brain of his ensured his mouth stayed shut. Dustin slid to the edge of his seat as his phone pinged with a notification from the Moodstr app: *You seem stressed. Try taking a long, slow breath in through your nose and holding it to the count of three. One ... two ...* He pressed ignore.

Chase was still staring out the window as his conversation segued into the sex scandal plaguing the office. It turned out Chase had found out about it from Francisco, the director of operations, who found out from Jeret, the overnight janitor, who found a used condom stuck to the side of the garbage can during his shift. Dustin was not surprised this kind of stuff went on. Chase might be a genius when it came to ideas, but when it came to managing people, he was like a dog trying to lay an egg. The company culture was akin to a college fraternity, except with cleaner clothes and nicer furniture.

Chase turned around and looked surprised to see Dustin still there. Guess the meeting was over.

Back at his desk, the first thing he did was google "what to do when you get turned down for a raise." He clicked on the first three sites that the search delivered, none of which gave solutions to his specific situation. Dustin closed the window and went to the kitchen to make himself a cup of coffee.

Mackenzie Sharma was standing in front of the toaster, spreading peanut butter on a sesame seed bagel. Mackenzie was new to the company, having joined four months ago. She was gorgeous, with big brown eyes, full pink lips, and a nose ring that drove him wild. She even smelled incredible, talcum powder with a hint of cinnamon. He thought about Jessica's advice and went for it.

"Hey," said Dustin. It was the third time he spoke to her.

"Oh, hey!" she said, turning around with one-half of a bagel in her hand. "That was a weird meeting, huh?"

"Yeah, I just hope they didn't do it on my desk."

Mackenzie laughed a delightful laugh. "Oh my gosh, gross! I didn't even think of that."

"How's your week—"

"Who did it?" said Mackenzie, giving him a calculated stare with those long-lashed eyes of hers.

"Oh." He gripped the back of his neck. "I'm just as clueless as you. Unless *you* know something?"

"No, no. But I saw you coming out of Chase's office. Thought maybe he might have told you something. That's why you were in there, right?"

Dustin placed a coffee pod in the machine. "Err, yeah but the guy is a closed book. Can't get anything out of him."

"Really? Even to you? You're like an OG around here," she said. *An OG who's severely underpaid,* he thought bitterly. His phone pinged again. It was the app, suggesting he listen to calming music. He put his phone on silent.

Mackenzie took a bite of her bagel and Dustin so desperately wanted to kiss away the sprinkle of seeds that were stuck to her lower lip. At least there was something about this job worth sticking around for.

"We were just going over production schedules, deadlines, things like that," he lied.

By Dustin's calculations, this was officially the longest conversation they had ever had.

A small group ambled into the kitchen. Mackenzie quickly grabbed the rest of her bagel and turned to leave.

"See you later, Justin."

Dustin clutched his heart. Close enough.

CHAPTER SEVEN

Debbie

For Debbie, the idea of luxury was not a mansion or a designer handbag. Luxury was having one day off to do whatever she well pleased. No customers to look after. No shop to keep clean. So simple, and yet it was all she longed for.

So when her first day off in who knows how long came around, she slept through the alarm, woke up around eleven o'clock, took a long shower, and spent a luxurious amount of time applying a soufflé blend of argan oil and shea butter to her entire body. She smelled heavenly.

Everything would have been perfect if she had the whole house to herself, but Jessica was home. She'd just come back from her job interview. It was her fifth interview this month and still not one job offer. Debbie couldn't understand why her kids were having such a hard time. Her daughter couldn't get a job. Her son couldn't get a raise. Wasn't a good education a sure ticket to success? Where was the better life that had been promised? The idea that she had sacrificed everything only for her children to still suffer horrified her.

But today was not the day to think such terrible thoughts. She patted on her skin care products, evened her complexion with a light layer of foundation, and sprayed herself with Elizabeth Arden's Red Door perfume, once on her neck, twice on her wrists, and a few times in the air to ward off evil spirits. That soapy rose scent always put her in a better mood.

For the rest of the day, she fought every instinct she had. Leave the laundry alone. Ignore the dishes piling up in the sink. Stay away from the stove. But Debbie couldn't help it. It felt good to be needed, to supply her family with freshly laundered clothing and cook them nourishing meals. Be more selfish, a friend once told her. But in her mind, doing those things *was* selfish. It gave her a sense of purpose and power. Ever since she turned sixty everyone assumed she needed help. Help getting out of the car. Help crossing the street. It was demoralizing. If she wanted to regain some dignity, she had to be more indispensable than ever.

Besides, she needed to get groceries for the big party this Saturday. She and Phil had been looking forward to it since the last party hosted by the Bùis. They won three hundred dollars at tiến lên and had a good feeling their winning streak was not over.

"Come to the farmers' market with me," Debbie shouted from the top of the stairs. She had recently discovered that you could bargain the price down at the farmers' market and no one would frown upon it like they did at the supermarket.

Jessica was sprawled out on the couch, buried under a blanket and a pink book called *Heartburn*. Debbie knew her daughter was still aching from the breakup and it pained her to see that. For Debbie, her children were like extra limbs. Whenever they hurt, she hurt, too. But my god, sitting on the couch all day was not going to do anyone any good. In one quick motion, Debbie yanked the blanket away from her daughter.

Jessica groaned, closing the book and wedging it between the cushions.

"Ah, so you're finished reading? Then you can come shopping with me."

Her daughter let out a guttural growl. It was only noon and her hair had already come undone, her makeup smudged all over the pillowcase.

"Don't make me go by myself. I can't carry all those bags around with my weak back."

Debbie's back was fine, perfect actually, but she knew how to draw pity out from her children like a tweezer to a splinter.

"I really don't want to be outside right now," Jessica moaned.

"Up, get up." Debbie began pulling on her daughter's leg. "You need to get some fresh air. You'll get sick breathing in this stale air all the time." She massaged her back and winced in fake pain for added effect. It worked. Jessica got up.

———

"So how did it go?" Debbie asked as they walked to the market.

"What?"

"The interview."

Jessica shrugged.

"Cheer up. I bet they liked you a lot, child. More than you think."

"The first thing they asked me was, 'Where are you from?'"

"That's good! That means they're interested in you!"

Debbie waited for her to respond, but she just shook her head and mumbled, "You don't get it."

She was right. Debbie didn't get it at all. She loved it when her customers asked her where she was from. Any chance she got to talk about how Saigon thrummed with feverish energy and how you could make a friend just about anywhere filled her with immense pride. Why that question filled her children with palpable discomfort never made any sense to Debbie. Maybe it never would.

The market was packed by the time they got to the park. Jessica made a beeline for the ice-cream stall. Debbie stayed put. The heat and crowd were nothing for her.

She weaseled her way to the front of a stall selling cucumbers of all shapes and sizes—long and straight, short and stout, curved and bumpy. She picked up five of the latter.

"Five dollars, sweetie," said the lady behind the table. Debbie had never been called sweetie before, especially not by a woman who looked two decades younger than her. Back in her country, this would have been grounds for a firm and ruthless lecture.

"Two dollars," Debbie said bluntly.

"Sorry?" she replied.

"I can pay two dollars."

The woman slowed her speech and enunciated her words. "Sorry, five dollars is already a good price for these. They're spray-free."

"Look at these," Debbie insisted, pointing at the rough bumps on the cucumber and the strange angles of their curves. "These are ugly. Nobody will buy these. That's why you still have so many left."

The young woman, whose forehead was now dewy from the thick humidity, looked incredulous. She glanced behind Debbie. There were at least four people standing in line, impatiently fanning away their sweat beads with whatever they could muster, be it a palm or a pamphlet. "Sorry, I can only sell these to you for five dollars, ma'am."

There. There was the magic word. Once Debbie was upgraded from a sweetie to a ma'am, she knew she had the upper hand. This was her opportunity to play one more card.

"Fine, I change my mind," she said as she exaggerated every single movement from putting down the cucumbers to zipping up her wallet to turning her body away from the stall—

"Okay, okay. Fine," the woman backpedaled. "You can have them for two dollars. Need a bag?"

Her family thought she went through a lot of trouble to save money, but saving a dollar here and there was one of the few ways she could feel in control. After all, she didn't have much control over anything that had happened in her life. The country she lived in was determined by a group of Canadian parishioners who offered to sponsor them. The job she had was carved out by a Hollywood actress named Tippi Hedren, who taught the first Vietnamese refugees how to do nails. If she couldn't govern such major aspects of her life, then she would seek rule in the small ways she could.

With a paper bag full of oblong victories tucked underneath her arm, Debbie walked away with her back straighter and her strides firmer.

That's when everything went black. A pair of clammy hands were placed over her eyes. They smelled like freshly picked lavender, calm and soothing like the voice that made itself known directly in her right ear.

"Guess who?"

Debbie immediately turned around.

"Angel!" Debbie took a few steps back just to make sure it was who she thought it was. It was Angel Võ all right. She used to be a regular at the Buddhist temple but stopped showing up after getting married and having a kid. Some said she became an atheist. Others said she converted to a different kind of religion: hawking dubious diet pills in a multi-level marketing scheme.

"I didn't know you came down to this area," Debbie said. "Don't you live all the way up north?"

Debbie wasn't sure why she asked. She knew exactly where Angel lived. How could she forget 76 Hedgewood Road in Hoggs Hollow? That detached brick house with the dramatic staircase and the double-sided fireplace and the outdoor pool with a rock waterfall. It had been several years since she was there for the baby shower of Angel's child, Coco, but she still remembered it as if it were yesterday.

"Sebastian and I just *had* to get out of the house," Angel said, pointing to her husband and daughter, who were standing in line for jam. It was strange to see Sebastian in a polo and khakis. The last time she saw him he was in a suit, at his law firm, where he graciously offered a free consultation for Phil's impaired driving charge. She waved sheepishly at him, embarrassed that he knew her family's humiliating past.

"We're upgrading all the bathrooms—*again*! I keep telling myself to wait just a few more months and then the dust and stinky men will be out of our house *forever*."

Debbie didn't know whether to congratulate or sympathize. *She* would have welcomed all that trouble if it meant she could finally get a faucet that didn't spray in every which direction.

"It will all be over soon. Just hang in there," Debbie said. She scanned Angel from head to toe. Angel was thin and willowy when Debbie last saw her. Now, she had filled out in her chest, cheeks, and lips. She was dressed like a teenager, with distressed denim cutoff shorts and a billowy, bell-sleeved white blouse. She was already nineteen years younger than her husband. Now she was practically a walking felony.

"Your English has gotten so much better since we last spoke!" said Angel. "Are you taking classes or—?"

"Thank you. Not really. Just talking more with my customers. Tiếng Anh có nhiều từ lạ," Debbie joked.

Angel looked confused, startled almost, as if she had not heard or spoken Vietnamese in a very long time. Debbie wouldn't be surprised if the woman had forgotten the language altogether. It'd been years since she'd been to the temple for a prayer session or even for Tết. "So, tell me everything. How are you? How is the salon these days? Summer been keeping you busy?" Angel asked, linking her arm into the crevice of Debbie's, causing Debbie's whole body to instinctively tense up.

"Good. The last two weeks of June were busy with prom and graduation. Young girls used to want short baby-pink nails. Now they all want long and pointy nails with diamonds glued on. It's *ridiculous*," said Debbie. Her cheeks immediately flushed. She'd only recently learned the word *ridiculous* from her kids along with a couple turns of phrases like "That is the worst" and "You've got to be kidding me." She prayed it didn't make her sound stupid.

"Oh, that reminds me," said Angel. "Did you see those protests on the news about that *New York Times* story? I have to say I agree with the journalist. It's absolutely atrocious how they treat those workers. Charging *them* to work there. Stealing *their* tips. Forcing them to work *twenty-four hours a day*. I keep thinking about the miscarriages those women had to suffer just so they could make, what, ten dollars a day? I can only imagine what years of inhaling all those fumes would do to your body. I can't stand the smell for *one second* let alone my *whole life*. No offense, but I've got to say it has changed my whole perspective about getting my nails done. You just never know what goes on in there."

Debbie tightened her jaw. How dare this woman insult her livelihood? It was bad enough to hear it from the media, but to hear it from a woman who sold weight loss shakes full of crap? She'd rather have her toenails ripped out one by one than listen to this.

"—and the coughs that went ignored for years turned out to be *lung disease!*" Angel carried on. "Did you know that was even possible? That the acrylic you are inhaling could cause *micro tears* in your lung tissue? I hope you're being careful, Debbie. Didn't I tell you it was not a healthy job? I'm sure I told you. Good money or not, it's simply not worth the risk to your health."

Debbie couldn't believe her. Yes, it was terrible what happened to those nail techs. But Debbie couldn't stand there and let Angel act all superior. She pulled away and pretended to check her phone. Where the hell was Jessica?

"I hear de Blasio is already raiding those people in Harlem," Angel continued. "It's about time they put a stop to this. Anyway, I'll send you a link. Fascinating read. There are translations in Spanish, Mandarin, and Korean . . . but *no* Vietnamese! What a mistake. We practically *own* the market!"

What do you care, you probably can't even read it anyway, Debbie thought. Was Angel always this infuriating? This must be what happens when people marry outside of their race and disassociate themselves from their culture and community. They sever their ties to their identity, then claim it back whenever it was convenient for them.

"Oh, I meant to ask about that new nail salon," said Angel. "It's right by you, right?"

"New salon?"

"Yeah, I'm certain it was in the Junction."

"I don't think so. You sure you're not thinking of someplace else?"

"Hmm, maybe you're right. I've been such a scatterbrain lately."

Debbie smiled weakly. This was the second time she'd heard of a new nail salon in the neighborhood. First that one-star review. Now this. Was there something she didn't know? Surely Phil would have told her. He knew everything that went on in the Junction.

"Hey!" Jessica finally appeared. Debbie considered making her escape right then, but of course Angel's attention was fully on Jessica now. For the next fifteen minutes, Debbie twisted the ring on her finger as she listened to them talk.

"Los Angeles! Wow! Can you believe I've never been there, like even once? What's it like?"

"It's all right. The weather is always nice."

"We're thinking of taking a family vacation there. You must tell us where to go. Now, do you think it's better to fly into Los Angeles first, or land in San Francisco and rent a car and make our way down? And do you think the scenic route is worth the longer drive? Oh, I hear that trip is breathtaking."

"There are tons of places you should check out. I can tell you more about it at the party this Satur—"

"Shoot!" Debbie interrupted, looking at her watch. "We have an appointment to get to."

The corners of Angel's mouth turned down. "Oh, that's too bad. Well, it was *so good* to run into you two." She beamed, revealing her gummy smile. "Oh, I almost forgot. Make sure you keep an eye out for an invitation in your mail."

"Invitation?" Debbie asked slowly.

Angel pressed her hands into her flowy shirt to reveal a slight protrusion of her belly.

"That's . . . *great!*" Debbie forced a toothy smile. "Congratulations!"

"I'm four months along! It's supposed to show much more with the second pregnancy, but my bump is not as noticeable this time around. Lucky me."

That explained the bigger lips and bloated face.

"Seriously? I couldn't even tell," said Jessica.

Angel beamed. "We've been trying for so long. We're just *so happy!*" Her eyes started to look glossy. "We hope you'll get to meet her when she's here. Both of you!"

"Of course." Debbie feigned a quick smile. "We'd be happy to attend. We really do have to get going though." Debbie pulled Jessica in the other direction. They walked and walked until they were a secure distance away from Angel.

"She seemed nice," said Jessica. "Did you invite her to the party?"

Debbie rolled her eyes as far back as she physically could. "Don't be ridiculous."

CHAPTER EIGHT

Phil

Phil had been dreading opening this bill, but the payment deadline was coming up and he could not put it off any longer. He grabbed a butter knife from the kitchen and cut open the envelope.

Just as he expected.

The car insurance premiums were still $4,300 a year. Dear god, even after a year of using the ignition interlock? Debbie was going to be so angry. His DUI conviction might have been two years ago, but the guilt and shame still followed him like a hungry animal. How could he be so stupid and get in the car after that party? He should've slept over like his friend told him to, but no, he had to be stubborn and get in the car anyway. Luckily no one got hurt. And yet, it was the biggest regret of his life.

He warmed up a bowl of minced beef congee and poured a dash of soy sauce and vinegar until the white soup turned a muddy color. With the bill tucked away in the drawer, Phil read the newspaper article again.

Take Ten has flourished following the New York Times's *exposé in 2015, which revealed widespread labor abuses and health violations in New York's nail salon industry. The investigation prompted Governor Andrew M.*

Cuomo to crack down on salons, most of which employed immigrant women from South Korea and China.

He skipped down to a quote from a patron. *"I used to shop around for the cheapest manicure. Now I'm going to have to think twice before I step inside a mom-and-pop salon."*

Dustin entered the kitchen. His hair was parted down the side and his eyes were crusted from sleep. It was striking how much his son looked like him in the mornings. But when Dustin stretched his long arms up in the air to reveal his defined abs, that was where the family resemblance stopped.

"Check out this article, child. I can't believe they're opening soon!" Phil slapped the news sheet on the kitchen counter. "How could that be? The For Lease sign is still up and for god's sake they haven't even removed the name of the previous store. The corpse is still warm."

"What are you talking about?" said Dustin, rubbing his eyes. "Holy mama, who is *that*?"

"Are you even reading the story?"

"Right. Give me a second." Dustin shook his moppy head and focused. Phil hovered over him.

Take Ten saw an opportunity to capitalize on the crackdowns, preaching a mani-pedi experience centered around wellness for their clients and prom- ises of employees being decently treated and fairly compensated for their work. Each station is even equipped with noise-canceling headphones so clients can listen to soothing sounds of nature as they get their nails done.

"Does Má know?" Dustin asked.

"No, how am I supposed to tell her? You know how worried she gets about these things. A small dip in revenue and she goes into full-on panic mode."

Dustin shrugged. "Well, this is what happens when nail salons are run like sweat factories. It leaves the door open for competitors to swoop in and then *BAM*! They get mauled by the competition."

"But that's not us! I'm not running no sweat factory."

"Don't you see, Ba? It doesn't matter. People are afraid of going to salons like yours now. They see an Asian person behind the table and they automatically think, 'Are they here against their free will? Do they get treated well?' You could be the most ethical salon in the world, but the white guilt will still be there. It's bullshit, I know. But that's just how it is."

Phil rubbed the loose skin at his temples. "These stupid Americans. They always ruin everything for us."

"They just got a whole lot stupider after nominating that imbecile for president."

"The *Apprentice* man? He won't make it far," Phil scoffed.

"Anyway, all I'm saying is salons like yours have a . . . reputation."

"And what reputation is that?" Phil snapped.

"Hey, old man. Don't get worked up over this. It's just a societal shift. Look, it happens in every industry. One day people want X. The next day they want Y. As a businessman, you've got to know how to change with the times and the tastes of your clientele. Or else—"

"Or else what?"

"You know what I mean."

"I don't. You're always telling me to speak more eloquently so please, my son, complete that sentence of yours."

Dustin released a deep breath. "Or else you'll go out of business. Kaput. Done-zo. I'm not saying this will happen to you. But it happens all the time. Remember Peter Abato and his barbershop? Or the Chantharas down the street? Remember that time I called to make an order but all I got was an answering machine saying they were closed indefinitely? No warning sign whatsoever. Just like that. And the place was filled with people the night before!"

"Ah, I remember the Chantharas. They were such a polite family. What was the owner's name? Parker? Patrick. Yes, that's right, it was Patrick. He dropped by the salon one night and gave us some leftover curry. We had green curry for dinner three nights in a row, that's how much he gave us!"

Phil sighed and thought about that short man with the pleated pants that were always belted too high. "Whatever happened to them?"

"I could have sworn I saw Mr. Chanthara scanning items at Costco."

"I hope not. It would be such a shame if he stopped making that delicious crispy snapper. That new restaurant that took over is absolutely awful. Twenty-five dollars for a burger that tastes just like a Big Mac? I can't believe people actually line up for those things."

Dustin sat down beside him, placing the gold chain of his jade Buddha necklace in his mouth.

"Stop that, it's disrespectful," Phil barked, slapping his son on the leg. "And please don't tell me you're wasting your money on that junk."

"If you had a bite of that burger, you'd see it's totally worth standing in a blizzard for thirty minutes."

"For a greasy hamburger that will clog your arteries? No thanks."

"I've seen you put away a box of Popeyes, old man. Don't act all holier-than-thou on me!"

"Is that what you do with your hard-earned salary? You waste it away on overpriced takeout instead of saving for your future?"

"Of course not. I also waste it away on drugs and hookers and lap dances and . . ."

Phil could feel his eyes bulging out of his forehead as Dustin laughed uproariously.

"Do not tell your mother about this," said Phil as he folded up the newspaper.

"Yeah, whatever. I better get in the shower before work."

"You're going to work? But it's a Sunday."

"We're working on a huge project right now and it's going to launch in— actually, you know what, no time to explain. Everyone's working overtime and I don't want to look like the slacker when everyone's pulling their weight. Boss said we don't have to come into the office, but we all know he's keeping tabs."

"And *you* kids think your mother and I are clogs in a machine. Look at yourselves!"

"*Cogs*, not *clogs*!" Dustin said with a mouth full of bread. "Besides, you guys are always working. What does it matter to you?"

"It's different for us. We didn't have a formal education. We don't have the luxury of taking a break. That's why your mother and I always wanted you and your sister to have a proper job, the kind that gives you sick days and vacation days. The kind of job that lets you come home by dinner. The kind of job that gives you weekends off. And now you tell me they're making you work on Sundays? What kind of job is that? You might as well work for me. At least you'll get Christmas off!"

"It wasn't so bad, Ba. They had a delicious turkey in the office."

Phil buried his face in his hands. "You know, I've never been prouder of you kids for having such a hard work ethic, but I never wanted you to work as hard as we do. What is the point of everything we've done?"

"Ba, you're being melodramatic. I've gotta go. Talk to you later?" Dustin ruffled his hair before double-stepping up the stairs.

Phil turned his attention back to the newspaper, locking eyes with the crinkly image of Savannah Shaw. What was he going to tell Debbie? She was stressed out enough as it was. Business was steady, but it was nowhere near as busy as it was the previous year, or the year before that.

He used to think the salon could survive anything. But for the first time in a while, he wasn't sure of anything anymore.

Besides, the party was coming up and his wife had enough to worry about. She did not need one more thing looming over her head and this article would surely put her in a mood for weeks, the kind of mood that made her lose all interest in intimacy and recoil at his every touch. When you're married to someone for thirty-eight years, you know what makes them tick and untick. Phil had been a very patient man, rubbing his wife's feet before she even had to ask and getting up early to make a fluffy batch of jasmine rice, since she loved waking up to the sweet, buttery smell in the morning. He knew she appreciated his gestures by the way she let her good-night kisses linger a little longer than normal and the way she looked in his eyes as she tamed the flyaway hairs on his head. Phil treasured those quiet, unspoken moments with his wife, but it had been three long, hot months and it was not the show of appreciation he was after.

Phil shoved the newspaper in the trash and rinsed the ink off his hands.

CHAPTER NINE

Jessica

The first Saturday of the month had arrived and the Tran party would be in full swing by sundown. It had been years since Jessica attended one of these and yet she remembered exactly how they went. Clusters of people gambling in different rooms of the house. Karaoke blasting from the basement. Children running around upstairs. The unholy marriage of cigarettes and Eagle Brand eucalyptus oil that stuck on every piece of fabric and strand of hair long after the party was over.

Her mother had been busy orchestrating every aspect of the party, down to the pattern of the table linens. She even divvied up the duties accordingly. Her father was in charge of marinating, skewering, and barbecuing all the meat: beef, chicken, pork, quail, shrimp, and squid. Thuy was responsible for washing the dishes and plating the food. Dustin was tasked with picking up the alcohol, cigarettes, and fresh decks of cards.

Lucky for her, her job was easy: Find the three dice that went with Squash-Crab-Fish-Tiger, a game based on pure luck that the elders went wild for.

Never in her life had Jessica wished so fervently to get out of a party. She was in no mood to be judged by her mother's nosy friends, and certainly in no mood to put up with drunk uncles who stared at your cleavage way too long.

She blamed Brett for all this, for stamping her with the indignity of being a dumped woman, for forcing her out of L.A., for putting her in close proximity to this party. Her body tensed up just thinking about how magnificently he had screwed up her life.

She wondered what he was doing right now. It would be so easy to find out. His number was still saved in her favorites. Just one tap.

She pulled out her phone and hovered over his name. Countless times she called him without giving it a second thought. He was the first person she called when anything good or bad happened. When she got the promotion at the agency. When she found out her grandmother had died. When the pregnancy test came up positive. Then a few days later when the test turned into a negative. This phone number was central to so many important moments in her life. And now, it sat in her phone like a relic from another dimension.

Dammit.

Tears streamed down her face. She fantasized about bailing on her parents' party and drinking an entire bottle of wine alone in the park. But she couldn't do that to her mother. Not after she laid on some classic guilt-tripping earlier.

"We're going to be very busy at the salon on Monday," said Debbie. "Poor Thuy has back-to-back appointments. Won't you please consider coming in and helping out?"

"Má, I told you I'm looking for a job. I'm supposed to hear back any day now from this agency and if I do, they're going to want me to come in for a second interview."

"Even just for a few hours?" Her mother sat on her bed.

Jessica gave her a definitive look. It was a no.

"Fine, if you won't help us out at the salon, then can you at least come to the party? I bought this for you." She held up a jade Buddha necklace with a dainty gold chain.

"Why?"

"I just thought you could use some luck in your life."

"No thanks. I have my own necklace. See?" she said, pulling it out from under her shirt.

"What, that cheap-looking thing?" she said. "It's got no mystical properties."

"And *that* thing does?"

"Can you please just wear it for the party?"

"Fine," Jessica relented.

It was obvious what her mother was trying to do. She had done this kind of thing in the past. When she was ten, her mother enrolled her in dance classes to improve her posture after noticing how she hunched during dinners. At thirteen, when Jessica refused to clean her dirty Chuck Taylors because they were part of the look, Debbie washed them in the middle of the night while she was sleeping. Her mother treated her like some kind of dented medallion that needed to be dusted and shined to presentability.

"She's only looking out for you," her father assured her as he was peeling a couple stalks of lemongrass. "She wants everyone to see what a wonderful daughter we raised."

Jessica rolled her eyes. "Remember the time she crashed my seventeenth birthday party and forced me to change into that hideous dress? In front of *everyone*? It's like I'm never good enough for her. She's such a—" Jessica could think of a number of ways to finish that sentence but she stopped herself.

Her father listened and nodded, keeping his gaze on the chopping board. She heard him sigh softly. "It's not because she thinks you're imperfect. It's because she wants everyone to know how perfect you are. Do you understand, my child?"

Jessica's head was throbbing like an infected tooth. She desperately needed to be anywhere but here. It was like nothing had changed in the past eight years. God forbid her public image be tarnished by failure, divorce, adultery, infertility, the list goes on. Her parents had been pulling off the greatest public relations stunt of their lifetime, and frankly she was sick of their shit.

"I'm stepping out."

"But the party is in a few hours," her father said.

She pretended not to hear and walked out the door.

———

Sipping a negroni, she waited for Sasha and Gigi at the Hotellium. The marketing agency Gigi ran was hosting a party to relaunch the restaurant's menu, so the night promised to be packed with celebrity chefs, reporters, and semi-recognizable socialites.

Jessica couldn't remember when the three of them officially became friends. Maybe third grade? Her memory was fuzzy, but she distinctly remembered molding papier-mâché masks onto each other's faces in art class. That school project became part of a mutual collection of memories that grounded them through what would become very long stretches of absence in each other's lives. With Jessica moving to Los Angeles, Sasha doing her dermatology residency in Vancouver, and Gigi growing her boutique agency in Toronto, their friendship became founded upon the assumption of distance, sustained by sporadic phone calls. Now they were all in the city at the same time. If Jessica were being honest, this newfound proximity to her very successful childhood friends was a little daunting.

"Wow. Do you ever age?"

Jessica turned towards the low, husky voice. Sasha's black hair was shiny while her skin glowed with the radiance of expensive laser treatments and highly concentrated serums. "I could say the same thing about you," said Jessica.

"Please, it's my job to look like this. You, on the other hand, have the skin of a baby angel who's never seen the sun," said Sasha.

They embraced, squeezing out all the time that had passed between them. "Oh, Sasha," Jessica replied. "Or should I say, Dr. García."

The DJ was playing upbeat tunes at a shout-from-your-lungs volume as the place quickly filled up with people.

"Come with me. There's a secret bar in the back. It's quieter and there's less people," Sasha said.

Jessica could feel the floor rattling from the heavy bass as they maneuvered through the crowd. Sasha whispered something to the hostess, who then led them through a door, a curtain, then another door, until they were in a new room that was just as busy as the one they came from.

They managed to get to the bar just as two seats opened up. Sasha ordered two Manhattans.

"A Manhattan? Who orders that anymore?" said Jessica.

"What? There's no filler, no frills. It gets the job done," said Sasha as she checked her reflection in a hand mirror.

Sasha was the same: high forehead, pointed chin, full eyebrows that never needed makeup. When they were younger, Jessica felt gangling and unremarkable around her. Sasha could put no effort into her appearance yet still somehow make people do a double take. That was still true today, only instead of feeling threatened or bad about herself, Jessica felt gratified to be in the company of such a vibrant woman.

Sasha was distracted by something behind her. "Stay still. Don't look but there's a James McAvoy dead ringer that's been eyeing you since we sat down. Cute, but looks a little young though. Might want to steer clear of that one."

Jessica didn't even desire a peek. Ever since the breakup, she had no interest in dating. At first she thought she did, which was why she inadvisably downloaded a dating app, then deleted it the moment people asked to meet up. Again, that fucking Brett.

"Sweetheart." Sasha stared directly into her eyes and snapped her fingers. "If you spend even a second missing that asshole, I'm going to pour this drink down your shirt." Sasha tucked a loose strand of hair behind Jessica's ear and began loudly spewing a string of clichés meant to mend a broken heart. They were nice and all, but in that moment, it was hard for Jessica to believe the pain could ever end. What if you could never ride out the pain, because the pain was everywhere?

Sasha finally changed the subject. "Any luck with the job hunt?"

"It's going all right," she responded. "I had a job interview the other day for an associate position."

Sasha's perfectly sculpted eyebrows rose to her hairline. "That's great! Tell me more."

"It's a small independent agency. They mostly do commercials, modeling, that type of thing. The people seem nice. And I think they liked me."

"Of course they did!" Sasha screamed, patting her on the back. "When will you hear back?"

"They wanted someone really soon. I think I might even hear back this weekend."

Sasha held up her glass and gestured for a clink. "It's going to be you. I just know it."

Jessica basked in the affirmations. She needed this job like a drowning person needed air. Years of living among career-obsessed, hypercompetitive individuals instilled a toxic yet firm belief that if she wanted to be someone people could respect, she needed to tick off as many external markers of success as possible. A coveted job. A place of her own. A six-figure salary. And if the proverbs were to be believed, love would happen when the rest of her life fell into place. It was comforting to think she could reinvent herself by simply having and following a to-do list.

"Anyway," Sasha carried on. "When you were living in L.A., did you ever come across a nail salon . . . What's it called? . . . Ten something or other?"

"There are, like, a million nail salons there."

Sasha looked up something on her phone. "Take Ten. That's the name of it. Have you heard of them?"

Jessica instinctively rolled her eyes at the mere mention. She had, in fact, heard of them. When a location popped up in her old neighborhood, it was all anybody could talk about. The lines were long, wrapping around the corner and blocking entrances to other businesses, including an urgent care clinic. It took months for the intensity to die down.

"Yes, what about it?" she asked.

"Have you ever been in one?"

Jessica shook her head.

"Wait, seriously. You've never been inside one? There must be a handful of locations there."

"Look at these nails," she shouted, holding up her hands to reveal her plain, ridged, sloppily trimmed nails. "I'm a lost cause. Besides, what's the big deal about this nail salon?"

Sasha paused to sip her drink. "Your parents never mentioned them?"

"Take Ten? They've never been to California. I tried to convince them to fly out one time but you know how they are. Always working. I swear if they won a trip to the Bahamas, they'd probably sell those tickets and put that money right back into the salon."

"Right . . ." Sasha took another long sip of her Manhattan.

"Seriously, what's the big deal about this salon?" Jessica asked impatiently.

"Any chance you've been by your parents' salon lately?"

"Lately?" Jessica realized she'd been back for a month and still hadn't paid a visit to the salon. She recognized how bad that looked, like walking through a cemetery and not visiting your loved one's grave. "No, not yet."

"Well, when you do, you'll see a shop under construction across the street. . . ."

"And?" Jessica was irritated now.

"It's Take Ten's new location."

"Okay. That still doesn't explain why you're being so cryptic."

"You don't get it? They're a freaking huge deal! They've got so much backing. Something like twelve million dollars in seed money. This is going to be their twenty-fourth location."

"So . . . Toronto is filled with these investor darlings."

"So? *So?* Aren't you worried they're gonna run your parents' salon out of business?" Sasha shouted.

The restaurant was filling up. Jessica shot a disgusted look at a man who was encroaching on their space. "Listen," she said. "My parents have been through *everything*. You know that. They've survived floodings, break-ins, recessions, PR nightmares." Jessica lowered her voice. "Well, you remember my dad's DUI. That was a rough time. If they could survive that ordeal, I think they'll be just fine. Besides, they haven't once mentioned this new salon."

"Oh, that's right! I forgot about your dad's . . . situation. Is he, you know, better now?"

"I think so. He has no more than one glass with dinner. And his driving record's been clean ever since."

"That's good. Your parents are so resilient. . . ." Her thought trailed off as if she had more to add.

"Tell me."

"Tell you what?" said Sasha, a mischievous look spreading across her face.

"Come on, you're hiding something from me. I can tell."

"Goddamn." Sasha gestured to the bartender for another round of drinks. "Fuck, okay, but when Gigi gets here you have to pretend you didn't know."

"Know what?"

"Promise?"

"*Fine.*"

Sasha looked over her shoulder before speaking, as if anybody could hear anything over the crushing music. "Gigi is taking care of all Take Ten's marketing and public relations. She's helping them drum up business in time for the big opening. That's why she's been so busy lately."

"Really? But why? I thought she had a full plate. Last I heard she was too busy to take on new clients."

"She is. But—and don't tell her I told you this—Savannah Shaw personally reached out to her agency. She liked the work they were doing and chose them to be their agency of record in Canada."

"Savannah?"

"Take Ten's head of global expansion. She's flying in to Toronto to oversee the grand opening of the salon."

"Ahh." Jessica leaned her body back, just this one time, to allow a woman to grab a napkin from the bar. She brought her glass up to her lips but nothing came out. Her body felt clammy and her clothes felt like they were clinging to her skin. She must have been beet red right now. Did she remember to take a Zantac before she left the house? She scanned the entire restaurant, looking closely for Gigi this time.

"Are you okay?" murmured Sasha.

"I'm fine. Why wouldn't I be?" To be honest, Jessica wasn't quite sure how she felt.

"Are you sure?"

"I'm *fine.*" She stretched out the vowel as long as her breath allowed.

"All right, now I feel bad. I knew I shouldn't have said anything."

"No, no. I'm glad you told me. It's a free market, right? People are allowed to open up new businesses. Besides, this must be so good for Gigi. She's probably so thrilled to get such a big account."

"Well, actually, because of this her agency's been able to hire four new employees."

"That's . . . nice." Jessica realized she'd been fidgeting with a loose thread on her pleated shirt this entire time. The hem had come completely undone.

A server came by with a long tray of shrimp satay and some type of honey glaze drizzled on top. A whiff of buttery garlic hit her senses and she grabbed two sticks from the server.

Finally, she spotted Gigi near the kitchen entrance, standing in a circle with three other people, laughing hip to hip and occasionally touching each other's arms. They looked chummy, like they were old college friends or buddies from her backpacking days. Knowing Gigi, they'd probably just met that night. She could turn a stranger from the cereal aisle into her emergency contact in a matter of days thanks to that Italian charm of hers.

"There she is. Come on, let's go save her," said Sasha, getting ready to scoop up her purse.

"No," Jessica said, probably more quickly than she intended. "Let her do her thing. She'll come to us."

Sasha gave her that look again.

"What? I swear, I'm *fine*. She's just doing her job. I can't be mad at her for doing her job."

"Okay, but if you tell her I told you anything . . ."

"I won't, *jeez*."

"You're paying for these drinks, as collateral."

"That's not how collateral works."

At some point a new DJ took over as the vibe of the night went from smoky lounge bar to high school dance party.

"Oh my god. Don't look," Sasha hissed.

"James McAvoy?"

"No, Savannah Shaw! She's here!"

"Who?" Jessica swung her head around. Sasha looked directly at a blond-bobbed woman with cherry-red lips in a forest-green jumpsuit. She was sitting at a booth with a group of people, drinking some kind of martini that was so green it looked radioactive.

"I told you, from Take Ten. She's here!"

"Really? How do you know that's her?" Jessica said, moving her head left to right to get an unobstructed look past the swarm of people.

"I saw a picture. She must be in the city for the launch of the salon."

"Already? That's so soon."

"You think Gigi invited her?"

Right on cue, both their phones pinged with a text message from Gigi.

Sorry, got caught up talking with some old coworkers. I'll be free soon,
I promise! Are you guys having fun? Make sure you try the spinach
artichoke cups.

Suddenly Jessica felt nauseated. She couldn't believe it, but she was start-ing to think being at her parents' party was better than this. "I think I'm going to head home."

"What? No way! You just got here. Besides, you can't leave me here alone. Let me get this next round of—"

Sasha suddenly stopped talking and pressed her lips tight. Savannah Shaw had gotten up from her booth and was now standing right next to them, try-ing to get the attention of the bartender. Jessica turned around to take a closer look. The woman wore store-bought lashes that were so long they cast shad-ows on her cheeks. Her nails sported a meticulous black moon manicure.

"What should we do?" Sasha whispered.

Jessica mouthed the words *I don't know* and pretended to stare out into the roomful of people.

"I'm going to the bathroom then. I really need to go," Sasha said. "Come with?"

"Actually, I'll stay here to save our seats. You know they'll get snatched up the second we leave."

"All right," she said before whispering in Jessica's ear, "Don't do anything stupid."

As her body disappeared into the dance floor, Jessica could hear Savannah ordering a glass of gin-gin mule. Without even thinking, Jessica turned around and said to her, "Good choice."

Savannah looked startled. "Oh, thanks. It's my go-to. I'm from New York so I can't not order it," she said.

"New York, nice! What brings you to Toronto?" Jessica said, probing her for the answers she already knew.

"I'm here to open up a new store actually. It's very exciting." She dug into her purse and pulled out a business card. "You should come to our opening when it's all done. Bring a few friends. You look like you enjoy getting pampered." She laughed.

Jessica tensed her jaw. What was *that* supposed to mean? She quickly glanced at the business card. The tagline read, *Take your nails from one to ten.*

"A nail salon? Very interesting. That's quite the bold undertaking."

"How do you mean?"

"I don't know if you've had a chance to explore the city but there's literally a nail salon on every block. Just take a stroll down Yonge Street and they're practically side by side. You're in for some competition."

"Oh, *those* salons," said Savannah, giving a half shrug. "I'm not too worried."

"Oh?"

"Come to the opening. You'll see what I'm talking about. It's got everything that those *other* salons don't have: modern decor, good hygiene practices, staff that can actually speak English, you know what I mean?"

Jessica clenched her drink.

"Honey, that's why you don't have boyfriend," Savannah shouted in a fake Asian accent.

"Excuse me?"

"It's a bit from a comedy skit."

Jessica knew the one. She'd repeated the line many times before, exaggerating the accent to get the most laughs from friends, but to hear it come out nonchalantly from a white woman made her downright cringe.

"Those little shops are just adorable, aren't they?" Savannah continued. "I have to give credit where credit's due. They're practically responsible for democratizing the industry and making a manicure something that everyone can treat themselves to. Did you know acrylics were once reserved for the upper class?" Her drink arrived and she placed a twenty-dollar bill on the bar. "But it's time we get a piece of this market, you know? They've monopolized the scene for far too long."

We? They? Jessica kept quiet as she tried to figure out which one of those camps Savannah had ascribed her to. Was she the *we*: honorable and deserving? Or was she the *they*: suspicious and untrustworthy?

"I just think customers deserve to go to a salon that doesn't cut corners, you know?" said Savannah.

"Not all of them cut corners," Jessica snapped back, suddenly feeling a swell of protectiveness.

"I know, but how can you *really* know that? Half of these salons are probably underpaying their staff and treating them like garbage. Seriously, it breaks my heart. I swear, if I think about it too much, I'll start to cry."

Savannah took a sip of her gin-gin mule, leaving a feathered red imprint on the rim of the glass and looking the exact opposite of someone who was about to cry.

"Look," she carried on, "our vision is much bigger than a salon. We're going to be offering something that's not yet out there."

"And what's that?"

"I guess"—Savannah briefly looked to the ceiling—"a more pleasant, transformative experience that's one hundred percent free of guilt."

Just then, a tall man slid up to Savannah from behind and wrapped his arms around her waist. His tie was slung over his shoulder, presumably from taking a piss, but apart from the sloppiness, he was remarkably handsome, clean-shaven and smelling of fresh mint. They looked like new lovers by the way their eyes became glossy and their hands lingered on each other's bodies a few seconds longer. He whispered something that made her blush, then she quickly slapped his hands away and acted as if she'd never met him.

Turning her attention back to Jessica, she gave a wink and said, "I have to go. It was nice meeting you. Hope to see you at our launch."

Jessica watched her walk away, the man trailing behind her. The densely packed crowd split open for her as if she were Moses.

Her phone pinged with another text from Gigi.

Finally, I'm free! Where are you guys?

Jessica turned off her phone and stormed out of the restaurant.

CHAPTER TEN

Dustin

There was only half an hour until the party and they still had no liquor. Luckily, there was no need for a long checklist. Only two types of drinks were served at a Tran party: Heineken and Hennessy. Dustin carefully loaded the shopping cart as Jack White screamed into his ears. It wasn't until the last guitar note struck that Dustin realized someone had been trying to get his attention.

"Hey! Hey! Justin! Is this all for you?"

Dustin turned around to see Mackenzie standing in a white tank top and red skirt. Her head bobbed in the direction of his cart, which housed about a dozen or so bottles of cognac. "I never pegged you as an alcoholic."

Caught off guard, Dustin quickly slid his headphones down his neck and attempted to come up with an equally witty remark. Maybe he should say something about how AA is for quitters? Or explain that these were actually gifts for his sponsor. Or maybe . . . Never mind. Everything sounded stupid in his head.

"Mackenzie. Hey, what's up? What are you doing here?"

"Picking up my dry cleaning."

Dustin's cheeks flushed. "Sorry, that was a dumb question," he said, fluffing his hair and desperately wishing he had worn a different shirt, something that didn't have a picture of an ear of corn above the words *I'm So Corny*. He folded his arms around his chest.

"How's it going?"

She looked different. Did she get a haircut? No. Wait. Yes. Yes, she definitely got a haircut. Should he compliment her?

"Thought I'd pick up some wine," she replied. "It's my parents' twenty-fifth anniversary tomorrow."

"Wow, congratulations. You're one of the few people I know whose parents are still together."

"Are yours?"

"What?"

"Are your parents still together?"

"Yes, of course. I don't even think they've uttered the word *divorce* before. That alone would be a rebellious act."

"What do you mean?"

"It's taboo in my culture."

"Pretty sure it's taboo in every culture. Besides, you don't have to convince the Desi girl. I know a thing or two."

"Yeah, my parents would rather argue till they die than divorce and be the talk of the town. I can't even imagine if that were to happen—"

"Excuse me, can I—?" A thick-bearded man reached between their bodies to grab a Crown Royal before continuing down the aisle.

"I know, right?" Mackenzie carried on. "Everyone deserves to get out of a relationship if they're not happy. Who cares what other people think?"

This was getting depressing. How did he end up talking about divorce with Mackenzie in the liquor store? This was not how he envisioned their conversations would go. When it came to women and first impressions, Dustin always stuck to his three tried-and-true subject matters: books, hobbies, and travel. He had an infinite number of things to say on these topics as a prolific reader who fenced every weekend and traveled abroad every year. Because he had so much to say, and because his companion almost always couldn't stop asking him questions, this tactic succeeded in helping him avoid any awkward lulls on first dates and second dates and so on.

But as he found himself standing silently across from Mackenzie for what felt like an unbearably long time, he didn't know what to do with himself. He simply turned to look at the shelf behind him, pretending to choose between the ice wine and the late harvest wine as if he knew the difference. He was certain that by the time he turned around, Mackenzie would be long gone, just like Amber and Fernanda and all the other would've, could've, should'ves.

"You can't go wrong with Cave Spring," she said, miraculously still there.

A security guard shot them a hard glance. Even though he was ready to pay, Dustin wasn't ready for their interaction to end.

"By the way," said Mackenzie, completely ignoring the security guard. "You never told me what's up with all the bottles of Hennessy there?"

"Oh, that? We're having a party tonight at our place. It's something my parents host every few months. They get together with their friends to drink and gamble basically. It's kind of entertaining, actually."

"How many people are going? You've got enough booze here for a hundred people!"

"More like a third of that."

"So you're telling me your parents have more of a social life than I do?" she said, chuckling.

"You would have to see it to believe it."

"Is that an invite?"

It wasn't, actually. Never in a million years would Dustin bring Mackenzie home to his parents, at least not before going on at least a few dates first, and even then, he would have to coach his parents on how to behave appropriately around a girl.

Dustin had never brought home a girl before. When he was a teenager, his parents were so relieved that he cared so little about girls, preferring to stay home and study in his bedroom. In reality, he was lying in bed jerking off to porn most of the time. So no, inviting Mackenzie to a party at his house was not the plan. But then again, neither was being single forever.

"You should totally come!" Dustin blurted out, realizing he could not take it back. "I mean, if you have nothing else to do."

"Sure, why not? I can stop by."

"Cool." Dustin started second-guessing everything now. "The party starts at seven. Give me your number and I'll text you the address."

After swapping cell phone numbers, they parted ways. It didn't cross his mind until he put the key in the ignition that perhaps bringing a new girl to a party full of no-filter Viets was quite possibly the dumbest thing anybody could ever do. What was he thinking? The girl of his dreams was going to meet his neurotic parents tonight. What would they think? What would *she* think? Oh dear god. This was going to be a disaster.

Dustin continued to drive east on Bloor Street, passing Keele, then Indian Road, then Dundas West. As he drove through each set of lights, his optimistic side began to peek through like the sun making its first crack over the horizon. On the bright side, he was going to get to hang out with Mackenzie tonight. The thought of her wearing something nice like a cute dress, sipping a drink that he poured for her, eating a bánh bèo that he showed her how to eat, was all too thrilling.

Dustin's head became lost in what could happen. Maybe he would take her upstairs to his bedroom and talk more privately, discussing everything from their favorite songs to their childhood memories to their dreams about the future. They would talk until there was nothing more to say. They would sit quietly on his bed, waiting for the inevitable moment when their lips would finally get to touch.

Before heading home, he quickly stopped at a Filipino grocery store and purchased a fertilized duck egg. He always ate one of these whenever he needed a bit of luck. He did it the night before a final exam, a big presentation, a job interview. And it worked every single time. If he could somehow get Mackenzie to kiss him tonight, that would make it four for four.

Back in the car, he peeled the eggshell and took a big bite.

CHAPTER ELEVEN

Debbie

I t was five minutes to seven. Guests would be arriving any minute now.

While Phil was in the kitchen stuffing bitter melons with ground pork, Debbie was upstairs in their bedroom getting ready for the party. After taking a shower, she sat down in front of a mirror and analyzed her complexion. Most days she simply saw her reflection. But today, all she could see was her past. The constellation of dark spots on her cheeks was from riding water buffaloes in scorching Saigon summers. The strong, stubby nose that did not get sharper despite her mother continuously pinching her bridge. The bald patch on her right eyebrow that came from not getting enough iron at the refugee camp in Thailand.

Debbie wanted no reminders of the past, so she spent the next half hour covering her face in a heavy layer of makeup. She filled in her eyebrows with a shade of espresso. She swiped her lips with a shade of Mars. These were all birthday gifts from Phil, one of many presents she received from him even though she was always saying she didn't need or want anything. Secretly, she liked receiving gifts.

On their last anniversary, Debbie came home to find a suitcase in the middle of the living room. A handwritten note was taped to the top. "Everything is packed. Now let's go on an adventure." Phil walked in behind her with a

65

bouquet of Peruvian lilies and whisked her away to Prince Edward County for the entire weekend. It was by far the most romantic thing he'd ever done for her. Did she admit it? Of course not. She spent the whole weekend berating him for not putting that money towards a new fridge.

Her husband was not a natural romantic. It was obvious to them that he was doing these things to seek forgiveness after what he put her through two years ago. It was bad enough that he had gotten in a car with a blood alcohol level significantly above the legal limit. Then he had to go and jack up their car insurance when finances were already tight.

For several months, they could barely afford to pay their bills, so she offered to clean customers' homes to make some extra cash. It was humiliating and exhausting. She still got furious just thinking about it, but she kept reminding herself, *It could be worse, somebody could have gotten hurt.*

She'd forgiven her husband since then. But he didn't need to know that. She enjoyed getting all these gifts and being pampered with little acts of love, like how he put toothpaste on her toothbrush every night before they went to bed.

The smell of onion and garlic rose from downstairs. They were just about done cooking. Only thirty-five people were invited, but there was enough food to feed double that.

"Don't forget to soak the bitter melon in tamarind juice! And not too long or else they'll get soggy!" Debbie yelled out, hoping Phil had heard her over the loud exhaust fan.

"You didn't hear me come up?" Phil was standing at the doorway of the bedroom.

Debbie jumped. "Oh, you scared me! One day I'm going to rip up that damn carpet on the stairs." She turned to face the mirror again, sitting extra still so she could apply a coat of mascara on her short lashes.

"That would have been helpful when the kids were younger and always sneaking out in the middle of the night," replied Phil.

Debbie and Phil chuckled simultaneously, remembering the countless times they found Dustin's and Jessica's bedrooms empty by midnight. She loved that they could still laugh together.

"Why aren't they home yet?" said Debbie. "The party's going to start any minute now and we still have no drinks! And look at you! Your face is as greasy as a deep fryer. Go on now. Time to hit the shower."

Phil did not answer her question, nor did he budge. Instead, he made that face he had made a million times before, the face that said, *Let's*.

"Oh, no, no, no. Not right now, Phil. It's nearly seven o'clock. People are going to get here soon!"

"You know no one ever shows up on time. Being late is in our blood."

"Yes, but this could be the one time someone actually arrives early for once," she said, brushing her already tangle-free hair. "Do you really want to take that chance?"

This was the silly charade they played before sex. He would beg. She would brush it off. Until eventually Phil's hands were underneath Debbie's blouse, her hairbrush knocked to the ground, their bodies on the bed and stripped of all clothing.

The pink glow of the sunset shone through the half-shaded window, spilling onto their intertwined bodies. "Keep it down," she whispered as the weight of his body repeatedly crashed into hers. "In case the kids come home."

And keep it down they both did for the next little while. It was strange how quiet the house was all the while her mind and her insides were screaming with pleasure. She sweetly kissed his neck, his chin, then made her way to his quivering lips. The moment the flash of ecstasy arrived, it was all too much for her to hold in. She cut the silence and released a satisfying moan, while Phil slid himself out and laid next to her.

"God, that was amazing," said Phil, waiting for her to agree. When she said nothing in return, only staring straight at the ceiling, he spoke again: "You look so beautiful tonight."

Finally, Debbie responded. "Did you remember to take the bitter melon out of the tamarind juice?"

CHAPTER TWELVE

Phil

Just as Phil predicted, the first guests arrived after 8:00 p.m. Eleanor and David Dang were at the doorstep carrying a plastic bowl of what appeared to be shredded chicken salad. The Dangs did not apologize for being one hour late, nor did the Trans expect an apology. The unspoken code with such parties was that no one should ever arrive at the designated time. This accomplished two things: It gave the host some buffer time, and it gave the guests the appearance that they had better things to do.

"The sauce is mostly peanut butter and rice vinegar with soy sauce, honey, fish sauce, a sprinkle of ginger and sambal oelek," said Eleanor. "Oh gosh, are these real? You have to show me how you get your peonies to open so fast. Is it okay that we parked in the driveway?"

Phil wasn't sure what part he should respond to, so he walked back to the kitchen and placed the salad strategically away from the rest of the food so no one would mistake that soggy salad for one of his own carefully prepared dishes.

The Dangs removed their shoes and placed them neatly against the wall. The couple was in their midseventies, making them the oldest friends in their social circle. David had retired as an immigration lawyer two years ago. Eleanor was still working as a professor at the University of Toronto, teaching human development and applied psychology. The Dangs were admired in the community for their well-rounded intellect, which they neither flaunted nor oversimplified in the company of people like the Trans who had no post-secondary education.

Despite their background, the Dangs were nice people who lived quiet lives and spent much of their time with their half dozen grandchildren, all of whom were mixed with some race or other. Every now and then, the Dangs stopped by Sunshine Nails to donate their finished copies of the *New York Times*, the *Wall Street Journal*, and *Financial Times*. The Dangs preferred slow journalism over twenty-four-hour cable news. You could always count on their conversations to begin with some variation of, "That reminds me of an article I read. . . ."

Debbie always complained about how long-winded they were, but Phil could listen to them talk for hours. They could speak with such confidence about anything, from politics to literature to pop culture. He wished he could be that knowledgeable on so many topics. Phil put on some traditional Vietnamese ballads at a low volume so he could hear David and Eleanor talk.

One by one, others started trickling in. The Trưởngs, who operated a nail salon in the Financial District. The Phạms, who had a restaurant in North York. The Bùis, also nail salon owners on St. Clair West.

The drinks were poured.

The money came out.

And the card games began.

Phil left the door unlocked and put a note at the front door for any late-comers. "Walk-Ins Welcome," it read.

He laughed at his ingenuity before heading back inside.

CHAPTER THIRTEEN

Dustin

Just after 10:00 p.m., Dustin got the text message: **I'm outside**. It was Mackenzie. He looked out the window and there she was, standing on their front lawn. She had showed up after all. He quickly checked his reflection, specifically his nostrils to make sure there were no crusty pieces of mucus in there, and sped down the stairs.

He met her on the front porch and closed the door behind him. No way was he ready to let her in the house, not with all those drunk people in there. He could picture it now: the women engulfing him like a tidal wave, Mackenzie being swept up by empty compliments about her youth, then both of them drowning in uncomfortable statements like, "When are you getting married?" and "Your mixed babies are going to be so cute!"

At least there was a cold breeze that night. He was already sweating underneath his Lacoste T-shirt, which only made him self-conscious about the wet armpit stains he was certain he was producing. Did he remember to wear deodorant?

Dustin suggested they have a seat on the front porch. It was quite nice out here. His mother had outdone herself. There were baskets of fresh cascading electric-blue flowers hanging from the porch roof. The steps were lined with decorative lanterns housing pillar candles. The wood bench was piled with delicate silk cushions brought out from the living room.

The two took a seat at the bench and Dustin suddenly became well aware that it all felt a little too romantic. He did not want Mackenzie to think he'd done all this for her. Coming on too strong was a death knell. He could not bear the thought of a rejection right now. He had come this far.

Vietnamese pop music blared from inside the house. They bopped their heads to the beat. It was incredibly catchy.

"Sounds really fun inside. You sure you don't want to go in?" Mackenzie said.

"Let's hang out here for a bit. It's so packed in there."

"How many people did you say?"

Dustin paused to think about it. "I want to say thirty. Forty, maybe? It's insane how many friends they have. I'm pretty sure they've got more friends than me."

"Well, you have one more friend now," she said as she untucked her hair from both ears.

He could see the moon out of the corner of his eyes, but his gaze was permanently fixed on Mackenzie's, a view he found to be far more mesmerizing. He wanted to know everything about her. What her favorite movies were, whether she liked dogs or cats, where she wanted to travel to next. He wanted to know these things so bad and yet another part of him did not want to know. He wanted to keep feeding his infatuation with mystery.

"What are you thinking about?" Mackenzie asked.

"Huh, what?" Shit, how much time had passed?

"You looked like you were staring off into space."

"Oh, uh, I was just thinking about the moon. It's weird how it looks gigantic near the horizon when in actuality it hasn't changed in size at all."

"Was that really what you were thinking about?"

Dustin paused to swallow. "The moon only looks huge when it's near the horizon because it's closer to things we see on an everyday basis, like trees and buildings and houses. It's one of the oldest optical illusions in the world, yet millions of people still think the moon grows and shrinks every night."

"Whoa," Mackenzie exclaimed. "I had no idea you thought this much about the moon."

"I guess I think about weird things a lot." He giggled nervously.

"I think it's fascinating," she whispered in his ear. "To be honest, I always thought the moon just traveled closer to the earth."

The heat of her breath made the tiny hairs on his ear stick straight out, and his whole body tingled. He didn't let himself look directly at her for fear his body might completely melt.

"You're not wrong. Every couple of weeks, the moon does come closer to earth, but not enough to explain the drastic size difference when it's at the horizon and when it's high in the sky."

He looked down at her hands. Since he was a kid, he developed a heightened awareness of other people's nails. His parents taught him to always look at people's nails because they revealed a lot about who they were. Nails could tell you how much self-confidence a person had, how spontaneous they were, their level of friendliness, and the degree to which you could trust them.

Dustin was happy with what he saw. Mackenzie's nails were trimmed close to the nail bed, her cuticles were crooked but clean, and the little crescent moons were so white they still shone through the light coat of cotton candy pink she had on. Bright lunulae were a sign of excellent health, kindness, and a hard work ethic.

"So how are you liking it at Moodstr?" Dustin inquired.

Mackenzie shrugged. "It's . . . good."

Dustin lifted an eyebrow. "Wait, why did you hesitate?"

"I didn't hesitate. Just want to make sure I say the right thing. For all I know, you're going to repeat everything I say back to Chase. Word on the street is you're his star employee."

Dustin turned to face her. "What? That's so far from the truth! I mean, yeah, I've been there the longest but the guy barely even knows me. I swear, anything you say stays between us."

Mackenzie slowly exhaled. "It's just . . . and I know I've only been working here for a few months, but don't you get the sense that this company, this app . . . that it's all just a . . . joke?"

Dustin became intrigued and waited for her to say more.

"It's just . . . their mission is to help people improve their happiness and yet they've got people working eighty-hour weeks and burning out so bad they're crying in the bathroom. The other day I walked in on someone having a panic attack in the stall after she got reprimanded for eating during a sprint. Can you believe that?"

This did not surprise Dustin. He'd had a breakdown or two in the bathroom himself. Once after receiving a deadline so unrealistic that failure was inevitable. Another time after being brutally scolded for writing code so inoperable it had to be scrapped altogether. In his defense, he'd been working twenty-two hours straight. No sleep. Not even a stretch. But excuses weren't tolerated at Moodstr. So he barreled through another eight hours until the code was perfect.

"That's just how things are done around here," Dustin said, shrugging. "You can't expect to grow at the rate we are without putting in a little elbow grease."

"So you're just okay with that? Don't you think it's a little hypocritical, given the whole point of the company is to, you know, reduce people's stress load?"

Dustin had never thought of it that way. It seemed obvious now that Mackenzie had vocalized it. Was the job stressful? Yes. But it was nothing compared to the torment his parents had to endure, grating people's feet like cheese. His gratitude for the job was so immense that the grind felt like nothing to him.

"Why are you working here then? Wait, don't tell me it's all sunshine and lollipops over at the customer success team," he said, smirking.

Mackenzie shrugged and folded her arms over her chest. "I thought I could make a difference, you know? Helping people brings me a lot of joy. And sure, every now and then, I'll get to meet a customer and hear how our app has helped them manage their anxiety. One person even told me it helped them cope with the loss of their dead husband! Don't get me wrong. It's an awesome feeling knowing it's helping some people. But I just thought working at this company would make me feel . . ." There was a moment of silence. "Never mind, it's so cheesy."

"No, go ahead and finish." He could listen to her for hours.

"I just thought I'd find my purpose here, you know?" she said softly. "I know, it sounds so stupid, right?"

He stared at her for a moment before speaking. "No, not at all. I think it's pretty normal to feel this way. Who doesn't want to feel like they're solving the world's problems and doing work that matters?"

"So you don't think it's naïve?"

"What?"

"To want to find fulfillment in a job?"

Dustin paused to think. "I think it makes you very human."

Mackenzie's eyes grew large. "You know, for a work robot, you're pretty good at the whole listening thing."

She placed her hand on top of his and held it there. He liked how soft her skin felt and how protected it made him feel.

Before he knew it, she gently tilted his chin up and kissed him. It took his brain a second to process what was happening, then another second before his eyes were fully closed, then another second for him to realize his heart was beating faster than normal. He was certain she could hear it reverberating in his chest. He felt so overwhelmed he broke the kiss and locked eyes with her.

"Did anyone ever tell you how handsome you are?" she said, smiling so wide he could see almost all of her top teeth. Her lips were glistening as if there was a slick of oil on top. He leaned his body back so he could see her whole face, but all he cared about were those lips. He put his hand on the back of her neck and pulled her in for another kiss.

"Dustin! Dustin!" His sister's voice boomed from the sidewalk. Jessica was running up the garden path towards them. "Where's Má? Is she inside?"

It was truly amazing how his sister always knew the exact moment to inconvenience him. "What do you want?" he groaned.

He saw her eyes dart over to Mackenzie, then quickly back at him. "Where's Má?"

"She's inside," replied Dustin, not bothering to introduce his sister to Mackenzie. He hadn't even thought about what he would even say. *Hey, this is my colleague?* No, that sounded too formal. *My girlfriend?* Definitely not. *My friend?* So vague.

Jessica ran inside and closed the door behind her.

"That was your sister?" asked Mackenzie.

"Yes, that's her. Sorry about that. I meant to introduce you but then she showed up out of nowhere and she seemed like she was in a rush and she's normally really cool. I'm sure she wanted to meet you since you're also really cool—"

"Hold up, your name is *Dustin*? I've been calling you Justin this whole time! Why didn't you correct me? Oh my god, I feel so bad."

Dustin let out a nervous laugh. "I just"—he stuttered, trying to come up with a good reason—"I just didn't think it mattered since we were just acquaintances."

Mackenzie smiled. "Still, I should have known. I feel terrible."

"Don't," said Dustin. "Happens all the time."

Their attention shifted to the house across the street. The neighbors, a Portuguese couple in their fifties, put their car in park, waved weakly at them, then disappeared into their home.

"So," said Mackenzie, jumping to her feet. "I parked my car on Spruce Street."

"Oh, you're leaving?" Dustin asked, disappointed. He wanted so badly to make out with her again.

Mackenzie stood up and grabbed his hand. "Come with me to the car."

This was not going the way he had planned at all. It was better.

His phone vibrated in his pocket. The Moodstr app detected an increase in his skin conductance and asked him to select what his current mood was. He clicked on the happiest of happy faces. Animated confetti exploded across the screen.

He smiled and looked up at the moon as they walked away from the house, the pop music fading gently into the night.

CHAPTER FOURTEEN

Jessica

Jessica was too flustered to introduce herself to that girl on the porch, though she was deeply curious. She had just spent the past forty-five minutes walking home in heels because she only had a ten-dollar bill in her purse and no cab would take her with that paltry amount of money.

If she had taken a second to stare at her reflection in one of the mirrored buildings she had passed by, she might have brushed off the flecks of dried-up mascara that had sprinkled her cheeks and flattened out the odd tufts that had formed in her hair. But she did not and so she stepped inside her parents' house looking like a raccoon in heat.

She used her entire body weight to push the door open. There were dozens of shoes piled up at the front entrance—sneakers, slip-ons, sandals. They'd been trampled on so many times they were all separated from their matching pair. Jessica exhaled a sigh of relief when no one noticed she had entered. She just wanted to find her parents and tell them about Take Ten and Savannah. They needed to be warned.

Peeking inside the living room, Jessica saw there was a game of tiến lên underway between Thuy and three other women. When she was five, her father taught her how to play. He used to cradle her in his lap during a game and let her take a peek as he slowly and carefully fanned out the thirteen cards he'd just been dealt. "The secret to winning is to use the heat of your thumb," he would tell her. "When you press down on the cards long enough, the suit will magically turn red. The more red cards you have, the more likely you are to win." After watching him win game after game, she believed for a long time that her father had magical powers. But then one night she watched him lose four hundred dollars in a single sitting and realized it was all a lie.

"Jessica? Is that you? It *is* you!"

She turned around. It was Mrs. Ho, a gossipy widow who, her mother had warned, solicited donations on a weekly basis for the local Buddhist temple. Mrs. Ho was wearing every possible shade of purple from head to toe. Her drop earrings were made of a rich, faceted amethyst glass and her eyelids shimmered from a powdery swatch of magenta. Not having a husband to take care of anymore served her well. Mrs. Ho looked like she should be at a charity gala clinking glasses with business elites, not here with people who believed gambling was a legitimate hobby. She even smelled important, her hair and skin giving off an accord of dark espresso and warm woods.

"We were so thrilled when your mother said you were coming back to Toronto. Did you gain weight?"

Mrs. Ho took a few steps towards Jessica and scanned her from top to bottom as if she were a barcode. Jessica tensed every muscle in her body. "You've got mascara all over your face, dear. Has your mother neglected to show you how to apply makeup properly?"

Before Jessica could pull back, Mrs. Ho yanked a Burberry handkerchief out of her purse and used it to brush the flakes off her face. "There you go, child. Much better. Now tell me, how long do you plan to stay for? A good daughter should never leave her parents until she gets married—" Mrs. Ho paused, grabbing her left hand. "Ôi trời ơi! Don't tell me you gave him back the ring!"

Down in the basement, someone had turned on the karaoke machine and set off a terrible rendition of Celine Dion's "The Power of Love." Jessica could barely hear herself talk and hoped Mrs. Ho couldn't, either.

"I gave it back. It didn't feel right to keep it," said Jessica, cautious not to say anything that would prolong this conversation. Her phone vibrated. Someone was calling. Thank god. "Do you mind if I answer th—"

"It's a shame what happened with you and that boy," continued Mrs. Ho. "To end a long relationship at such a young age, it's a tragic waste of youth. But if you take care of that face of yours and lose a little bit of weight, you'll find a new man in no time. It's a good thing you moved back home with your parents. It shows you're a good girl. Look at you, such a good daughter. That will impress lots of men. In fact, I might know someone for you—"

Shit. The phone stopped ringing. Jessica looked around, hoping her mother or father would show up to scold her for coming late to the party, anything to get her out of this conversation. Instead, all she got was the karaoke singer passionately screeching into the microphone. " 'Cause I'm your laaaadaaaaay."

An idea occurred to her. "Hey, have you seen Dustin yet?" she said abruptly. "He's outside on the porch. With a *girlfriend.*"

"Girlfriend?" Mrs. Ho nearly spat out the red wine she was drinking. "Little Dustin has a girlfriend? I must meet this girl. Be a darling and take my glass for me." She left Jessica with an empty wineglass stained with crusty lipstick and sped down the hall towards the door.

Jessica's head throbbed from all the smells wafting in the house, an ungodly combination of reheated fish, spicy cologne, and cigarettes. She made her way to the garage to get herself a cold drink. Where the hell were her parents?

The garage door had been left open. Standing on the driveway was Văn Đỗ, smoking by himself. He was wearing a button-down white shirt and Ed Hardy jeans with a colorful embroidery of a serpent intertwined around a skull. He turned to look at her with the cigarette still in his mouth.

Văn was an alcoholic with two grown sons, one of whom he hadn't talked to in three years on account of the way he treated their mother. A few summers ago he had lost over six thousand dollars at the casino and slapped his wife across the face, right at the poker table, because he blamed her for convincing him to stay at almost every hand. Afterwards, he tumbled into a legal hole so dark and mysterious it was as if the earth had swallowed him whole. He was working on getting sober, but the only person who bought it was Debbie. She was a fervent believer in second and third and fourth chances, which explained why he got an invite to the party.

When Jessica walked into the garage, Văn flicked away his cigarette butt and gestured for her to come over. She spotted the compass tattoo on his left shoulder.

"Debbie's daughter, right?" said Văn, his bloodshot eyes blinking incessantly. From afar he looked like a cool twenty-one-year-old, but as Jessica got closer, she saw the soft sacs under his eyes and fine lines across his forehead. "You look just like your father. You know, I was invited to one of your birthdays many, many years ago. You must have been turning nine or ten. I got you a pink teddy bear. Do you remember?"

Jessica had no clue. She did not remember ever receiving a present from him. Not knowing what to say, she tightened her grip on a can of beer and took a long sip. They both stood on the driveway in silence, their interaction resorting to halfway smiles as his question vaporized into nothingness.

"Ack, what am I saying?" continued Văn. "You're probably too young to remember every single present you got." Jessica simply nodded and drank her beer, wondering why he brought her over here in the first place.

He put his hand in his denim pockets, pulled out his phone, and showed her the screen. There was a picture of a scrawny young man in sunglasses sitting on a stoop. He had no remarkable features but his spotty mustache and a couple of missing teeth were striking enough on their own.

"This is my nephew in Vietnam. He's single and a good boy. What do you think of him?"

Jessica was baffled by his quick candor. "Look, whatever my mother told you, I'm not looking to get married anytime soon," she said, taking in three gulps of beer.

"I can give you forty thousand dollars."

Jessica nearly dropped her can. Was he being serious? She knew fake marriages were a thing in their community, a last resort when immigration applications were rejected or taking too long to process. But she thought they'd at least be a bit more discreet about it.

As Văn went on to explain, his nephew's paperwork had been sitting in decision pending mode for five years. In that time he had gone through puberty, learned how to drive a motorbike, and completed a traineeship at a hotel. His dream was to work at a Ritz-Carlton in Toronto one day. He just needed a way to get here.

"You don't have to stay married to him for that long. Just until he becomes a permanent resident and then you can get divorced and go your own way. Of course, this is only possible if you agree to this. We would never want to pressure you to do anything you don't want to do, but you would be helping my family a lot."

Văn smoothed back his hair and tucked his phone back in his pocket.

"Anyway, I have a lawyer who can help explain how everything works. Whatever questions you have he can answer. I trust him with my life. What do you say? I don't know, have I said too much? Fuck. I've scared you off, haven't I? Fuck." He lit another cigarette and took a long drag, his eyes still on her.

Jessica stared at him for a moment before laughing maniacally. Maybe it was the money or the trembling desperation in his voice or the fact that he was standing outside by himself being the social degenerate of the party that he was. She kind of felt bad for him. Too bad it was an outrageous idea.

"You know how crazy this sounds? Sorry, but I can't help you. You've asked the wrong person," Jessica said.

"Is it because you're still in love with your ex?" Văn said abruptly.

"Excuse me? No, no, it's not," said Jessica, blushing. "Trust me, it's not."

"Is it the money then? Is it not enough? If you give me a couple weeks I can offer fifty."

Jessica groaned. She didn't care that her irritation was showing. It was true what people said about him. His aggressive boldness was unbecoming for someone who stood no taller than five foot five and wore shoes that she was pretty sure came from the kids' department.

"Thank you but I don't need the money that badly," she said before turning her body back towards the house. "I need to go find my mom. I hope everything works out for your nephew."

Văn dropped his head, seeming to surrender.

"Please," Jessica continued. "Help yourself to any beer in the cooler over there. It's still very cold."

"I don't drink anymore." He yanked at the heavy stainless steel chain on his necklace and pulled out a bar pendant that was dangling behind his shirt. It was stamped with a column of numbers. He brought the pendant to his face and let the cold aluminium linger on his lips for a couple of seconds. "Seven months sober."

"Oh," replied Jessica, suddenly feeling embarrassed.

"I'm no fool, kid. Do you know why I'm out here by myself?" He took a sharp inhale of his cigarette. "I know what everyone in there thinks of me. They're all making bets on when I'll fuck it all up again. But I'm not going to. Not anymore."

Jessica took a few steps towards him. "My parents would never—"

"I won't let them know me better than I know myself. And what I know is that I can't be surrounding myself with people who look at me and only see failure. The only reason I came to this party was because your mother is a nice lady." He shuffled his feet. "And to talk to you."

Jessica was speechless. She watched as he fumbled for his car keys.

"Tell your mother I'm grateful for the invitation," he said. "Treat your mother well, okay? When she becomes old and frail and unable to speak because it hurts too much to even open her mouth, you'll wish you appreciated her more. Trust me, I know."

He paused, taking one long drag of his cigarette before crushing it on the driveway. "Take care of yourself, kid."

As he walked away, Jessica noticed the back of his jeans had a pair of washed-out angel wings cascading down each thigh.

She checked her phone. Two missed calls. Two voice messages. She clicked to listen to the first one.

"Hey. It's Gigi." There was a pause so long Jessica thought the message was over. "Where did you go? Can we talk? Sasha told me what she told you and I want to make sure we're cool. Call me back. All right, bye."

Jessica clicked to hear the second voicemail. "Hi, Jessica. This is Robyn from Ivy Harper Casting Agency. We wanted to thank you for coming in for an interview. We were highly impressed with your background and experience, and we all think you would make a good fit with the team. However, we did have several highly qualified candidates for the position and have chosen to pursue another candidate. We do thank you for your interest in our company and wish you good luck in your job hunt."

Jessica's heart sank like a rock. Without thinking, she threw her phone into the front yard. It hit the soft lawn on impact, then bounced off and hit the sidewalk pavement, cracking the screen straight down the middle.

You've got to be fucking kidding me.

Why was nothing going right in her life? How many more blows could she take? Her head throbbed even harder, and she ached for anything that would flush the bitterness sticking to the back of her throat.

Then in one flash of a second, a moment of clarity settled in. She wasn't going to take this anymore. If the universe was going to keep throwing punches at her, she was going to duck, swerve, hit back. Whatever it took to take back some control. She would not let her life be a joke. She knew exactly what she had to do next.

The interior door of the garage opened. Two dark figures stood at the top of the ledge.

"Jessica, there you are!" Phil shouted.

Debbie appeared from behind. "What are you doing out here? Trời ơi, have you been smoking? It smells so foul in here my head is beginning to hurt—"

"Guys!"

"And your hair! Hurry in, child, and brush that hair out until it no longer looks like a rat's nest. My god. Do you want to embarrass me in front of my friends? And where is that necklace I gave you?"

"Má! Stop!"

"Let's go, come inside now."

"Wait. I need to— Did you know?"

"Know what?" Debbie asked.

"About Take Ten. The nail salon opening up across the street? They're opening up any day now. They're all over the States. And now they're here in Toronto." She paused, waiting for a response that didn't come. "Don't you get it? It's going to change everything! They're going to drive you out of business!"

Debbie looked confused. "What is she talking about? Phil?"

When Debbie turned to look at him, she must have seen something in his eyes that said everything she needed to know. Never had she seen her mother look so humiliated.

"You knew . . ." Debbie mumbled.

"I was going to tell you!" Phil cried.

"Quỷ sứ! You lied to me!"

"I swear I was going to—"

"Stop! There's something else," Jessica interrupted. "I'm coming to work with you at the salon."

Phil's jaw dropped. Debbie's eyes grew large.

"You—you what?" Debbie said before a loud and unexpected laugh escaped her mouth.

They both ran up to give her a hug. As they squeezed her tight, Jessica told herself repeatedly that this was the right thing to do. It had to be.

CHAPTER FIFTEEN

Thuy

C an anyone give me an example of a homophone?" The instructor stood
up from his desk and paced the front of the room.

Thuy quickly flipped through her notebook to find the week they had discussed homophones. Surely she had written a few examples down.

Bobby Santos raised his hand.

"Flour and flower," he said.

"Very good." Mr. Krupinski scrawled Bobby's words on the whiteboard in all caps. "Anyone else?"

"Dear and deer," said Youngju Sohn.

"Nicely done." Two more words were added to the board.

"Pear, pare, and pair," said Mariam Abdalla.

"Excellent job, Mariam. Very excellent."

Thuy found the page she was looking for. There wasn't much to go off of, just some scribbled notes of what a homophone was, but no examples anywhere on the page.

Words that sound the same but have different meanings and spellings.

She could think of at least a dozen of the Vietnamese variety, but English? Nothing was coming to mind. As she sank deeper into her chair, every student took turns shouting out words, receiving praise from the instructor and basking in the reward of having their answers immortalized on the board. By the time the instructor realized Thuy was the only person left who had not ventured an answer, there was no more white left on the whiteboard.

"Thuy, do you have an example you'd like to share?"

Looking down at her notebook again, she hoped that maybe an answer would magically appear on the page. It did not. She spat out the first words that came to her head.

"Fall and fall?" she guessed.

"Actually," Mr. Krupinski said, stretching out the first syllable for what felt like an unnecessarily long time, "those words you just shared is what we call a homonym. Words that sound the same and are spelled the same but have completely different meanings. Thanks for helping us transition into our next subject, Thuy."

Mr. Krupinski—or Sutton, as he preferred to be called—was a former backpacker turned English instructor who had a knack for telling students they were wrong in the nicest way possible, especially with that open smile of his, the kind that allowed the top of his tongue to peek through. He didn't believe in making people feel bad for learning, especially a group of international students who had only just started speaking English less than a year ago. Thuy tried to remind herself of this, but the fact of the matter was she was the only one in the room who'd gotten the answer wrong.

She picked at the eczema on her wrist, watching the flecks of dead skin trickle down to her desk as her skin turned drier and redder. Maybe this wouldn't have happened if she hadn't been so busy at the salon. She would've had more time to study and brush up on her notes and get up to speed like all the other students. After grating the eczema down like lemon zest, she moved on to a dry spot on the inside of her elbow.

Thuy knew she should be grateful for everything she had. Some students here had no job or family at all. She snapped herself out of her pity party. No way did she go through all that immigration headache just to forget how good she had it, how so many of her friends back home would have shaved their heads if it meant they could live in North America. Thuy reached into her bag for her steroid cream and applied a thin layer over the areas she'd been scratching.

When class ended, everyone pushed their chairs away from their desks and packed up their belongings. Outside, the same group that always lingered behind was standing in a circle, talking, smoking, and passing around a bag of chips. Thuy usually walked right by them but today, she was called over.

"Hey, you, come here," said Youngju.

Thuy couldn't stand cigarettes, the smell, the cancer-causing chemicals, the way they yellowed nails so badly that no amount of buffing could whip them back into a healthy-looking state.

"It's Thuy, right?"

She quickly nodded, straightening her spine.

"Cool nails. Where did you get them done?"

Thuy looked down at her nails, forgetting that she'd painted a sunset gradient on them.

"I did them myself," she answered.

This set off a series of exclamations from the rest of the group.

"No way!"

"Are you for real?"

"You *have* to do mine!"

"If *I* did that, there'd be polish all over my knuckles."

Thuy felt embarrassed and quickly crossed her arms. She did not have much practice being the center of attention, so she diverted it elsewhere.

"I like your shirt," she said, gazing at the lace collar on Youngju's sheer white blouse. Youngju moved to Canada from Korea about a year ago and already her English was the envy of the class. There was a confidence to her cadence, and the words cascading out of her mouth sounded like a smooth waterfall.

The students began talking about fashion, what styles they liked, what stores they went to. Thuy didn't say much but enjoyed listening to the conversation. It was like a master class in human interaction. She took note of the ease in which they segued into the next topic. How they used sarcasm to strengthen their statement. The way they offered up a personal anecdote without seeming vain. She was learning more in these few minutes than she had in that last hour of class.

"Anyway, we're all going to check out that Captain America movie later. Wanna join?" Youngju looked at her, flicking ashes onto the ground.

Thuy had never hung out with anyone outside of class. There was usually no time. She'd either have to rush back to the nail salon or head home to help make dinner. She'd also never been invited before.

"Sure, I will come," she responded with a hint of joy in her tone.

"Which number is this one now? Two, three?" said Samra Begum.

"Three. *Civil War*. I've heard really good things about this one," said Bobby.

"Okay, I confess. I see it already. I love it. It's the best of all the Marvel movies," Amy Agmata said, spreading her arms wide.

"That good?" replied Bobby, pulling out his phone to check something.

"Yeah, just wait until you see the part where—"

"No spoilers, please!" shouted Samra.

Thuy covered up her giggle as Samra stuck her fingers in both ears and sang the alphabet as loudly as she could.

Thuy loved action movies. It didn't matter what language you spoke or whether you could understand the dialogue. The stories were always universal and the endings always satisfying. Good versus evil. Good triumphs over evil. It gave her hope that even if you get beaten down and lose everything you love, you could still win in the end.

"We better get going then, it starts in forty-five minutes and I want to get good seats," said Youngju.

All eight of them walked in groups of two. Thuy partnered with Samra, a bubbly girl roughly her age who moved from Pakistan nine months ago. She asked Thuy some questions about herself, then followed up with more questions. They were simple and routine ("Where do you work?" "Do you have family here?") but had the effect of making Thuy feel interesting and important.

She indulged in the spotlight for the next several blocks, but it wasn't long before she wondered if maybe she was talking too much, maybe not asking enough questions about Samra, so her last answers were kept short and to the point. Desperately wanting to make friends, Thuy wished herself more smart and pleasant, not gabby and egotistical.

As they entered the theater and waited in line for their tickets, her cell phone rang.

"You need to come back to the salon. Right now!" said Phil. "Six customers just walked into the salon. Your class is over now, yes?"

Thuy sighed and lowered her head. What was she supposed to say?

"Okay. I'll be there soon."

Everyone was already at the counter buying tickets from the cashier. She didn't want to make a fuss, so she waved goodbye, knowing no one was looking, and quietly walked out of the theater.

CHAPTER SIXTEEN

Jessica

I t had been two weeks since Jessica started working at the salon. The days were long. The headaches were violent. It wasn't just the nail polish and acetone fumes that got to her. It was also the disinfectants they used and the perfumes the customers wore. Wearing a surgical mask helped, but she did not enjoy wearing one. Not only did it smudge her makeup, it made her feel cold and inscrutable, as if she had something nefarious to hide.

The only solution that worked was to take lots of breaks. As soon as two o'clock hit, she stepped outside and breathed in as much air as her chest could possibly take. She walked past an antique furniture store, a juice bar, and a series of restaurants before reaching her usual coffee shop.

One of the few things she relished about working at the nail salon was the location. The Junction was one of those neighborhoods built for the flâneur, one where you could pass the time wandering the streets, heading nowhere in particular but always ending up somewhere.

But some things had definitely changed since she'd been here last. Having lived in urban cities her whole life, Jessica had developed an eye for signs of gentrification. And the Junction ticked off every one of them. Restaurants charging fifteen dollars for eggs and bacon. Check. White women jogging alone with their headphones on. Check. Well-dressed babies being pushed around in $1,000 strollers. Check.

She sat outside waiting for her order. A beagle stopped to sniff her legs, then looked at her with curious eyes as if she had a treat in her hand. She gently rubbed its ears as its eyes rolled back luxuriously.

That was the other thing that was different about the neighborhood; there were so many dogs now. Little ones, big ones, pure breeds, mystery mutts, many clipped with monogrammed collars and leashes.

Her iced latte arrived. She sat back down and scanned the neighborhood from left to right. The Junction—between Runnymede Road and the West Toronto Railpath—was an area of contrasts and contradictions. There were bars everywhere, bars that would have been outlawed during the alcohol ban of twenty years ago. There was a men's clothing boutique that sold Oxford shirts for two hundred dollars, just a mere block away from the pawnbroker whose glass display was still shattered from a robbery the previous week. There was a juice bar on the corner where drug deals happened in the open. There was a seven-story condominium being erected across from a former sandwich shop that closed due to rising rents. In every pocket of the neighborhood was a battle between new and old.

Jessica could see Take Ten from here. Its entire facade was painted in a blush pink, including the door and window frames. It was still wrapped in scaffolding and the windows were covered up in kraft paper, a cheesy message splashed across the front: "Excuse us as we freshen up."

She walked up to the store and peeked through a tiny slit in the paper. It was dark but she could make out the inside. Even with construction material everywhere, she had to admit it looked nice. Like something out of a magazine.

She turned around to look at her parents' salon down the street. The knockoff Patrick Nagel decals were yellowing on the edges. The "Walk-Ins Welcome" neon sign was crooked. And the last word on "Nails Nails Nails" had burned out. Smack-dab between a fancy French bakery and a high-end baby furniture store, Sunshine Nails looked tacky and outdated, like the overly airbrushed square nails once popular in the mid-nineties. Their salon did not complement the vibrancy and newness of the stores around it. It was like the glum person standing in the corner, minding his own business but still managing to put a damper on the party.

"Excuse me?" came a voice behind her.

Jessica turned around. A man wearing sunglasses and a Blue Jays baseball cap beamed at her from ear to ear. He was tall and lanky with a noticeable dimple on the right side of his mouth, like a period at the end of a sentence.

"Sorry, I don't have any money," she said instinctively, turning to walk away.

"Wait!" he said. "Do you live around here?"

"Um . . . yes . . . why?" Jessica said hesitantly.

"My name's Hamza. I'm collecting signatures for a petition," he said, pulling out a clipboard from his backpack. "You might have heard? There's rumors the historic Henderson building could be destroyed and turned into a large commercial building."

"I'm sorry, which building?"

"The bank at Dundas and Keele," he said, pointing towards the intersection. Jessica nodded and let him continue.

"We want to preserve this iconic building. It's an important part of this neighborhood and without it, the Junction will lose a piece of the architectural beauty that makes this area so special." He paused to lift his sunglasses up off his face.

"Some members of the community, including myself, are concerned it will further strip the neighborhood of its unique characteristics and turn it into another bland commercial district." They stepped aside to let a woman with an overpriced stroller go by. "If the rumors are true, this new building could have upwards of nine hundred employees and a parking lot big enough to accommodate at least two hundred cars. It will bring a lot of traffic to the neighborhood and disrupt our residential streets."

It was clear he'd made this speech dozens of times before. He seemed very driven, very passionate, in a way that made Jessica feel like she had a moral obligation to do something. He pulled a pen out from his pocket. "Would you care to sign the petition to stop this demolition from proceeding?"

There was a long list of signatures on the page. The guy had a point.

Somebody needed to do something about all the changes happening in the Junction. The city was already riddled with too many cranes. The last thing they needed was another whitewashed neighborhood. She took his pen and signed. The man handed her a bright green leaflet before walking away.

The salon was packed when she got back. She could hear the girls discussing the ethnicity of one of the customers.

"Her nose says Filipino but her jaw says Japanese," said Kiera.

"What if she's Vietnamese and she can understand everything you're saying? That would be so embarrassing for you," Thuy whispered.

"Vietnamese? No way she can be with those monolids."

"My cousin has monolids. Not all Vietnamese people have double eyelids, you know?"

"Didn't your cousin get the surgery recently?"

"She told everyone she got it to look that way with just eyelid tape. But we all know her parents paid for that surgery as a birthday gift. She looks so different now. I'll show you a picture after I'm done here."

Jessica never understood the power of gossip until she worked at the nail salon. It gave people who had nothing to talk about a reason to engage with one another, to create closeness through the exchange of closely guarded information.

"Jessica, for today."

Debbie handed her a piece of paper. It was a list of tasks that needed to be done: Disinfect the pedicure basins; refill the containers with cotton balls; call customers to remind them of their appointments tomorrow; order two dozen cuticle nippers, ten buffers, and three gallons of pure acetone.

These were the types of tasks her parents trusted her with. She wasn't allowed to do anyone's nails, nor handle any vendor payments, but most of all she was not allowed to throw anything out. Not even old gossip magazines from 2009, when Robert Pattinson and Kristen Stewart were still a thing. Her father kept receipts, expired coupons, and grocery flyers, while her mother had a penchant for take-out containers, plastic bags, and disposable cutlery.

"Do not throw anything out without telling me first," her mother said on her first day. "I don't want to end up like that family that died of beriberi because all they had to eat was white rice. They had so little in their home that the communists stole everything they had in just twenty seconds."

Jessica didn't protest. Their breed of hoarding was steeped in trauma, as if they were stuck in the 1970s and the Vietnam War had never ended. No way was she going to mess with that.

She walked straight to the back of the salon towards the break room, a small seven-by-eight-foot room lit with hot fluorescent fixtures that made everyone look their worst. She slipped her arms through her white spa jacket, the sunshine logo emblazoned on the right breast pocket. With her hair tied up, she started with the pedicure basins.

Getting down on her knees, she swept up yellowed nail clippings and dead skin shavings from people's feet. She'd done it dozens of times by now, but it did not get any less humiliating. Last season she sat in meetings with agents of A-list actors where fresh flowers and chocolate-dipped croissants were artfully presented in the center of the table. Now here she was, collecting a pile of human sheddings on the cold tile floor. It was not the big "fuck you" to L.A. she was hoping for, but at least she was no longer unemployed.

"'Scuse me, miss," said a customer. She stretched her neck up to see an older woman wearing a white T-shirt tucked inside a lilac skirt. "Just letting you know I used the last of the toilet paper."

Jessica stayed on her hands and knees and nodded to the customer. *This is better than no job. This is better than no job.* She muttered it over and over again until those six words became one.

"Is that a new employee over there?" she heard a customer asking.

"Who? Jessica? That's my *daughter!*" her father replied.

"Your daughter?!"

Phil got up to point to the dust-covered baby picture that had been taped to the wall since the salon first opened. "That's her!"

"*That's* Jessica? *That's* the little girl that used to run around here back in the day? It can't be!"

"Jessica!" her father said. "Come meet Allegra. She's one of our oldest clients."

"I beg your pardon? Old?" said Allegra.

Her father laughed uproariously.

Jessica took off her sopping-wet latex gloves and walked towards them.

"I remember you when you were this tall," said Allegra, putting her palm to her knees. "You used to have these cute little barrettes in your hair."

Jessica smiled back. The barrettes she remembered. Allegra, not so much.

"Do you remember I let you choose my designs one time? And you chose this bright orange color with black airbrushed palm trees?"

Still nothing was ringing a bell. It was scary how strangers like Văn and Allegra held more memories of her than she did of herself.

"Phil, I can't believe you didn't tell me until now that this is your daughter. Debbie's daughter maybe. But *yours*? She is *waa-aa-y* too pretty to be yours."

The entire salon bellowed in a chorus of laughter. Her father bitterly brushed off the comment.

"So what brings you back to *Tronnuh*? It can't be this muggy heat wave, I know that for sure," said Allegra.

Jessica shuffled her feet. "I was sick of L.A.," she lied. "Thought I'd come back here and help out my parents."

Her father let out a low guttural sound.

"That is so sweet of you. Phil, your daughter is an angel! Who'd she learn that from? Certainly not *you*!"

More laughter erupted, even from customers in the waiting area who were furiously fanning themselves with flimsy magazines.

"Hot tip," said Allegra, covering one side of her mouth with her hand, "if you ever get tired of your parents, you can always hop over and work at that new salon across the street." She winked and turned her attention back to her nails.

Debbie, who'd been steadily concentrating on painting her customer's nails, stopped and raised her head. The existence of Take Ten had been a sore spot for her mother. Any mention of it would send her into a fit of two things: anger or anxiousness. And who did she blame it all on? Her father of course. He may not have summoned the salon, but he knew about it and did not tell her the minute he found out. That was a betrayal, as far as she was concerned. So for everyone's sake, Jessica prayed Allegra would change the subject.

"What did you think of the article in the *Globe*, Phil? The one I showed you? Sure does look beautiful inside. Never thought a salon like that would ever set up shop here but here we are—"

Phil stepped on the grinding drill, making it rev up even louder and faster.

"*Ouch!* That's hot," Allegra shouted, pulling her hand away.

"Sorry," he mumbled.

Debbie was about to say something, but she put her head back down and continued with a second coat of polish on her customer. An awkward tension settled in the salon.

Sunshine Nails was no stranger to competition. In 2001, there was Amazing Nails, which opened near Willard Avenue and was run by the Nguyễns for four years before a heart attack forced the owner to retire early. Then, in 2009, there was Tips 2 Toes Nails, managed for two years by the Trươngs until a failed health inspection tarnished their reputation so badly that they had to relocate their salon to North York and rebrand it to Five Star Nails. But Take Ten was different. It was a Goliath and they were barely a David.

"Speaking of the devil, look over there!" Allegra pointed out the window.

Everybody stood up and turned to look outside. A construction crew had started mounting Take Ten's name against the pink brick storefront. The "T" and the "A" were installed. Now they were on to "K." It was like watching your enemy prepare for battle while you could do nothing but stand there paralyzed.

Jessica took one huge gulp. It wouldn't be long now before they opened.

CHAPTER SEVENTEEN

Dustin

While the rest of the city was going to church or brunch or a combination of the two, Dustin was going to work. This was the third Sunday in a row he was in the office. Not because anyone had asked him to come in but because he liked working in a quiet space. No unnecessary meetings. No distracting conversations that had nothing to do with work. No obnoxious air horn that set off every time the sales department scored another contract. He wondered how anyone got any work done in that tyranny.

To his surprise, there was someone else in the building.

Chase was in his glass office, pacing the room as he talked on the phone. He was supposed to be in San Diego (or was it San Juan?) until Wednesday. What was he doing back so soon? Dustin suddenly felt like an intruder.

Or maybe not. Maybe being seen in the office on a Sunday was a good thing. Maybe it would finally convince Chase that he was wrong, that Dustin *was* the hardest worker in the office and that he *should* have gotten that raise after all.

He walked to a random door and slammed it so hard that his presence could not be ignored, then fake coughed a few times for good measure.

"Who's there?" Chase popped his head out, the phone still in his hands. "Dustin? Is that you?"

"Hey, good morning, boss," he said casually with a wave of his hand. "Don't mind me. Just coming in to get some work done. I won't be too loud."

"But it's Sunday."

"Oh, it's no big deal. I like working in the office when it's quiet. More productive, you know?"

Chase paused and put his ear to the phone, then turned his attention back to Dustin. "Could you wait a moment, actually? Once I get off this call I want to talk to you." Chase closed his office door and did not wait for Dustin to answer.

Holy shit. Was this it? Was Chase finally going to give him the recognition he deserved?

Forty-five minutes later, Dustin was seated across from Chase. Turned out he had just come off a red-eye from San Antonio, yet the man looked as impeccable as ever. The Texan sun made his freckles more pronounced and the high points of his face a little sunkissed. It had the effect of making his teeth look brighter than they already were.

"I came back a few days early because I need to make an important announcement tomorrow."

"Oh," Dustin said, confused by where this conversation was going.

"And since you're here I might as well tell you. You've been one of the most loyal employees I've ever had. Did you know you've been here the longest out of anybody here?"

Yes, Dustin was quite aware of this, especially that time Chase overlooked him for a managerial position because, like everyone he'd encountered in his life, Chase mistook his introversion for incapability.

"You can't run a business without loyalty, and these next few months are really going to test just how loyal people are to this company. I know I can count on you to stick around during the rough patches."

Dustin nodded and shifted uncomfortably in his chair. He couldn't count the number of times he got to know every new intrepid employee, only to never see them again after they suddenly quit. Retention was not something the company was very good at, but according to Chase's book, high turnover was a good thing. He called it "liver management," a natural purging of toxins that were bound to disrupt the ecosystem. The sooner people quit, the sooner he could bring in better talent.

"Tomorrow I'm going to make an announcement and I want you to know first." Chase paused for effect. "We're moving our offices. We've secured an entire floor to ourselves in a building on the west end. Top floor, sixteen stories high, unobstructed views. It's going to look sleek as hell. Huge meeting rooms, wraparound balconies, floor-to-ceiling glass windows, you name it. Our team is growing, and we need a space that can accommodate all these new people. We need a space that reflects the awesome things we're doing here." Chase leaned as far back as he could on his chair. An inscrutable smile stretched across his face. "Exciting, yeah?"

It took Dustin a moment to figure out where he fell on the spectrum of reactions. It wasn't the news he wanted to hear. But still, a new office meant private cubicles, wider hallways, a bigger kitchen, anything that would nix the need for small talk, which he went to great lengths to avoid. It could even mean he'd never have to hear those raucous salespeople ever again.

"Where did you say it was again?"

"The corner of Dundas and Keele. Are you familiar with the area?"

Dustin was familiar with it all right. It was only a few blocks from the nail salon. But he couldn't pinpoint the exact building Chase was describing. There was nothing taller than three stories in that section. "And which building is it again?"

"That's the best part. It doesn't exist yet. They're tearing down an old building right at that corner and in its place will be the tallest, most epic office tower you've ever seen in the neighborhood. We're moving on to bigger and better things, mate. Bigger and better things."

Dustin was certain he was talking about the Henderson building beside the parking lot, a beaux arts relic with intricate stone molding and balustrades perched on the roof like soldiers standing guard. An architectural gem over a hundred years old, it was an institutional reminder that so much history had come before him. Call him sentimental, but without these buildings, there would be nothing tethering the city to its past. It would be no different from tearing down the family altar. Severing his one and only tie to his ancestors.

"I think I know the building you're talking about. The one with the arched doorway, right?" Dustin said.

"Sure." Chase shrugged his shoulders. "Whatever it is, it won't be around much longer once they demolish it."

"Really? They're allowed to just . . . tear that whole place down?"

"You seem disappointed."

"No, no, that's not it. I just thought heritage buildings were protected."

"I know, right? Worked out so well for us! The city gave the owners the demolition permit a few days ago. Soon it'll be a pile of rubble. Then it'll be our new home."

"Mm-hmm," Dustin responded. "You're not worried about the backlash?"

"Not my problem." Chase raised both palms in the air. "We're just the tenants. Besides, what are they going to do once it's ripped down? Hot-glue it all back in place?" Chase slapped his knees and laughed obnoxiously at his own joke. Dustin went along with it, letting out a halfhearted chuckle.

"You know, my parents work right around there," said Dustin.

"Oh, that's right. Don't they own a Laundromat or something?"

"Nail salon."

"Of course, of course." Chase's eyes wandered down to his phone.

Dustin had mentioned the nail salon a handful of times in the past. Chase had even promised he'd come in for a pedicure, unironically at that, but it never happened. He should've known, though. It was Chase after all, not exactly the best at remembering the names of his employees' partners or pets or kids, or even the employees for that matter. The man was constantly doing something or going somewhere so that it felt indisputably trivial to expect him to remember every single detail of your life.

"Well," continued Chase. "You know better than me how ratty that neighborhood can get. But our real estate agent said this development was a once-in-a-lifetime opportunity and we should take advantage of the low rent right now while we still can. For what we're getting, it's a steal! *Fuck*, I'm just so fucking excited we got into this development. Once you see mock-ups of the new office, you'll be shitting your pants."

Dustin could tell Chase was earnest in his excitement based on the amount of profanity he used in one breath.

"If I may ask, sir," Dustin said. "Why did you tell me this? Why not wait to tell me along with the others?"

Chase received a message on his phone and he glanced down as he spoke.

"Why not? You were here. I'm here. And the deal was just finalized. That was the real estate agent I was on the phone with earlier. Sandra will be sending out meeting invites to the whole staff and soon everyone will know."

Chase still hadn't looked up from his phone, furiously typing something that was clearly more interesting than whatever Dustin had to say next. "Until then, keep this to yourself, all right, mate?"

Dustin didn't show it, but he felt special being the first to hear this news. To be seen was the kind of affirmation he had sought from men like Chase all his life.

"So when do we move in?"

"Not for a *looong* time," said Chase, looking directly at him now. "The proposal still needs to get approved and obviously the building needs to get built. If I could invent something that would speed up the process, I would do it myself. But it'll be worth the wait. Trust me, this place is going to be a million times better than what we've got here. It's going to be *sooo* nice."

Dustin hadn't seen Chase in this good a mood in a long time. Maybe this was the perfect time to bring up the matter of his raise again.

"Well, it sounds like the company is in really good shape. I wondered if we could possibly revisit the topic of my raise again, since our meeting was cut short last time and—"

"Dustin, Dustin, come on, mate. Didn't we just go over this a few weeks ago? Now is not the right time. Didn't you hear what I said? There's so much in flux right now. Let's just wait for the storm to pass and then we can have a proper chat, yeah?"

"But if we could just talk about how I can improve my skills or any areas you think I can focus—"

"Are you quitting on me?"

Dustin was stunned by his candor. "What? No, I just—"

"Do you have another opportunity lined up?"

"No, no. I want to stay here and—"

"Then let's drop it, all right? We can table this until next year." Chase's phone conveniently rang. "Anyway, I'll see you tomorrow? Get out of the office and enjoy your weekend, will ya? I don't want people thinking I'm overworking you. What are we? Google?" He laughed as he turned to face the window.

Dustin was not done talking, but Chase was already well into his phone call. There was nothing he could do except leave. He thought about slipping back to his desk and drowning himself in work, but what use was that? No matter how much he devoted to this job, it was never going to love him back.

At least there was something worth sticking around for. Glancing over at Mackenzie's desk, his insides started to tickle. The past couple of weeks with her had been incredible. They'd gone on three dates. A drink, a dinner, a walk in the park. Each date lasted longer than the one before. And for reasons he could not explain, she kept inviting him over to her place afterwards. At first it was just to watch a movie. Then it became clear. She wanted him, all of him.

It was a wonderful thing to be wanted with such frequency. He knew things were moving fast, but their chemistry was instantaneous, like being zapped with electricity in the most pleasurable way. She was the only thing that soothed the current disappointments of his job. And when he told her this, she confessed the same. They were each other's balm to the existential dread they were both feeling about their careers.

He thought about calling her. Hearing her voice always made him feel better. Maybe she could tell him what to do now that Chase had turned him down once again. He couldn't quit without another job lined up. And he certainly wasn't going to keep making a fool of himself begging Chase.

Screw it.

There was only one thing Dustin could think to do. He walked to the fully stocked beer fridge, filled his backpack with as many bottles as he could, and defiantly drank one on the way out as he flipped a middle finger to Chase's back.

CHAPTER EIGHTEEN

Debbie

The scaffolding came down on a sunny September morning. Take Ten was officially open. The fallen leaves on the sidewalk had been brushed away to make room for a pink-and-white balloon arch over the doors. Upbeat pop music blared from inside as two thin women, one blond and the other even blonder, stood outside handing out flyers to pedestrians.

Debbie counted close to thirty customers who had come and gone from Take Ten. It was only eleven o'clock. Sunshine Nails only had one customer that morning: Nancy, a tired-looking mother of three who hired a babysitter for the first time in five years so she could treat herself to a full day of pampering. In the end, she only wanted a manicure with clear polish, spending just twenty dollars plus two for tip.

Busy mothers had never been their bread and butter. They were too practical and too precious with their time. It was the young, child-free, and precariously employed who brought in the most money. They always wanted more. More glitter. More rhinestones. More pointy. More long. It was as if there was no limit to how much they could optimize themselves.

"Do you think they're handing out gift cards? Why are so many people going inside? How are they allowed to play music this loud?" Debbie asked, not particularly interested in getting a response from anyone. Her face was so close to the window her breath created a small patch of fog that came and went like a flame flickering in the breeze.

"You've been staring at their shop all morning, Má," said Jessica.

"She's right," Phil chimed in. "Get away from there, you'll go crazy."

"Crazy? If you had told me about this salon earlier, we could have done something about this!"

"What exactly do you think you could have done? The salon was going to open no matter what. It was far too late by that point. I'm sorry for not telling you about the article, but you were going to find out anyway. It was better to save you from a couple weeks of worry."

"*Save* me? You saved me from nothing, Phil. All you did was make me look like a fool. I was probably the last person on earth to know."

"Get away from the window," said Phil, cupping her shoulders gently. Debbie flinched at his touch. "I'll make you a glass of hot water and lemon. You'll worry yourself sick standing there."

"Did it even occur to you," Debbie said, turning to look at him, "that this salon could take everything away from us? We were barely breaking even when we had to compete with Five Star Nails. And they weren't even that good! Their nail art looked like something out of a toddler's drawing book! If we were barely scraping by with them, can you imagine what Take Ten will do to us?"

"You think that thought never crossed my mind?" Phil said, his voice rising. "Of course it did. I'm terrified just as much as you. But there's nothing we can do. What's done is done. All we can do is work hard, do our best, and not focus on what other people are doing. That's how we got through the past twenty years. And that's how we'll get through the next twenty. Now get away from the window and sit down!"

Debbie relented. She didn't want to believe that there was nothing that could be done. Taking a passive approach when it came to her salon—or to anything for that matter—didn't sit well with her at all. She needed to do something.

Just then, two women walked into their salon. From a distance, they looked like replicas of one another. Both wore a heavy layer of makeup with overlined lips in the same burnished plum shade. A suede fanny pack was wrapped around waists that were at most twenty-four inches or less. Debbie perked up at the sight of their youth and style-conscious appearance. They looked like the type who spent more money on looking young and beautiful than they did on rent.

"How can I help you?" Debbie said, a bit too eagerly. It was about time things picked up around here.

The tall one pulled out a stack of postcards from her fanny pack and handed them out to everyone in the store. She even left one beside Thuy, who had been napping on the pedicure chair.

"I hope we're not interrupting," the girl yelled out, so loud it startled Thuy awake. "We wanted to introduce ourselves. I'm Victoria and this is Mimi. We work at Take Ten across the street and we wanted to let you know about our grand opening. We're inviting all of our neighbors as a thank you for welcoming us into the neighborhood."

Nobody knew what to say or what to do. Debbie looked down at the postcard. The words "Mimosas & Manicures" were splashed across the page.

"I'll leave a couple more flyers here on the table in case you want to hand them out to any of your customers," said the tall one.

"Hope to see you there!" the other one said, winking at Phil. As she turned towards the door, she whipped her head so fast that her long ponytail nearly whacked Debbie in the face. They exited the salon, setting off the bell chimes.

Everybody stood still, mouths agape.

"I can't believe they just did that!" cried Jessica. "Who do they think they are?"

"Don't they realize we're a nail salon, too?" added Thuy.

"Did you see the smirk on that girl's face? She knew exactly what she was doing," Kiera joined in.

"Look at this!" yelled Jessica. "They left like a dozen flyers on our table. I'm throwing these in the trash."

"Girls, girls! Settle down," said Phil. "We can't let them bother us. We have important things to worry about."

"Like what? Can't you see? There are no customers in here because they're taking them from us!" said Kiera.

"Look! I just saw three more people walk into their salon with the flyers in their hands! Look how busy they're getting!" said Jessica.

"Get away from that window!" cried Phil.

"But they can't just march in here like that and pretend they're the only salon in town. It's so . . . rude and arrogant! This is how they treat their neighbors?" said Jessica.

The girls continued their banter as they desecrated the flyers with nail polish.

Debbie felt all the things the girls were saying. Shock. Anger. Humiliation. She, too, did not want to sit there and do nothing.

"I'm going over there."

"What?" said Phil, staring at her with bulging eyes.

"They invited us to come over so why not? As a good neighbor, we should accept their invitation. It would be rude if we didn't."

"What? That's the stupidest thing I've ever heard. Don't do it," Phil pleaded, shaking his head.

"I'm going over there. If you want to join me, then you can. But I'm going anyway."

Phil paused before speaking. "Why do I feel like you're up to something, Debbie? What exactly are you going over there to do?"

Debbie looked down at her feet, hiding the smirk on her face. She did not have any plans per se, but she liked being the sort of woman who seemed mischievous. Without saying anything, she grabbed her purse and turned towards the door.

"Okay, okay, fine," Phil gave in. "If you're going to go, at least take one of the girls with you."

"I'll go," Jessica said.

"I'll go, too," Thuy echoed.

Just before Kiera could volunteer as well, Phil stepped in. "Not so fast. You two can go but I'll need one person here for the lunchtime rush."

Kiera huffed and sat back down. Phil added one more thing just before they left. "Don't do anything stupid."

The raspberries were the first thing Debbie noticed. Some were bobbing at the top of the glass water dispenser while the majority had sunk to the bottom, giving the water a slightly pink tinge. Stacks of paper cups and napkins were placed neatly beside it, along with trays of cupcakes topped with nail polish bottles carved from fondant.

"Well, aren't they clever?" Debbie whispered to Jessica.

"Did you say something?" her daughter asked.

Take Ten was too loud for whispering. A couple dozen people were chatting away while a nondescript beat played in the background, the DJ discreetly tucked away behind the receptionist table. Despite the crowd, the salon felt luxuriously roomy. The decor was minimal and modern, if a little bland. Birchwood shelves lined the blank white walls, displaying rows and rows of colorful nail polish. A tufted pink sofa marked the seating area, with iPads taking the place of magazines on the tempered glass table. There was no hint of acetone or nail polish fumes. Just an overwhelming scent of peppermint and lavender, as if someone was preparing the world's most epic bath.

A demonstration was taking place at the manicure station, which Jessica and Thuy had already huddled around. Debbie decided to walk around the salon.

Every pedicure chair was occupied by giddy customers who were taking photos of their feet soaking in a copper bowl of fresh petals. Despite all these feet, there was no hint of spoiled cheese smell. The section smelled divine, actually. Debbie tried very hard not to enjoy it, but she couldn't help but breathe a little more purposefully.

There was a letter board displaying the Wi-Fi password on the wall. Installing Wi-Fi was something their customers had always bugged them about, but they never buckled under the pressure. It would cost them an extra fifty dollars a month plus installation and maintenance. Also, it wasn't crucial to how they ran the business, so they decided to upgrade their cable package instead to keep their customers entertained. No one seemed to mind that there was no internet when *Judge Judy* was playing on repeat.

There was no television inside Take Ten, nor were there any massage chairs. Instead, they had pink velvet armchairs facing aerial shots of beaches framed in birch.

How could a nail salon not have motorized massage chairs? Those were a favorite at Sunshine Nails. For a moment, Debbie felt proud that her salon could offer things this salon could not, but that momentary confidence floundered as soon as Savannah Shaw got out a microphone and addressed the patrons.

"One, two, three . . . Mic check, mic check." Savannah cleared her throat. "Can I get everyone's attention, please?"

Everyone turned to face her. Debbie recognized her from the news article. She wore a yellow dress brighter than the sun and rose-gold pumps with metal vines spiraling up the heels. Her hair was more ghostly white in person.

Debbie reunited with Jessica and Thuy, who were now carrying flutes of something bubbly.

"First of all, I'd like to thank everyone for coming out to the grand opening of Take Ten." A few members of the audience clapped softly while others held their phones up to record the speech.

"I can't believe it when I say that this is our twenty-fourth location—and our first location in Canada!"

Cheers and whistling rang out from a group of people in the back.

"This could not have been possible without our hardworking team, some of whom you may have already met. We're excited that so many of you took the time out of your day to come say hello," continued Savannah. "It means a lot to us to have the support of our neighbors and we look forward to growing with you and making this the best damn nail salon in Toronto! May it be the first of many more to come!"

Savannah raised her champagne flute, prompting others to do the same. Debbie suddenly felt naked for not having anything in her hand to hold up, except maybe a middle finger if she had been feeling bolder.

"So please have a look around the salon," Savannah continued. "Let all of your friends know that we're here. And one more thing, if you haven't already gotten your complimentary manicure or pedicure, what are you waiting for? Just grab a table or ask one of our lovely nail techs. You can't miss them. They're the good-looking folks in black aprons."

The audience laughed. As they dispersed and the muffled chatter resumed, Debbie perused the three-panel menu and stared straight at the prices. Fifty dollars for a single-color polish? Seventy for a pedicure? Ninety for gel? Who could ever afford these ridiculous prices? Debbie was flabbergasted at the upcharge, but then a wave of relief washed over her like a cold glass of water. There was no way people were going to pay that much money when they could walk down the street to Sunshine Nails and pay a fraction of the price. Absolutely no way.

Debbie helped herself to one of the many mimosas and nibbled on a warm lavender hibiscus donut as she watched Savannah conduct an interview with a journalist. There was a ring on her finger, an emerald-cut solitaire diamond as bright as the high-beam setting on a car. It was cradled by a delicate sterling silver wedding band. Debbie wondered if her husband was here. But of all the men she saw in the room, none looked wealthy enough to comfortably afford at least a three-carat diamond.

As soon as the journalist put her recorder away and shook hands with Savannah, Debbie knew this was her chance. She scarfed down what was left of her donut, chugged the rest of the drink, and marched towards Savannah with purposeful strides. She could see Jessica and Thuy from the corner of her eye watching with anticipation and a little bit of horror.

"Hi, Savannah. I'm Debbie Tran," she said, extending a hand. With those heels, the woman was at least a foot taller than her. She could practically see up her nose, which had not a single hair in sight. Two stripes of radiant highlight graced her cheekbones, while a faint crack in her foundation ran from her nose to her mouth. Her makeup drew attention to her round eyes, which were as dark as holes. "You've got a lovely shop here," said Debbie.

"Thank you for saying so. That is so sweet of you. Have we met before? Oh wait, were you the one that came in last night to clean the salon? You are a lifesaver. The person we originally hired canceled at the last minute."

Debbie feigned a smile. These were the sorts of assumptions Debbie often encountered when she first moved to Canada. The fact that people thought so little of her fueled her desire to be anything but small and meek.

"Actually, I own the salon across the street with my husband. We've been working in this neighborhood for twenty years, back when your salon was just a Laundromat. Since then it has been a restaurant, a law office, a convenience store, a barbershop—"

"A barbershop? The landlord told me this was a coffee shop before."

"Yes, a barbershop that sold coffee, too. Mr. Mendoza made the most delicious lattes. He would always add a happy face on my foam. It's terrible that he had to leave but he went through a personal tragedy and just couldn't keep up with the rent anymore. When he got the notice that it had nearly doubled, he practically stormed into our salon and slammed the letter on my table. I could see the blood vessels popping out of his eyes. Anyway, maybe it was good timing. He had been complaining more and more about his carpal tunnel. It was probably time for him to settle down and retire anyway."

"Mm-hmm," said Savannah, circling the rim of her empty wineglass. "Why yes, that is too bad. But when one door closes another one opens, right?" Savannah spread her arms wide as if she wanted to hug the entire room. "Tell me again, which one is your salon?"

Debbie described the place in as few words as she could. She had a hard time believing this multimillion-dollar corporation had not already scoped out the competition long before crossing the border. Maybe Sunshine Nails wasn't even a blip on their radar. This wouldn't surprise her at all. People that looked like Debbie tended to get ignored.

"Oh yes!" said Savannah. "I think I might have driven by your salon the other day when I was looking for parking. It's the one with the vintage decals on the windows, right? I love how cute that looks." Savannah bent down slightly to give Debbie's shoulder a good squeeze. "It's amazing that you've been around for as long as you have. We'd be so lucky if we lasted as long as you and your family have."

Lucky? Did this woman think luck was what it took for their business to weather an economic recession, a rapidly gentrifying neighborhood, a natural beauty movement that called on women of all creeds to let their hair, skin, and nails "breathe"? If this woman thought luck was all it took to get through these calamities, then Debbie relished the thought of seeing Savannah's salon crash and burn along with her complacency.

"Look at those nails!" Savannah grabbed ahold of Debbie's hand. Her nails looked sad and naked against Savannah's nails, which were long, pointy, and encrusted with tiny golden gems. With nails like that, it was obvious this woman had never worked on another person's nails a day in her life.

"How about we treat you to a manicure? You look like you need it. Andee, come over here!"

Savannah waved to one of the workers, a curvy pale woman with brown hair that ran the length of her entire torso. "Could you take care of—sorry, your name again?"

"Debbie."

"Andee, could you treat Debbie to whatever she desires? She's our neighbor! Isn't she just the cutest little thing you ever saw?"

Debbie shook her head and pulled her hand back. "No, no, that's okay. If I get my nails done, they'll only be ruined as soon as I get back to work."

"Then how about a pedicure?"

A pedicure? Debbie craned her neck to look across the street. With the glare of the sun, it was hard to tell whether there were any customers back at their salon, but considering how deserted it was this morning, it was most likely still as dead as winter. "I guess I could make time for a pedicure."

"Wonderful!" Savannah was practically squealing. "Andee will take good care of you. She's one of our very best."

Debbie followed the worker to the back of the salon. She peered behind her, only to see that Savannah had already been swarmed by another journalist.

Jessica appeared out of nowhere. Her cheeks were extra pink as if she had just been pinched really hard. She got this trait from her father who, despite having trained his body to tolerate alcohol since the age of twelve, still turned a sunburned red whenever he drank. For Debbie, it served as useful evidence when Jessica was in high school and attempted to mask her Asian glow under copious amounts of foundation.

"Má, we're going to head back to the salon. This place is *sooo* pretentious. C'mon, let's go."

"You two go ahead. I want to look around some more."

"Would your friend like a pedicure as well?" asked Andee.

"Are you serious? You're getting a pedicure?" cried Jessica.

Debbie grabbed her daughter's arm and pulled her aside. "Don't make this a big deal. It's not like I'm paying for it!"

Jessica lowered her voice into a hissing whisper. "But you hate them and everything they stand for! I saw you talking to Savannah over there. What did you even say to her?"

"We were just making small talk."

"Ba is going to find this hilarious. After all the shit you gave him."

"He's not going to know. Because you're going to go back to the salon and tell him that I went for a walk afterwards."

Jessica straightened her back and lifted her chin, as if posing for a photograph. "Wait a minute. What are you up to?"

"Why does everyone think I'm up to something? Can't I enjoy a little time for myself once in a while?"

Thuy broke up their huddle. "Are we ready to go?"

Debbie gave Jessica a desperate look, begging her to drop it and leave. "You two go. I'll follow behind in a little bit." She gently pushed them out the door.

"Care to have a drink?" Andee's voice came from her left, and it suddenly dawned on Debbie that she had an English accent. "It's rose water with agave syrup."

Debbie grabbed the drink and flicked out the petal that was floating inside.

As her feet soaked in the tub, she tried very hard not to luxuriate in the warm bath, but she surrendered. The lavender eucalyptus soak that Andee had prepared for her was just too lovely. She had even managed to set the water at a perfect temperature without having to ask once, "Is this too hot?"

Five minutes into the soak, Debbie couldn't help but lean her head against the curved back of the pink velvet chair. She closed her eyes for just a second, drowning out the chatter and the synthetic beats until it became one dull, soothing sound.

When she opened her eyes again, her feet were dry and blue foam separators were wedged between her toes.

"You're all done here, Debbie. What do you think?"

Debbie looked down at her toes. They were pure white and extra glossy. They looked like teeth.

"You fell asleep before I could ask you what color you wanted so I thought I'd match the color of your shirt," said Andee. "I think it looks great with your skin tone."

Debbie smiled and thanked her. She was rather embarrassed that she had let herself fall asleep on enemy territory. She pulled the separators from her toes, being careful not to smudge the wet polish. The color may have not been her first choice, but at least her calluses no longer felt like tree bark.

Debbie handed her five dollars, then immediately regretted tipping her. She hated that she liked Andee. She hated that her feet were the softest they'd ever been. She hated that she felt so rejuvenated, like she'd slept for a week.

With her shoes in her hand, she wobbled back to Sunshine Nails in her bare feet. For the first time in a long time, Debbie was scared.

CHAPTER NINETEEN

Jessica

A week passed after the opening of Take Ten. Then two, then three. In that time, Jessica noticed a strange thing happening. Business was doing well. Really well. In fact, some days were so busy they didn't have time to eat.

The opening of Take Ten had generated a lot of buzz for the west end neighborhood. There were lineups for everything. A sandwich, a sneaker, an elaborate ice-cream cone. With more people came more business. Was Take Ten's arrival actually a good thing? Neither Jessica nor anyone else at Sunshine Nails dared mention their fortuitous circumstances. They knew better than to jinx a good thing.

Since Jessica didn't have to worry about rent—her parents refused to cash her checks—she was able to put away money into a savings account. She had enough to treat the entire family to an all-you-can-eat dinner at the Royal Dragon Buffet for her father's sixty-third birthday. He was going to be thrilled. Plus, it would make up for all those years she phoned it in and sent him e-cards on his birthday, which she later discovered he never opened because he thought they would give his computer a virus.

Royal Dragon Buffet was a massive restaurant located northeast of the city just off the Don Valley Parkway. They made the best duck and scallion pancakes in the city, and the enormous golden dragon statue it was named after attracted plenty of flashing lights from camera-wielding patrons. What her father liked most about the buffet was that it served every kind of cuisine under the sun: Chinese, Thai, Japanese, Vietnamese, Korean, Indian, Italian, Western. While other people found buffets to be gauche and wasteful, her father liked the dream that buffets sold: that you could bridge cultural divides and break down prejudices one heaping plate at a time.

Dustin was already there when they arrived. And he'd brought a girl.

"Everyone, this is Mackenzie," Dustin said with a huge grin on his face.

Mackenzie stood up and warmly hugged everyone.

"The girl on the porch. Nice to finally meet you," said Jessica. She could see what her brother saw in this girl. She was classically beautiful but not intimidatingly so. The way her eyes did not yield to various distractions in the room hinted at an implacable intelligence. She wore a long, olive-green dress that reached the floor, covering every inch of her body save for her wrists and clavicle. "Good job," she whispered to Dustin.

After all the hellos were said, everybody headed their separate ways: Phil and Debbie made a beeline for the seafood counter, where a lineup had already formed for the hot batch of lobster tails that had just come out. Dustin and Mackenzie were more methodical with their approach, preferring to see everything first before picking up a plate. Thuy started slow with a few rolls of sushi, while Jessica went straight to the scallion pancakes.

"Mackenzie, what do you do for work?" Phil asked once everyone got back to the table.

"I work with Dustin," Mackenzie said.

"Ah yes, that's right, I remember now."

Jessica jumped in. "Remember what? Dustin never told you that."

Phil's cheeks turned red as he ignored her. "And what do you do there?"

"I work in the customer success department."

There was a pause as they all waited for her to say more.

"I answer calls and respond to customer feedback. Make sure they're happy with our app and answer any questions they have. You know, that kind of stuff. It's nothing as exciting as what Dustin does."

Dustin jumped in. "She's selling herself short. Mackenzie is really good at what she does. She can upsell and cross-sell better than anyone on that team. Actually, maybe you guys can take a few pointers from her."

Mackenzie blushed before looking down at her food.

Phil nodded, loudly sucking the juices out of a lobster shell.

Debbie chimed in. "You sound like you work very hard, just like Dustin. Do you have to work on weekends like he does?"

"Oh no, definitely not. I leave at five like a normal person."

"Can you please tell my son that work is not everything?"

"Excuse me, hypocrite much?" said Dustin. "Besides, I'm working hard so I can save up and get my own place someday. Rent is just insane right now, even with roommates."

"Well, you're right about that," said Phil, turning to face Mackenzie. "When we first moved here, Dustin's mother and I only had to pay nine . . . no wait . . . eight hundred and seventy dollars a month and we lived in a two-story home with two bathrooms and two bedrooms. No roommates, just us. Now I see all these young kids moving into apartments smaller than my broom closet and the amount they're paying for rent is crazy. I'm thinking, 'Who in their right mind would ever pay that much to live like this?' You can get much more real estate living in the park—and that's free!"

Phil gulped some of his beer and accidentally slammed the glass down so hard that some of it splashed on his shirt. "That's why Dustin is still living at home with us, saving up his money and waiting until this real estate bubble crashes. Want my advice? Stay at home with your parents until you get married." Phil winked at the couple.

"Ba, some people prefer their independence," said Dustin. "Not everyone loves living with their parents."

"Are you saying you *looove* living with us?" joked Phil, who shot up from his seat, clasping one hand on his heart and the other in the air, mimicking a dramatic reading of a sonnet. "My son, on my birthday, has finally admitted to loving me! Oh what better day could there be?"

"Oh my god, can you not be so loud?" said Jessica, covering her eyes.

Thuy and Mackenzie both chuckled into their plates while Dustin desperately tried to lower his neck into his dress shirt like a turtle in retreat. Phil tipped his head back and roared with laughter.

"I must say, Dustin is very lucky to have parents like you two," said Mackenzie, shooting Dustin a smile.

"Like I said, young children should not be paying so much for their rent just so they can claim to have some kind of false sense of independence," said Phil. "You're better off saving it and spending it on your future family."

"Don't listen to him, Mackenzie," said Jessica. "He's just being a typical Asian parent. I practically had to cross the border to gain any kind of freedom whatsoever."

"And how did that turn out for you, daughter?" said Phil, his mouth full of greasy noodles now. "With great freedom comes great changes."

Jessica buried her face in her hands and let out a groan. "That's not how the saying goes."

"Well, I think it's very noble to let your children stay with you as long as they can," said Mackenzie. "Especially given how expensive everything is in this city."

Debbie smiled. She seemed to be liking this girl. "So where do your parents work?"

"My mother runs a catering company and my father is an angel investor."

"Angel investor? That sounds lovely. What is that?"

"Basically he gives people money if he thinks they have a good business idea."

Debbie laid her utensils down, looking intrigued. "What sorts of businesses does he give money to?"

"There have been so many I can't remember them all. Some have done well. Others not so much. My mother and I *never* hear the end of it when one of his investments fails. You never want to be in the room when he gets *that* phone call."

"Ooh, like what?" said Debbie, leaning into the table.

"There was this one company that created a self-brushing toothbrush. You just stick it in your mouth and it cleans your teeth for you. I tried it. It actually worked. But some shipments went out with malfunctioning equipment. One customer's gums got all cut up. A total liability nightmare. Not to mention the company's founder was a narcissistic train wreck. Always late to board meetings. Disheveled appearance. One time he showed up to a media interview reeking of tequila. Anyway, it didn't end well and my dad lost six figures on that company."

Jessica nearly choked on her deep-fried shrimp wonton. "Six figures? Low end or high end?"

"Take a guess," Mackenzie said nonchalantly. "But seriously. Don't feel bad for him. My dad is not hurting."

"So you're rich?" Debbie asked.

"Má!" Dustin shouted. "Jesus, you can't just say stuff like that!"

"What? It's a compliment! Anyway, Mackenzie, your father sounds like a very smart and capable man. Maybe one day Phil and I will get to meet your parents."

Dustin's face immediately lit up. Jessica, too, was stunned. Their mother never took kindly to anybody they dated. They were either too quiet, too loud, too strange, too boring. When she first started dating Brett, her mother said his jawline was too weak, how it was a sign of someone who was selfish and bad in bed.

Come to think of it now, she wasn't wrong.

Debbie raised a glass in the air. "To my husband and my love. Happy birthday, Phil!"

"Happy birthday!" everyone cheered, joining their glasses.

As Jessica took a sip, she saw the blurry silhouette of a tall woman through her fingerprint-smeared wineglass. That's when she realized it was Savannah Shaw emerging from the bathroom.

What was she still doing in Toronto? And *here* of all places? She did not seem like the kind of person who would be caught dead gorging on a bottomless pit of greasy food among a cacophony of screaming infants and clumsy servers.

"Savannah!" Jessica hadn't expected to blurt out her name, but she did, and she couldn't take it back now. Savannah spun her head around and looked in their direction. Immediately Jessica blushed, untucked her hair from her ears, and curled one corner of her lip upwards. Savannah was clearly mortified to be recognized. Jessica took much pleasure in seeing it, so she decided to yell some more. "Come over here!"

Her entire family stared at her like she was a rabid animal. "What the hell are you doing?" Debbie hissed. But it was too late. Savannah was approaching them, if a little hesitantly, and gave a weak wave with her peachy ballerina nails.

"Do you remember me? From the Hotellium?" Jessica asked.

"Yes, yes, of course. What a small world," said Savannah, fixing a smile on her face.

"And my mother, Debbie? We stopped by your salon the day it opened."

"*This* is your mother? Wait, do you work at the salon, too?"

Jessica nodded and watched as Savannah absorbed this information, waiting for a furrow of the brows or a widening of the eyes. But there was none of that. She looked preoccupied by something else, her head continuously turning back as if she was expecting something or someone. Clearly she had more important things to do.

"Sorry," Jessica sneered, "I didn't mean to interrupt what you were doing. You probably need to get back to your—"

Just then a man with heavily hooded eyes swooped in behind her. He wore a blue button-down shirt that was light enough to reveal the outlines of his nipples.

"There you are! I just settled up. Ready to go?" He stared at the Trans, confused.

Savannah spoke up. "This is the family that owns the nail salon across the street from Take Ten."

"Oh!" he remarked with the widened eyes Jessica had been waiting for.

"This is the daughter and the mother," she said, pointing at them like they were hippos at feeding time. Jessica pushed her plate away, suddenly wishing a waiter had collected the heaping pile of king crab legs she had consumed. "Sorry, and the rest of you are . . ."

"I'm Dustin, the son. That's my dad, Phil. My cousin, Thuy. And this is my girl . . . friend girl. She's my Mackenzie . . . I mean my friend." Dustin looked like he wanted to die.

"Hello, it's a pleasure to meet you," Mackenzie said merrily, shifting her body and extending a hand to them.

"What a beautiful family you have," Savannah said, looking directly at Jessica. "I had a feeling that was your father. You two have the same almond eyes. Just beautiful."

Her father blushed so hard it showed through his already tinged cheeks. "Thank you, thank you." He stood up and nearly bowed, as if he was greeting a senior member of the monarchy. Debbie tugged on his shirtsleeve and he quickly sat back down. Plastered on everyone's faces was a tight-lipped smile.

"What are you doing in Toronto? I thought you were only here for the launch," Jessica said.

"Oh god no," she exclaimed. "I wish that's how it worked. There's still so much to do. I'm practically here every other week tying up some loose ends."

"And you?" Debbie chimed in, looking at the man. "You don't mind your wife traveling so often?"

"Theo? Oh no, no, no. He's our operations manager," Savannah corrected. "My husband's home in New York." They both laughed, seemingly not at the misunderstanding but at their stupidity.

Jessica's eyes darted back and forth between the pair. If they had just finished eating, she couldn't tell. There were no signs of expanded bellies, or belts that clipped at the last hole, or cheeks that flushed from the sudden intake of salt, or lips left shiny from a film of grease. These two exhibited none of those features; instead they looked like they'd just stepped out of a Calvin Klein ad.

"Don't tell my nutritionist I'm here," continued Savannah. "She'll kill me if she finds out how much MSG I've just eaten. I could literally feel my heart racing right now."

"Actually," said Dustin, pushing his chair back so he could face the two directly. "It's a common misconception that MSG is a harmful ingredient. If you think about it, it's actually in everything we eat. Tomatoes, asparagus, bouillon cubes. It's even found in breast milk. It wasn't until some people started complaining about their limbs feeling all tingly after eating at Chinese restaurants that scientists began linking it back to the MSG. But most of the time if people didn't know there was MSG in their food, they would experience no symptoms at all. I mean, it's kind of like if I told you the milk you just drank had gone bad. You'd suddenly feel your stomach start to churn right? But the milk is fine. And if I didn't tell you it had gone bad, you would be feeling perfectly fine. In fact, you *are* fine! That's probably a bad example, but you know what I mean. It's the nocebo effect."

He paused, waiting for a response that never came, so he carried on. "Basically, if you think something will make you sick, it will make you sick. The brain is very powerful. That's why you see those 'No MSG' signs everywhere. As soon as people see those words, the tingling fingers and heart palpitations magically disappear. And I can guarantee you some of those restaurants still sprinkle a little bit of it on. You can't keep them from using MSG. It's like telling a chef not to use salt!"

Jessica looked up at Savannah and Theo, who were at a loss for words. Then she looked over at her mother, who was beaming from cheek to cheek. This was why they were always telling Dustin he should've gone into politics or law or teaching, a job where the whole point was to be persuasive.

Dustin turned to look at their mother. "Don't you use MSG when you make phở, Má?" He turned his head back to them. "She makes the best phở."

"Debbie, you know how to make foe?" said Savannah, pronouncing it incorrectly despite having just heard the word. "I absolutely love Korean food. My nutritionist"—Jessica fidgeted in her seat, preparing to correct her if only she could stop talking for a second—"keeps going on and on about how many probiotics are in kimchi. She says, just one spoon a day is all you need. It took me so long to even get over the look of it. What does it remind me of? It reminds me of . . . yes, a wad of wet toilet paper. You know exactly what I'm talking about, don't you?" Savannah slapped Mackenzie on the shoulder, who in turn let out a nervous laugh.

"I had to close my eyes the first time I had it. Norah practically forced it down my throat. Thank god she did! My skin has never looked more amazing. Who knew such an unpleasant-looking thing could be the key to a youthful complexion? It's no wonder your entire family has such glowing skin. You Koreans have all the beauty secrets, don't you?"

More nervous laughter ensued from the table, and everyone seemed resolved to ignore her and move on.

"They're Vietnamese, actually," Mackenzie spoke up.

"Oh, right, of course! You know what I meant! The chardonnay must be getting to my head." Savannah swung her arm back and nearly hit a server who was carrying a very precarious tray of colorful cocktails. The server gave Savannah the kind of stare that could freeze an entire ocean.

"We should probably get going," Theo said.

"Nice meeting you all," she said. "Enjoy your dinner!"

Jessica watched them disappear through the front door.

No longer in the mood to eat, she proceeded to play around with the remnants on her plate. It seemed no one else felt like eating, either, except her father, who took a huge bite out of a deep-fried shrimp ball. "Is it true, son? Breast milk, really?"

———

Dustin took Mackenzie home in a separate cab. Jessica drove everyone else home, traveling westbound on the highway and relishing the lack of bumper-to-bumper traffic. The radio was on, something about a dead whale that washed up on a beach in Indonesia with a bunch of plastic bags in its stomach.

"The news gets more and more depressing every day," said Debbie, who had claimed the passenger seat to prevent post-meal nausea. "You'll go to the grave with a heartache if you keep listening to this stuff. Change the station."

Jessica turned the knob and stopped when she heard Sam Roberts's sinewy voice.

"So . . . that Savannah is a piece of work, isn't she?"

"That woman's got something going on in her head," Debbie said. "How could she possibly think we were Korean? Look at this stubby nose! They don't make it like this in Korea!"

Everyone burst out laughing.

"That's a first though," said Thuy. "I've gotten Chinese, Thai, Cambodian. Even Hmong! Not Korean yet."

"Better tick it off on the map. You've almost got all the Asian countries!" said Phil.

"How about you, Jessica?" asked Thuy. "What have you gotten?"

Jessica checked her blind spot and merged onto the middle lane. "Let's see. I've definitely been mistaken for Korean before. I even got Japanese one time. Filipino, too! And you, Ba?"

"Hmm, a customer thought I was from Laos. I didn't mind. It's flattering, really. Those Laotians are beautiful people."

"I think we've almost got all the countries! Just need a few more to complete my collection!" joked Thuy.

Jessica laughed, then got quiet. It was a weird thing to laugh at. Sarcasm could only do so much to mask the ugly truth that society still saw them as one huge monolith.

"So what did everyone think of Mackenzie?" Jessica asked, curious.

"Who?" replied Phil, sitting up straight.

"Dustin's girlfriend," Thuy said, letting out an audible exhale.

"Was that her name? Are you sure? She looks more like a"—he paused to burp—"like a Caroline."

"Phil, stop joking around. What does a Caroline even look like?" said Debbie.

"Like *her*."

"You only say that because a woman named Caroline came into the salon yesterday and she had the same long black hair as Mackenzie did."

"Well, don't you agree then? They looked very similar."

"There's about a thirty-year difference between the two."

"Guys!" Jessica interjected. "You didn't answer my question."

"What?" Debbie replied. "About Dustin's girlfriend? She was a lovely girl. Very well-mannered."

"That's it?"

"She was very pretty," said Thuy.

"Má, you're not going to say anything about the fact that he's not dating a Vietnamese girl? You were always nagging me about that when I was younger!"

"We only want happiness for our children," Debbie said in a rather robotic manner, as if it were one of her dozen preprogrammed statements.

"This is a free country," Phil added. "Everyone can date whoever they want to date."

Dear god, what cult did her parents accidentally join? When did her parents become so unconcerned with whom their children were dating? When she was as young as seven, her mother had always tried to impress upon her the importance of preserving traditions, and the ultimate way to do that, they said, was to marry within the culture. By the time Jessica was seventeen, her parents had already amassed a list of suitable Vietnamese boys she could possibly marry, a third of whom were named Brian. The idea that there was one kind of person that Jessica could end up with was so off-putting that she gravitated towards men who were the exact opposite of what her parents wanted for her.

"Hold on," Phil said. "I got a text from the landlord. Can we stop by the salon? He said he dropped off a letter. Just take this exit. It's on the way home anyway."

Half an hour later, the car was parked outside the salon as the Tran women waited inside the car.

"Is this for real?" Phil screamed, waving a piece of paper in the air.

"What? What is it?" asked Jessica.

"Doyle is raising the rent. I *fucking* knew it. I knew that motherfucker would do this!"

Debbie sat up straighter. "He does that every year. We knew that was coming. What's the big deal?"

"It's fifty percent!"

"Phil, please, not right now. It's late. We're all tired. Your jokes just don't have the same effect anymore. Get back in the car and let's go home. I'll make you a cup of tea before bed."

"Take a look for yourself."

Phil shoved the sheet of paper through the car window. His outburst was beginning to attract glares from a group of drunk men who looked far too young to be barhopping.

Debbie turned down the radio, switched on the interior car light, and squinted her eyes to read the small type on the page. "Jessica, read this to me. My glasses are at home."

Jessica leaned over and concentrated on the first paragraph. Her father paced the sidewalk back and forth with his hands clasping his hair.

Please be advised that effective January 1, 2017, the monthly rent for the rented premises of the above address shall be increased to $4,100 per month, payable on or before the 10th day of every month. This is a change from your present rent of $2,050 per month. All other terms of your tenancy shall remain as presently in effect.

The rest of the letter went on to describe the commercial tenancy act, a blurry block of legalese that Jessica didn't bother to read out loud. She confirmed the news to her mother.

"How can they do this to us?" Debbie cried out.

"Maybe this is a mistake," said Thuy. "Maybe it was meant for someone else."

"Are you an idiot, child? It's addressed to us!" Phil shouted from the sidewalk.

Thuy sank deeper into her seat and remained silent.

"Nobody is an idiot." Debbie turned around and squeezed Thuy's knee. "Please, Phil. Get back in the car. Everyone is staring at you. You look crazy. It must be an error. Get in the car and we'll figure it out when we get home."

"Fuck it! I'm doing it."

"Phil, what exactly are you doing? Where are you going? Get in the car right this second!"

Jessica watched as her father walked towards the back of the car. With his back to them, they heard the sound of a zipper followed by a heavy stream of urine crash-landing on the pavement. Her father's head was tilted back, the moon's reflection perfectly bounced off his shiny forehead. Like a wolf, he let out a long, primal howl that practically scared every underage drinker on the street into going home.

CHAPTER TWENTY

Phil

After failed attempts to negotiate a new agreement with the landlord, Phil sat down in the kitchen and did some math.

The car insurance was bad enough. Now that they had to pay four thou— Phil couldn't even say the number. It felt like a sick joke. They were going to have to make a lot more money now. How were they supposed to keep up? If it was simply a matter of working harder, faster, longer, then that was not a problem. But there were only so many hours in a day. And the timing was absolutely terrible. As temperatures dipped, people were less inclined to leave their homes, let alone take their hands and feet out of hibernation.

Phil had no choice but to call an emergency meeting. He even asked Kiera to rush over to their house right away; this was news that everybody needed to hear.

"If we want to keep the salon open, there's only one thing we can do," said Phil, standing stoically at the head of the dining table.

He paused to stare at the bewildered faces peering back at him. It was times like these he felt like an imposter. He was supposed to be the protector of the family, the one who made everyone feel safe, who could wipe away those worried expressions with a hard day's work or, at the very least, a witty joke. What a trap it was to be given this expectation. It was too much for any man to live up to.

"You're not going to like what I have to say." Phil chugged the glass of water that was on the table. "It's going to make sense when I show you the spreadsheet."

Phil tapped his hand to his groin to make sure his zipper wasn't down, an old habit. "We had it color-coded and everything. Even our bookkeeper complimented us. He said it was the most organized balance sheet he had ever—"

"Oh just tell them, Phil!" shouted Debbie.

"Spit it out, old man!" said Dustin, who was not asked to join the meeting but was standing in the corner of the room anyway, sucking on a cherry Tootsie Pop.

"All right, all right," Phil said, scratching his temple. "Girls, how do I put this? Well, this is not easy to say, and I promise it's temporary . . . it's the only way." He let out a huge breath. "You're all going to have to take a pay cut."

Jessica leaned into the table. "Are you serious?"

"How much are we talking here?" said Kiera.

Even Dustin, who had no skin in the game, let out a reaction. "Wow."

Thuy remained silent. Her eyes became glassy and she looked like she might cry any minute.

"How is this possible?" Kiera blurted. "Business has been good! Last week we were working past nine! The other day we had a bachelorette party that spent over five hundred dollars!"

Phil stood up, puffing out his chest like a fat rooster on the strut. "I know, I know. It seems like we're doing well, and we are. It's just . . . we went through the numbers so many times. The rent, the taxes, the winter . . ." He felt so defeated. Why hadn't there been Hennessy in that glass?

"The good news," he continued, "is that this is only temporary until we figure out our cash flow situation. I am confident that by spring, our profit margins will be up and you'll all go back to your usual pay. For now, I have no choice but to cut thirty percent from your monthly paycheck."

"*Thirty?*" Kiera cried out, sinking back into her chair with arms crossed. "This is so unfair. Why don't we raise the prices instead? Did you see what that other nail salon was charging? Seventy dollars for a pedicure! Why am I breaking my back on two customers when I could make the same amount with just one?"

"We can't go changing the price from thirty to seventy overnight," said Phil. "The customers will hate us. They'll start a riot! Or worse, they'll boychuck us!"

"Boycott," Dustin corrected from the corner.

"There has to be another way," Jessica chipped in. "If we can't raise the prices, why don't we cut back on expenses? I'm not going to name names but I've seen some of you use, like, a dozen cotton balls to remove nail polish. For *one* hand! It's such a waste."

"Why are you looking at me?" cried Kiera, her eyes expanding.

"I didn't." Jessica shook her head. "I'm just saying we could all be a bit more cautious with our supply use. I know it doesn't seem like much but the costs add up over time."

"Jessica has a good point," said Debbie, who also darted her eyes at Kiera. "If we could all not be so wasteful, then Phil and I wouldn't have to reorder supplies as often."

"Okay, seriously. Why is everybody looking at *me*?" said Kiera. "It's not like I'm the only one that's doing it. The other day I saw Thuy pour almost half a bottle of dead sea salt in the pedicure bath."

"I told you a million times. It was *not* half a bottle!" Thuy yelled, banging both of her fists on the table so forcefully that it stunned everyone.

"Okay, okay," Phil jumped back in. "Let's all calm down. These are all very good ideas but even if we cut down on our supply orders, we won't be saving nearly enough to cover the rent. I'm sorry but it's going to have to come out of your pay. We're taking a cut, too! Trust us, we've thought of all the options. Like I said, this is only temporary. To make it up to you, any tips that Debbie and I receive will be divided up between the three of you."

"This is bullshit," Kiera said, rolling her eyes.

"Unbelievable," exclaimed Jessica. "Thuy, how can you sit there like that? Aren't you angry? Don't you have anything to say?"

Thuy didn't say anything. Her eyes were getting red and puffy despite any evidence of tears. She curled back into her usual meek self and offered no further words on the subject.

"She doesn't care. Why would she? She gets to live in this house rent-free and doesn't have to pay for anything," Kiera interjected. "Mr. Tran, unlike some people I have books and rent and food to pay for. This is my last year of university. I don't have time to work another job. My grades will suffer!"

Phil peered at all the girls sitting across from him. If only his father could have seen this. He would have been disturbed at the level of talkback he was receiving from these kids. This would have never happened back home. Growing up in Vietnam, Phil attended weekly classes on how to make your grandparents and parents happy. By the time he was a teenager, the filial piety was drilled so deeply into his bones that he would rather chop off his fingers than get beaten for being disobedient.

"Wait, I have an idea!" said Jessica. "Why don't we run a promotion?"

Phil rubbed his eyes. "I don't know . . ." he said, shooing the air as if there was a pesky fly circling his head. "I don't know if we can afford to give away discounts at this time."

"It won't be any regular discount. We'll encourage them to bring people. We'll run an offer they can't resist." Jessica paused, seemingly waiting for an idea to strike. "Aha! Bring one friend, get twenty percent off. Bring two friends, get thirty percent off."

"Thirty?!" Phil shouted.

"Trust me, Ba! This is the way to attract more clients. Once they see how great we are, they'll keep coming back long after the promotion is done. You won't even have to do a thing. Let me handle the advertising. I'll get some friends to spread the word. It'll all work out! We'll make the difference in rent in no time."

Phil and Debbie looked at each other. In all their years of marriage, they formed an ability to reach an agreement without ever uttering a word to each other.

"Fine," replied Phil. He walked towards the bathroom before turning back around. "Just don't get your hopes up, okay?"

Everybody gave a halfhearted nod before dispersing.

Despite having his doubts, Phil couldn't help but cling on to some hope. He *had* to believe everything would be okay. It was the survivalist in him. If he could overcome war and displacement, then he could make it out of this, too.

He walked to the family altar and stared directly at the gold, cross-legged Buddha perched in the center.

Surely, the gods wouldn't punish him any more than they already had.

CHAPTER TWENTY-ONE

Thuy

There was so much Thuy wanted to say at the meeting. But she choked. A familiar lump of frustration had swelled in her throat, preventing her from letting anything out.

Kiera was wrong about her. They were all wrong about her. She *did* care. She *was* angry. She *did* need the money. Did they forget she had a family back home to take care of? Of course they forgot. She was always being treated like a brief speck. Nothing but a pair of helping hands.

For what it was worth, she did not think the promotion was going to work. If money was as tight as Phil and Debbie said, then what good would a discount do? It was bad enough they were docking her pay, but now she'd have to do the same amount of work for less money? How unfair. She felt so unappreciated, like a falling star that nobody bothered to look up and notice. But of course, she couldn't tell them any of this. As an immigrant teenage girl, grateful was the only feeling she was allowed to express.

So here she was, wrecking her wrists trying to staple promotional flyers all over the neighborhood. It was Jessica's idea to strategically place them near businesses where a potential Sunshine Nails client might frequent: hair salons, tanning beds, yoga studios, coffee shops, gyms. Once the last flyers went up, all they had to do was wait.

"I've gotta say," said Allegra, "I've been coming to this salon since day one and never once has there been a promotion. I kept telling Phil and Debbie they should do some kind of discount, at least during Christmas or something. Or they should hand out those punch cards like they do at the bubble tea shops, you know, buy ten get one free. Think of all the free sets I would have had by now!"

Allegra was sitting in her favorite chair, waiting for her month-old acrylics to soak off. This time, she wanted to try out a bold new design: bright magenta camouflage on long coffin tips.

"You know how they are. They don't like things to change," replied Thuy.

"Sure they do. They hired you, didn't they? Finally got some young blood around here. I bet you'll take over for them one day."

"Me? Oh no. I—" The thought of claiming anything as her own was so absurd that Thuy found herself giggling. "This is their salon. I can't take it from them."

"Why not? They're not getting any younger." Allegra peered towards the back room where Phil and Debbie were eating lunch. "I mean, no offense to them but they're not as spry as they used to be," she said, lowering her voice. "Why do you think I asked *you* to do my nails? You're fast. You're precise. You, Jessica, Kiera—I can see you girls running the whole thing. And I'm not just saying that so you'll knock off the price of those rhinestones."

Allegra winked as Thuy found herself reddening. She was startled to hear someone sound so confident about her abilities. Did someone pay Allegra to say these things? She looked out the window, expecting to catch Jessica and Kiera peering through the glass and laughing their heads off as they watched her fall for their prank. But nobody was there. Just a pigeon with a broken wing.

Thuy put her mask on and lifted Allegra's fingers from the bowl to check the progress. The acetone was fully seeped into the acrylic, bloating it out and melting it off the nail, but it needed a good five more minutes of soaking.

"What kind of pink would you like?" Thuy walked to the wall of polishes and held up three contenders. "Cha-Ching Cherry, Feelin' Hot-Hot-Hot, or Aurora Berry-alis?"

Unlike most of their clients, Allegra needed only half a second to decide. "The one you're holding on the left. The brightest one. And let's also go for that light pink one that's on the wall, up top and to the right . . . yeah that's the one. Do you have any cool gray tones? I've got an exact idea of how it'll all look in my head."

Thuy marveled at how Allegra knew exactly what she wanted and declared it so boldly. She wondered if it was something people were born with or if it was learned over time. If it was the latter, perhaps there might be hope for her after all.

Phil stepped out from the back, wiping his mouth with a tissue. "There she is, the traitor who didn't want me to do her nails."

Allegra let out a loud, thunderous laugh. "You know me, Phil. I've gotta spread the love. Besides, I need a super-steady hand for this one. The design I've got in mind is very complicated."

"I'm just kidding. Thuy's got the steadiest hand on this earth. We don't know what we'd do without her. I swear she could be a surgeon."

Thuy clenched her jaw as she vigorously wiped off the acrylics one by one. She couldn't believe the words coming out of Phil. First, he slashes her pay. Then, he hails her as his most invaluable worker. The worst part was she detected no ounce of awareness over his hypocrisy. For the first time, Thuy realized she deserved better. It was a sickening feeling.

"Remember the time you made her cut up that ten-dollar bill?" Phil slapped Thuy's back in a way that felt more violent than playful.

Thuy looked up at Allegra, preparing herself to hear the story again, a story made possible because of her.

It took place six months ago. Allegra had walked in with a rolled-up magazine under her arm. She flipped to a page featuring nails adorned with ripped-up American dollar bills, said it was designed by Bernadette Thompson of Yonkers, New York, a nail legend who gave Lil' Kim her famous money nails in the nineties, back when no one cared about nail art. Allegra went on and on about those nails to anyone and everyone that walked into the salon, how the design was so revolutionary that it had a permanent display at the Museum of Modern Art. "I've got to have these!"

"Allegra," Phil had shouted. "We don't have any American bills. And it's illegal to mutilate banknotes. The last thing I need is to have the police raiding our store!"

"Don't worry, Phil," Allegra responded as she reached into her purse and took out a ten-dollar bill featuring Sir John A. Macdonald's purple-tinged face. She grabbed a pair of scissors and proceeded to cut up the bill like it was split ends. Everyone's face lit up with equal parts horror and awe. The nail techs, the customers, even the repair guy who'd come in that day to fix the television, were shocked.

"Jesus Christ, are you crazy?" Phil said. "I'm not doing it. I'll do anything else. I'll paint you a peacock, I'll make your nails as long as my arm, I don't care. But I'm not going to put money on your nails!"

Debbie also refused, and Kiera didn't dare say a word. The entire salon froze into a state of awkward discomfort. Until Thuy spoke up. "I'll do it."

When she finished, Allegra was as happy as a child at a carnival. She posted a picture of her nails on social media, and it garnered so many likes that even journalists were calling the salon asking for an interview. Thuy was too shy to talk to anyone. She was afraid her English wouldn't be good enough. Now, she regretted not claiming her spotlight.

Allegra wiped tears from her eyes. "I still won't forget the look on your face, Phil. I'd never seen a grown man look so scared in my life."

Phil handed her a tissue. "Can you blame me? You were paying money to lose money! Who does that?" Now Phil was dabbing his eyes.

Thuy was glad for her mask. She didn't need to feign amusement for anybody. She just focused on correctly sizing and applying the translucent tips to each nail.

"Anyway, our Thuy did an excellent job. Your best work yet." Phil patted her on the back. Thuy tried her hardest not to flinch.

"Oh, did Thuy give you these?" Phil handed Allegra a stack of flyers featuring their upcoming promotion. "Would be great if you could hand these out to your friends."

"You don't think I haven't already converted all my friends? I even convinced my brother to come here once! A fifty-two-year-old man who eats his bananas sideways because he thinks it makes him look more manly!" Allegra rolled her eyes so far back only the whites were visible.

Phil turned around to wipe down the mirrors with Windex. "Maybe he's got friends he can convert," he joked.

"What's really going on?" said Allegra, her tone becoming serious. "Why are you giving out discounts all of a sudden? You never do that."

Thuy held on to Allegra's hand firmly as she glued each tip down, making sure to push out all the air bubbles.

"What do you mean?" said Phil.

"Is business slow? It's that damn nail salon across the street, isn't it? I knew it!"

"No, it's not—"

"Those people," Allegra continued, shaking her head. "They think they own this neighborhood just because they've got every subway and streetcar covered in their ads. I swear, if I catch anybody I know walking into that salon, I'll never talk to them again. I mean it."

Thuy warmed at her sentiment. She desperately wanted to tell her that the future of the salon was not looking good. But what was the point? Nobody could do anything about it. Like death and taxes, rising rent was just an inevitability. This was something they'd have to figure out on their own.

A fresh breeze rushed into the salon along with a scattering of leaves as Jessica and Kiera returned from lunch. "We picked you up something."

Thuy thanked them and offered a half smile. As hungry as she was, she did not feel like eating one bit.

CHAPTER TWENTY-TWO

Dustin

On the first Friday of October, the entire staff of Moodstr had gathered in the boardroom for a two-hour-long meeting. It was the biggest room available, but there were hardly enough chairs for all eighty-nine people in attendance, so latecomers were forced to lean against the walls or sit on the floor.

Dustin and Mackenzie were off in another boardroom where they had lost track of time, as two people in love tended to do. It was Dustin's idea to have sex in there. Mackenzie looked so irresistible with her hair tied up in a knot. He couldn't help but want to thrust it loose.

Besides, everyone knew this kind of stuff went on at Moodstr. So much so that the "quickie mart" caught on as the official office nickname. It wasn't like Dustin to participate in lewd conduct, but as of late he'd been asking himself, *Why should I act any better than the rest?*

When they were finished, they rushed to button any buttons that had come undone, pat down any hairs that were out of sync, and check for lipstick that had transferred anywhere it didn't belong. Mackenzie exited first and Dustin followed a couple of minutes later. He couldn't believe their relationship had progressed to this level. It certainly made the long days go by faster. But most of all, it felt like a giant, gratifying fuck you to Chase.

Despite being late to the meeting, they had missed nothing, and their tardy arrival elicited zero attention. Chase had not yet arrived, so the room was buzzing with chatter as people made predictions for this major announcement that Chase was about to make. As far as Dustin knew, he was the first person to know about the big office move. Mackenzie was the second. Nothing strengthened a bond like sharing a secret.

Chase strode in twenty minutes later, wearing a smartly cut navy blazer, fitted white shirt, and denim jeans. He did not apologize for being late and got right into the PowerPoint presentation that his assistant had already set up for him.

Up on the projection screen, Chase clicked through image after image of architectural renderings of a glistening building featuring stacked horizontal platforms with floor-to-ceiling glass. On the inside, where the future location of the office would be, he revealed an open-concept floor plan that was flooded with natural lighting. The photoshopped people looked happy and excited, even if they were merely sitting at their desks. It was hard to imagine a building like this could ever exist among the low-rise, century-old buildings that lined the Junction neighborhood.

"As long as there are no hiccups, we'll be one of the first tenants to move into this new building," said Chase. "We'll have four times the square footage that we do now. As you all know, we've been rapidly growing our user base, which means we need to rev up our back end to keep up with demand. This new space will allow us to hire more people, and the best part is we'll be working alongside some of the top tech companies in the country."

An unprompted applause burst out from the corner of the room, forcing a trickle effect of more clapping.

"This plan has been in the works for a long time but we've finally got traction on the deal and I could not wait to finally tell you all." Chase pressed his hands underneath his armpits. "Does anybody have any questions?"

"Where will it be located, again?" asked one of the senior developers.

"In the Junction, at the corner of Dundas and Keele."

Some employees let out eye rolls and audible groans.

"I know, I know," said Chase. "It's not the most ideal location for some of you. I've been told that the number forty bus can be atrocious. There will be some growing pains, indeed. And I did, I swear, I did try my best to find us a new home closer to the downtown core. But this was the only neighborhood that wasn't charging ridiculously high rents. Trust me, this place is perfect for us at this stage of our business."

Another employee raised his hand. "When do you expect the building will be ready?"

"Best guess is a year. Like I said, we have to wait for the demolition to be completed and proposals to be approved. They're building approximately four hundred thousand square feet of office space from scratch. Once it's done, it'll be the tallest building in the neighborhood."

Another person raised their hand. "What's happening to the old building?"

Chase jutted out his lower lip. "Who cares?" he barked, seeming annoyed. "Apologies, I didn't mean it like that. What I meant to say was, why dwell on the past when there's a whole exciting future waiting for us?"

Chase's eyes grew large and he snapped his fingers in the air. Suddenly, two servers entered the room carrying trays of bubbling drinks. They handed one, sometimes two, to each person and did not take no for an answer. Leave it to Chase to show up late to his own meeting, get his employees drunk off champagne before 11 a.m., and abruptly end the Q&A portion of the meeting.

Not that anyone minded. Everyone clinked their glasses and reveled in the excitement of moving into a brand-new building.

"Holy shit, this is *huuuge!*"

"I know, I didn't see that coming at all!"

"I knew the company was doing well but not *that* well."

Dustin couldn't mimic these feelings of hope and excitement. Maybe he could a year ago, back when he thought he was helping move society towards something better. But Mackenzie was right. This company, this app, was a joke. It did nothing to undercut the everyday stresses of people's lives. It was nothing but a mirage.

He looked down at his phone. Since his last encounter with Chase, he'd removed his biosensor and turned off Moodstr notifications on his phone. It was the best thing he'd ever done. No more reminders that his cortisol levels were too high. No more questions about how he was feeling. No more prompts to breathe and relax. He took a huge gulp of his champagne in hopes it would numb the deep hatred he had for this company.

He turned to Mackenzie and tapped his glass against hers. They exchanged a sly glance while standing an appropriate distance from each other. Looking at her always washed his problems away.

"I can't believe everyone's head over heels for this news," Dustin said to her.

"Can you blame them?" Mackenzie said. "Chase didn't say a thing about the heritage building that's being demolished."

"Even if he did, I doubt they'd care at all. They don't know the neighborhood like I do."

"Well, I care," she said, reaching out to touch his arm before realizing they were in a room packed with people. She always knew exactly what to say, and it made him want to open up to her even more.

"Did I tell you that old bank building was where my dad took me to get my very first card? I must have been nine or ten at the time. He handed me a twenty-dollar bill and showed me how to deposit the money into an ATM. I thought it was so cool, how it got eaten up by the machine like that. He would take me to the bank every month to update my little bank book and show me how much interest I'd made. It was something stupid like one or two cents, but it made me feel so adult. I always thought if I ever have kids, I'd do the same thing with them."

He examined her face, waiting for a grimace at the mention of having kids. But there was none. Just a softening of the eyes. "That's so sweet," she said. "That makes me feel even sadder that the building is coming down. There must be something we can do."

Her thoughtfulness and desire to help—even if it all seemed hopeless—made his heart melt a little.

"I wouldn't know the first thing about saving a building," he said. "Even if I did, you know Chase. Men like him always get what they want."

Dustin scanned the room to look for his boss. Chase was standing by the door, surrounded by employees. He eventually broke free and made his way to the center of the room. He climbed up on the boardroom table and let out a sharp whistle.

"I've got one more surprise for you all," he said, turning his body a full three-sixty like he was a rockstar onstage. "You're free to go home and start your weekend early! You've all earned it!"

The room exploded in stadium-level types of cheering. As everyone spilled out of the room, Dustin and Mackenzie stayed back. He noticed her collar was inside out and gently untucked it.

"You should be worrying about yourself," said Mackenzie, her eyes shifting to his waist. His shirt was inside out, exposing the long white garment label.

"We're really bad at this, aren't we?" he said.

From the corner of his eye, he noticed Chase looking at his untucked shirt like it was a pile of dog shit. Dustin lifted his glass in the air and gave his boss a smug grin. As soon as Chase left, laughter broke from them like fireworks hitting the sky.

CHAPTER TWENTY-THREE

Debbie

The promotion was a bust, just as Debbie had expected. There was no lineup of customers waiting outside. No voicemail overfilled with appointment requests. No influx of revenue to melt away the dread that January was coming up fast. At least Debbie wasn't surprised like everyone else. Because to be surprised was to have been hopeful in the first place.

"I don't get it," said Jessica, sulking in her swivel chair. "The flyers were up for weeks. The people I talked to promised they'd come by."

"Maybe they were lying to you," Thuy said, her voice fading into silence.

"Come on, guys," Kiera chimed in. "What kind of attitude is that? It's still early. Just watch. They'll all trickle in at once. That's how it always works."

The salon was so dead, the girls kept busy by checking each other's hair for white strands. To Debbie, they looked like three monkeys cleaning each other of dirt and debris. Gullible and foolish.

By the time afternoon came around, only two regulars showed up. Sylvia for a shellac manicure and Judy for a dip powder fill. There was still no promised wave of new faces, and while Debbie tried not to feel any type of way about it, she was beginning to feel uneasy. Was it anxiety? Fear? Panic? She wasn't experiencing shortness of breath, a racing heart, or sudden nausea. She just felt off.

A curse. It had to be a curse. That had to explain why all the hairs on her neck were standing. Debbie got up and did something her mother taught her to do whenever it seemed as if bad omens were everywhere. She filled up a cup with cold water and threw it out the doorway to wash away all the bad things that were blocking customers from coming into their salon. The pedestrians stared at her like she was a madwoman, but she didn't care. Where she came from, superstition was just common sense.

For the rest of the day, Debbie kept her hands busy, cleaning all the mirrors with great intensity, dusting away any gray film that had accumulated on surfaces big and small, including the grooves of the laughing golden Buddha. She offered hot tea and several incense sticks to the altar, bowing three times to complete the purification of the space. The statue hadn't moved since the first day they opened the salon. She liked how large his belly was, representing an abundance of good fortune and wealth. With his red-lipped laugh, he rested on a bamboo step stool near the entrance of the salon, serving as the greeter of all that was good and banisher of all that was not.

Debbie put on her winter coat and headed to her favorite bakery. There was still room on the altar for one more offering.

The Portuguese store owner waved as soon as Debbie walked in.

"Mrs. Tran! Long time, no see. It's been months. Are you avoiding me? Don't tell me you're on a diet or some nonsense like that."

Debbie laughed, gleeful that someone had finally noticed the five pounds she had lost just from swapping white rice for brown.

"No, no. It's nothing like that. I'm just watching my sugar levels."

"Well, it's good to see you again. We just put out some fresh pasteis de nata and chocolate salami. Care for some?"

They looked delicious, but Debbie had her eye on something extra decadent, something that would really appeal to the god of abundance and bring good fortune to their salon.

"What's this?" Debbie pointed to a colorful round cake dotted with crystallized fruit, sliced almonds, and an assortment of other toppings.

"That's the bolo rei, cake of the kings. We're testing out a new recipe for Christmas. Want to try a piece?"

"Actually, can I get the whole cake?"

The store owner's eyes lit up. "You may have a dozen cakes if you like."

Debbie grinned. "Just the one cake for now." She dug through her purse for her wallet. "How's business going? Cold weather slowing things down for you, too?"

"Not really," the owner replied nonchalantly. "The cold is when we get the most action around here. Everybody wants to feel warm and cozy and what better way to do that than with a warm pastry?" She shot Debbie the widest grin she'd ever seen. "Besides, the holidays are coming up and people have been buying us dry and leaving us orders weeks in advance. We can't keep up. We had to hire a part-time student from the Catholic school just down the street. He's a good kid, a little clumsy but he catches on real quick."

She looked behind Debbie's shoulders towards a bespectacled adolescent who was scrubbing coffee stains from a table. "Hey, Vincent!" she yelled. "Say hi to Mrs. Tran. She works at the nail salon down the street. Be a dear and bring her a glass of water!"

"Oh, that won't be necessary. I'm going to be leaving shortly," said Debbie. She funneled her change back in her coin purse and was about to head towards the door until the craving sank in. "Actually, can I get one of those tarts?"

"See? I knew you were looking at those earlier." She beamed, holding up a pair of tongs. "I'll give you an extra one on the house. Vincent will take care of you. I've got to tend to some business in the kitchen. It was nice seeing you, Debbie. Don't forget to add the cinnamon and powdered sugar on those natas."

"Thank you." Debbie managed a stiff smile and took the plate from her. What a kind, sweet woman. She even remembered her name after all these months. Still, Debbie couldn't help but feel jealous about her thriving bakery.

Debbie found an empty seat beside a group of elderly men talking in another language. On the table in front of her was a glossy pink postcard with the words in bold, black type: "Cuter. Cleaner. Classier." Debbie bit into the tart as loose pastry flakes rained down on the plate. She used the postcard to gather all the flakes until she noticed more text on the back of the card. "Bring a friend, get thirty percent off. Bring two friends, get fifty percent off." Her eyes moved to the bottom. There it was. A Take Ten logo.

"What the fuck?" she screamed, startling the busboy, who nearly dropped the glass of water in his hand.

Debbie left the water and half-eaten tart on the table and stormed out of the bakery in a dramatic flurry. She caught a flash of her reflection in the mirror. Her eyes were bloodshot, and her skin was as pale as death.

"How dare they?" Kiera shouted after Debbie showed everyone the postcard. "Copying our promotion? On the same exact week? They must have seen our flyers in the neighborhood and thought they could one-up us. They're clearly sabotaging us."

"I knew that promotion was a bad idea," said Phil, pinching the space between his eyes. "No wonder our store is empty. Who wants thirty percent off when they can get fifty percent off right across the street?"

"Don't blame all this on me!" cried Jessica. "I was just trying to help out the salon. How was I supposed to know they would rip off our idea?"

"Well, it was *your* plan to post the flyers all over the neighborhood for everyone to see," said Thuy.

"How else am I supposed to get the word out? This is how promotions work," said Jessica.

Kiera shook her head. "It can't be a coincidence. The same week we decide to run this promotion, they decide to run theirs? It's obvious they're trying to steal our customers."

"So why don't we go over there and confront them? They can't get away with this!" Jessica said, standing up with her arms outstretched.

"That's not a bad idea," replied Kiera. "Let's show them who was here first. Thuy, what do you think?"

Thuy gave a firm nod.

"That's my girl! Look who came to win!" said Kiera, high-fiving her.

Phil stood up so fast the momentum caused his swivel chair to roll backwards. "No!" he shouted. "You girls will do no such thing! Look, I agree. It's messed up what they did but technically, they did nothing wrong. Every business has a right to set discounts whenever they like and if it happens to coincide with ours, then so be it. We can't go over there and tell them they can't do that. That would be childish!"

"But aren't you mad they're taking away all our business?" said Kiera.

"I am, but—"

"But what?"

"I'm not letting you storm over there like a bunch of bullies, not in front of all their customers. Look at their postcard. They think they're classier than us. Don't let them prove they're right."

"You think they care about our little salon? You're just the ugly store across the street that's a blight on their view," Kiera fired back. "I bet they can't wait for this block to be demolished so some store selling twenty-dollar chopped salad can take over."

"Ba, she's right," said Jessica. "If we shut down tomorrow, they won't even remember our names."

"I don't care what they think of us," said Phil. "But I care what customers think. If they hear that you girls picked a fight with the neighbor, what are they going to think of us?"

"What will they think about *you* when they find out *you've* been cutting our pay?" said Kiera, folding her arms over her chest.

"That's—" Phil stuttered, seeming to be at a loss for words. "That's temporary. Debbie, back me up here."

Debbie, who had been kneeling in front of the altar the entire time, did not say anything to defend her husband. She wasn't sure what to say. It seemed everyone had said everything she had been feeling, so it made no sense to waste her breath. Instead, she saved her breath for her prayers.

Debbie kept her gaze on the altar. She pushed the laughing Buddha farther back towards the wall to make room for the colorful cake. When she set it down, she could have sworn the corners of the Buddha's mouth grew wider, his laugh lines deepening ever so slightly. She couldn't remember the last time she laughed so hard it carved out semipermanent lines around her mouth.

Once she lit the incense, she allowed the smoke cloud to engulf her entire head. She took a long whiff of the leathery, cigar-like scent, a comforting aroma she'd come to rely on for clarity in times when she felt hopeless. There was something about the scent that made her feel as if peace had taken over.

One bow. Two bows. Three bows. She kept bowing until the incense burned down to her fingers and a resolve formed in her mind. She was going to fix this. She wasn't sure how, but when it came to her family, nothing was off the table. "Leave it to me. I'll take care of this."

CHAPTER TWENTY-FOUR

Phil

Phil had no idea what his wife meant when she said that. When he asked her later that night, she simply told him not to worry. He knew she was keeping something from him, but if thirty-eight years of marriage had taught him anything, it was that when two people trusted each other enough, the truth was overrated.

Besides, Phil had his own ways of keeping the salon afloat, and it involved cooking a series of spicy meals for his family. It was a trick he learned from his grandmother: Whenever money was tight, just add more bird's-eye chili into everything. The spicier the food, the less everyone would eat, the more money they'd save on food. It was the reason why Phil preferred to make his own fish sauce; Debbie insisted one chili was enough, but to him there was no kick without at least five.

His scheme was working. Their grocery trips were stretched out a bit longer, their credit card bills not as high. But by no means was it a perfect solution. The other day, he had overdone it with the bún bò Huế, causing Dustin to have a continuous bout of explosive diarrhea in the middle of the night. Dustin could eat nothing but crackers and bananas for the next week. Phil felt so bad. Then again, having one less person to feed pushed their savings up even more.

For Phil, it was a small price to pay if it meant having financial security.

He even switched to a discount grocery store, even though it added an extra thirty minutes to his drive. He'd done the math and determined that the savings he'd reap from shopping at this particular store made up for the extra cost of gas. His family agreed no gifts would be exchanged this Christmas. He also resisted the temptation to buy anything unnecessary, including a pair of shoes he'd tried on during a sale. Even though they felt heavenly on his sore bunions, he walked out and opted for generic aspirin whenever the pain flared up.

When it came to the salon, he instructed everyone to be a little more pushy. If someone wanted a polish change, suggest a relaxing pedicure while their nails dried. If someone wanted acrylics, tell them biogel was more natural-looking. If someone didn't want designs on their nails, show them a picture of a celebrity sporting a trendy design.

Bless the girls. They were naturals at this. Something about the stylishness of their youth gave them an air of authority as they casually pointed out flaws ("Your nail bed's a little short," "They're looking a little yellow today") in hopes the customers would get bummed enough to fork over more money. It worked. Some of the time.

The toughest change of all was telling his relatives abroad that he'd have to stop wiring them money. That phone call nearly killed him, especially when his younger brother protested that he would have no food for his family, that the state would cut their power, that he only had a month's worth of asthma medication left. . . . Phil wasn't sure how long the list went on for. He tuned him out in order to save his heart. What was he supposed to do? He had already done his brother a huge favor by taking in Thuy. It was time he put his own family first.

It was the cruelest of punishments. Moving all the way across the world, risking your life on a rickety boat, and working until your back ached, only to have to tell your impoverished family back home that you had no money for them. None of it seemed fair to him. Where was the dream he was promised?

On the first of January, the new rent officially kicked in and despite all their efforts, the Trans did not have enough money to cover it. Not even twenty-four hours later, the landlord stormed into the salon. For a brief moment, Terry Doyle smiled at the customers before turning to Phil with a serious expression on his face.

"Phil, a word, please?"

Phil walked towards the reception desk, pulling down his mask. "Phil, you know why I'm here, don't you?" said Terry.

Phil instinctively bowed his head like some kind of servant. "Yes, yes. I know we're late on the rent, but I promise I will get it to you soon. I just need to wait for some payments to clear. Shouldn't be too much longer now," he lied.

Terry sighed. "I gave you plenty of notice," he said. "More notice than what was required of me."

"I know, I know. Please, sir." He hated that he called him sir. Not because Terry was a few years younger, but because Terry was a pathetic, patchily bearded man who did not deserve respect.

"Please be patient," Phil pleaded. "We just need a couple more weeks. I promise." He wasn't sure why, but he instinctively reached his arm out over the receptionist counter and lifted his pinkie finger.

Terry scrunched up his nose and looked at Phil's finger as if it were contaminated with fecal pathogens. Terry was probably the kind of man who dropped his wife off in front of the salon and aimlessly drove around the neighborhood instead of sitting in reception because he would never dare be caught inside a beauty salon. That's how fragile his masculinity was, which explained why instead of returning Phil's pinkie promise, he simply stood at the doorway and cupped his crotch as if to check that it was still there. By now the customers were all gawking at him.

"Phil, come on, man," said Terry, motioning for Phil to come outside. There was no time to grab his jacket so he went out with just his uniform, goose bumps elevated all up his arms.

"Look at me in my eyes. Am I a scary guy? I don't think so. I'm actually a very nice guy. Ask any of my friends," Terry said as he lit a cigarette. "But listen, I'm a business guy. I have my own bills to pay, and I can't keep extending these kind gestures to everyone that looks like they're about to cry."

Phil wanted to point out that he was not about to cry. His eyes were just a bit glassy because of the cold air, but it was irrelevant at this point. "One more week then," said Phil, clenching his arms as close to his body as he could. "That's all I ask. One more week."

Terry blew out a cloud of smoke and took his time to respond, which only unnerved Phil even more. One week, really? Phil replayed the words he just uttered. *Why did you say that, you idiot? How are you going to come up with four thousand dollars in one week?*

"Fine. One week," said Terry, stubbing out his cigarette with his wingtip oxford shoe, the shoe of a man who probably spent the Trans' rent money on annual winter vacations to Santorini or Aruba.

Terry saluted him goodbye and drove away. Phil made sure Terry's car was completely out of sight before he kicked down their sandwich board.

——

Phil was desperate. He refused to let down his family again.

He sought a solution the only way he knew how: the casino.

After two hours of placing bet after bet after bet, he came away with nothing. Twelve hundred dollars less than nothing, actually. If Phil thought the world was out to get him before, he was damn sure of it now. Why could nothing go his way? At least he got some free drinks out of it, which numbed the pain of his badly bruised ego.

He took a cab home and stumbled into the house in the middle of the night. The house was dark and quiet. He kept the lights off as he walked towards the kitchen. With his arms stretched out, he felt for a chair and pulled it out, making sure not to scrape it against the tile. His entire body felt numb, so he started picking at a scab on his arm just to make sure he could still feel something.

He heard soft footsteps coming down the stairs.

"Where have you been all night?" Debbie stood at the doorway, one eye half open. Even in the dark, he could tell she was wearing those silk pajamas in his favorite shade, bloody Mekong sunset.

"Out," said Phil.

"It's almost three in the morning. Where could you be out?"

He accidentally knocked something off the table (a cup? a bowl?) and heard it hit the floor and shatter into pieces. "Trời ơi, you're drunk! You went to the casino, didn't you?"

The lights turned on as his wife scanned the mess.

"Tell me, did you go to the casino or not?" Debbie screeched.

Phil said nothing.

"How much did you lose?"

"It doesn't matter. I will win it all back tomorrow."

"Tell me right now!"

"It doesn't concern you."

"Đồ ngu. How could you do this to us?" said Debbie. She knelt on the ground and started carefully picking up the bigger pieces of broken ceramic.

Phil remained silent.

"We need that money more than ever right now and because of your stupidity it's all gone. What are we going to do now? How could you go back there? You didn't need to do that. We were going to have enough—"

He tuned out what she was saying and continued to pick at the raw skin on his arm. It was soft, warm, and a little bit sticky.

Nobody had any idea what it was like to be in his position, no idea the things he was doing to take care of his family and the business, and how embarrassing it was to have the wife you adored tell you to your face that their problems were all your fault. But it was going to be okay, he told himself, because he had a plan. A new plan.

"—and you don't think I know we are overdue on our rent?" Debbie was still talking. "You don't think I've been working extra hard to make ends meet? You think going to the casino is your way of helping out around here? Ông có khùng không? Hey, hey, are you even listening to me?"

Either fatigue or the sedative effects of alcohol had set in, because Phil was feeling rather tired and it was becoming awfully hard to keep his eyes open. Debbie dragged him to the living room sofa. He could feel his wife lifting his legs onto the couch and pulling his socks off. He was then shrouded in the softness of a faux fur throw as he heard footsteps go up the stairs and the sound of a door closing. The last thing he heard before he passed out was the tick-tock of the kitchen clock.

CHAPTER TWENTY-FIVE

Debbie

After her last appointment walked out, Debbie decided to treat her sore feet to a bath. She filled the pedicure tub with warm water but skipped the Epsom salts and tea tree oil. She didn't want to waste supplies on herself.

Leaning back into the massage chair, Debbie closed her eyes and thought about many things. About the money Phil lost. About the money they couldn't give their relatives. About the money they owed to the landlord. Money, money, money. It was all she could think about.

It would be so easy if they were back in Vietnam. The amount they were making each month would be enough to live in a luxury condo in Saigon's gated communities. They wouldn't have to work every day. Instead, they could go for leisurely swims in the rooftop pool, ride around the city in their shiny scooters, then come back to their air-conditioned home and eat like kings. They would have lived a happier life, Debbie was sure of this.

She looked out the window. It was ten minutes past five and right on cue, Savannah was leaving Take Ten with two bags slung over her shoulder, one for her laptop, the other for god knew what. Even though the Toronto location had opened without a hitch, she was still coming to the city on a regular basis, her arrival confirmed by the company car parked across the street, a white metallic Mercedes-Benz with a brown leather interior.

This was Debbie's chance. If she was going to do it, she had to do it now.

Ever since their run-in with Savannah at the buffet, Debbie couldn't shake the feeling that this woman was up to something. She didn't belong here. Everyone knew it. Even Savannah knew it. So why was she constantly coming back here? She remembered how Savannah pretended she'd never heard of Sunshine Nails. That was bullshit. Then there was that awkward encounter at the buffet followed by the copycat promotion. The more she thought about it, the more she deduced these could not have been coincidences. Was Savannah watching them? For what? To make sure Sunshine Nails crashed and burned so they could have a monopoly over the neighborhood? Debbie wouldn't put it past her. The woman had greed in her eyes. It was always the ones with power that were the hungriest for more, wasn't it?

Debbie told her family she was going to the grocery store. To her relief, nobody lifted a head or asked her to pick something up. Just as planned, she slipped out without any fuss.

Her car was parked just a couple vehicles away from Savannah's. Debbie eyed the gas. Only an eighth remained. She'd been waiting for prices to drop to fill it, so wherever Savannah was going, she hoped it wasn't very far.

Ten minutes passed and Savannah was still in her car. Debbie could see her swiping on a lipstick, applying a bit of blush and highlighter, curling her eyelashes, and applying several coats of mascara. Then she tilted her head back to apply some eye drops and proceeded to take a phone call.

Another ten minutes went by and Savannah was still sitting idle in her car. Debbie was starting to feel stupid. What was she doing, sitting here freezing in the car? She hadn't turned on the engine for fear of wasting fuel. Her hands were so cold she had to sit on them. She'd gotten so bored she pretended she was a dragon breathing out swirls of smoke with every exhale. After counting thirty clouds of smoke, she realized just how silly this all was. She reached down to take the key out of the ignition.

That's when Savannah inched out of her parking space. Debbie quickly turned the engine on and followed the car, being careful to leave at least a car or two between them. By the time they got to the highway, Debbie was certain she'd lost the car. Why the hell were there so many white cars in this city? Then she spotted a vehicle up ahead switching lanes and in that quick second, she caught a glimpse of that bright blond bob peeking out at the top of the headrest.

Gotcha.

If someone had asked her in that moment why she was doing what she was doing, she wouldn't have had a good answer. She wasn't sure why she was driving in this crippling rush-hour traffic, following a woman she barely knew to a location she couldn't anticipate. Debbie couldn't explain it. It was just a feeling, like when a mother instinctively knows something is wrong with her child.

A husky female voice on the radio said there was an accident between two delivery trucks that was causing a terrible backlog on the highway. Debbie groaned and peered at the dashboard. The skinny red arrow on the gas gauge was creeping closer to empty.

Savannah's right taillight flickered and she finally took an exit. Debbie followed behind but not so close that she could be recognized. She remembered this exit. It was the exit Jessica took when they drove to the buffet. What was Savannah doing all the way up here again?

Eventually the car entered a sleepy cul-de-sac where every house had a minimum of two cars parked outside and blue recycling bins neatly lined up along the curb. Debbie stayed farther back and lowered the volume of the radio just as Aretha Franklin was saying a little prayer for her.

Savannah parked on a driveway beside a black SUV. She knocked on the door, then disappeared into the house. Debbie caught a quick glimpse of somebody standing in front of a staircase, but not much else. She could only assume the inside was as luxurious as the outside. Detached, slate brick all over, two garages the color of a rainy-day sky, driveways pristinely cleared of snow, lights that turned on at the first detection of motion, a world of protected lush forest sitting behind it. It was easily mid seven figures.

This was the kind of house Debbie and Phil spent many nights telling themselves they would one day buy for their family. After the first ten years of running the salon, they had saved up a decent amount for a down payment on a three-bedroom home, but by that point housing prices shot up. So they continued to save and save, stowing as much money as they could into a risk-free savings account. But after another ten years, prices went up even more. They just couldn't catch up. Staying where they were, a semidetached town house with slightly sloped floors and a perpetually damp smell, seemed to be as high as they could reach.

Debbie checked the time. Savannah had been inside the house for at least half an hour. It was dark out now. Cars were filling up the driveways as owners were coming home from work. Windows were lighting up on every side of each house. Blue bins were being begrudgingly dragged out to the curb.

The house Savannah was in remained completely dark, not even a porch light was on. How much longer would she have to wait? Debbie wasn't exactly sure what she was waiting for, but she needed to know more about this woman. She owed it to her family to get answers as to why everything was slipping out of their grasp. Debbie switched to another radio station, settling for one that was still playing Christmas songs. There was something about Frank Sinatra's velvety baritone voice that convinced her maybe someday her troubles, too, would be miles away.

Finally, the front door opened. Savannah came out with a man. She kissed him on the lips, her right leg slowly lifted as if being pulled by an invisible string. Debbie didn't think women did that in real life. She took a picture on her phone to capture the absurdity. Savannah got in her car and drove back the way they came. Debbie quickly sank into her seat to avoid being seen.

She waited a few minutes before straightening her posture, making certain the car had disappeared into the pitch blackness of suburbia.

Every window in the house was now lit. As Sinatra crooned smoothly into her ears, Debbie looked at the photo. It was dark and grainy, but once she zoomed in it was unmistakable what she was seeing. Their bodies were so intertwined it was hard to tell which parts were hers and which were his. Savannah's neck was covered by a large, generous hand adorned with a wedding band. His baggy crewneck sweater was draped so loosely over his body it seemed as if there was nothing but air inside. She zoomed into the photo as far as she could.

Debbie gasped.

It was the man from the buffet. A million thoughts raced through her mind, but only one came to her as clear as day: Savannah was having an affair.

So that was why she was in the city? Debbie was disappointed. It wasn't the smoking gun she was hoping to find. She'd only wanted proof that Savannah was sabotaging their salon, not that she was gallivanting around town cheating on her husband. This information, as scandalous as it was, did nothing for her.

A terrible thought popped into her mind. Was Sunshine Nails faltering through no fault of Savannah's, but of their own? Did they only have themselves to blame for everything that had gone wrong? The idea made her entire body quiver. She stopped herself from ruminating any longer and told herself she'd delete the photo as soon as she got home.

Debbie turned on the engine, noting the little red arrow perilously hovering over the empty marker, and drove back home. The steering wheel was so cold it physically hurt to touch, so she drove with one hand at a time, switching as soon as it felt like her fingers were going to fall off.

At a stoplight, Debbie pulled off her jade ring. The stone felt so icy against her delicate skin that it practically turned her finger white. She stared at it, remembering with vividness the night the pirates attacked their boat. She wondered what happened to the girls that got kidnapped. Did they survive the night, the week, the year? If they escaped, did they survive the trauma that surely violated their every waking minute of life?

The glow of the red traffic light bounced off the surface of the ring. She never realized how much history a ring could hold. How the subtle swirls carried the stories that were too hard to talk about. How the muddiness of the milky tone masked a past too painful. How could she ever forget the feeling of that imperfect circle shoved so far up her inner lip? Even to this day, Debbie swore she could still feel the bruise.

The light turned green and she hastily put the ring back on. She thought about what she just saw back at that house and wondered how anybody could look at their ring—a wedding ring no less—and strip all meaning from it? Debbie had never once thought about cheating on Phil, not even when he screwed up so badly. She had witnessed the untold depths of pain and suffering that were possible—lovers being thrown into the ocean, babies being snatched from their mother's arms, parents being shot in front of their children. That's why she could never hurt her husband. She couldn't stand to break any more hearts in this world.

Debbie thought about Savannah's poor husband. At home in New York, clueless that his heart was being stomped all over. If only someone would let him know.

Would it be so terrible if she kept the photo?

She imagined this was what it felt like to hold a gun, having the unstoppable power to completely alter the life of another person. Never in her life had she been granted such a power. She didn't know what to do with it, but it didn't feel like something she should relinquish.

When Debbie got home, she pulled up the picture on her phone and pressed the delete icon. A message popped up asking if she was sure. She hovered her thumb over the delete button, then swiftly hit cancel.

CHAPTER TWENTY-SIX

Phil

Phil searched all over the house for his black book. Where was that thing? He hadn't used it in a long time, not since he opened the salon. When he was looking for his first job in Canada, a kind woman at an information session gave him one piece of advice that stuck with him ever since: Write down the address and phone number of every person you ever work with. After that, Phil got in the habit of carrying around a tattered black address book that fit perfectly in the back pocket of every one of his pants. It contained pages and pages of scribbled names and numbers: Chann, the line cook from Great China Restaurant; Mateo, a janitor at the GoodLife gym; Julius, a delivery driver at Swiss Chalet.

There it was. He found it in the closet and frantically flipped until he saw the name he was looking for: Eamon Harsanyi, his old friend at the bank, the last job he had before opening Sunshine Nails.

Eamon, like him, was a new immigrant to Canada, making his way over from Hungary to follow promises of a grander life. Unfortunately, he got arrested for stealing money from the vault, and the last thing he said to Phil as he was being dragged out by the police was, "It wasn't even that much! Fuck these dick-sucking greedy bastards! Fuck 'em all!"

Despite Eamon's predilection for crime, Phil quite admired him. He never let setbacks derail his dreams. Last Phil heard, Eamon had gotten married, bought a house, had a kid or two, and was running a successful moneylending business. Just the person Phil needed.

He dialed Eamon's number and suggested they catch up for old times' sake. Eamon immediately called him out on his bullshit.

"Phil, my buddy! You don't got to pretend with me. Nobody ever calls to ask me how my life's been except my mama. Now how much do you need?"

Phil was relieved. He hated fake niceties and besides, he had no time to waste.

"When can you meet?" asked Phil.

Eamon paused. "How about right now?"

———

Phil had never been in this part of the city, and that was the point. He wanted to be as far away as possible from the salon and every person he knew. He did not want anyone, especially Debbie, to know what he was doing or who he was meeting.

The moment Eamon stepped inside the Coffee Time, Phil's head felt heavy. Walking towards him was a man who hadn't changed all that much. He was still tall, eyebrows still bushy, cheeks still hollow. Wearing ripped black jeans, a beanie that was barely on his head, and an oversized puffer jacket in a lemon meringue shade, he looked like a man desperately holding on to his youth.

"My man, you're nearly gray! How much time has gone by?" Eamon was practically shouting. Everyone in the café turned to look, causing Phil to feel embarrassed and momentarily regretful of this entire plan. Fortunately, Eamon sat down across from him and lowered his voice to library-level volumes. He reeked of cigarette smoke.

"Thank you for meeting me on such short notice, Eamon. I am sorry we haven't been in touch since you . . . left," said Phil, remembering the moment his friend got handcuffed.

"No, no. Don't worry about it, man," said Eamon. "What a long time ago that was. Man, I was a dumbass. I should have just kept my head down and done my job. I had a good thing going, you know? But I was so restless. You know that feeling when you got an itch and you scratch and scratch and it don't go away? Man, that was me. Never shoulda taken that job in the first place! Too many temptations, you know? Thank god I only done three years in jail. Any more and that woulda fucked me up. Now look at me, I don't need to rob no bank anymore. I'm my own bank. The Bank of Harsanyi." He cackled so loud that people were staring again.

"Coffee? I'll pay," Phil said.

"Let's just cut to the chase, Phil. Have you seen it outside?" They both stared out the window at the falling snow, which was quickly coating everything in sight. "I don't wanna have to brush that shit off my car again."

Phil never understood why people complained about snow like clockwork every season as if they never saw it coming. He felt pressured to play along, saying what everyone wanted to hear just so he could feel like he was part of a Canadian tradition. "Summer can't come soon enough!" "That's it, I'm moving to Florida!"

The truth was he loved the snow. It was clean, white, and odorless, and god knew he'd been buried under far worse. He recalled his time on the ocean, the feces and vomit that piled up at his feet making him wish the boat would just capsize. Snow? He'd happily eat it for dinner.

"O-o-okay, well then," said Phil, keeping his voice low. A gush of freezing air came in, and Phil quickly turned around. It was nobody, just an old man. *Get it together*, he thought to himself.

Eamon smiled at him. "Look at you, you're so nervous! You're still the shy guy I remember. Always so quiet. You're as green as they come."

Phil smiled back. If only Eamon knew about his DUI. Would he be impressed or horrified? "So, the reason I called you, as you are aware, is that I'm in some need of help." Phil scanned his surroundings. There were empty tables on each side of them. Some people were wearing headphones, others seemed to be reading or staring off into space. How could he be sure they were not listening to their conversation? Phil lowered his head and his voice even more.

"I know, I know. Say no more," Eamon said. He whipped out a pen and checkbook from his jacket pocket with the grace and movement of a seasoned ballet dancer. It was clear he had done this hundreds of times. "How much we talking here?"

"You don't want to know what it's for?"

"Your business is your business. You want to use it to pay off a hit man? You want to use it to buy your mistress some diamond earrings? I don't care. As long as you pay it all back."

"Of course, I promise you will get this money back. You need me to sign any papers or anything . . ." said Phil. He had not taken out a loan before, not even officially from the bank, but he was certain that papers and signatures were involved.

"Nah, I don't work like that. You know how many loans I hand out on a given day? I can't keep track of documents and shit or else I'll go crazy. All I need to know are names, faces, and addresses. Now did you say you worked at a beauty salon or something like that?"

"Yes, Sunshine Nails in the Junction. Near Dundas and Keele Street."

"And you're aware of my interest?"

Phil shook his head. Everything was moving so fast.

"For you, ten points every week. Cash or check, it doesn't matter. We can meet here or you can come to my place." Eamon handed him his card. "Now how much will it be?"

"F-f-fifteen thousand," Phil whispered. This should be enough to get through winter.

Without hesitation, Eamon wrote the number on the check. He scribbled his signature on the bottom right corner, blew on it to let the ink dry, and handed it to Phil.

Phil shuffled in his seat. "Um, so this thing. Is there any risk . . . I mean, is all of this . . . legitimate?"

"What are you talking about, Phil? I been doing this for seven years, you don't think I know what I'm doing?"

"No, no, no. That's not it. I know you're a good businessman."

"Good. Now if you don't mind, I've got to run to another meeting. Good to see you, old pal. Glad to know two guys who started with nothing can finally call the shots. What goes around comes around, am I right?"

Phil watched him walk out before glancing down at the check. There it was, the answer to all his problems. On the drive home, he came up with an airtight story. He told his family that he'd gone back to the casino, that he hit a streak of luck playing blackjack and won big. They all cheered loudly, ran up to hug him one by one, and Debbie forgave him, even gave him a kiss on the cheek. Everything was going to be all right. He was a hero again.

CHAPTER TWENTY-SEVEN

Jessica

'm here to visit thirty eleven."

"Name, please?"

"Tran. Jessica."

The concierge was neatly shaven and dressed in a crisp black suit that, if not for the gold-plated name tag, made him look as if he were the best man at a wedding. He made a quick phone call, then gave Jessica the okay to head towards the elevators.

A group of friends rushed in just before the doors closed, cheering loudly for making it at the last minute. They proceeded to indiscreetly drink from a wine bottle wrapped in a brown paper bag and asked Jessica if she wanted a sip, which she politely declined.

Gigi's condo attracted the kind of young professionals who worked hard during the week and partied even harder on the weekends. It was a newly built high-rise located in the entertainment district, towering so high above everything else like it was an extraterrestrial threat looming over humankind. Gigi had snagged a one-bedroom unit before the balcony was even completed and paid rent to a landlord who didn't even live in the country. As Jessica walked down the dimly lit hallway, she checked the time. Twenty minutes after seven.

Sasha texted her earlier saying she was running late. Jessica prayed she wasn't the first to arrive at the dinner party.

Things had been weird between her and Gigi ever since she bailed at the Hotellium. She never told Gigi about Savannah's microaggressions, the promotion fiasco, nor the fact that she started working at her parents' salon. What would she even say? Take Ten was Gigi's biggest client. There was no way she was going to drop them for her. Besides, things were okay now thanks to her father's big win at the casino. Everybody thought he was crazy for going back, but once they saw all that money they changed their minds.

Gigi answered the door wearing ripped jeans and an emerald velvet top with a deep V-neck and peplum hem. There was makeup on her chest as her collarbones shimmered bright against the light, and suddenly Jessica felt like her chest was dry and bare. She handed her a bottle of cabernet sauvignon that she'd purchased at a liquor store on her way here.

"Am I the first one?"

"Nope. Paras and her partner are here. You remember Paras, right? She was in our chem class. You'll recognize her. Anyway, wine, vodka, gin, soda, all on the counter. Help yourself."

Gigi took her jacket and disappeared into the bedroom. The condo was narrow but long, with floor-to-ceiling windows wrapped around one corner. On the opposite wall was a large canvas of the Prada Marfa sign. The entire place smelled of roses thanks to the Diptyque candles that had been scattered throughout the condo. Jessica poured herself an ample glass of red wine and slowly walked towards the couple sitting on the couch. They were picking over a beautifully laid-out platter of meats, cheese, and crackers.

"Is that you, Jessica? I didn't even recognize you with that hair!" Paras got up and gave her a sticky kiss on her right cheek.

Jessica touched the ends of her strands like they were a prize.

"Hard not to go lighter when you live in California."

"Oh, that's right. You were living all the way out there. Weren't you in film production or something like that?"

"Casting."

"Like an assistant?"

"Associate."

"Wow . . . you must have met some pretty famous people then."

"Sometimes."

"Oh my god, don't be modest. Spill the details!"

Jessica blushed and tucked her hair behind her ears. She always found it gauche to name-drop the celebrities she'd met, but she had to admit it felt really nice to be showered with admiration and respect. This feeling was why she stayed in casting for so long, despite the stagnant salary and lack of upwards mobility. It was one of those jobs that made people think she was important and successful due to her close proximity to some of the richest and most recognizable people in the world. In reality, she spent most of her time on the phone with extremely persistent and often rude agents.

By now a few more people had arrived. They were crowded around the counter, laughing loudly and clinking glasses. Paras's partner abandoned the cheese platter and walked over to greet someone. The condo was starting to feel warm and Jessica regretted wearing such a densely knit wool sweater that trapped in all her body heat.

"Are you working on any exciting shows these days?" said Paras. "Or wait—you're probably not allowed to tell me, huh?"

Jessica tensed her jaw. "Actually, I'm going through a bit of a"—she paused, searching for the right words—"career change right now."

Paras widened her eyes. "I knew it! You're gonna be an actor, aren't you? I swear, you've got the cheekbones for it."

"Oh god no."

"Director? Screenplay writer?"

Jessica shook her head.

"Really? So what then?"

"I work at my parents' nail salon."

The light in Paras's eyes instantly went dark. She looked like she had just discovered that the expertly crafted cocktail in her hand was actually piss. "Oh, that's nice, too. Your parents must be happy to have you around to help."

Now that it was clear to Paras that Jessica's life was not as interesting as she was led to believe, Paras proceeded to talk about her life like it was a

LinkedIn profile. After high school, she lived in Ghana for a year, helping poor families start up small businesses. She came home, got a degree in political science, followed by law. Passed the bar. Opened her own practice, where she spent her free time doing pro bono work for transnational migrant workers facing unfair treatment and wrongful repatriation.

"And now I'm getting married in two months," she said emphatically, raising her manicured fingers in the air to hammer home the proof. Her cuticles were still shiny from oil, giving away the fact that she'd gotten her nails done less than an hour ago. She pointed to the kitchen. "That's my hubby—sorry, I'm just so excited—*soon-to-be* hubby over there."

Jessica gulped down the remainder of her wine. She could feel sweat beads forming at the roots of her hair. "He's very cute," she said, indulging in Paras's need for a compliment.

Once Sasha arrived, dinner was ready to be served. A series of string quartet covers played gently in the background. All seven guests hovered around the dining table, unsure which seat to take. Sasha pulled out a chair on one end of the table as Jessica promptly grabbed the one next to her. Beside her was a gum-chewing young man named Murray, who owned a clothing boutique near Chinatown. The boutique sold "luxury, contemporary streetwear," which he emphasized twice in a pompous tone. It turned out he had only met Gigi a couple months ago at a launch party for a magazine he was profiled in.

"The photo shoot was sick," he said. "The photographer is apparently a super-big deal in Dubai so they flew him all the way from there." He pulled out his phone to show her the profile. His face took up the entire screen. Those stern, deep-hooded eyes looked back up at her with such intensity it made her uneasy. Underneath the photo was a headline in large, bold type. "The Next Stüssy?"

Everyone here seemed so successful, which came as no surprise. It was Gigi, after all. Ever since high school, she always surrounded herself with people she deemed to be accomplished. It made Jessica wonder whether they would have stayed friends had her casting career not taken off. That's perhaps why she hadn't told her about working at Sunshine Nails. She didn't want to find out the hard way.

They started with some bruschetta. It was seasoned perfectly with just the right amount of garlic, basil, and salt, though it could've used another half hour or so to get to room temperature. Next up was the Bolognese, made with fresh pappardelle and topped with a fluffy helping of fragrant Parmesan. Jessica's body was turned to Sasha as they caught up on everything. Sasha told her about a trip to Argentina that she was planning. Jessica told her about the run-in with Savannah at the buffet.

For the first two courses, they talked to no one else but themselves. By the time the cannoli and coffee came out, Gigi scowled at them from across the table, nudging them to break up their one-on-one. Annoyed, Jessica shifted her body and made an effort to join in on the larger group conversation that was taking place.

An attractive redhead at the other end of the table was talking about bidding wars. Jessica nodded along as she tried to figure out whether the woman was buying a home or selling one. It turned out she was neither. She was a real estate agent, and she was boasting about how she'd recently closed a property for $1.9 million, resulting in her best commission yet. The whole table raised their glasses and congratulated her. As everyone took a sip, Jessica wondered what was so celebratory about someone paying nearly $2 million for a three-bedroom house with one bathroom and no parking.

The conversation deviated to Paras and her fiancé, whose name still eluded Jessica. Within ten minutes, she learned where their wedding was going to be held, who was officiating the ceremony, the brand of her dress and his suit, the song they were going to do their first dance to. She knew their entire itinerary from wake-up time to sparkler send-off, and yet the fiancé's name still didn't come up once.

"Now we just need to figure out what gifts to get for our parents," said Paras.

"Gifts? For your parents? Shouldn't it be the other way around?" replied Gigi.

"They've done so much for us. I mean, they practically paid for the whole wedding. Getting them a thank-you gift is the least we could do."

Everyone took turns spewing gift ideas to the engaged couple. How about some engraved jewelry? Did they like the opera? What about a spa day?

"Ooh, they could use a spa day actually," said Paras.

Murray, the one who made the suggestion, put on a proud smile and pretended to flick his nonexistent long hair.

"Jessica, do you know any good spas in the city?" Paras asked. "Someplace that's got a really nice steam room? My dad is constantly complaining about his sinuses."

Before Jessica could recommend a few places, Gigi cut her off.

"Why are you asking Jessica?" She laughed, pouring red wine into Paras's glass until she was told to stop.

"Because she's in the industry, *duh*. She probably knows all the horrible places to avoid."

"Who? Jessica? What are you talking about, hon?" Gigi paused, quickly shifting her eyes between Paras and Jessica. "Oh, I see. It's her parents that work at the salon. Not *her*, hon."

Jessica wiped her lips before speaking up. "Actually, I *am* working at my parents' salon at the moment."

"What—" Gigi spit out. "You are? Since when?"

"A couple of months now."

"Oh," Gigi remarked, blushing to the tips of her ears. Throughout their entire friendship, Gigi was always the first to obtain and disseminate information. It was how she was able to enhance her social capital and be firmly rooted in so many different networks. To be caught uninformed was, in her eyes, one of the worst forms of humiliation.

"I didn't know you were desperate to find a job," said Gigi with a flicker of disappointment in her voice. "You should've told me! I would've helped you find something."

"I wouldn't exactly say I was desperate. . . ."

The table fell quiet. Everyone had quickened the pace of their drinking.

Sasha quickly jumped in to save the night. "Has anyone here been to Argent—"

"Do you— Do you actually like working there?" Gigi interrupted. "I thought you were in touch with a few casting agencies. Didn't you get to the final round at one of them?"

"None of them worked out. And I needed a job, so . . ." Jessica shrugged, letting her shoulders finish the rest of her sentence for her. She pressed her fork into her cannoli, watching as the creamy ricotta filling gushed out of both ends like a broken fire hydrant.

Gigi forced a tight smile. "Well, I mean, if you like it there, then good for you."

"I do like it there," Jessica said confidently. "I really do."

If someone else had asked her whether she enjoyed her job, she would have had a completely different answer. But after seeing the secondhand embarrassment on Gigi's face when she found out that her childhood friend was no longer grazing Hollywood celebrities and was instead sweeping up nail clippings and callus shavings at her parents' salon, she refused to feel inferior. Not in front of all those high-achieving, thirty-under-thirty types. What was it about some jobs that made them more revered than others? When did it become mortifying to want to feed yourself and have a roof over your head?

That night, as she took the streetcar home, it became clear what she needed to do. She would keep working at the salon until her bones crumbled beneath her. She could not bear to have another job come and go like a bad hangover. No way was she giving Gigi the satisfaction of seeing her fail. She was going to make this one work. She *had* to make this work.

CHAPTER TWENTY-EIGHT

Debbie

The weekend after Tết, the Trans were due to attend the first-month celebration of Angel Võ's baby. As hard as Debbie tried, there was no way to get out of this one. After bailing on the baby shower, she couldn't decline yet *another* invite. In the circles they ran in, it would be considered downright hostile. She thought about pretending they never received the invitation, but Angel was the type of person who included a tracking label on all her invitations.

There was no way they could have missed the envelope anyway. It was heavy and gold, the words "To the Tran Family" professionally hand-lettered on the front. There was a pink wax seal on the back, and inside was an illustrated map with directions to get to their house in Hoggs Hollow. Word was they had hired the entire staff of a Chinese restaurant to cater the event, which would consist of a ten-course meal starting with crabmeat soup, climaxing at Peking duck, and ending with a sweet red bean soup. Debbie perked up when she heard this. If she had no choice but to drag her family to this event, then she was going to make certain they were coming home with a week's worth of leftovers.

"What's the point of a one-month celebration? The baby's not going to even know what's going on," said Dustin from the back seat of the car. He was squeezed between Jessica and Thuy, who held the presents while he clutched the bag of mismatched, empty Tupperware containers.

Phil was driving well above the speed limit. They needed to get there early to find street parking close to the house. These kinds of parties tended to get so packed that latecomers would practically have to park in a different postal code.

"It's tradition," said Debbie. "Back in the day, it was a miracle if a baby lived past the first month. Your father and I had a đầy tháng for you kids. Nothing as fancy as this. We had a few friends over and got a cake. We have pictures somewhere in the house."

"But we have things like penicillin and vaccines and modern medicine now." Dustin snickered. "It's not a miracle anymore. It's just science and good health care. This whole thing is just a gift grab for what's-her-face."

"Who?" asked Debbie.

"The baby. What's her name?"

"We don't know yet. They'll announce it tonight."

"They haven't given the baby a name yet? It's been a month!"

"It's bad luck to name the baby early. The spirits will snatch her soul."

"Okay, now *that* is even more ludicrous than the mortality thing."

"Why must you question everything we do?" Debbie snapped. "It's tradition. You guys don't appreciate it because you're mất gốc—" She stopped herself. It dawned on her the irony of calling out her children's loss of culture by using a term they did not even understand.

"I thought you didn't even want to come to this thing anyway," Jessica piped in.

"At first, but—"

"But peer pressure, I bet," Dustin quipped.

Debbie didn't retort. She didn't care that they thought what they thought. Ever since Phil won all that money, she'd been feeling a lot lighter, like her body could float up to the sky with one deep inhale. By no means did she approve of what Phil did, as she believed gambling was for the weak-willed, but she figured a little bit of celebratory fun wasn't the worst thing in the world. That's why she gave herself permission to spend money on a new dress, plus a couple of onesies and a stuffed giraffe for the baby.

An Asian woman in a black vest greeted them at the door. She took their jackets and presents and escorted them to the entrance hall, which was brimming with people of all backgrounds. The first familiar face Debbie spotted was the man of the house, Sebastian himself. How could she not, with that six-foot-six frame that naturally commanded attention everywhere he went?

A large crowd had gathered in the living room, circled around what was presumably the baby girl, dressed in a frilly pink polka-dot dress, cradled soundly in the arms of her mother. As Angel walked her baby into the middle of the hall, someone somewhere had cued up "Isn't She Lovely" for the grand entrance.

"This party is so extra," said Jessica. "All for a newborn? The shit rich people do with their money."

"Look at all this wealth," said Thuy, turning her body a full three-sixty. "There's got to be food somewhere. I'm going to explore."

"Head for the kitchen. I think that's where your uncle and Dustin are," said Debbie.

"Did you see the champagne fountain over there? It's five tiers!" Jessica cried. "Why are they even serving appetizers when there's a ten-course meal coming up?"

A man's voice interjected.

"It wouldn't be an Angel Võ party if there wasn't a fountain you could drink out of."

Debbie turned around. It took her eyes a few seconds to recognize the man standing in front of them, but sure enough, it was Văn Đỗ. His hair was neatly combed back, imparting a slight sheen. He wore a tie with a shawl neck collar sweater and for once, the waistband of his pants sat where it should: his waist. It was a jarring transformation. Amazing what sobriety and a shower could do to a person.

"Văn," said Debbie. "Wow. You look . . . great. Did you . . . how are you? It's nice to see someone we know. There are so many people here. I didn't realize you knew Angel."

"Angel is my cousin's cousin. So technically we are related, if you can believe that at all."

"If you looked like this all the time, I think I could." Debbie brushed her hand through Jessica's hair. "Văn, have you met my daughter, Jessica? I wanted to introduce her to everyone at our party, but I think you had already left at that point. She's been working with us at the salon."

Văn grinned at Jessica, exposing his yellow teeth and a dull gold cap.

"We met," he said, looking at Jessica. "It was brief. It's nice to see you again." He extended his hand.

Jessica didn't move. So Debbie nudged her to extend a hand in return. Such rotten manners. Surely her daughter did not learn it from her.

"How have you been?" continued Debbie. "I heard your mom isn't feeling well. Is everything okay?"

"Yes. I mean no. Not really. She's come down with a bad cold. It could be nothing but she's ninety-six, you know? I'm trying to think positively but I can't help but think, is this the thing that takes her down? A fucking cold?"

"I'm so sorry to hear that," Debbie said sweetly, laying her hand on his shoulder. "I agree. It can sometimes be the most unexpected thing. Many years ago I flew to Saigon after my mother called and complained about a pain in her stomach. I was so scared it was something bad. Turns out she had eaten too much fruit that day. They're just so fragile, you never know."

"It's a miracle she's even made it this long considering she still smokes a dozen cigarettes a day," said Văn. "Half the family keeps telling her to quit, and the other half tells her to keep doing what she's doing. If she's lived this long, maybe she's doing something right."

"Hmm, I think you're right. Routine is so important for these elders. If my mother gets her breakfast even thirty minutes too late, she'll complain of feeling faint."

Everyone was jostling to take a picture of the fountain. The crowd had gotten so tightly packed it was hard to move around. She was standing so close to Văn she could smell his breath, spearmint layered over cigarettes.

"So, Jessica." Văn turned his body to face her. "Do you have a boyfriend yet?"

"No, nobody at the moment," she said dully.

"Is that so? A girl like you should be married by now. Start a family, buy a house, have a kid, throw a đầy tháng just like this." He laughed, revealing another gold cap in the back of his mouth.

"I've been saying the same thing to her," Debbie chimed in. "Do you know someone for her? A handsome man with a good job?"

A group of boisterous people attempted to snake through the crowd. Someone knocked into Debbie, which launched her so far forward that both breasts nearly bounced out of her V-neck dress. Embarrassed, she pointed across the room.

"Look!" said Debbie. "Angel is finally alone. Let's go over and see the baby before she gets swarmed again."

Before Debbie could even move an inch through the crowd, a loud bell rang out, reverberating against the walls of the house and echoing down the large hall. Everyone's eyes cast upwards towards Angel, Sebastian, and their two girls, all standing like Roman statues at the top of the spiral staircase. From this unfortunate angle, everyone could see the cheetah-print underwear Angel was wearing under her body-con dress. Knowing Angel, it most likely wasn't an accident.

"Thank you, everyone, for coming to our daughter's one-month celebration," Sebastian said into a wireless microphone. His voice boomed through speakers that were nowhere to be seen. "Your support and presence mean the world to us. Most of you know the journey my wife and I had to go through to have our baby girl and now that she's here, healthy as ever, we know we couldn't have done it without your prayers." Sebastian stopped to look up towards the ceiling, dabbing tears away. Angel beamed down at the crowd, compensating for her husband's emotional whims.

"Somebody get him a towel," jeered a person from the back.

The entire room broke out into laughter.

"Sorry!" Sebastian said. "I know you're not here to see me cry." He gently took the baby from Angel's arms and lifted her Rafiki-style as the crowd half cheered, half gasped. "I'd like to introduce you all to . . . Amethyst Cassidy Cope."

Everybody clapped and hollered. Once it died down, Sebastian and Angel pointed their arms towards the living room. "Please make your way to your tables for dinner," said Angel, before screaming into the mic, "and be prepared to eat!"

By the time the fifth course arrived, a plate of steamed fish drowning in a pool of soy sauce, ginger, and cilantro, people began to slow down their food intake, leaning back in their chairs and loosening their belts. Phil was the only person at their table to keep funneling food into his mouth. Ever since Debbie had known him, he'd never complained about having too much food. It wasn't a thing to complain about. Especially not after those days at the refugee camp where they sometimes had to split small bowls of rice with up to six people. So Phil kept eating and eating, telling his children to eat some more and putting more food on her plate.

"Phil, it's like you haven't eaten in days," said Debbie. "We brought the plastic containers for a reason."

"Leftovers aren't the same. Best to eat it when it's fresh and hot right now."

Phil turned towards his kids, their faces resembling those of zombies as they peered into their phones. "Look up, guys." Phil had shoved two chopsticks in his mouth so they stuck down like vampire fangs.

"Oh god, are you serious, Ba? You're so embarrassing," said Dustin.

"Phil. Stop that," said Debbie, who couldn't help but snort out a chuckle.

"Are you five years old?" said Jessica. "Maybe you should sit at the kids' table."

"Being a vampire really *sucks*." Phil chuckled.

"Oh my god, that's it! I'm going to the washroom," Dustin said before getting up. The five other people at the round table, an Asian couple and three white women who appeared to be related in some capacity, all pretended not to notice the silly behavior ensuing across from them. There was simply not enough context to deduce whether this man was harmlessly quirky or downright deranged.

"Looks like someone's having a lot of fun here," Sebastian said, standing behind Phil's chair. Even with his towering frame, this man's gait was as light and airy as a feather, gracing him with the ability to sneak up on people at their most idiotic moments.

"I got those chopsticks custom made in Japan," said Sebastian. "Randomly found this tiny little store in Tokyo when I was walking back to my hotel. The old man there made a set for me right on the spot. Loved them so much I went back the next day and ordered two hundred more sets. He screamed with joy. Guess he'd just made half a year's worth of earnings."

Phil removed the chopsticks from his mouth and laid them neatly on the table. Debbie shook her head. Such a fool, that one.

"What a story!" Phil's voice tended to come out two octaves higher when he was caught off guard. "Anyway, the food here is phenomenal. You must tell me where you ordered all of this from." Debbie felt embarrassed by his overcompensation.

"Do you know Lee Garden in Little Chinatown? They make the best suckling pigs in the city. Of course, I was fine with serving everyone soup and steak, but Angel insisted that baby Amethyst's celebration not go by without an abundance of food surrounding her. She said it was a Vietnamese tradition and how can I argue with that? I don't want to be that guy that says no to cultural traditions. We think it's very important for Amethyst to be in tune with her Vietnamese side. She should know her language and identity and if this will help her get off on the right foot, then why not?"

Everybody at the table cooed praise at Sebastian for doing something that seemed obvious to Debbie.

"Where is the baby anyway?" she asked.

"Upstairs in the nursery. She's a fussy girl. Can't sleep with all this noise and smell."

"Ah." Debbie picked up her glass, realized there was nothing in there, and let it sit awkwardly in her hands.

"Jeez, have you been dry this entire time?" Sebastian waved over a waiter. "Please get these people here a drink. How about a vodka tonic?"

Debbie nodded. She wasn't about to say no to a man who probably didn't hear the word *no* a lot.

"By the way, Phil, did you see Eamon Harsanyi? Table six or seven, I believe." Sebastian's gaze fell over the sea of people who had filled up his oversized living room. "God, we went overboard with the guest list, didn't we?"

Debbie looked at her husband, whose eyes suddenly widened. "Who's Eamon?"

Sebastian turned to face Debbie. "I represented him way, way back in the day. Before he ever became a private lender. He told me he met up with Phil a few weeks ago. What a small world, huh?"

A tray of vodka tonics arrived and Phil grabbed them so fast the straws flew out.

"Ah yes, a small world indeed. Yet I never run into Michael Jordan," said Phil, his voice cracking.

"Look, I won't pry into your financial matters, but I'll tell you this, Eamon is a class act. A great guy. When it comes to money, you're in really good hands, my man."

Sebastian took a handkerchief out of his jacket pocket and dabbed the beads of sweat collecting on his forehead. "Anyway, I've got to make my rounds. Enjoy the rest of the meal." He waved at the entire table and walked away.

Debbie forced a smile. She tried to look at her husband, but he wouldn't even look back at her. That's when she knew.

How could she have been so gullible? He'd been lying to her this whole time about where all that cash came from. She felt as if her heart had dropped into her stomach, and suddenly she felt sick. Debbie scanned the room. This was no place for a public uproar, a dramatic exit, or even a disparaging comment or two about his poor sense of judgment.

Instead, Debbie pierced a piece of fish full of tiny bones and handed it to her husband. "Eat this."

CHAPTER TWENTY-NINE

Phil

Fuck. Shit. Fuck. That was all Phil could think on the ride home. Debbie knew what he'd done, and in one night he'd gone from family hero to degenerate loser.

The car was silent. Phil wished someone would turn the radio on, or talk, or hum, something to slice through the noise in his head. A few times, he thought about saying something, but he took one look at his wife's expression in the side-view mirror and sank deeper into his seat, staring at every passing billboard on the highway. He envied his son, who had the presence of mind to take a cab and sleep at his girlfriend's place. The smells from the leftovers were starting to seep out of their containers and fuse in the air to create one amalgamated aroma that smelled equal parts delicious and disgusting.

When they pulled into the driveway, Debbie finally spoke. "If it wasn't so cold out tonight, I would've made you sleep in the car," she said, keeping her gaze straight ahead. And in one swift movement, she exited the car and disappeared into the dark house.

A wave of relief swept over Phil. Anger was much more comprehensible than silence. Of course, he would have preferred if she hadn't found out about the loan in the first place, but at least he could go to sleep knowing where she stood on the spectrum of moods. She always forgave him, even when he had done far worse in the past. This, he was certain, was something she would get over, too.

Jessica and Thuy looked at him like he'd just been prosecuted to the highest extent of the law.

"Go inside, kids. Go on," Phil said. "We'll be okay. Really."

They reluctantly got out of the car while he stayed put. The cold air was quickly swallowing any residual heat left in the car. His muscles violently shook every few minutes. Despite all that, he felt safe in there, protected by the impenetrable steel surrounding him on all four sides, top and bottom. Even though Debbie thought it too cold to sleep in the car, he could probably do it just fine. Maybe it was the savage in him, hardened over many years of sleeping inside precarious structures like that makeshift tent at the refugee camp: stained, moldy tarpaulins strung over perilously thin wooden sticks that could be knocked over by the sound of a screaming baby. He might wake up with blue lips and frostbitten toes, but at least he knew the roof of the car would not come crashing down on him that night.

Phil lay down, bending his knees so he could fit his entire frame on the back seat of the car. He played a song on his phone. There was nothing quite like the sound of a sixteen-string zither to transport him home. He closed his eyes and allowed each pluck to fly him back until he had landed at the Tan Son Nhat International Airport, greeted in the arrivals area by Mr. Heat and Mrs. Humidity. He'd hop on a motorbike and excessively beep his way through traffic (god, how he loved the madness of those roads) until he got to his parents' grave. He'd pay his respects by setting on fire the things they needed to navigate the afterlife: stacks of fake money, two pairs of sandals, shirts and pants, and a pack of cigarettes. This time he would throw in an empty iPhone box. That way they could check Facebook from heaven and see how big their grandchildren had gotten.

From there, he'd drive to his favorite restaurant, sit himself on a small plastic chair on the sidewalk, drink cà phê sữa đá and snack on rare beef soaked in lime. For the rest of the day he'd do nothing else but watch beautiful women walk by as the sticky breeze made the backs of their áo dài flutter in the air. Pluck, pluck, went the zither. Oh, to be home and—

The song stopped. Eamon was calling. Phil froze, unsure what to do. This was the call he had been dreading. He was three weeks late on his payment. If only he had more time. Surely, Eamon would understand. He knew better than anyone that money was as fickle as the wind, moving in any which direction it wanted without regard to whoever was in its path.

The ringing stopped. He was expecting Eamon to call again but nothing. He checked his voicemail. There was a message from Quân Phạm, a friend from the Buddhist temple. He was having some men over for cards and beer tonight and asked him to come over. Phil looked at the time. It was close to ten o'clock. Perhaps he could go for just an hour, take his mind off things for a little while. His problems were still going to be there tomorrow, so what was the harm in letting future him deal with it then? He was tired and deeply in need of a night out with his boys and Hennessy.

Before he could even ring the doorbell, Quân opened the door and waved him in. "Get in, get in, we're about to start a new round."

Quân's droopy-eyed face had more freckles than Phil remembered, like someone had blown cocoa powder all over him. He still smelled the same, though, like an official Tiger Balm ambassador. "You still got that back problem?" asked Phil.

"It comes and goes. Today I had to deliver a box of dumbbells over a hundred pounds. Nearly popped out my eyeballs trying to lift that thing. Probably made everything worse." He rubbed his lower back, wincing when he hit a sore spot.

Phil took off his shoes and neatly placed them against the wall. Quân's home had all the classic markers of a Vietnamese abode: a wooden clock in the shape of the motherland, a daily tear-off calendar whose pages hadn't been ripped in three days, a gigantic wall-mounted fan depicting the tranquility of rural life, a wife and daughter in the kitchen making glutinous rice balls from scratch. Simmering pots of coconut cream and ginger syrup wafted in the air.

There were two games going on in the living room: one was in progress, the other group was waiting on him. Phil sat on the floor next to Quân, and before he could even fully cross his legs, shots of Hennessy were already being passed around. "One, two, three, drink!" they all shouted before synchronistically pouring the cognac down their throats. On the second round, they shouted even louder, this time screaming, "One hundred percent!" On the third round, they boisterously clinked their glasses, spilling some alcohol on the cards, and recycled the first cheer: "Một, hai, ba, dô!"

The dealer passed around the cards. His hands were veiny and spotted with age, and the whites of his eyes were slightly red. He looked defeated, which probably had something to do with the fact that he had the least amount of money in front of him, while the others were all up by at least sixty dollars. Phil was determined not to be more of a loser than that guy.

He slowly fanned out his thirteen cards and refrained from smiling. What luck. With two twos and the highest-ranking sequence of three, he was guaranteed a win. When he got down to his last card, a two of hearts, he slammed it down so hard it made the other cards bounce and the other men scowl. Just like that, Phil was up twenty. Here came another round of shots. "Yo!"

On his next hand, he had no twos, but a sequence of six and three. Someone in this circle had at least two twos, so he avoided playing singles or doubles until the very end when slam! He couldn't believe it, he'd won again. Now he was up forty. Hello again, Henny. "Yo!"

Quân's wife broke through the circle to set down some longan fruit and sesame rice crackers. Phil hadn't even noticed that the whole house had filled with a warm, almost-burnt nutty smell from the roasted black sesame. He broke off a piece and bit down on a cracker. It was not very good. Too thin and mealy, unlike Debbie's, which was far superior on all fronts, from texture to thickness to taste.

He wondered what Debbie was doing right now. Had she noticed the driveway was empty? Was she tossing and turning in bed? Or did she fall soundly asleep because she didn't have to sleep beside the burden of a bad husband? Maybe leaving her alone was the one right thing he'd done in a very long time.

He continued to eat more rice crackers, punishing himself with tinder-dry blandness until there were no more left. He popped in a longan, letting the sweet, candy-like juices coat the insides of his mouth before spitting out the shiny black seed into his palm. The pupil of the dragon, as his people called it.

Was the tale really true, that when you pressed the seed against a snakebite it would absorb all the venom? He pressed the seed against a scab on his arm, but nothing happened.

They continued to play more rounds, capping each game with a shot. Cards. Shot. Cards. Shot. Phil had lost track of how many times he'd won and lost. He'd lost track of everything, in fact. What time it was, what day it was, who he was with, where he was, why it smelled like something was burning, why his hands were so sticky.

The next thing he knew, he was lying down on an unfamiliar couch with a heavy velvet blanket draped over him. His phone said it was nearly four in the morning. It also said there were nine missed calls from Eamon, three voicemails, and one text message.

Pick up you fucker.

Phil's head was spinning like a spool of silk, his vision too blurred to trust what he was really seeing. Rubbing his eyes only made it worse, and now he could see nothing on his screen, like there was a viscous film over his eyeballs. He proceeded to text Eamon anyway, assuring him he'd call in the morning. Hoping he'd pressed all the right keys, he hit send. There was nothing that tomorrow couldn't fix.

CHAPTER THIRTY

Debbie

Debbie did not sleep well that night. She'd become dependent on the presence of Phil's body to lull herself to sleep. It was a maddening kind of dissonance, to be furious at somebody while aching for them at the same time.

By morning, she discovered the car was not there. The driveway was empty, blanketed by a light layer of snow that fell overnight. No tire tracks left behind, which meant the car had been out the entire evening. A worry started to form, but immediately she squashed it. For far too long she bore the mental load of worrying about him, and she was tired of it. He was a grown man. He could take care of himself.

With no car, Debbie took the bus to the salon. When she got off, the first thing she noticed was an unshaven man in a puffy yellow coat smoking in front of their salon. It was not unusual to find clients standing outside the salon before it even opened, hoping to snag a walk-in appointment before the seats filled up. But Debbie did not recognize this client. Perhaps he was looking to buy a gift certificate. Or maybe he was trying to sell something. Lately there had been a canvassing blitz in the neighborhood and salespeople were visiting them on a regular basis, pitching them things they didn't need like magazine subscriptions, credit card terminals, and cable and internet bundles.

"Good morning, sir," said Debbie, kicking the snow off her boots. "We don't need anything today."

The man took a drag of his cigarette. "I'm looking for Phil." He had a deep timbre to his voice that was hard to ignore.

"Phil? He's not here yet." She pointed to the store hours sign that was hanging crookedly on the front door. "We don't open for another hour. There's a coffee shop right across the street if you'd like to stay warm before we open."

"That won't be necessary. I've had my coffee already," he said, throwing his cigarette butt to the ground, where it disappeared beneath the snow. "Is he on his way?"

Debbie detected a European accent, his *w*'s morphed into *v*'s. "What's this about? We already have cable. The best cable package around. Nothing you sell can be better than the deal we've got."

The man laughed in her face. "I'm not here to sell you cable, lady. I'm a friend of your husband's. I just need a few minutes with him. That's all." He turned his head to spit on the sidewalk.

His body was still blocking the door, and Debbie was getting cold standing outside. It was clear he wasn't going to leave her alone, so she let him come inside and told him to stay seated in the reception area. Debbie was certain this was the man Sebastian was talking about, the one who loaned Phil the money. Why was he here? What did he want? And what the hell had her husband done now?

"How do you know Phil?" said Debbie, pretending to be clueless.

The man took off his hat, revealing hair that looked expensively cut. He twisted his face in discomfort. "I always hate this part."

"Hate what part?"

"I'd rather discuss this with your husband. When does he get here?"

"I told you. He'll be here in an hour," Debbie lied. The truth was, she had no idea where he was.

The man leaned back on the chair, his puffy coat spilling over the armrests. "Why didn't he come here with you? Probably drank too much last night, huh?"

Did he know something she didn't? Debbie acted as if she didn't hear him and went on as if it was any ordinary morning. She lit up three incense sticks, held them up against her forehead, and bowed three times before offering them to the Buddha.

"What are we praying for these days?" he said, both hands casually tucked inside his pockets.

Debbie stayed silent, filling up the three small cups on the altar with tea. She stared at the phone, wondering whether she should call Phil. He would know what to do. The only problem was, as soon as she picked up the phone, she'd be surrendering to this man's intimidations. No way was she going to let him win.

"I'm guessing you have no idea where your husband is, do you?" he said. Debbie continued to say nothing. "You know, I tried to call him last night. Multiple times . . . He sent me a message just a few hours ago. I'm wondering if you could help me decipher it."

Debbie hesitated before stepping towards him. She leaned down to see his phone. It was indeed a text from Phil's phone number.

Ueill csll uoi tumlfrrow

Oh, Phil, you fool, Debbie thought. She tried to hide the displeasure on her face, but she feared he'd already seen it.

"Marriage, it can be hard. Trust me, I get it," he said. He paced around the nail salon, touching everything he could. "Nice shop you got here. Where did you get that Buddha? Been thinking of getting one of those for my place."

Debbie's back was turned to him, so she rolled her eyes freely and fiercely for no one to see but the Buddha himself. "Vietnam," she replied begrudgingly.

"Vietnam," he echoed, raising his eyebrows to his hairline. "I want to visit one day. I've never even been to Asia but it's on my bucket list. The Great Wall, Angkor Wat, Taj Mahal. That's stuff everybody has to see once before they die, right? Don't tell me you haven't been to any of these places."

Debbie turned to face him. "We don't have time to travel."

"Ahh, the classic tale of the hardworking immigrant. How many times have I heard this before? I'm an immigrant, too, you know. Came here with nothing. All by myself. Did not know the language one bit. Now look at me. I've got Diamond Medallion status with Delta." He paused, waiting for a reaction, but she had none to give. "It's a big deal." He paused once more, and again she said nothing. "You people need to relax. Look at you right now. You're so tense and stressed all the time. What's the point of busting your ass if you can't even *relaaaax*?" He stretched out the last vowel as if it was supposed to loosen every knot in her body.

Debbie turned her back again and wiped away the week-old incense dust that had collected on the altar.

He stood up and stared at the wall of polish bottles. "One of these days, you're going to get bad news. A death in the family, cancer, car accident, whatever. And when something happens, *BAM*." He punched his fist into his palm so hard that the sound startled her.

"Don't get me wrong, I'm all about the hustle. Last year, I found out my father had stage-four testicular cancer. Stage four! It doesn't get any worse than that." He pulled out a dark red polish, then put it back on a different part of the shelf, messing up the color coordination. "Doctor said he had five, maybe six months to live. Well, guess what? He died the week after we found out. Didn't even get to see him. That wrecked me for months."

He ambled towards the altar and Debbie stepped aside, keeping at least a broomstick's distance away. Both of his hands were clenched as he hovered over the Buddha like an impending storm. "No dying person ever wishes they worked more."

Debbie examined his face. His brows were knitted in a frown and his eyes glistened against the light. Did he really expect her to buy any of this? *What bullshit*, Debbie wanted to say. He fed off people's financial problems and then threw those same problems back at them and called it work? Secondly, it always infuriated her when people said work wasn't everything. How could it not be everything when it was all this country had told her she must do in order to be worth the trouble of accommodating her? She needed to survive, and because of that, working was like breathing to her. It could never stop.

The man brushed his hand through his shiny hair as his eyes wandered around the room. He seemed to grow more and more impatient with her silent treatment. She could tell he was the kind of person who believed that if he could overcome adversity, a nobody who came from nothing, then everyone else was capable of success, too. No excuses.

"You may be small but I can tell you probably don't take shit from nobody," he said, looking her up and down in a way that made her feel uneasy. He unzipped his puffy coat, releasing a wave of cologne that was much too strong for the morning. He sat down. "I like that about you."

Debbie peered out the window, hoping that Phil would show up. Surely, he would have driven straight to the salon as soon as he realized she'd left the house. She wished so badly to see her husband's face right now, more than she wished that this man would leave the store, but the way his body was sinking deeper into his seat showed her he was willing to wait as long as it took.

"Phil should be here soon," Debbie lied. She had a lot of work to tend to in the back room, but she didn't want to leave him out here alone. Too many times they'd had things stolen from them—cash, polish bottles, nail clippers. Someone had even taken a plant one time. Debbie pretended to tidy up around the salon so she could keep an eye on him.

His cell phone rang. "Yeah? I'm working right now. For fuck's sake. Again? There must be something going around in that school. How bad is it? Where is he right now? Why can't you go? Fine, fine, fine. Yes, I'll pick him up. When will you be home later? Yes, yes, I know where the medicine is. What about Leah? Do they think she's got it, too? All right, all right, I'll call you when I get home."

Debbie breathed a sigh of relief. Finally, he was leaving. "This isn't over. I'm going to be back," he said with a sneer on his face. "Your husband is late on his payments, you know?"

"What payments?"

"Don't play me, bitch!" he shouted. "You know exactly what I'm talking about."

His tone startled her, but she stood her ground. "I don't know anything."

The man continued to grin at her, his stare unrelenting.

"You're good," he said. "Debbie, is it?"

She tried not to look flustered at the mention of her name.

"Your husband hasn't paid me yet. Wouldn't you be angry, too, if your client promised they'd pay you and then they didn't? It ain't a good feeling to be left dry like this." He peered down at his coat and flicked away some lint. "I've called your husband many times, but he won't pick up. Don't you see how this puts me in a bind?"

"I told you. I don't know anything," Debbie repeated.

His eyes veered down towards her neck. "That necklace you're wearing. That real gold?"

Debbie grasped the chain, pressing it into her clavicle as if to make it disappear inside her body.

"Queen and Church. There's a guy there that will pay good money for that. I bet that would get you a couple hundred. It's not enough to pay off your husband's debts, but enough to buy you time."

"Please leave," she pleaded.

"Look, I like you, Debbie. I helped your husband when he needed help. And since he's not stepping up, I'm gonna need you to help me out. You understand?"

Debbie nodded.

Then it happened so quickly.

He grabbed the Buddha statue and smashed it on the ground. Gold shards scattered everywhere. A jagged edge of the Buddha's hand rested at her feet.

"Tell your husband to call me," he said, leaving a business card behind before slithering out of the salon.

Debbie quickly ran to lock the door. She bent down, being careful not to rest her knees on any sharp pieces, and slowly picked up the shards. A piece of the belly. A piece of the foot. A piece of the robe.

"Shit," she yelped. One of the pieces pricked her finger and the cut pooled with blood. "Đồ ngu, đồ ngu, đồ ngu," she cried. She wasn't sure who she was calling an idiot, herself or her husband. They both were, it seemed.

Debbie taped a cotton ball around the cut and swept up the remaining pieces. She was sick of having to clean up her husband's mess. It wasn't just the DUI. When he hired an unlicensed contractor to fix their roof, she was the one who called the Better Business Bureau and got all their money back.

When he accidentally ordered four hundred dollars' worth of the wrong wax, she was the one who was able to sell it and recoup the costs. She was always the one fixing things. Just for once, why couldn't he deal with the problem on his own?

Debbie knew this was a rhetorical question, but she pondered it anyway because it felt cathartic. Their lives were inextricably tangled to the point of perplexity. This mess Phil created was now her mess. His actions were her actions. His consequences were her consequences. No amount of untwisting and untwining could get her out of this bind.

As she swept, she saw that the gold ingot was still intact. She held it delicately in both of her open palms, just like the Buddha did, and begged for forgiveness for what she was about to do.

———

Debbie took the bus home and was relieved to find the house empty. She sifted through her jewelry box in search of anything that could fetch some money: a pair of tiny gold hoops (Jessica's first earrings), a gold link chain (Dustin's fifth birthday present). She touched the necklace she was wearing (her tenth anniversary gift from Phil). Unclasping the necklace, she held all three items carefully in her palms, treating them as preciously as if they were the beating hearts of the people she loved.

Memories flashed through her mind. Baby Jessica crying the whole car ride home after getting her ears pierced at the mall. Little Dustin laughing uncontrollably because the chain felt ticklish against his chubby neck. Phil's eyes crinkling with joy when she opened the box and told him she'd never seen a necklace more breathtaking.

Debbie shook her whole body as if she were covered in a layer of silt. It appalled her to think about giving these away. What would become of those memories if there was nothing physical rooting them to the present? Would they just evaporate like snow left out in the sun?

She checked on her cut. It was deeper than she thought, the blood still pouring out of her as if it were weeping.

The jewelry was just stuff, she told herself, just stuff. Debbie thought back to something a monk had recited at the temple. *Be attached to nothing. Happiness arises after letting go.*

As she recited the mantra in her head, she pulled her jade ring off and on until her finger was raw and red. The faces of the pirates flashed in her mind, their sunken cheeks and sunburned skin, their chapped lips, their menacing eyes that carried in them no ounce of mercy.

Debbie threw all the gold jewelry into a plastic bag. If she was going to the pawnshop, her face needed to look as nice as possible, like the face of someone who bought gold jewelry as if it was a loaf of bread. She swept on an onyx shadow, drew on her eyebrows, applied blush and red lipstick, and topped it off with a few spritzes of perfume.

———

"I can give you one eighty for all of this," said the man behind the counter. He had a compact body and a slight stubble that coated his bloated cheeks. The way his eyes halfheartedly examined the jewelry suggested he was uninspired, like he could tell they were mass-produced in a factory.

"That's it? Did you see the chain necklace, too? It's nine karat."

The man held up the necklace. "It's already rusting in this area. See here?"

Debbie didn't look up. "These hoop earrings were only worn a few months when my daughter was a baby. They're like new condition."

"One eighty, ma'am."

Debbie looked down at her hand. She hadn't planned on selling her ring, but she was curious to see what it was worth. "What about this ring?" The man held it up and peered at it through a scope. Debbie's heart was beating fast. She didn't know what kind of answer she wanted to hear.

"It's certainly a beautiful piece, but I can't guarantee the origins of this. Ten is the best I can do."

"Dollars?"

The man gave a terse nod.

Debbie cried out a sigh of relief. Would she have sold it if he were offering more? She didn't want to find out. "Never mind. Are you sure the rest isn't worth more?"

"One eighty," he repeated, sounding more impatient each time.

The amount was much too measly to make a dent in Phil's debt. She placed the items carefully back in her bag, making sure they didn't get tangled, and turned towards the exit.

"I don't just do gold, you know?" the man called out. "If you have diamonds, we pay good money for that. Rings, earrings, necklaces, anything like that. We get engagement rings all the time."

"How much do you pay?"

"Depends on the size and clarity. I'll need to take a look. If it's a real nice one, we could give you about eighty percent of the retail price."

Debbie didn't own any diamonds, at least not real ones. They didn't look good on her. The icy coolness of the gem clashed against the yellow undertones of her skin. But she did know someone who wore a diamond ring. Someone whose pale skin, silvery blond hair, and cold blue veins were made for diamonds.

No. She couldn't possibly. Savannah might be having problems in her marriage, but that didn't give Debbie the right to take her ring. It would be wrong. So wrong.

Then again, this was her family she was talking about. Her blood. Her everything. She couldn't sit back and watch Eamon do something terrible to her husband. Phil made a mistake, but he did nothing wrong. How could it be wrong to protect the people you love?

Next thing she knew, she was driving straight to Take Ten.

———

"Do you have an appointment?" the receptionist asked.

"No," Debbie said nervously. "I'm here to see . . . well, I'm wondering if Savannah Shaw is in town."

"She is, but she's currently out having lunch with her husband. Did you have a meeting with her? I can call her—"

"No, no," Debbie spat out. "That won't be needed. I'll just wait here for her until she gets back."

So Savannah *was* here. With her husband. Debbie was not expecting this at all. Was this a sign? Should she really do this? Debbie pulled up the photo on her phone. Proof of betrayal. This was power. She'd be a fool not to use it.

She took the last seat available. There were no magazines to flip through and the iPads were currently being used, one by a tanned woman with horn-rimmed glasses, the other by a woman whose eyebrows were drawn in a quizzical expression.

Debbie squirmed in her chair, eyes glued to the door, spinning her jade ring round and round as she counted each rotation. Two hundred and fifty-five, two hundred and fifty-six, two hundred and fifty-seven . . .

Thirty minutes went by, and Debbie was starting to feel sick with guilt. This was a terrible idea. What would her family think if they found out what she was doing? This was not who she was at all.

Debbie got up to leave. Just as she was about to pull the door open, Savannah entered and walked right by her. It was as if Debbie were a speck of dust to her, seemingly everywhere but never visible.

"Savannah," Debbie blurted.

She turned around, a startled look appearing on her perfectly spotless face. "Oh, I'm surprised to see you here . . ." Of course she had forgotten Debbie's name.

"It's Debbie."

"Of course, of course. I remember. From the cleaning crew, right? How are you?"

Debbie was seething with fury. Was this woman joking? After two encounters with her, this woman still thought she was the hired help? Savannah deserved no mercy. And this conviction freed Debbie to do what she did next.

"From Sunshine Nails, actually. I need to talk to you."

Savannah loosened her smile. "Who? Me?"

"Can we go somewhere private?"

Savannah knitted her eyebrows and cocked her head, gesturing for her to follow. Debbie kept her eyes low as they passed the row of customers getting their nails done. She kept her focus on the back of Savannah's skintight white jeans, which sculpted her body like a cake. Green fuzz from her thick-knit sweater sat on the denim surface like sprinkles.

"I have something of yours." Debbie spoke as soon as the door closed behind them.

"What is it?"

She pulled out her cell phone and showed her the picture.

Savannah leaned in to take a look, then quickly covered her mouth.

"How did you get that?"

"I don't want to hurt you."

"Who sent that to you? Who?"

Debbie's nervousness was now replaced with indignation. Did she really think so little of her that she thought someone *else* had taken this picture? That she was too docile and innocent to be capable of taking this photo of her own accord?

"I know your husband is here." Debbie paused to catch her breath. "And I'm not afraid to do it."

"Do what, exactly?"

"When you marry someone, you become a team. You let go of your selfish instincts and you stay loyal no matter what." Debbie paused, playing back in her head the words that just came out of her.

"Why are you doing this?" Savannah cried out. "Is someone making you do this? Who is it? You can tell me."

Debbie snapped. "Nobody is making me do anything! This is me. *I* am the one doing this."

"I don't understand." Savannah looked at Debbie like she just found out she had two weeks to live.

"I need something from you."

Debbie glanced down at Savannah's left hand. It took her a moment to realize what Debbie was insinuating, then her eyes became enlarged like a dead fish.

"Are you serious?" She clutched her hand like it was a baby. "You're crazy. You're absolutely fucking crazy."

Debbie didn't let her decisive tone dissuade her. "That ring is a lie. You don't care about your husband or your marriage. It doesn't mean anything to you."

"Fuck you. I knew you people were fucking uncivilized. You think you can make something out of yourself? You're nothing! All people see when they see you are your hands. That's all you'll ever be good for!"

Debbie felt a boiling sensation in her stomach. "This would never have happened if you hadn't come here."

Savannah scoffed. "You're delusional!"

"You could have gone anywhere. Anywhere else in the city. But you didn't. You came here. Right across from us."

"What are you talking about? You don't *ooown* this neighborhood. This place doesn't *belooong* to you. You're lucky we even let you *live* here! If you can't handle a bit of competition, then you're not cut out—"

The door opened slightly. An employee with a high bun peeked her head through the crack. "Your husband is here. Said he needed to get something from you," she said before slipping back out.

Savannah glared at Debbie like one of those menacing lion statues that sat at the entrance of the temple. Debbie held up the phone again and gave her a piercing look that said, *I'll do it.*

Her husband appeared at the door. His cheeks were tinged red from the cold, and flecks of snow sat perched on his padded shoulders. "Hi, I'm Lionel," he said to Debbie, not bothering to ask her who she was. "Honey"—he turned to Savannah—"you forgot to give me the key card to the hotel."

Debbie clutched her phone even tighter. Her hand was so clammy she thought it might slip and break. Savannah looked like she was going to charge at her with so much force that both their bodies would go right through the drywall and into the art gallery next door. Instead, she gently pushed her husband through the door and told him to wait in the car.

They were both alone in the room again. This was it. Debbie tightened every muscle in her body as she prepared to get screamed at, slapped at, anything that would relieve the molten anger that was flashing in Savannah's eyes.

But nothing happened. Savannah stayed as still as stone before dropping her shoulders and slowly sliding the diamond ring out from her left hand. Of all the scenarios Debbie could have imagined, this was by far the scariest one.

"Give me your phone," said Savannah.

Debbie handed it over and watched as she furiously deleted the photo, then emptied the trash folder.

Savannah passed her the ring. "Fuck you. And fuck your family." She paused, then snickered. "I just find it absolutely laughable that you think you have any power." And with that, she walked out the door.

Debbie had done it. She'd won the war. People like her never won the war. They were always the casualties, relegated to a statistic too enormous for the human mind to make sense of.

But not this time. With the diamond ring now in her hand, Debbie closed her fist and allowed herself to feel every sharp edge of the stone as it pierced into her palm. She put the ring on. It was too big for any of her fingers, but she marveled at how nice the diamond looked against her skin tone. That was a first.

Back in her salon, Debbie pulled out Eamon's business card and called his number.

"Hello?"

"I've got something better than fifteen thousand dollars." She had no time to waste.

"Who's this?"

"It's a diamond ring. Three carats. Emerald cut. White-gold band."

"Well, well, you really pulled through, didn't you? Phil married a good one."

"Do you want this thing or not?"

"I'll need to come by and inspect it first."

"Then?"

"Then, if it's as good as you say it is, your husband will be off the hook."

"There's just one thing," Debbie said. "You can't tell Phil about any of this."

Eamon laughed. "Lady, I like you."

They both hung up. Debbie stared at the ring. Her heart was beating so fast, pumping a quick succession of feelings through her veins. Triumph, then relief, then ecstasy, then anxiety, then . . . queasiness? Suddenly, Debbie clutched her stomach as she felt a burning sensation travel up her throat. She hunched forward and puked all over the floor.

CHAPTER THIRTY-ONE

Phil

Phil knew he was in deep shit. He was still at Quân's house, having slept in late into the afternoon and missed all his nail appointments. If Debbie was upset at him last night, she was probably burning with rage by now.

As he came to, he remembered the voicemails from Eamon. They were laden with so many slurs it had to have qualified as a hate crime. To make matters worse, he was severely hungover. The most vicious, unrelenting hangover he'd ever had in his life.

He quickly grabbed his jacket, car keys, and shoes and quietly left Quân's house. There was a bottle of water in the car, half-frozen from being out in the cold. He sucked out as much water as he could. *Agh.* A sharp, intense pain vibrated across the front of his head.

As he drove to the salon, he called Eamon. Before he could apologize profusely and beg for more time to pay off the loan, Eamon stopped him.

"Don't worry about it, man. We're good now."

Phil was stunned by how chirpy he sounded. "W-w-what do you mean?"

"Listen, I've been thinking a lot about our friendship. We go way back. I know you're a decent man. An honest, hardworking man, much like myself. So I'm going to let you off the hook. You're good people, Phil. You *and* your family."

Phil was still confused. "So you'll give me more time then?"

"Time? For what?"

"To pay you back."

Eamon snickered. "Like I said, forget about it. Consider your debts officially paid off."

Phil couldn't believe what he was hearing. "B-b-but . . . why? I mean, really?"

"For Christ's sake, yes! Do you want me to change my mind or what?"

"No!" Phil shouted. "I don't understand. The voicemails. You were so angry."

"That's all in the past, man."

The line went dead silent.

"I think the words you're looking for are 'thank you,' " Eamon offered.

Phil was so flustered he didn't realize the light had turned green. "Of course, thank you. Thank you! THANK YOU!"

Phil hung up the phone. Did that just actually happen? What changed between last night and now? Whatever. He was too ecstatic to probe. A wonderful thing had happened, and his luck had finally turned around. For the rest of the drive, Phil laughed and laughed until his raging hangover went away.

———

Now he just had Debbie to deal with. He didn't know what to expect before walking into the salon. Silent treatment? A tongue-lashing? A fist to the face?

When he walked in, *Entertainment Tonight* was playing on the TV. The girls were busy tending to customers. Debbie was standing at the sink, disinfecting a handful of clippers and pushers. He walked slowly towards her with the anticipation of a man on death row.

"Are you okay?" she asked without looking up.

The casual normality with which she said that threw him off. "Excuse me?"

"Are you okay?" she repeated. "You didn't come home last night."

"I . . . I was at Quân's."

"Just you two?"

"No, there were a few of us. Bảo, Hải, Trương. And a couple other men. I don't remember all their names."

"Did they give you anything to eat?"

This small talk was killing him. There were so many more important things they needed to discuss. Why was Debbie doing this to him?

He listed off all the food that was there last night and then quickly changed the subject.

"I'm sorry I didn't tell you about the loan. It's the only thing I could think of to help us pay the rent. I didn't want to tell you because I know you didn't want to add to our debt load, but listen, it's all taken care of now. It's not going to be a problem. I promise."

"Okay."

"What?" Again, Phil was expecting her to lash out.

"I said okay."

"Y-you're not mad?"

"You did what you had to do for your family. How can anybody fault you for that?"

A look of profound agony flashed across his wife's face. It was clear something was bothering her. He waited for her to say what was on her mind. But all he got was silence. He knew better than to ply her with a million questions. The only thing he could do was hope that whatever she was carrying would not torment her any longer.

He took a step closer and kissed her on the forehead. She leaned into him and rested her head against his shoulder. How was it possible to be so close to someone and still feel oceans apart?

CHAPTER THIRTY-TWO

Jessica

"S hit, I messed up the polish!"

The last customer of the day had accidentally smeared pink polish all over her wallet just as she was about to pay. Jessica assured her it was no problem at all.

"Flip-Flops and Crop Tops?" Jessica asked. The woman nodded.

By now Jessica could tell the names of polishes just by looking at the color. It was a skill that seemed completely useless at first but had come in handy many times. Like the time someone came in with chipped nails and wanted a touch-up (Udon Know Me). And the time someone asked if they could copy Rihanna's latest nails (I Just Can't Cope-acabana).

Jessica loved seeing customers' faces light up when she found the exact shade they wanted. It was a wonderful feeling to be able to bring little bursts of joy to the most ordinary of people.

She was surprised how much she was starting to like this job. As soon as she stopped focusing on the negative aspects, she could finally see all the hidden delights. The fun people she was meeting. The fast-paced nature. The unpredictability of each new day.

Phil came up to show her something on his phone. "Did you see this?"

"See what?" said Jessica.

"Another five-star review that mentions *you*."

Jessica blushed. She didn't want to be the one to bring it up, but she had noticed a string of positive reviews for Sunshine Nails lately:

> Ever since the new girl came in, the salon has become impeccably clean.

> The receptionist is absolutely lovely. Some of the nicest people I've ever met.

> Jessica is a LIFE SAVER. She squeezed me in at the last minute and I felt really taken care of.

She beamed. There was something truly fulfilling about helping her parents' business thrive. She always wanted to repay them for all the sacrifices they made. And this seemed to be the perfect way to do it.

"You know," said Phil, "in my twenty years of running this salon, I've always felt there was something unfinished about this place. But now I realize what we were missing. You. You being here. It just feels right."

"I couldn't agree more," Debbie joined in. "I don't know how we ever managed without you."

Jessica smiled. Her parents would never realize how much those words meant to her.

———

Later that night, Jessica texted Gigi to let her know she'd be late for dinner. They hadn't spoken since that awkward dinner party, and the way things left off was less than ideal. Jessica wanted to patch things up with her. But mostly, she wanted Gigi to know that despite her life not turning out the way she wanted, she was happy.

By the time she made it to the restaurant, Gigi still hadn't arrived.

That was weird. She was never late to anything.

Jessica took a seat at their table. Time passed like molasses as she called Gigi over and over until she finally picked up.

"Where are you? I think they're gonna ask me to leave any minute," cried Jessica.

"You seriously thought I still wanted to see your face after what happened?"

Jessica plugged one ear to drown out the atmospheric buzz. "What are you talking about?"

"Don't act like you don't know."

She double-checked the number on the phone, making sure she was talking to the right person. "Gigi, what is happening right now? Did I miss something?"

"You know, I wouldn't have been so surprised if she told me it was your father but your *mother* . . . wow. If I wasn't so angry right now, I might have been a little bit impressed."

Jessica's brain was whirring as she tried to make sense of Gigi's words.

"Please tell me what's going on."

"Seriously? You're just gonna pretend like you don't know?"

"I swear! I have no idea what you're talking about!"

There was a pause. Loud sirens whizzed by on the other end of the line. A waiter with dark-rimmed eyes and impeccable skin came and unenthusiastically filled her glass with water.

"Your mother came to Take Ten yesterday."

Another pause as more sirens screeched through the phone.

"She took Savannah's engagement ring! Straight-up *blackmailed* her!"

Jessica covered her mouth but a chuckle managed to crawl its way out between her fingers. "You can't be serious right now. My *mother*? Really? Come on, this is a really weird joke."

"I'm dead serious." There was disgust and fear in her voice, which was worrying Jessica.

Gigi went on to reveal that Debbie had been spying on Savannah and was secretly taking photos of her. She revealed that the photos were damaging to her client's reputation and that her life would be ruined if anybody saw them. She revealed that Debbie had accosted Savannah in the nail salon, blamed her for all her family's problems, and threatened her into giving up the ring.

"And what sucks the most," Gigi said, "is that I tried so hard to make our friendship work when we both know it expired a long time ago."

For Jessica, it was all too much to process. She needed a drink and she needed it now.

"Okay, let's back up here," Jessica said. "Why would my mother even want her ring in the first place? She doesn't even wear diamonds. It has to be a lie. It has to be."

Gigi groaned loudly. "Why would Savannah make something like that up? What does she have to gain from this?"

"Don't you see? She has *everything* to gain from this," Jessica shouted, startling a few of the patrons around her before lowering her voice. "A rumor like this could ruin our business. Don't you understand she's trying to take us down?"

The waiter was making his way over again, shooting daggers directly at her.

"Can you hear yourself?" yelled Gigi. "Why would a company as heavily backed as Take Ten worry themselves over a nobody shop like yours?"

Nobody. That word felt like a punch in the gut. "You're wrong, Gigi. My mother would never do something like this. She would never."

The waiter loomed over her. "Excuse me, miss? Will your guest be arriving any moment? Unfortunately we will have to offer this seat up to other guests if they don't arrive in the next five minutes."

Jessica forced a smile and told him, "She's literally crossing the street right now," and put the phone back against her ear.

"You know," Gigi went on, "it's *sooo* easy to point the finger at Take Ten and make them out to be the bad guy that's taking customers away from you. But it's a dog-eat-dog world out there. Some people just work harder than others. And some just have better ideas than others. Take Ten has earned their right to be there. That's it. That's all it is. The universe doesn't owe you anything. Don't turn it into something it isn't and definitely don't play the victim card when we all know your family is far from innocent."

Jessica could not believe the bullshit coming out of Gigi. Who gets to decide what hard work looks like? Who decides what ideas are the best? And what of privilege and luck, as if they didn't overwhelmingly shape the trajectory of our lives?

"That is *not* fair," Jessica said.

"Fix this."

"You are fuck—"

Gigi hung up. The waiter came back and before he could say anything, Jessica kicked herself out.

———

When she arrived home, she found her mother hovering over the kitchen sink, vigorously scrubbing a yellow stain on her salon tunic. The room smelled putrid and sour, like someone had just thrown up spoiled cheese.

"Má, I have to ask you something," said Jessica.

"What is it, my child?" she replied without lifting her head.

"Did you . . ." Jessica suddenly felt so silly asking this of her small-framed, sixty-year-old mother. "This is going to sound crazy, but did you take Savannah's engagement ring?"

Her mother stopped what she was doing and turned to look at her with fiery eyes. "What kind of nonsense question is that? Where did you get such a ridiculous idea? Why on heaven's earth would I need that woman's ring?" Her mother turned back to the sink and furiously wrung out the uniform, staring at it as if it were Jessica's neck. "Silly child! Your dead grandparents are more likely to burst out of their tombs before I'd ever do anything stupid like that."

Jessica was never good at reading her mother, but she knew one thing for sure: She was lying. Her mother would never, ever joke about resurrecting the dead.

She continued to deny anything ever happened. "Do you think I'm your father? I'd never do such an idiotic, reckless thing without thinking of what it would do to our family. And why would I want anything to do with that woman—"

The more her mother denied, the more confused Jessica became.

Who was this person? It didn't make any sense. Throughout her childhood, her mother's strict moralism was the one thing she could count on to remain consistently and wholly a part of her identity. *Do not steal. Do not lie.*

Do not disrespect your elders. Children grew up and evolved based on the lessons they were taught, but parents were supposed to stay the same.

Jessica leaned against a doorframe as she watched her mother pour all her strength and might into making the yellow stain disappear. She'd seen this look before, back when her father got arrested for his DUI. It was a look that was hard to describe. Not anger, not disappointment, not hopelessness. She just looked spent, like a plant that was constantly being watered without time to breathe. Jessica wondered what that must be like, to be such a devoted wife who sacrificed herself for her husband like it was an uncontrollable tic. What was it that made her do it time and time again? Was it love? Loyalty? Pride? Perhaps this was the secret to a lasting marriage. If so, then maybe it was a good thing she never married Brett. She had zero desire to give up so much of herself.

She walked up to her mother, who peered at her not with fury but with a forlornness that it physically hurt to see. Jessica tucked some rogue strands of hair behind her mother's ear and with that one gesture, her mother told her everything, spilling it all out like a dam under pressure.

She told her about the loan shark, the shattered Buddha statue, the ring. She told her how she never meant for it to get this far. How she was just trying to fix a mistake her father had made. How terrible it would be if anybody discovered what she'd done.

Jessica was stunned. She didn't know how to respond. What could she say exactly? That she was angry, disturbed, disappointed? Sure, she could say all those things. But when tears started cascading down her mother's cheeks, the only thing she could do was cry, too. They wrapped their arms around each other and cried over the life they loved so much. The life that seemed to be crumbling all around them.

How did Jessica not see that things had gotten so bad? Of course she couldn't blame her mother for doing what she had to do for her family. When you spent your whole life doing the right thing and the world suddenly stopped rewarding you for it, it was only a matter of time before you lost sight of what was right and what was wrong.

Her mother had sacrificed enough for the family. Now it was Jessica's turn to do the same.

With technology-powered neighborhoods and endless glass towers that nobody could keep up with, it was evident that Toronto was barreling towards
the future. However, one pocket of the city still allowed residents to feel like
they'd been transported back in time: the Galleria Mall. Located in the Duf-
ferin Grove neighborhood, the tumbleweed mall was perpetually stuck in
the 1970s, with its shiny brick-like floors, kiosks that sold rotary-dial phones,
and coin-operated rides that did nothing more than go up and down and side
to side.

This was where Jessica told Văn Đỗ to meet her. She arrived fifteen minutes early, so she saved a table beside the El Amigo food counter and ordered
a corned beef sandwich from the smiling Asian woman behind the counter.

"Good choice, but I would've gone for the chicken clubhouse," said Văn.

Jessica's heart sank when she heard his voice and smelled the correspond-
ing aquatic cologne that went with it. There was no turning back now.

The two took a seat. "Thanks for coming here," said Jessica. She paused for
a second. "Do you want to grab a coffee or something?"

"No, no. I'm trying not to drink caffeine after one o'clock. Keeps me up all
night, you know?"

Jessica nodded. She tucked her hands underneath her thighs for warmth.
"I . . . I think you might know why I asked you to meet me here."

"I think I have an idea but why don't you go ahead and tell me why I'm
here?" Văn leaned back in his chair and rested both of his hands on the table.
Jessica stared at the dead skin hanging off his cuticles and realized she had
disgust written all over her face. She quickly softened her eyes.

"I gave it some thought and I . . . I'm willing to marry your nephew," said
Jessica, not believing the words that just came out of her mouth. "That is, if
the offer is still on the table."

Văn's eyes bulged. "Wow . . . wow, really? Are you sure? I thought you
hated my guts after I asked you the first time. Wait, this is not a joke, right?"

She could still back out; there was still a chance, but then she remembered
the agony on her mother's face. She had to get the ring back to Savannah

and pay off her father's debt. She had to do this for her parents. It was the only way.

"Yes. At first I thought it was a crazy idea . . . I mean, it *is* crazy in so many ways. But then I thought about it some more and I realized that it's actually one of the most altruistic things a person can do." Jessica paused to scratch an itch on her nose. "I'd be giving someone less fortunate than me the opportunity to live out their dreams in Canada. What could be more amazing than that? And besides, we can divorce after like, what, a year or something? A year is nothing."

Văn took a slim, crisp cigarette out of a crumpled box and tucked it behind his ear. "Two years, actually."

Jessica pondered this small but significant difference. "I'm sure it will fly by just like that." She snapped her fingers in the air, but no sound came out.

"Listen, this is a very nice thing you're doing. Believe me, my nephew would be so happy to hear this," said Văn, "but I get the sense that you're not really ready for this."

Jessica straightened her back. "Look, I know I might have thrown you off before when I said I wasn't interested. But I mean it this time. I really do," Jessica said. She hadn't expected to grip Văn's large hands. As soon as she realized what she'd done, she released her hold immediately.

Văn looked to his left and right, like he was afraid of being caught. "Tell me, what has changed since then? Why do you want to do this all of a sudden? What's in it for you, the money aside? You can't tell me you're doing this out of the goodness of your heart. No woman possessing your beauty and intelligence would give up two years of her life to make some scrawny kid's dream come true."

Jessica sagged her shoulders. Maybe he was right. Maybe this was ludicrous.

"So it *is* about the money then?" said Văn. "What do you need it for? New clothes? A down payment? Credit card debt?" He paused to examine her, but something she did must have given her away. A lip twitch? A shuffle of her seat? She couldn't figure out what the tell was. "Jesus, I heard rumors your family was having troubles with the salon, but I didn't know it was that bad. Did they send you to me?"

"My parents? Oh god no. They have no idea I'm here. They would never have forced me to do this. This was all my idea. Completely and totally my idea."

"How bad is it then?"

"What?"

"The debt. What do you owe to the man?"

"How do you know about the man?"

"No. I meant *the* man. Not *a* man. Why? Is there a man involved?"

Jessica massaged her temples. This meeting was supposed to be quick, one minute in, one minute out. She hadn't expected to go into the whole story, least of all to be sharing it with a man whose presence alone made her body quiver with discomfort, but here she was spilling everything in one continuous stream like a waterfall.

"And that's why I need to marry your nephew. That money will be more than enough to pay our debts and keep our shop afloat for a while."

Văn looked straight at her, but his gaze went beyond her eyes. He pulled on the straggly strands of black hair growing out of his chin.

"Listen, I should have said this sooner, but we can't go through with it. At least not now."

Jessica felt like her heart was shriveling up, but she let him finish.

"The government has been cracking down on sham marriages like this. If we do this now, we could risk getting caught. Or worse, he might lose any chance he has to get to Canada."

Once again he looked to his left, then his right, and continued speaking at a low volume. "His family has decided to get him through the international student sponsorship route. It's going to take longer. But the kid is smart, and I bet he'll get in eventually."

Jessica felt like she'd been handed the world only to have it snatched away from her. "Are you fucking kidding me? You had me sit here this entire time, begging you to let me do this and spill all my family's secrets—and you didn't even have the courtesy to tell me that this deal was already off the table? Screw you!"

Jessica got up and grabbed her purse. But Văn grabbed her arm.

"Sit down. I can still help you out."

Jessica turned her head. "How can you possibly help us out? You're a terrible person. I've heard about your"—she didn't want to take it there, but he didn't deserve her decency—"your wife and your gambling addictions. Your sons don't even want to talk to you because you're a piece of shit and the whole community knows it!" She took a step towards the exit.

"I can pay off your entire debt right here, right now."

Jessica stopped in her tracks. "Excuse me?"

He had to be bluffing, but when she saw that he had pulled out a worn-out black leather checkbook, she sat back down. "Do you have a pen?" he asked.

"Why would you do that?"

"You might not know this, but your mother was the only person who didn't treat me like a piece of shit when I was going through all that legal bullshit. This community of boat people—my god—you think with all the parties and events that we're a tight-knit group, but these people are quicker to kick you to the curb than embrace you with warm arms."

He scraped his chair a few inches away from the table, as if he needed to make room for the words that were coming out of his mouth. "Did you know that your mother drove me to my AA meetings every week when my license got revoked? She would drop off food at my apartment—the one I lived in after my wife left me and my kids stopped talking to me. It was this shithole of a bachelor apartment where the floors would slope so much that you couldn't put a cigarette on the table without it rolling off—and that wasn't even the worst part. There was this stench—god I can still remember it—that smelled like cat piss that had been out in the sun too long. I lived there for a year and never found out where it came from."

He stopped, waiting for the woman behind the counter to finish chopping so loudly.

"Anyway, your mother didn't care about any of that. She'd always come inside to put food in the fridge and then she would take me to the meeting. And when she picked me up, she never asked me any questions. She'd just pat me on my shoulder and put on a song. It was always some nhạc vàng, you know? The slowest, saddest bolero music you'd ever heard. I swear they were designed to extract tears from your eyes. We'd sit in the car and listen the whole drive. We never talked, but by the time we got to my place we'd bond over the fact that both our cheeks had gotten wet and shiny."

Jessica had never heard any of this before. She had so many questions, all of them just long-winded variations of, why? But she kept her mouth closed, her body firmly planted in her seat.

"I remember getting out of the car one time and before I shut the door, she looked at me and said, 'Cái nết đánh chết cái đẹp.' Do you know what that means?"

Jessica shook her head.

"Good character is better than beauty," he said, gazing down at his hands as if the exact proverb had been scribbled on his palms. "Your mother is a very good woman. I can see that everything she does, she does for her family—and the fact that you came to me looking to see how you can help your family tells me you're exactly like her."

"D-does my father know all this?"

"Your father? He's the one that signed me up for those meetings. He wouldn't admit it but I think he'd been to a few meetings himself, after the DUI I'm guessing. I think your parents know a thing or two about being ashamed and ostracized. That's why they were the only people who didn't disappear from my life. If it weren't for them, I'd probably be dead in a ditch somewhere, rotting for weeks before some dog walker accidentally found me."

Just as Jessica was about to say something, the woman behind the food counter waved her hand to get their attention. "You want a tuna sandwich? It's on special today."

Văn shook his head. "No thanks. I'm fine. Maybe next time."

Jessica smiled at the woman and shook her head as well.

"Well, come back soon then. We may not be around for long."

"What do you mean?" said Văn.

"You didn't hear? They're demolishing this entire mall and putting up new condos. It's going to be huge. Very big. This place will be no more."

"Really? Well, I can't say I'm surprised." He looked up at the ceiling, marred by a flickering light and rusty brown stain.

"And a park, too. There's going to be a big park with lots of trees. Can you imagine such a thing in this area?"

"What are you going to do?" asked Jessica.

"Don't know yet. That's why I asked you if you want a sandwich. Could be your last chance."

Văn reached for his wallet. "Well in that case, give me two on white. I'll have it later for dinner."

The woman flashed him a smile, the fluorescent light bouncing off one of her front teeth.

Văn turned back to Jessica. "I'm serious about wanting to help your parents out. Just tell me how much they need, and I'll write you the check."

"But how? I mean, you're very generous and I appreciate that and all, but I thought you were . . . struggling."

"I may have fucked up a few things in my life, but the smartest thing I ever did was love my mother."

"What do you mean?"

"She died a month ago. And she left me with a lot."

"I didn't know. I'm sorry." She felt an urge to reach across the table and grab his hands again, dead skin and all.

"Your parents are coming to the funeral this weekend. I told them to bring the whole family."

"They hadn't said anything to us."

"You know how Vietnamese people are. They're afraid to talk about death. They're scared of that word more than they're scared of death itself."

He grabbed a napkin from the dispenser and started writing something on it. "Have you ever noticed how the Vietnamese words for *mother* and *ghost* look nearly identical?" He turned the napkin around to show her.

Má   Ma
Mother Ghost

Back and forth he uttered those words like he was going up and down a curb, raising his tone sharply when he said *má*, then dipping it back down when he said *ma*. Over and over, he repeated until it became difficult to hear the difference.

Then he scratched out the accent.

Ma Ma

Ghost Ghost

"Funny how it doesn't take much to become a ghost," he said before his face fell to a sullen sadness.

Jessica wasn't sure what to say, so she said the only thing there was to say. "I have no words."

"It's okay. Don't you see? She's free now. There's no stress hovering over her anymore."

Văn changed the subject and opened his checkbook. "Let me help. Tell me how much you need."

How could she possibly quantify the amount they needed to go back to the way things were? Jessica spit out the first number that came to her head.

Văn scribbled some words and numbers on the check, ripped it off in one smooth move, and handed it over to her.

"Are you sure? Shouldn't you use it on the funeral?" she asked.

"Take it." He put the cap back on the pen and proceeded to zip up his coat.

"Thank you. I don't even know what to say or how to repay you."

"Just . . . just be good to your parents. That's all."

Jessica nodded at him and smiled.

The woman behind the counter held a brown paper bag in the air. "Here are your sandwiches, sir. Four twenty-five."

"Let me at least pay for those sandwiches," Jessica said, before realizing how embarrassing it was to offer him a pittance in exchange for his profound generosity.

Văn nodded. He grabbed the bag and used it to wave goodbye. "See you around, kid."

As she watched him amble down the hallway towards the doors, Jessica looked at the check. There was a mark on the bottom left corner in the memo section. It was tiny and slightly smudged. Maybe it was just a fleck caused by a slip of his hand, but Jessica could have sworn it was a diacritical mark, an acute accent just floating on the paper all by itself, looking for a letter to land on. But then it moved and fell off the paper. It was just an eyelash.

CHAPTER THIRTY-THREE

Dustin

s this the kind of thing you wear black to?" asked Mackenzie.

Dustin watched his girlfriend as she stood in front of the full-length mirror, holding up a black blazer against her chest to figure out what to wear to a Buddhist funeral. It had been forty-nine days since Văn's mother died and the Trans were invited to mark the end of the mourning period. When it came to death, RSVPing no was not an option.

His body was still glued to the bed. He liked sleeping over at Mackenzie's. Not only was the mattress more comfortable, but it was also nice not having to ask his girlfriend if she could grab her stuff and sneak out before his parents woke up. She was always cool about it, telling him that it was no problem, that it gave her a reason to get some work done early, but part of him still felt foul about the whole situation. His parents liked Mackenzie, they said so themselves, but he'd been living in his parents' house for twenty-eight years. It was hard to break the rules that kept everything running smoothly.

Dustin stretched out his arms as if begging her to come back to bed. "You can wear whatever you want."

"I'm serious, Dustin. You need to give me more. What's the protocol? What do I wear? Remind me who's going to be there again? Are you sure you asked your parents if I can come?"

"Yes, Mackenzie, you can come. You've met Văn, haven't you?"

"No, never actually."

"No? Well, he'll want to meet you anyhow. He's an old friend of my mom's and it would mean a lot if you came."

"To you or to your parents?"

"What?" Dustin replied. "Me. Everyone!"

"Well, I just want to make sure I make the right impression. It's a *goddamn* funeral! It's the last place I would want to offend someone by doing or saying the wrong thing."

"Just wear black. And don't wear anything too tight. There's going to be a lunch after the ceremony."

"A lunch? See, that's what I mean. That's the kind of stuff I need to know."

"Sorry I thought it was obvious. Isn't that what normally happens at all funerals?"

"This is different."

"Why? Because it's at a Buddhist temple?"

Mackenzie looked through her closet again, sliding items of clothing to the right, seemingly rejecting every piece of clothing she owned.

"Look," said Dustin, sitting against the edge of the bed. "I'm going to be honest with you. I have no idea what we should wear or how long this thing's going to last. All you have to do is look cute and follow my lead." A tuft of hair hung perilously over his forehead and he blew it up and out of his face. He started doing it a lot more after Mackenzie said she liked it when he did that. "Besides, we don't have to get there for another four hours. You're up so early."

"Hard to sleep in when you get in the habit of getting up at six a.m." Mackenzie gave him a snicker and whipped out a yellow knee-length wrap dress.

Dustin shook his head. "Sorry, it won't be forever. I just want my parents to get used to the idea of us together before I introduce them to the fact that we're sleeping together."

"We've been dating eight months. Wouldn't they have assumed that by now?"

Dustin fell back onto the bed. "Dear god, I hope they have never given it any thought."

Mackenzie pulled out a long gray satin dress with skinny straps and put it back in the closet. Dustin liked watching her do ordinary things. It gave him time to think about how amazing these past eight months had been. It was strange how being in love made the world around him look so different. He wasn't a hopeless romantic by any means, but he swore he could see the faintest of rainbows these days.

"Have you ever seen your parents kiss?" she asked.

"Sure I have."

"When?"

Dustin paused. "I can't remember when exactly but I'm sure I've seen it a dozen times."

"It's just interesting."

"What is?"

"We've had how many dinners with them now, for the past few months, and I've never seen them kiss or hold hands or rub each other's back. Nothing."

"You like it when I do that?" he said, caressing her thigh.

She shot him a sly smile. "You don't think that's weird?"

"That my parents aren't physically affectionate? I think it'd be weirder if I *wanted* my parents to exhibit more PDA." He came up from behind her and gave her two quick squeezes on her shoulders.

Mackenzie slipped out of her pajamas and into the yellow dress. The fabric was cinching her body so tight he could see her belly button. He looked at her body in the mirror, admiring the fact that the dress lifted her breasts in ways no bra had ever achieved. Before she could take it off, Dustin picked her up and threw her on the bed. He kissed her on the lips, then on the neck, then on the inside of her thigh. She reached down to lift her dress off. "Keep it on," he said before going down on her. She grabbed his hair with both hands and when she came, she yanked on his scalp so hard he thought it was going to peel right off. He kind of liked it.

After they were finished, Mackenzie laid her head on his chest.

"What's that?" She pointed at the floor where his pants lay crumpled, a folded piece of paper sticking out of the pocket.

Dustin looked down. He completely forgot to tell Mackenzie about the leaflet. He found it in Jessica's room when he went in to steal some of her weed. There was no way he could miss the neon-green sheet and big, bold letters. "HELP THE HENDERSON." It was about the building that was going to be demolished. Someone had organized a campaign to save it from being destroyed and had even started a petition to get politicians and city officials involved.

"Let me see!" She scanned the sheet. "How are we just hearing about this now? Where can I sign?"

Dustin searched up the petition on his phone. There were already well over 12,000 signatures.

"Whoa, check this out," he said. "There's going to be a protest in front of the building."

"Really? When?"

"February eighteenth. Shit, that's next weekend!" Dustin paused to read some more. "Looks like there are tons of people who are not happy about this demolition. Turns out they hadn't even consulted the community! The province just went ahead and granted the demolition permits. The councillor didn't even know!"

"Wait, can they do that? Just tear down a building without running it by the councillor?" said Mackenzie.

"Says here they've been given the green light," he replied. "There are already bulldozers on-site getting ready to tear that place down."

"Do you think Chase knows about it? The protest?"

Dustin paused to ponder. "Hmm . . . he has to know."

"Could they actually stop this demolition from happening?"

"I don't know," said Dustin. "Chase made it sound like it was a done deal. I'm glad there are people out there raising hell about this. Give him grief!"

They were both glued to their phones reading an article about the proposed demolition. Moments later, Dustin turned to look at her, only to discover she was already looking at him.

"Should we go?" she asked.

He smiled at her. "Did you even have to ask?"

CHAPTER THIRTY-FOUR

Thuy

Thuy smoothed out a wrinkle in her dress and told herself for the fifth time that what she was wearing was fine. Her dress was black, unembellished, and not too tight, which effectively checked off all the requirements of standard funeral dress code.

It had been a long time since she'd attended one of these. The last time was when she was eleven and someone obscurely connected to her had passed away, a great-aunt once removed or something like that. Everything about the funeral was loud and theatrical. The chanting, the music, the crying. Oh, the crying. It was a sound one could never forget, wailing and howling so loud it traveled through dimensions so that even the dead could hear.

But today, there was none of that. Văn and his siblings stood at the front of the temple with faces awash in stoic solemnity, not a sound to be made. The lack of crying somehow felt sadder.

The Trans were among sixty worshippers at the funeral. The room was silent except for some whispers and shuffling of bodies. Thuy stood next to Dustin's girlfriend, who looked puzzled by the whole business. Two monks draped in burnt-orange robes entered the room, joining Văn and his family members at the front. They all wore black outfits and white headbands around their foreheads. A photo of their deceased relative was displayed on an altar, accompanied by bowls of fruit and cups of tea.

The entire family repeatedly bowed and kneeled to the photo, silently praying that the deceased would get reincarnated in human form. Anything else, especially a dog, would be a travesty.

Once that was done, the monks began the chanting, a melodic string of words that Thuy knew by heart. The whole room chanted along, except for Dustin, Jessica, and Mackenzie, who kept quiet. Thuy handed her cousins a booklet so they could follow along, but they shook their heads, whispering that they couldn't read it.

Was this what happened when you lived away from the motherland for too long? All the strings that connected you home slowly got snipped off one by one? Thuy hoped it wouldn't happen to her. She continued chanting and kneeling for the next forty minutes.

Mackenzie leaned into her. "How long is this thing going to take?" she whispered.

Thuy shrugged her shoulders.

"Do you know how she died?"

"Old age."

"I'm sorry. What?"

"She died because she was old."

"You mean she died from an ailment of some kind?"

Thuy didn't know what else to say. "No. She literally died of old age. That's what we were told."

The other story going around was that she died of breast cancer. Nobody could confirm it, but then again nobody wanted to talk about it for fear they'd be afflicted with the disease. If Thuy knew anything about Vietnamese people, it was that they had absolutely no problems taking stigma and secrets to the grave.

After the ceremony, everyone slowly made their way to the basement, where lunch was being served. The monks were strictly meatless, so the day's menu consisted of hot soup, tofu stir fry, yellow noodles, and red bean pudding. Everyone did the respectful thing and waited until the monks took their seats before loading up their plates.

The Trans sat at a long table next to a group of friends they hadn't seen since their party. Thuy saved two empty seats for Jessica and Debbie, who had been upstairs for quite some time. She went to go look for them and found them whispering in the corner of the main hall. Debbie looked frantic—her arms and legs were restless and the veins in her neck were bulging. Thuy stayed as far back as possible so they wouldn't see her.

"His mother just died! Why would you accept money from him?" she could hear Debbie saying.

"He wanted to help. He wanted to do it for *you*! Because of everything you did for him!" replied Jessica.

"We must pay him back."

"He says we don't have to."

"But we must!"

Jessica grabbed Debbie's shoulders to stop her from pacing.

"Má, we're going to be okay. I've paid off Eamon. I've paid off the landlord. The rest is in the bank account. We don't have to worry for a while."

"And Savannah?"

"I got it back from Eamon. Took some convincing, but he couldn't say no when I showed him an envelope of cash."

Thuy watched as Jessica pulled something out of her purse. It was small and shiny, a stone or earring of some sort. No, wait, it was a diamond ring.

"We need to give it back," said Jessica.

"Child, I can't go back there. Not after what I did to her."

"You don't have to. I'll do it."

"You're going to see her?"

"No, I'll put it in an envelope and drop it off with the receptionist after the funeral."

Thuy leaned in to get a better look as Jessica took the ring and placed it on her finger. She stretched her arm out towards the ceiling, peering at her newly bejeweled hand from various angles as if trying to catch the light. Next thing she knew, they began walking towards her. Thuy quickly ran back downstairs and sat in her seat.

Her food had gotten cold, but she didn't want to complain or waste the food, so she ate it reluctantly as Jessica and Debbie took their seats. Without missing a beat, they seamlessly inserted themselves into the conversation happening at the table.

Thuy quietly ate her food as she tried to decipher what she just heard and saw. Maybe it was a business thing. Though Thuy worked at the salon every day, she knew nothing about what went on behind the scenes, how they kept the lights on, how the supplies were constantly replenished, where the money went as soon as the customer swiped their card. It wasn't like she didn't care to know. More like everyone assumed she didn't need to know. Maybe this was one of those things she didn't need to know, too.

She tuned midway into a conversation Dustin was having with Phil.

"Maybe you should close the salon on Saturday," said Dustin. "It sounds like this protest is going to close down the main street. Might make it hard for customers to get inside."

Phil put his cup of tea down. "Close? No, no, that won't be necessary. Son, we've worked in blizzards, in heat waves, in earthquakes. We're not closing for some protest. Besides it has nothing to do with us. You kids just worry about yourself." Phil dipped his pinkie finger in his teacup to gauge the temperature. "Thuy, can you text Kiera and tell her the salon will be open on Saturday? I don't want her finding out about this protest and assuming she can take the day off."

Thuy was still thinking about what she heard upstairs. All she could muster was a gentle nod.

"If they're going to protest anything, they should protest those nasty nail salon owners in Orange County who treated their workers like shit. They make us look like bad people! Did anyone see that on the news?" said Phil.

The topic caught the attention of other people at the table. The news of four Vietnamese nail techs suing their employer for docking their pay and faking their paychecks was all anybody could talk about.

"I hope they win," said one man with a goatee.

"I heard they forced those women to clock out even though they were still working!" said a woman at the end of the table.

"Apparently, it went on for ten years! Trời ơi, why didn't they just leave?" said the first man.

"But where would they go? They need to feed their families," said an older woman, wielding her spoon in the air.

Phil piped in. "I feel so terrible for them. But if things were really that bad, they should've spoken up sooner. Not let it go on for so long. There are hundreds of other nail salons they could've worked for. Why not just get a job somewhere else?"

Thuy was normally one to listen, but she had an urge to vocalize her opinions. "But it's not that easy. Some of them barely spoke English. They were scared of getting in trouble. They didn't even know their rights until that *New York Times* article came out. There was no way they could—"

"I get they were scared," Phil interrupted. "But if they were unhappy, I don't see what's stopping them from leaving. If they were good at their job, they should have no problem finding work."

"But they were immigrants. They were probably terrified of getting deported."

"I don't care how desperate they were!" Phil barked, the rims of his eyes getting redder. "If you don't like where you work, then get out! It's that simple!"

Thuy sank into her chair. She couldn't believe his lack of empathy. Had he forgotten about those vulnerable first days in Canada? How scared and lonely and powerless he was? Maybe all these years of living comfortably had blinded him to the hardships—*real* hardships—that still existed out there. He must be blind, for how did he forget that he, too, had cut her pay and made her work those long hours? He was just as bad as those bosses being sued.

Debbie yanked on Phil's shirt. "Keep it down! Thầy is standing over there." She pointed her head in the direction of the monk, who was ladling some soup into his bowl.

Thuy looked over at Debbie and Jessica, the ring nowhere to be seen. What exactly were they up to? She did not know, but she knew one thing for sure. They were hypocrites. All of them.

Fed up with how cold her red bean soup had gotten, she dumped the entire contents in the trash and got herself a fresh, warm bowl.

CHAPTER THIRTY-FIVE

Jessica

The protest outside was getting bigger and bigger. The police had closed off the entire strip of Dundas West from Keele Street to Runnymede, but inside Sunshine Nails, it was like any other day.

As most Saturdays went, it was a constant cycle of go, go, go. Thuy stayed home because she wasn't feeling well, which left the others to take on more work than usual. Jessica barely had a moment to wipe away the smeared mascara below her eyes, or shake off the nail dust that flecked the top of her head, let alone pay attention to what was happening outside. She had been running around cleaning up each station, taking credit card payments, grabbing supplies that were running low, brushing on top coats, checking to see whose nails were dry so they could leave and make room for the next. The energy was frenetic. And she loved every minute of it.

Perhaps they might have heard the chanting outside if it weren't for all the gossipy chatter that was going on inside. Jessica had become invested in a conversation between two women at the drying station. They had spent their entire appointment going over everything that had happened to them in the past month: Sheila had a lazy coworker who somehow got a promotion over her, a leaking toilet that caused thousands of dollars in water damage, and a new, troubling discovery that her hairline had been receding. Karla's month, on the other hand, consisted of a father who had quit smoking after they found a benign tumor in his esophagus, a new job at a swanky law firm with an incredible view, and an insecurity about a man who had not called her since their date last week.

Jessica's eavesdropping was interrupted when the salon's phone rang.

"I got the ring." It was Savannah. "Never step inside this salon ever again, you hear me? You and your entire despicable family."

"We won't."

"Don't think you've gotten away with this."

Before Jessica could say anything, Savannah hung up the phone.

She gently put the phone back in the receiver. Was that it? Was it over? Short of donating bone marrow or ripping Savannah out of a burning vehicle, there was no way they were ever going to earn her trust. This would have to be good enough.

She turned to look at her mother, who was exfoliating a lady's feet. They exchanged a nod. Everything was handled.

Jessica exhaled deeply, letting the tension in her body melt like rock sugar in boiling water. Just for a second, she let herself bask in the glorious satisfaction of having cleaned up the biggest mess of her parents' life.

A reporter abruptly walked into the salon, a microphone in one hand, a phone in the other. Everyone in the salon stopped talking. Even Sheila and Karla paused to see what was going on. A man with a lengthy beard stood behind her, wielding a bulky camera over his shoulder.

"My name is Angela Jacobs, I'm a reporter for CP24. Can we talk to the owner of the salon?" asked the reporter. She was wearing a green parka that went all the way down to the floor.

"What is this for?" said Jessica.

"There is a demonstration happening not too far from here. We're told they are making their way down this street to protest the demolition of the Henderson building. We wanted to get a small business owner's perspective on all this. Do you work here? Are you open to sharing your comments on this?"

Jessica brushed past the reporter and rushed out the door to look down the street. Shit. A group of about a hundred protesters were marching closer and closer to the salon, their signs becoming more legible as they approached. Whistles were blown as the group repeatedly chanted, "Don't. Demolish. Our. Heritage." A line of police officers moved in sync with the group, deliberately and precisely.

The reporter had followed Jessica outside. "Are you the owner of the salon? Do you have any opinions on this protest taking place today?"

Jessica ignored her, too busy observing the protest. Now her mother had come outside. "What's going on, Jessica? Should we be worried?"

"It's nothing, Má. Go back inside. I'll be right back." Jessica motioned her to turn around.

She ran towards the protesters and scanned the crowd. One man with a tired expression held up a sign that said "People Over Profits." She looked down at his border collie. A cardboard sign with a similar message was clipped to its back: "Puppies Over Profits."

"Jessica, over here!"

She craned her neck to see who was calling her. Straight ahead were Dustin and Mackenzie, both waving frantically to get her attention. If not for that, she would have glossed right over them, just a pair of bodies moving among a pack of other galvanized bodies. When she got closer to them, her eyes went straight to the large blue stickers on the front of their jackets. They had a line of bold red text that read: "Help the Henderson."

"What are you guys doing here?"

"We came to check out the protest. And now we're part of it." Dustin raised a fist in the air and pulled out the same blue sticker, slapping it on her uniform before she could pull back. "Now you are, too."

The crowd continued to move down the street, so Jessica turned to march in the same direction.

"But isn't your company supposed to move into that building? The one they're trying to keep from being demolished?" she yelled as loud as she could. The chanting was twice as loud now that she was in the heart of the pack.

"Fuck it. I don't care about that shithole anymore. This is *our* neighborhood!" Dustin yelled back.

Jessica was taken aback. This was the first time she'd seen her brother exhibit any ounce of rebellion. Years of growing up poor and feeling unworthy had programmed him to be grateful for any and all jobs, even if they made him miserable.

"You're not worried your boss will find out?"

"What?" Dustin leaned in to hear her better.

"What if your boss finds out?" she said louder.

"What's he going to do about it? *Not* give me a raise? Again?"

Mackenzie squeezed between them. "When we heard what the organizers said at the rally, we wanted to join," said Mackenzie, the lower half of her face covered by a thick-knitted scarf. "The guy made some good points."

"What guy?"

She pointed to a man standing on the back of a pickup truck. "That's Hamza. He's one of the people who put this event together."

Hamza? She looked up. He was wearing a gray toque and blue parka, unzipped enough to reveal a faded Nirvana shirt underneath. She'd met him before. He was the one that stopped her on the street and got her to sign the petition.

Jessica wrapped her white smock tightly around her body, wishing she'd put on a jacket.

"Here, take this," said Mackenzie, who generously offered up her scarf, which was large enough to wrap around Jessica's body twice.

The crowd stopped as Hamza brought a megaphone to his face. "The demolition of the Henderson building is unjustified!" The crowd roared and whistled.

"Not once did they consult the community. *Our* community!"

"Shame!" the crowd shouted in unison.

"Our heritage buildings and conservation areas are under threat by our government and they think they can get away with it! They consulted tech firms, multimillion-dollar companies, real estate investors, all while completely ignoring us!"

He paused to let the crowd collectively expel their pent-up rage.

"We believe in the preservation of our heritage buildings. We deserve to have a say! We will not allow this demolition to move forward! Our heritage should be embraced, not erased!" He stretched one arm out, pointing towards the street as the crowd resumed its march and echoed his last words, "Embrace, not erase! Embrace, not erase!"

More onlookers filled the sidewalks, cheering the protesters on and taking videos with their phones. This fueled the crowd even more as they bounced their signs and fists further into the air. When they walked past Take Ten, Jessica glanced inside. There was no sign of Savannah, only a pixie-haired receptionist staring at the crowd with a confused look on her face. Behind her were two customers, stuck to their chairs by fake acrylic extensions that still needed to be sealed down.

The reporter was still standing in front of Sunshine Nails. This time she had managed to find someone to interview, a restaurant cook by the looks of his dirtied apron, baseball cap, and permanently hunched back. Her mother and father stood behind the window, hands and noses pressed against the glass as they stared out at the crowd. Jessica wondered if they'd ever been part of a protest, or been so moved to publicly call out injustice. Surely it was in the blood of people who'd ignited one of the largest antiwar protests in history. As she waved to them, they returned a look of what she could only describe as horror.

Suddenly, a deafening sound jolted the crowd to a complete halt. Multiple people began to scream.

Something was happening on the north side of the street. The three of them weaved through the crowd to get a closer look. Someone had thrown something through the windows of Take Ten and now their storefront was smashed to pieces. Police officers rushed to the scene as several people shouted, "He's not with us! He's not with us!"

"Who the hell did that?" one person shouted in her ear.

Another person pressed against her and yelled, "What the fuck, man!"

Everyone was getting worked up, pushing and shoving each other to get to whoever had shattered the window.

"He did it!"

"No, the guy was wearing a blue bandanna."

"I think he ran over there!"

"Was it one of us?"

"It can't be!"

"Instigator!"

Hamza picked up his mic. "Everyone, please calm down. Calm down. This is a peaceful protest. Do not make this situation worse."

A bulky police officer stepped up on the truck beside Hamza and one-upped him with an even louder, bigger megaphone. "Everybody must leave this street. Now!" he said. "This has become an unlawful assembly."

"Help the Henderson!" someone shouted.

The crowd echoed the words back again and again and again, each time getting louder as people joined in.

"Disperse immediately and go home," the officer's voice boomed.

Nervous families and curious onlookers started to peel away from the crowd and walked in the other direction. Some protesters lowered their signs and began to walk back, while a few stayed put, keeping the chants going in an even louder, more uniform fashion.

As the crowd slowly dispersed, all of Take Ten's employees and customers came outside to scan the damage. They tiptoed over the glass, making sure not to step on any shards. One woman still had foil wrapped around her fingertips.

Savannah frantically ran out of the salon. She looked like she'd just gotten off a roller coaster ride, her hair disheveled, her eyes wide and alert. "What the hell happened?"

"This your store?" a police officer asked.

"Yes!" she screamed, before turning her attention to the thinning crowd. "You're all nothing but a bunch of hoodlums!"

The police officer took her to the side to talk, while the employees huddled together and consoled the ones who were crying. There was still one more person inside the salon. Jessica couldn't tell if it was an employee or a customer. Whoever it was, she found it unsettling how they were just standing there, as still as a painting behind velvet rope stanchions. Jessica waited for the crowd to dissipate some more before inching closer to get a better look, first at the shattered storefront, then at the—

No, it couldn't be.

Thuy? What was she doing dressed in Take Ten's uniform?

Thuy hadn't noticed her standing there. She appeared to be stuck in a trance, staring at all the glass that had accumulated on the ground, a dazzling mound of blue and white pieces that used to be one. Finally, Thuy lifted her head up, pulled down her dust mask, and looked straight at Jessica.

Debbie appeared by her side and yelled at Thuy. "Child, what are you doing in there? It's not safe. Come out, there is glass everywhere!"

"Má . . . don't." Jessica grabbed her mother's arm, a suspicion taking hold in her mind.

"She had a fever this morning. She couldn't tell her left hand from her right. That girl must be so sick and confused. Bring her out here."

"Má, I don't think she's sick." She kept her gaze on Thuy, searching for any hint as to why she had done what she'd done. But nothing. Not even a slight grimace at being caught. Instead, Thuy maintained her defiant stance.

How could she betray them like this?

Debbie ignored her, refusing to believe what her eyes were telling her. "Thuy, it's okay, you can come out now!"

Jessica continued gripping her mother's arm, convinced it was the only thing keeping her from nose-diving right into the pile of glass.

Dustin, Mackenzie, and Phil had joined them now. Thuy still hadn't moved, hadn't responded, hadn't given any signs as to what she was thinking. So many questions rushed through Jessica's head.

"Why is no one helping her?" Phil cried, running up to a police officer. "My niece is trapped inside! She needs help coming out!"

The officer, a bald man with meaty cheeks and lips so thin they were barely there, looked at Thuy, then back at Phil, and gave a lackluster shrug. "Sir, all these folks managed to come out fine. I don't see any barriers blocking the way, do you? The path is safe and clear. She can come out anytime she likes."

Phil muttered something under his breath and begrudgingly walked over to the family. A female police officer began blocking off the store with yellow caution tape.

"Thuy!" Debbie yelled frantically. "It's okay, child. The police said it's safe to come out!"

Glass crunched under someone's shoes. Savannah stood right in front of them, blocking their view of Thuy. From under a thick layer of lashes, her dark brown eyes flicked over Jessica's frame before settling on Debbie's. The look she gave was not warm, not even lukewarm. It was something closer to annihilation.

"You took something of mine. I took something of yours," she said.

Expecting her mother to lunge with full force, Jessica gripped her arm even tighter this time, but Debbie didn't move. Her biceps didn't even flex.

"B-but we gave you back the ring," said Jessica.

Savannah glanced down at the diamond ring on her hand with an air of ambivalence. "You think this is about the ring? You were *stalking* me, crazy lady," she said, looking at Debbie. "You threatened to ruin my life, my marriage. You thought you had power over me."

Phil came to their side. "What are you talking about?"

Savannah peered down at his small frame. "He doesn't know? Well, well. I hate to break it to you, but your sweet little wife is actually a blackmailing bitch."

Jessica flinched as her parents locked eyes. He looked disappointed. She looked ashamed. Was this it for them? Was this the thing that would finally crack their marriage?

The expression on Phil's face quickly melted as he whipped his body back towards Savannah.

"Don't you dare talk about my wife like that! Stealing our customers wasn't enough, you had to go and steal our niece?" he said.

Her chest heaved with a throaty chuckle. "I didn't have to do much of anything. The girl came to *me* and asked *me* if she could come work with us. Poor girl nearly cried of happiness when I said yes. It was like someone saw her for once. It's like she'd never been appreciated in her whole life." She shifted to look at Debbie. "Maybe instead of spying on me, you should've focused on keeping your niece happy."

The bald police officer came back with both arms outstretched, corralling them all to move back.

"I'm going to have to ask you all to go home. We need this place cleared out," he instructed, waving his arms in a sweeping motion.

Before taking a step back, Jessica figured she'd try one more time. "Thuy, we're leaving. Please come with us!"

Finally, Thuy moved. It was just a few steps, but she moved. She was now standing in the stream of light that flooded the front half of the store. Jessica felt hopeful. If her parents could put loyalty above all else after everything that had happened, then her cousin could, too. There was a saying her father loved: A stiff tree that resists will crack in the wind, but a bamboo that bends can survive and adapt. Jessica shot her cousin a half smile from across the yellow tape, but Thuy only deflected, shook her head, and slipped back into the shadows of the salon.

CHAPTER THIRTY-SIX

Thuy

That night Thuy dreamed the house was on fire. Smoke seeped into her room, but her body stayed stuck to the bed, not even a finger could be lifted. Everyone else was rushing down the stairs to escape but no one came to help her. With every scream she let out, smoke filled her lungs until all her air passages swelled. Just when it felt too unbearable to breathe, she woke up with clammy skin and a racing heartbeat.

It was fifteen minutes to nine and the winter sun hung low in the sky, doing a pathetic job of lighting up her room. Thuy stayed put so she could pay attention to the rumblings of the house: footsteps trudging down the stairs, kettle coming close to a boil, faucet running in the upper-level bathroom. In the last twelve hours, she'd become acutely perceptive to the domestic sounds produced by the Trans for the sole purpose of avoiding them. She knew exactly when to step out to use the bathroom or when to quickly run downstairs to grab a glass of water without bumping into anyone. It was as if she were a ghost floating through the house, unseen and unwanted. Perhaps she'd been successful thus far because they, too, were doing the same thing.

Since she got home last night, nobody wanted to talk to her. Not even Dustin, the most empathetic of the bunch, could return a slight nod when she walked through the door and saw everyone eating dinner at the table.

Of course, she didn't have anyone to blame but herself. She didn't have to do what she did, but when she saw Savannah smoking a cigarette outside Take Ten the day after the funeral, she knew this was her chance.

"You're Savannah, right?"

"Yeah," she said, startled.

"I'm Thuy, from the salon across the street."

"Oh for fuck's sake! What do you people want from me now? My necklace? My car? You want the keys to my fucking car, don't you?"

Thuy was baffled. She wasn't expecting such vitriol.

"Don't look all doe-eyed innocent on me," Savannah fumed. "You know exactly what your family has done."

"I—I—I really don't know anything. I swear."

Savannah put the cigarette to her lips and eyed her up and down.

"Quit lying."

Thuy shrugged her shoulders.

"You really don't know?"

Thuy shook her head. She noticed a faint tan line on Savannah's finger. A line where a ring should have been.

"They took your ring," Thuy said, waiting for her to fill in the blanks.

Savannah flicked her cigarette and nodded.

Thuy was stunned. She had a hunch, but she didn't believe it until now. How could Debbie do this? This was a woman who routinely donated to the temple, who once scolded her for squishing a spider. Maybe she had changed. Or maybe she was that kind of person all along and Thuy just hadn't seen it.

"You happy now?" Savannah said. "Isn't that why you're here? To rub it in my face?"

"No," Thuy replied. "I actually came to ask . . . I came to ask if I could work here?"

"Excuse me? Why the hell would I hire *you*? I want nothing to do with your disgusting family."

Thuy was going to give her a spiel about how hardworking she was, how her designs were unmatched by anyone else. But looking at Savannah right then and there, she knew that was not the answer she wanted to hear.

"If you want to get back at Debbie, hire me."

Savannah swiftly turned her head. "What?"

"I'm their best nail tech. I bring in lots of loyal customers. You bring me to work at Take Ten and it'll devastate her."

There was a grand pause. Savannah squared her shoulders, inched closer to Thuy, and reached out to shake her hand. "Glad to hear I'm not the only one who hates that bitch."

Savannah might have only hired her out of vengeance, but Thuy didn't care. She was finally going to get what the Trans had long denied her: respect and autonomy. Plus, with the kind of money Take Ten brought in, she could buy her parents a new bed back home, one of those memory foam ones that would hug them in their sleep so they'd never again complain about the pain of sleeping on a concrete floor. Once they sank into that mattress, they'd forgive her for betraying the Trans. They had to. When you're poor, money becomes thicker than blood.

Still in bed, she heard the front door being locked and the car doors slamming shut. She was finally alone in the house. So she got ready for work.

The late February winds were merciless. They slapped Thuy across the skin and tied her hair in knots. The bus shelter was full, so she stood on the outer edge, hoping it would shield her from winter's violent lashings. It would have been simpler if she had just gotten a ride with the Trans, if she had just stayed at Sunshine. . . .

Thuy shook off that thought and reminded herself she did the right thing for her and her family. It was a mantra she repeated every time a twinge of guilt ran up her spine.

When she arrived at Take Ten, she was instantly greeted by the receptionist and the three technicians working that morning. She walked over to her station—her very own station—where her trusty tools were neatly lined up on a marble tray, disinfected and sanitized from the day before. Thuy scanned the salon. All the broken glass had been cleaned up and the window had been replaced in the middle of the night. It was as if yesterday never happened. Thuy marveled at how money and clout could make problems go away so easily. At Sunshine Nails, it took months and many frantic phone calls to get one burned-out fluorescent tube replaced.

After she was finished with her first customer, a broad-shouldered woman named Letitia who wanted simple black shellac, Thuy balked at the total cost of such a basic manicure (sixty-eight dollars). Then she beamed when she saw the tip (fifteen dollars). For a half hour's work, it felt almost criminal to accept the money.

For lunch, Thuy ate fried rice with Spam, which she quickly cooked at one in the morning when she was certain everyone was asleep. She made enough to last a week. That way she wouldn't have to sneak into the kitchen so late in the night.

Her coworker Andee sat across from her. Thuy remembered her from the launch party; her English accent and exaggerated but perfectly winged eyeliner were hard to forget. Today, her eyeliner was a vivid shade of admiral blue, popping between each strand of thick, black lash. She looked cool and confident. Just the type of person Thuy wanted to be. She made a mental note to buy herself some eyeliner.

"I read about you in that article," Andee said. For the next several minutes, Thuy blushed as Andee praised her for her talent and ingenuity, for quickly learning the art despite her age, background, and education. "You have to teach me how you get your lines so thin and crisp like that."

"Sure." Thuy flashed her a smile. She used to feel embarrassed by compliments. But something inside her had switched. She learned how to finally accept praise, especially when it was hard earned.

Another technician walked into the break room. She was tall and baby-faced, and preferred to be called Shelly, short for Michelle, even though it required the same number of syllables.

"Andee, did you tell her?" said Shelly, her voice turning up at the end.

"Tell me what?" asked Thuy.

"Oh, right!" Andee slapped the table. "We're taking you out to a tiki bar tonight. It's our tradition for every new girl. You've gotta say yes."

Thuy rarely went anywhere after a long day of work. Not just because she was bone-tired, but also because this was Toronto and if you went anywhere for fun, you'd be out at least fifty dollars. It just didn't make sense to work so hard only to waste it that same night.

At the sight of Thuy's hesitation, Shelly chimed in. "It's on the company dime, girl. Take Ten's paying for the whole thing."

Wow, thought Thuy. Her suspicions were officially confirmed: Money really did make everything better.

After closing up the salon, they walked arm in arm down the street to keep from falling on the ice-shellacked sidewalk. Thuy nearly slipped when she spotted Debbie way up in the distance heading towards them. It would be so awkward to run into her right now. She didn't want Debbie blowing up in her face in front of her new coworkers. She considered convincing the girls to quickly cross the street, but as they got closer, Debbie was the one who scurried across the road and escaped to the other side.

Thuy released her grip on the girls' arms. "Can you guys wait here? I just need to check something."

Thuy tried to run after Debbie, but the road was so slippery she was forced to go slowly or risk cracking her skull against the pavement. By the time she crossed the road, she lost sight of her. All she saw was a couple walking their dog.

She walked over to Sunshine Nails. It was closed. The only light on was the neon "Nails Nails Nails" sign dangling crookedly on the front window. She cupped her hands around her face and peeked inside. All the chairs were neatly tucked into their tables. Fresh rolls of towels sat on top of each pedicure station. Tattered magazines were neatly fanned out on the coffee table.

Something looked different about the reception area. She couldn't figure it out. Had they moved the chairs around? It looked bigger, less crowded somehow.

Then she realized the altar was not there anymore. The Buddha, the bowl of incense, the fruits and flowers, all gone.

How strange, thought Thuy. As she strolled back towards her coworkers, careful to avoid any black ice, she got a sick feeling in her stomach. Had they gotten rid of the altar because of what *she* did? Because *she* made them lose hope? People were sensitive like that. All it took was one unfavorable event to make them no longer talk to God.

CHAPTER THIRTY-SEVEN

Dustin

"Hey, check your inbox."

Dustin sat up straighter at his desk. He'd been daydreaming about a vacation, somewhere warm and lush where the street food reigned supreme over any Michelin-starred restaurant. That dream was quickly quashed when his coworker Kane notified him of a company-wide email that Chase had just sent.

Dustin leaned into his computer and clicked on it. The subject line read, "In response to Saturday's protest." The email needed a TL;DR at the bottom. It was much longer than it needed to be. Dustin skimmed it, getting the gist from some key sentences that pretty much said everything he needed to know. "We do not condone the violent actions of the protesters. . . . We stand by our decision to invest in the lawful development of the new building. . . . We're excited to inject new jobs and an ethos of innovation into the neighborhood."

Dustin couldn't help but roll his eyes. The email was full of generic statements that only served one purpose: to make the company look good. Three successive beeps came from his phone. It was the Moodstr app, telling him his sweat secretion levels were unusually high and asking if he cared to practice the box breathing method to bring his stress down. He selected no. Then the app suggested he try a quick five-minute guided meditation starting in ten, nine, eight . . .

249

"Fuck this." Dustin regretted putting the activity tracker back on and ripped it off. "I swear to god this place!"

Kane, who hadn't heard him or did but chose to ignore it, leaned back in his chair after he finished reading the email. "I heard the crowd got so rowdy the police threw tear gas and rubber bullets at them."

Dustin shook his head. "Seriously? That's the word going around? That didn't even happen. I was there!"

"You were? So what really happened then?"

"It was nothing like that. Some random idiot threw a brick into a store to get everyone riled up. He wasn't even part of the protest."

"Did they catch him?"

"No idea. We were told to go home after that."

"So what are people all worked up about then? I mean, that development is going to bring in tons of new jobs. And look around, there's not a lot of real estate left in this city. It's time that building got put to better use, you know? A tech darling like ours moving into the neighborhood is a good thing, right? Do you know how much money politicians would pay to get Amazon to open an office here? Hell, they'd probably get up on a stripper pole to bring in all those jobs."

Dustin leaned back on his chair with his hands behind his head. He considered what Kane said but couldn't get Hamza out of his mind. Everything he said about how the residents were ignored, about embracing the past instead of erasing it. He knew he had nothing to do with the demolition. He was just a powerless employee, after all. So why did he feel so guilty?

"I don't know, man," said Dustin. "Us moving in, it's gotta change some things."

"Well yeah, that's the point! That section can get real sketchy at night and I'm saying that as a dude!"

"So that's it then? We're demolishing a centuries-old building so we can get more streetlights on the corner?"

"I was just kidding, man. Think of the new businesses it'll attract, the new restaurants and stores. Come on! You're saying you don't dig that new fried chicken sandwich shop that opened up near your place?"

In that moment Dustin regretted posting all those photos of his visits to the Crunch Spot. Sure, he treated himself to an overpriced-but-so-worth-it sandwich every now and then. But that didn't mean he supported the rapid pace at which the neighborhood was changing, did it?

He thought about his parents and how they were struggling to make ends meet. Even Thuy saw how bad it had gotten and dashed on over to a higher-paying job. He'd never admit this to anyone, considering how betrayed his whole family felt, but the first thing he felt when he found out Thuy was now working at Take Ten was respect. Respect that she dredged up the courage to get out of a low-wage job and secure herself a more self-sufficient life. She found shelter before the storm hit.

Dustin glanced around the office, observing the frenzied energy of programmers slamming on their keyboards and salespeople taking phone call after phone call. Was Moodstr the impending storm?

"Trust me," Kane continued. "Moodstr being there, it's going to change things for the better."

Dustin turned his body towards the computer. There were already eight unread emails in the short time he was speaking to Kane. He didn't want to open any of them, knowing that behind each one was some type of demand on his energy, of which he had a dwindling supply right now.

But of course he had to open them. There were people who relied on him. That was how these things worked: He came in, did his job, and in return he received a biweekly paycheck that enabled his subsistence.

Behind his monitor, he spotted Chase in the glass-encased meeting room with three other men. Dustin had never seen them before. Clients, maybe? Whoever they were, they were acting like old friends, knocking their heads back with each laugh, spreading their legs as far wide as they could go.

"Who's Chase meeting with?"

"Investors," said Kane. "Apparently he's getting close to securing the first round of funding. And by the looks of it, I think he's got it in the bag."

"It's Chase; he can headlock a cub and still get the mama bear to like him."

"Well, whatever he's doing, it's getting him one step closer to securing a cool fourteen million."

"Are you fucking kidding me?" Dustin said. "Fourteen million and he can't even give me a ten percent raise?"

Kane said nothing and looked down at his phone, pretending to scroll through messages that appeared to already be read.

"What is it?"

Kane looked up, feigning an expression of confusion. "Nothing."

Dustin lowered his voice and leaned in. "Did he give you a raise?"

A guilty nod.

"Recently?"

Again Kane nodded.

"That motherfucker!" Dustin hissed under his breath. He didn't even want to know how much of a raise his coworker got; it might drive him over the edge. Besides, it didn't matter. The whole thing was unfair. He had been at Moodstr way longer than Kane, had come in many Sundays in a row to fix bugs and write code until his brain was fried. And for what? To make his boss even wealthier? He watched Chase through the glass with the intensity of a sniper. The vision of him once evoked godlike levels of adoration. Now, it just pissed him off.

Five more emails appeared in his inbox. He ticked them all, hit delete, and composed a new email.

Chase,
01001001 00100000 01010001 01110101 01101001 01110100 00100001
00100000
Respectfully up yours,
Dustin

He hit send and smirked. Picking up his jacket, he headed to Mackenzie's desk to inform her that he had just quit.

CHAPTER THIRTY-EIGHT

Debbie

The Trans didn't get many impromptu visitors, so when the doorbell rang as they were having bò chiên bơ for dinner, Debbie's immediate thought was that it was Jehovah's Witnesses.

"Everybody, be quiet. Turn down the TV. Don't answer the door. Sit right where you are!"

Ten seconds later, the doorbell rang again, and then again. *That was strange*, thought Debbie. They usually left after the first ring. Certain there were no preachers on the other side of the door, Debbie wiped the grease off her lips and got up to see who it was.

Thuy was standing there, her hair pulled back in a French braid and her eyes rimmed with black liner. She was holding something in her hand, but Debbie couldn't see past the opacity of the plastic bag.

"D-did you forget your keys?" she asked. It was the first time they'd spoken in days. Debbie knew it was a matter of time before they would inevitably have to talk. This game they were playing, living in the same house and avoiding each other, wasn't sustainable. Debbie had racked her brain coming up with an alternative. Kick her out of the house? Phil's brother would never forgive her. Pretend the betrayal never happened? Debbie would never forgive herself. Ultimately, she concluded there was no alternative.

"I must have left my keys upstairs," Thuy replied.

Debbie stepped to the side, waiting for Thuy to come in and walk straight upstairs as she'd done the past couple of nights. But this time, her feet remained planted on the stoop.

"Well, aren't you going to come in?"

Thuy's eyes went past her and straight to the dining room. "It smells really good in here."

Debbie didn't respond. She shuffled her feet and impatiently waited for Thuy to move along so she could shut the door and return to her meal. But Thuy didn't move. Her expression was like one of a dog who hadn't been fed in a long time.

"Oh just let her come sit with us," Dustin yelled from his seat.

"No." Debbie was surprised how fast that came out of her mouth. Thuy looked bewildered. "I don't . . ." She paused. "I can barely look at you much less have a meal with you."

Thuy lowered her head. "I understand," she said, walking towards the staircase. Debbie let out what felt like her last breath as she watched Thuy go up the stairs, stop midway, and turn around.

"You know what? I'm sick of eating in my room," Thuy said. And in one fell swoop, she came back downstairs and took a seat at the dining table. Debbie blinked a few times to make sure she was seeing correctly.

"I can't believe this girl. Look at the nerve she has to sit down as if she has done nothing wrong," said Debbie.

She could feel her armpits getting hot and sweaty as she glanced at Phil, waiting for him to back her up. Instead, he kept his gaze lowered at his food, his shoulders sagging as if he'd given in to the weight of resentment. It was times like these she wished her husband could match her level of anger.

Thuy was about to get up, but Jessica grabbed her arm.

"No, stay," said Jessica, before turning to look at her mother. "Má, this needs to stop. You can't hold on to this much bitterness towards her. It will kill you."

Debbie clutched a bowl of mắm nêm and stirred it with her finger to keep it from getting clumpy. She licked her finger clean, savoring the pungent pineapple and anchovy flavor that stuck to the back of her throat.

"You're taking her side, Jessica? My god, you were just as mad as I was!"

"I know," said Jessica, "but we need to try to understand where she's coming from."

"Understand? She has brought nothing but shame to our family."

"I—" Thuy tried to say something, but Debbie made certain to stop her.

"What can you say to make it better? That you did it for your family? What about us? What about the family that brought you here so you could live a better life? Are we less important to you?"

"No, that's not true," Thuy replied in a flustered manner. "You are like my own mother. I didn't mean to hurt you. I just—"

"You just what? Thought you could do better than what we've given you? We have given you everything from the first day you arrived in this country. A home, a job, an education. You should be grateful. Do you know how long it took us to find work when we got here? Trời ơi! If only you knew how many toilets we had to scrub before we opened this salon. Did you take that for granted as soon as you stepped on the plane? Where is your humility, child?"

Thuy raised her chin. "I *am* grateful for everything you've done. I'm sorry, thím. I did what I had to do for my family. They needed the money. And you guys said so yourself, family comes first. I'm truly sorry. I don't know what else to say."

"Leave! Just leave!"

Debbie looked down at the electric griddle and threw in a handful of raw shrimp and thinly sliced beef. She waited to hear the sound of Thuy's chair scraping against the floor, the whoosh of the door being swung open, followed by the footsteps of Thuy walking away from the house and out of their lives for good.

But she heard none of that. Instead, Thuy dipped a rice paper in the bowl of hot water and began making a beef roll for herself.

"What do you think you're doing?"

"I'm eating."

Good god. How did she learn to be like this? So defiant and disrespectful. It took all of Debbie's might not to reach across the table and shake some sense into that girl. She would have, if not for her husband and children, who all had that same desperate, pleading look in their eyes. Even Jessica was giving her that "just let it go" look. The last time she was met with this unanimous appeal was when she locked a customer in the nail salon for calling her a "chink bitch."

Fine. If her family so desperately wanted her to pull out the proverbial white flag, then so be it. Debbie grabbed a plate from the cupboard and set it in front of Thuy. For the next few minutes, everyone sat quietly and ate their beef rolls.

Debbie threw some more beef onto the grill along with some sliced onions. It sizzled with fervor, forcing everyone to lean back to avoid getting hot grease on their skin and clothes. The room quickly filled up with the smell of charred sweetness as everyone watched the red meat turn gray, then brown.

Phil turned on the TV. It was the third period and the Leafs were trailing the Sharks, one–nothing. It didn't seem like they were going to win, but there was no use telling her husband that. His entire life was dedicated to believing in comebacks.

"They're going to win this one, I just know it. You know how I know? I just wrapped the perfect beef roll. It's a sign. I have a good feeling," Phil said in that naïve, vulnerable way that only a man who had given in to self-delusion could.

"Everything is a sign for you," said Dustin. "Last time, he thought the Leafs were gonna win 'cause he caught the elevator just as it was about to close."

"Or that time the cashier forgot to charge him for a pack of gum and he took it as a sign from the heavens," Jessica joined in, both of them now cackling.

They took turns teasing Phil. It was clear what they were trying to do. Pretending like things were normal and injecting levity where there was none. Debbie could not play that charade. She wasn't built like that. Forgiveness had to be earned, not handed out to anyone and everyone like candy. Forgiveness to all was forgiveness to none.

From the corner of her eye, she observed Thuy and the way she was assembling her beef roll. The rice paper was much too thin. There were too many ingredients and too many air bubbles in the roll. It was going to fall apart the minute she took a bite. Debbie tried to ignore it, but she couldn't avert her eyes.

"You're doing it all wrong," she said, abruptly standing up. "This is how you roll it properly."

Debbie gently submerged the stiff rice paper into a bowl of warm water and placed it on her plate. The key to making the perfect roll was to lay down a thin layer of vermicelli on the rice paper, one or two pieces of beef, a couple of shrimp, a strip of onion, a sprinkling of garnishes, then carefully roll, roll, fold, and fold, keeping everything tight and compressed so no air pocket was trapped inside.

"There," said Debbie, handing it to Thuy. Her niece dipped the roll into the anchovy sauce and bit into it. She swallowed, quickly and satisfyingly, then looked up and smiled. Debbie did not dare return a smile.

Commercials came on and Phil looked away from the TV. "Child, it's about time we all ate together."

"I agree, chú," Thuy said, covering a mouth full of food.

"Listen, I'm sorry for everything," he told her. "I've been so stressed out with the salon that I haven't been treating you right."

"It's okay," said Thuy.

"No, it's not. Several times I made you cry, and I just ignored it. I didn't think about your feelings. It was wrong of me." He paused, his voice cracking. "I want you to never forget that we are so grateful you're here. I don't want you to feel like you're just a guest in this house because you're not. You never will be. You are like my own daughter."

Thuy looked at Phil and reached her arms out for a hug.

Debbie watched how easily the two of them set aside their differences and embraced each other like the past never happened. She had no idea how they did it.

Phil took a seat back down. "So tell me, Thuy. How is the job? How do you like it?"

"It's good. The people are nice. I have my own station and somebody else takes care of my appointments."

Thuy shot Debbie a quick but worrying glance. The fact that she was constantly checking on her reaction, squirming uncomfortably in her seat and choosing each word deliberately, was confirmation that Thuy felt guilty, and that meant Debbie was justified in her coldness.

"You have a new job. Dustin has no job. Who would have thought?" said Phil, holding up a roll dripping in mắm nêm.

"Hey!" Dustin shouted. "The other day you said you were grateful I didn't have a job because now I could help you shovel the driveway."

"I've been shoveling snow for half my life, I don't need you," cried Phil.

Jessica jumped in. "Just admit you need him, Ba. You can't even bend down to sweep dirt into the dustpan. I saw you the other day kicking it in with your feet." The whole table laughed except for Debbie, who threw more raw meat onto the griddle, sending another flurry of grease into the air.

Suddenly the TV roared with cheers as the Leafs scored for the second time that period, now up by one with thirty-nine seconds left on the clock. They all abandoned their half-eaten rolls and watched the screen. One second before the timer ended, the Sharks took a shot, but the Leafs blocked it as the puck bounced off the wall. The Leafs had won. Debbie stayed seated as the others jumped up and cheered and watched as the players in white and blue skated off the screen.

By the time they got back to the table, the beef had burned to a crisp on the grill pan.

"What happened here?" Jessica asked.

Debbie couldn't do it anymore. "I can't."

"You can't what, Má?" said Jessica.

"Pretend everything is okay. It's not okay. We're supposed to be a family. Family do not betray one another"—Debbie turned to Thuy—"especially not when we did everything to give you a better life."

Thuy's shoulders sank. "I will leave then. I will find a new place to live, starting tomorrow."

Without looking, Debbie could feel the searing stares coming from her husband and children. She ignored them and proceeded to scrape the burned meat off the pan.

"I have something for you," Thuy said. She bent over and handed her a plastic bag. It was weighed down by something solid and bulbous.

Debbie hesitated, but with everyone's eyes on her, she felt like she had to accept it. When she reached in, she felt something cold and heavy, something with many bumps and ridges. Her heartbeat quickened when she pulled it out and saw it was a laughing golden Buddha.

"Trời ơi! It looks just like the old one." Debbie covered her mouth. She turned it around and around, examining it from top to bottom to make sure it really wasn't the old one somehow magically fused together from a million shattered pieces. The rational side of her mind knew there were countless sculptures manufactured to look just like this one. But a part of her wanted to believe it was the original reincarnated. Debbie pressed the statue against her chest as if it were a baby she just birthed.

"I saw the salon didn't have one anymore so . . ." With her head down, Thuy turned around and headed towards the stairs.

"Wait," Debbie said. She looked at Phil, then down at the electric griddle. The large cube of butter she'd dropped in earlier was now congealing around the edges, the rich, nutty aroma fusing with the bitter smell of burned beef. Debbie leaned over to turn it off. "Stay, I'll make you another roll."

CHAPTER THIRTY-NINE

Phil

That night, Phil tossed and turned in bed but he wasn't sure why. He was happy to see his whole family in one room again. And even happier to have made amends with Thuy. So why couldn't he fall asleep?

Quietly, he slipped out of bed and snuck out of the room. He made himself a cup of tea and thought about everything that had happened over the past couple of months. The things he did. The things his family did. All to keep their little salon afloat.

When he found out what Debbie had done to fix *his* mess, and then what Jessica had done to fix *Debbie's* mess, he was outraged. Especially towards his wife. Blackmail? How could she have been so wicked? He never thought she was capable of such things. Perhaps that was why he couldn't sleep lately. He didn't know who he was sleeping beside.

Phil stared at the pile of mail sitting on the counter. His car insurance bill was at the top. It was still as exorbitant as ever, thanks to his terrible record.

A thought came to him.

Was this how Debbie felt when he had his DUI? Did she also feel like he had become someone she no longer knew? He paused, letting that revelation sink in. He truly, deeply hoped not.

Right then and there, he made himself a promise. If Debbie could love him for all his flaws, then he would learn how to love her for hers. It was an honor to be with a formidable woman who cast aside her judgments and was ready to forfeit everything for him. Phil might have done some dumb shit in his life, but building this perfectly imperfect family was the smartest thing he'd ever done. Holding tightly on to that thought, he went back to bed and slept soundly that night.

———

Thanks to Văn's generosity, the next three months went by without any problems for Sunshine Nails. The rent was paid in full every month. Jessica and Kiera got paid their original wage. For once, money wasn't even on their minds.

But when June started approaching, Phil quickly realized they were running out of money again. There was no way they could keep running the salon at this rate. It was the thing he'd been most afraid of. They were reaching a dead end.

Phil kept poring over spreadsheets and budgets and bills, trying to get all these numbers to make sense, but no matter how many different calculations he tried, everything kept coming up red. At one point, he looked up from the table and stared at his reflection in the mirror. It was his father, staring right back at him: the multiple creases on his forehead, the dark purple bags under his eyes, and the deep grooves along the sides of his mouth. Had he always looked this tired?

Phil thought about those early years when they opened the salon. How dizzyingly busy it was, how the salon seemed to always hum with a palpable energy from customers who couldn't get enough, how giddy they'd all get counting the day's earnings. That top-of-the-world energy had fizzled out so slowly, so subtly, like a roaring bonfire on its last flames.

A part of him was excited by all the possibilities of not working anymore. No more catering to women who were rude and picky. No more worrying about whether they'd have enough money for rent. No more headaches from inhaling chemicals all day long.

Then the worries kicked in: Who would he be without Sunshine Nails? What would he wake up for? What would tether him to society?

It wasn't only that he was afraid of the boredom and irrelevancy. He loved that damn salon. He loved being the person people unleashed all of their problems on. They walked in with overgrown cuticles and walked out with a good mood. This made him feel important, like he had given these people a level of peace they couldn't get anywhere else. The salon represented the first time in his life he got to call the shots. He would miss it all very much.

The only other person who loved that salon as much as he did was Debbie. That was why he had to break it to her.

"We won't last long at this rate," he told Debbie one night. She was slathering on a thick layer of face cream before bed and just like that, the sparkle in her eyes lost its luster. "We can keep trying. We can keep the salon open for as long as we can, but we won't be able to keep up with the payments." He walked over and held her hand. "I'll do whatever you want to do."

He waited for her to retaliate, to point out how he had failed so miserably by admitting defeat so soon. But instead, she squeezed his hand and said, "I know."

"You do?"

"I know this is what we must do. It's become too hard. It shouldn't be this hard."

"But everything you . . . *we* did, everything we fought for. I thought you wanted to save the salon so badly."

"I did," she said before moving to the bed and pulling a corner of the blanket out from under the pillow. "But ever since Thuy left to work at Take Ten, I knew it was time."

"Time for what?"

"Time to let go. Not just of Thuy. But the salon." She looked down at her hands. "Look at these. It's getting worse." There were red splotches all over. The skin had started to peel around the webs of her hands, and the joints of her fingers had deep, dry fissures that looked painful to bend. She grabbed the jumbo-sized tub of petroleum jelly on her nightstand and slathered her hands in it, making sure to seal in every single crack. Phil couldn't remember a time when her hands weren't like this. It had become such a ritual, her covering herself in emollient every night, filling the room with what he swore was a faint smell of gasoline. But for the first time, he saw her wince in pain as she rubbed her hands together. How did they get here?

Phil grabbed a clean pair of cotton socks from the drawer and slipped into bed beside her. Just as he had done every night for as long as he could remember, he covered her sticky hands with the socks, making sure to pull each one down past her wrist. He gently held both of her sock-covered hands in his and melded his forehead into hers.

"What will we do for money?" Debbie said it so softly he tried to pretend he didn't hear it. But try as he might, it was something he couldn't ignore.

"I will worry about that. I can clean. I can drive. I can wash dishes. I'll do whatever it takes. You don't have to lift a finger. Things will be easier from now on," he promised her.

"What do we tell the kids?"

Phil sighed. He thought about all the times he pretended things were okay when they were not.

"We tell them the truth."

CHAPTER FORTY

Jessica

Jessica came home to find everyone seated around the dining table. There was a single cup on the table as black coffee dripped slowly down the phin filter onto a thick layer of condensed milk. Something weird was going on.

"What's everyone doing in here?"

"We were waiting for you," said Dustin. "Má and Ba have some news to share with us."

Jessica's heart sank. This did not sound good. She examined all their faces for clues as to what it could be. Her mind raced to the worst-case scenarios: divorce, cancer, death. She took a seat and braced herself.

Phil uncrossed his arms and leaned into the table. "We've decided"—he paused to clear his throat—"we've decided not to renew the lease on the salon. We're closing the salon next month. For good."

Jessica's eyes widened. Thuy's jaw dropped. Dustin's face froze.

"W-what?" Jessica sputtered. "I don't understand. Why?"

"Your mother and I talked yesterday and we are getting old and . . . the numbers aren't adding up, and we . . ." He lifted his chin a little higher, not looking at anyone or anything in particular. "If we keep going, we're not going to survive."

Thuy started to cry. "Oh my god, no! Is it because of me? I'll come back. I can come back and help!"

Debbie spoke up. "No, my child, it has nothing to do with you. Our business was struggling way before you even arrived. It was just a matter of time before it caught up to us."

"There must be something we can do!" Jessica said, standing up. "Are you sure this is the only way?"

Her parents looked at her with sad eyes and nodded in tandem.

"I can't believe it," said Jessica. "After twenty years. This is it? This is really it?"

The coffee was still dripping into the cup. Everyone sat in silence, unsure what to do except watch until the very last drop fell down like a wilted leaf off a tree.

Later that night, Jessica locked herself in her room. She smoked an ungodly amount of weed and called her ex-fiancé three times. Fortunately for her, he didn't pick up and his voicemail was full, so she couldn't even leave a message and make a fool of herself if she wanted to.

She scrolled through his most recent photos. A picture of a baseball stadium. A picture of a basil-topped margherita pizza. A picture of him shirtless in the mirror, biceps flexed, stomach sunken in. Then she saw it. A picture of him and that woman he was fucking against their marble counter. There was a pear-shaped diamond ring on her finger. The caption read, "Yes. Yes. A thousand times yes."

Jessica felt like an air mattress that had just been slashed, deflated, and turned shapeless beyond recognition. Then she felt sick. She rushed to the window and hurled up the contents of dinner. On the last heave, thin white noodles flew straight out of her nostrils. She looked down. Vomit was splattered all over her mother's newly opened tulips.

After taking a hot shower and changing into clean clothes, Jessica splayed her body across her bed. She closed her eyes and imagined she was lying on train tracks, listening to that rhythmic rumbling sound in the distance. The picture became clearer with each breath, but the sound never got louder, the train never got closer. No matter how hard she tried, she couldn't imagine her own death. Maybe she was too high or too nauseated. Or maybe she was just the kind of person who never got what she wanted in life. No fiancé. No home of her own. And now she had no job.

She involuntarily laughed, remembering a moment she had earlier when she was sitting beside her mother at the salon, toweling off people's feet and giggling at how ticklish the customers were. It was just a flash, as quick as a blink, but it was there, that glowing feeling of purpose. She felt like her family needed her, the salon needed her, hell, the entire world needed her. She loved that feeling. But now that the salon was closing, what did she have left?

At least she had candles. Lots of them. They were covered in dust and were probably as old as the nineties, but they still smelled strongly of whatever the label claimed they smelled like (Christmas Cupcakes, Swimming in the Rain, Midnight Tobacco). She went around the room and lit every single one of them before lighting another joint.

Minutes or maybe hours later, she wasn't quite sure, Jessica woke up to Dustin frantically stamping out a fire on her desk with a pillow. "What the fuck, dude!"

The fire was extinguished by the time she could rub the sleep from her eyes and see things clearly. Black paper ashes were everywhere. A candle jar had exploded on her desk, leaving a pool of hardening orange wax all over loose sheets of paper.

"Are you crazy? Why did you fall asleep with all these candles on?" Dustin whispered harshly, gritting his teeth. He shut the door quietly so as not to wake everyone up.

Jessica shrugged. She didn't have a good explanation.

"What time is it?" she asked, her voice croaking from dryness. She could still taste the sourness of the vomit.

"Three, almost four. Seriously, you're fucking crazy you know that? Good thing I came in here. I only woke up 'cause that smell was driving me crazy."

Jessica breathed in the air. The room smelled downright awful, not just from the burned paper but also from the Frankensteinian mixture of weed and vintage candles. She stood up and blew out each flame.

"Thanks, I guess."

"You guess? I just saved your sorry ass. The least you could do is share some of your weed." He picked up her roaches from the orange Café Du Monde tin. "These can be composted you know? If it was once alive, it can be necrotized."

Jessica rolled her eyes. "Did you just make that up?"

"Registered the trademark and all."

She let out a half smile.

"So I guess we're both unemployed losers, huh?" said Dustin, sitting at the end of her bed.

"Can you believe they're closing the salon? After all these years?"

"Definitely didn't see that one coming."

"What are they gonna do now? They barely had a life outside of work. They don't even have hobbies."

"Hey now, who said gambling and gossiping aren't hobbies?"

"I'm serious," said Jessica. "I can't picture them without the salon. It would be like . . . like . . . picturing them without their heads!"

"Thanks for the image."

Jessica licked her lips and scanned the room for her ChapStick, only to find it was in her pocket. "I just think it's a bad idea is all."

"For you or for them?"

"Come on, I didn't need this job."

"Didn't you, though? You seemed to like it."

"Please, it was a stopgap."

"Okay, well, what happened to the job search? That's all you talked about when you got home and now nada. You haven't even gone to an interview in months. With your experience, you can't tell me you didn't get at least a few more callbacks."

Flattered, she pulled out her phone and checked her unread emails. There were three interview requests that she never responded to. Things had been so busy at the salon that she never got around to it. And now those emails were several months old. There was no way those positions were still open.

"And what about you? You're the idiot who quit a decent-paying job."

Dustin produced a flatulence-like sound from his mouth. "I *am* an idiot. I let those greedy bastards undercut me for too long. The guy that sits next to me makes five thousand more. And he *just* started. Most people in the office don't even know his name yet. Do you know how much I busted my ass to get a promotion? It's actually embarrassing how much I gave to that company."

"That really sucks. And here I thought you had it good."

"Nope." Dustin lay down on the bed and gazed at the popcorn ceiling.

Despite feeling sorry for herself, Jessica felt even more sorry for her brother. He was smart but a late learner, always had been. He once believed that friends stayed friends forever, that love was like a rom-com, that bad things only happened to bad people. Today, she got to witness the moment he learned the lie that hard work always gets rewarded.

"So what are you going to do then? Look for another job?" said Jessica.

"Actually, I've got a meeting tomorrow."

"That fast? With who?"

"Well, it's not a job per se. You remember Hamza? From the protest? I reached out to him to see if he needed any volunteers, you know, see if he needed any help keeping this demolition from happening."

Jessica was stunned. "I had no idea you cared all that much."

"I mean, I didn't at first. But this is our neighborhood. I wanna be able to look up and see the sky, not a bunch of carbon-copy office towers, you know?"

"What's Mackenzie think of all this?"

Dustin turned around to lay on his stomach. He grabbed the ChapStick from her and smeared it across his lips twice. "At first she thought I was crazy. But eventually she mustered up the courage to quit, too. She wasn't happy at that job. Neither of us were. It just took us some time to realize the reason we were sticking around was because we were scared of the future."

Jessica nodded. It was chilling how much she could relate. She thought back to the day she caught Brett cheating and how, for a split second, a part of her was ready to forgive him because she didn't want to start a new life from scratch.

She took off her socks and inspected her feet. The corners of her big toe-nails were digging into her flesh, making the sides tender to the touch. She'd trimmed so many toenails but couldn't remember the last time she trimmed her own. There weren't even any nail clippers in the house. They'd always cut their nails at the salon.

"I guess Mackenzie can dump your ass now that you're no longer working together, eh?" Jessica joked.

Dustin let out a fake laugh. "No way would she dump me! Not with these good looks. Besides . . ." He was about to say something, then stopped.

"What? Tell me!"

He hesitated. "We said 'I love you' the other day," he said with a wistful twinkle in his eye. "Whatever happens, I think we're forever."

She cringed, unable to say anything back because it was just incredulous how much delusional optimism he still had. Always an idiot, that one.

Getting up very slowly, not wanting her head to spin, Jessica hovered over the desk and felt flush with embarrassment over the fact that she nearly burned the house down. She carefully set aside the broken glass and picked out anything that had come into contact with flames or wax. An old teen magazine with a young, red-lipped Gwen Stefani on the cover. A stash of yellowed tax documents from the eighties. A binder filled with grade seven math notes. She threw them all in the waste bin.

That was when she noticed the bottom of the binder. Old sepia-toned photos had melted and stuck to the back panel, their edges blackened by the fire. Jessica desperately prayed that these weren't the few photos her parents had managed to bring to the country.

Fortunately, one photo was still intact. It was a pixelated picture of her parents standing side by side on a beach, a row of huts in the background. Their faces were youthfully plump and darkened by the sun. His smile was wide and relaxed while hers was reserved. At their feet was the green vinyl suitcase that they'd brought to Canada. It was bulging on the top and sides as if all the dreams and trauma they'd shoved inside were about to explode any minute. She turned the photo around and found a faint scribble. *Songkhla camp, 1983.*

"How do they do it?" Jessica asked, not looking up from the picture.

"Do what?"

"Pack up and leave everything behind, just like that? First their country, now the salon."

Dustin sat up on the bed. "You tell me."

"What?" She whipped her head towards him.

"You left us. All those years ago. It seemed perfectly easy for you."

"Come on. That was different. I moved for love, for opportunities."

"I really don't see how that's different."

Jessica looked back at the photo. Their worlds felt galaxies apart. She never stopped to see the ways in which they were similar.

Dustin looked pleased with himself as he walked towards the door. "To answer your question, maybe it's easier to leave when you don't look back so often."

"Yeah. Maybe that's it," she said before climbing back into bed.

Before Dustin could fully exit the room, she had one more question to ask. "Hey, we're not going to let them close the salon without a party, right?"

He tapped his temple. "You read my mind." Dustin let out an audible yawn, which made her do the same. "So what are you gonna do now?"

"Hmm." Jessica stalled. She hated that question. It implied she should have a blueprint for her life. But what was the point? Mapping out your future meant believing in a universe that favored you. Not her. She'd seen enough to know that that was wishful thinking, reserved for people who already had the resources to make their desires come true. For people like her and her parents, planning was futile. Instead, they would have to ride out into the ocean and hope for the best.

Dustin didn't wait around for an answer. He got up and flicked the switch, leaving her alone in the dark. Then, just for a second, she felt that glowing feeling again.

CHAPTER FORTY-ONE

Phil

With only twenty days left before the end of the lease, the salon needed to be cleaned and emptied. Not even a stray nail clipping was to be left behind.

Phil focused on selling off the inventory. With Debbie's help, he used his phone to take pictures of the supplies, and with Dustin's help, he posted them on Craigslist. It would take at least a week before they made their first sale; someone wanted to buy the four gallons of pink, pearlized, cherry-scented hand soap. Phil was so excited that someone, anyone, was interested that he got a little overzealous and asked if the person also wanted to buy the matching hand lotions, the paraffin wax, or perhaps a dozen or so orange buffer blocks.

No, just the hand soap, they wrote back.

Oh well, who could blame him for trying? It was a habit he couldn't shake.

On a very humid day in June, Phil and Debbie carved out a part of their afternoon to drop off all the items they managed to sell online. They didn't feel comfortable giving strangers their address, so they insisted on driving to each buyer's home.

The first stop was located on the east end, just past the Riverside Bridge. The address the person gave was a town house among a sea of similar-looking,

273

brick-clad town houses with tiny front lawns. Phil texted the person when he arrived. He was surprised when he saw Rebecca, a client of theirs.

"Hey, guys!" she yelled from the stoop, waving at them. They almost didn't recognize her. She had no makeup on, her brown hair was in a loose bun that looked like it could unravel at any second, and she was dressed in sweatpants and a baggy green shirt.

"Rebecca! What a weird coincidence," said Phil.

"I was so sad when I heard you were closing down the salon." She stretched out her arms and showed Phil and Debbie her red gel nails. There was at least half a centimeter of growth, but all Phil could see was his fine craftsmanship and how well the gel had still bonded to her nails.

"We're still open until the end of the month. You should come in and get those looked after. One last time," he said.

"One last time. I can't believe it. I guess I'll be saving lots of money once the salon closes," she laughed, revealing her straight white teeth.

Phil opened the trunk to reveal the box of industrial-sized soap. "What do you need all this soap for anyways?"

"I'm addicted to the smell. It's like strawberry shortcake. Now every time I wash my hands, it's going to remind me of your salon."

Phil smiled. He examined her face, trying to remember whether she worked as a massage therapist or a chiropractor. Or maybe it was a physiotherapist? He might not have been able to remember what she did for a living, but he could describe in intricate detail how she got her pit bull mix. He remembered when she first adopted the dog from the animal shelter, how she was so worried when he had contracted cherry eye and had to wear a cone for two weeks, and how she nearly had a heart attack the time he somehow got unclipped and went sprinting down the road, stopping traffic from every which way.

"How's Mykonos?"

She turned and pointed at her house, where the dog had been peering at them through the window. "Do you want to go inside and meet him?"

"No, it's okay. We've got other drop-offs to make. It was nice to see you again. Stop by before the end of the month, okay?"

"You bet. Bye, Phil! Bye, Debbie!"

The next buyer was located closer to home, so they headed back west towards the Junction. Of all the items he was selling, he was surprised anybody wanted a box of five hundred orange nail buffers.

"Who needs that many buffers?" said Debbie. "Are you sure we're not going to some maniac's place?"

"I'm sure they don't let those kinds of people on the internet."

"Still, just in case they try to kidnap us, I'll stay in the car and be ready to call the cops if you get snatched inside."

Phil chuckled. "Debbie, that's not going to happen." He paused to let his mind consider this possibility, and then chuckled again. "You've always had problems trusting strangers."

"You would, too, if you read the news," she replied.

"I read the news."

"Listening to people bicker back and forth on your TV screen is not *reading* the news." Debbie used air quotes when she said "reading," looking quite proud of herself.

For the next fourteen minutes, the amount of time the GPS said it would take to reach their destination, his wife sat quietly, looking out at the street, closing the window each time they passed a dusty construction site.

The directions took them down a narrow, one-way residential street. They found parking directly in front of the house. Debbie stayed in the car as Phil carried the box to the front porch. Despite there being hundreds of pieces in the box, it felt like carrying air. He rang the doorbell.

A broad-shouldered man in his forties, maybe fifties, answered the door.

"Hi, I'm Phil. You wanted to buy the buffers?" He opened the box to show him.

The man looked down at the box, then at Phil, then he pressed his glasses back up towards his face. "Allegra!" he yelled. "Somebody's here for you."

Allegra came to the door. She wasn't dressed in her corporate attire like she always was when she came to the salon. She looked like a completely different person in her bright orange ruffled shirt and loose-fitting denim.

"Surprise! Bet you didn't know it was me that was emailing you!"

Phil was stunned. And confused. "What? Wait, but why? Why do you need all these buffers?"

"I don't. But I heard you were closing down, and then I saw all your stuff being sold online. It's not hard to tell from those pictures you took. Would it kill you to get better lighting?" She laughed. "Anyway, I wanted to help out and told some of your other customers to chip in."

"Wow, I don't know what to say." It warmed him to the core knowing how loved their salon was. "But what are you going to do with five hundred buffers?"

"Listen, I've got dozens of cousins who can take these off my hands. I'll be fine." Allegra stepped out into the sunlight and closed the door behind her. "So only a few more weeks left, huh? Are you going to invite me to your party or what?"

"Party?" said Phil. "No, no, there's no party. We don't want to make it a big deal."

"A big deal? Phil, it *is* a big deal. You've been on that block for two decades and you're moving out, leaving our nails out to dry. Now I'm going to have no choice but to go to that stupidly overpriced salon across the street. This *is* a big deal. You *have* to have a celebration."

Phil scratched the back of his head. "I don't know, Allegra. There's so much to do in the next few weeks, I don't think—"

Allegra pursed her lips. "You were always a stubborn man. Maybe it's a good thing you're closing. You were getting on my last nerve."

They laughed until Allegra let out a snort, causing them both to cackle uncontrollably.

Allegra took out some bills from her pocket and handed them to Phil. "What's this for?" he asked.

"The buffers!"

"Oh right," he said. "Please, you don't have to. You've helped us out so much already."

"There you go again with the stubbornness. Take it!" It was as if she knew he wouldn't extend his hand, so she leaned in and stuffed the money into his shirt pocket.

He smiled and nodded. There wasn't much left to say. They both waved Allegra goodbye as they drove away.

Back in the car, Debbie seemed as if she wanted to say something.

"Phil?" she asked.

"Yeah?"

"This is the right thing to do."

Phil wasn't sure if it was his ears, but it sounded like a question. *This is the right thing to do?* There was a big difference between a statement and a question, and he desperately wanted to ask for clarification. Was she suddenly having doubts? Or was he the one having doubts and his brain was subconsciously imagining an upwards inflection where there wasn't one? He stayed silent through several intersections, then decided that it didn't matter. He was sixty-three years old and had become very familiar with that insistent tug of self-doubt. His mind would frantically cling on to those thoughts, let it cripple him and make him feel worthless.

But this time, he let it wash over him like a gentle lapping wave. For the rest of the drive home, he let himself forget how terrified he was of the future.

CHAPTER FORTY-TWO

Dustin

More than a century ago, there was a notorious hotel located on the north-west corner of Weston Road and St. Clair Avenue called the Heydon House. People from all over North America would travel to the hotel to place their bets on the infamous cockfights. When the fight was over and the money was exchanged, these men did not go into the night quietly. Fights, public drunkenness, and all sorts of disturbing debauchery spread out onto the streets like an oil spill, despite police attempts to rein it in.

One night in 1903, a massive fight broke out between the cattlemen and the railway workers, causing irreparable damage to the property and the arrest of three people. The residents of the Junction, most of whom were working-class immigrants, had had enough and voted to ban the sale of alcohol altogether. That prohibition would not get lifted until 1997, the year Sunshine Nails opened.

Dustin was standing in that very hotel, except it was now a brewery. He had been eavesdropping on a tour guide who was recounting the building's history. He found it rather fascinating.

"And the irony of it all is that there are now multiple breweries in this neighborhood," the tour guide said before quickly adding, "Ours is obviously the best." This elicited a couple of laughs. Then the group disappeared behind a door.

"Order for Dustin Tran," the cashier called out. Dustin raised his hand. A scrawny, heavily tattooed man brought out a 24-pack of beer cans, followed by another 24-pack. He paid the man and carefully placed the cartons in the trunk of the car. He hoped this would be enough for the party.

His parents were going to freak. They didn't want to draw attention to the fact that Sunshine Nails was closing forever. Sad events warranted a sad send-off, his mother said. But Dustin and Jessica ignored her. This was the end of something big. It deserved a celebration.

Before heading to the party, Dustin drove to the Henderson building and parked right in front. The bulldozers were gone. The building was still intact. The protest had worked.

When word of the demonstration got out, media outlets went wild for the story. Help the Henderson received thousands more signatures for their petition. And dozens more volunteers stepped up to do whatever they could to save the building. Collect donations. Call councillors. Camp outside. Dustin, with his skills, volunteered to revamp the website. He even made it easier for people to sign up for shifts to guard the building.

Eventually, their hard work paid off. Several politicians stepped in and demanded the demolition be stopped. The proposed sixteen-story commercial building was officially canceled. The future home of Moodstr would no longer be.

A coworker messaged him that day and said Chase had smashed his laptop to pieces when he found out the news. It was the best text Dustin ever received.

It felt good to finally do something that made a real difference. But he had no idea what he was going to do next with his life. Up until he quit, every move he made had always been carefully planned out. Now he was lost, directionless.

Maybe that was okay. Maybe it was okay to not know what you were doing. He buckled up his seat belt and put the car in drive.

CHAPTER FORTY-THREE

Thuy

Thuy was quickly finishing up with a customer. She didn't want to miss the party.

Swipe, swipe, swipe, and done. She turned on the UV nail lamp, carefully placed the customer's hand inside, and waited for the gel to cure.

It saddened her to see Sunshine Nails close. She made so many memories there. Learned so many new English words. Discovered a talent she didn't know she had. That place taught her more than any teacher ever could.

She couldn't help but feel like she had done something to cause this. If she had never taken this job at Take Ten, then maybe they wouldn't have had to shut it all down. But Phil and Debbie kept assuring her it wasn't her fault. They said she did the right thing by finding a better opportunity, that they would've done the same thing. She just had to trust their word.

The customer left a ten-dollar tip and asked if Thuy had any openings two weeks from now. She did not. Her calendar was full from now until the end of August. It would be a long summer of seventy-dollar pedicures, ninety-dollar gel nails, and very generous tips. By the end of the season, she would have enough money to send home to Vietnam. Now her family could finally dig out that squat toilet and replace it with a Western-style toilet. Her family had been begging for that thing for months.

Thuy hoped by next year she would have the means to go to school and become a nurse like she originally wanted. Ever since she came to Canada, she set aside all her dreams to put other people first. In doing so, she had shrunk herself so small she forgot who she was and what she wanted. Fortunately, these past few months had taught her that she was capable of so much more. That she had a voice and she could use it. Thuy took off her black apron and told the other nail techs she was going on break.

Her friends from the ESL class were waiting outside. Youngju. Samra. Bobby. She had finally worked up the courage to invite them to the party and to her relief, they all said yes.

"Are you ready to go?" said Samra.

Thuy nodded. She was ready for anything.

CHAPTER FORTY-FOUR

Jessica

Helium balloons layered the ceiling. Sparkling garlands were strung up on the walls. There was even an ice-cream cart outside, serviced by a teenager who happily accepted twenty dollars and a free manicure to do the job. Had Jessica overdone it? Probably. But it was her parents. She would blow up a billion balloons for them.

"Jessica!"

She couldn't miss the unmistakable silhouette of Gigi. From across the street, she could see her yellow stiletto nails waving vigorously in the air.

"Wait for me! I'm coming to you," she yelled over the buzzing of cars whizzing by at speeds too fast for the street limit.

"Here," said Gigi, handing her a white box. She licked her lips and wiped a bead of sweat off her forehead. The air was brisk but the sun was warm.

"What's in here?" Jessica asked.

"You'll see," Gigi replied, flashing a sly grin.

Now Jessica was starting to feel warm. Based on the slight whiff of vanilla frosting, she deduced that it had to be some kind of cake.

"Why are you giving me this?"

"I heard about the salon closing and the party and I wanted to contribute somehow." Gigi stuffed her hands in her pockets. "Listen, I feel terrible about everything that happened between us—"

Jessica interjected, "Let's not get into this now. It's really not a good time."

"No wait! It'll only take a few minutes. I just— I just wanted to say that I shouldn't have said those things about your parents. It was completely wrong of me. And I shouldn't have judged you for working at the salon. I put my job first before our friendship. I was just so obsessed with impressing Savannah and this huge company that I lost sight of what's important."

Jessica stared at her. "Do you remember what you said?"

Gigi shook her head.

"You said our friendship had gone way past its expiration date. You said we were only friends because you felt bad for me. You called me a *nobody*! That really fucking hurt."

Gigi lowered her head. "I know, I know. I'm so sorry! You mean so much to me and I would really hate to lose you as a friend. You know me. I can be a total bitch sometimes."

Jessica unexpectedly laughed, nearly dropping the cake. Jokes aside, she could sense Gigi's desperation to make everything right.

"I'm glad I can still make you laugh," said Gigi.

"Well, admitting you're a bitch is a first step."

Gigi shifted from one foot to the other. "I dropped them. Take Ten."

"You what?"

"They're no longer my client. Thank god! To be honest, they were a night-mare to work for. Unnecessary meetings. Endless back-and-forths. Passive-aggressive emails. I feel so much lighter now that I never have to deal with Savannah ever again."

"Wow. This is big. You never quit anything!"

"I know! I'm like a Pokémon; I'm evolving."

They both burst out laughing.

"Honestly, I feel bad for everything that happened, too," Jessica said. "I'm sorry I put you in an awkward situation. It was so messed up what my mother did to Savannah."

"Are you kidding?" said Gigi. "I was literally so impressed when I found out. Your mother is such a badass! Like, that is some boss level stuff."

Jessica chuckled but said nothing in return. She wasn't sure what would become of their friendship going forward. Could they go back to the way things were? Probably not. But maybe they could forge something new, something better than the one before. She had to try, right?

Jessica refrained from dropping everything and giving her a hug. It was too soon. Instead, she tilted her head in the direction of the salon.

"You want to come to this party or what?"

Gigi flashed her a smile. "Yes!" She paused before going inside. "But wait! I have a surprise for you. Are your parents here?"

CHAPTER FORTY-FIVE

Debbie

Debbie and Phil were told to come to the salon at four o'clock sharp. When they arrived, they could hear George Michael belting "Freedom" inside.

If it were up to Debbie, they would have shut down quickly and quietly. No fuss. No decorations. Just fade into history. Stores closed down all the time. Laundromats turned into bakeries. Hotels into breweries. Soon, something would come to replace Sunshine Nails and it would be like it never existed.

A handful of customers were already there, as well as some of their friends. Văn and Angel chatted by the pedicure station. Allegra and Kiera clinked beer bottles. Eleanor and David Dang were here, too. Even Mrs. Ho put on her brightest magenta dress to bid farewell to the salon.

Debbie did what was expected of her. Said hello to everyone. Thanked them repeatedly for coming. Smiled for impromptu photos. Made small talk.

There was one question that seemed to be on everyone's mind: "How does it feel?" She wasn't quite sure how to answer. Were they asking how does it feel to no longer work? Or how does it feel to say goodbye to the one job that gave her purpose? Regardless, what she really wanted to say in return was: Does it matter anymore?

By the time she made it to the back of the salon, the kids were just about to bring out plates of cheese and crackers.

"You're here!" said Dustin.

Thuy walked up and gave her an effusive hug. She'd been doing that a lot lately.

"You don't have to work today, child?"

"I'm on break. I can't stay for long."

Debbie smiled, reaching out to tug on the lobe of Thuy's ear. Such a hard worker, that girl. She reminded her a lot of herself.

"And she . . . Savannah . . . doesn't mind you're here?"

Debbie had been avoiding saying that name ever since the protest. Not because she felt guilty for what she'd done. But because that wretched woman had won. The neighborhood was all hers. She had everything, and Debbie had nothing to show for her twenty years of running a salon except for contact dermatitis. Who was she kidding anyway? People like Savannah always won. She couldn't believe she'd been so naïve in thinking she could rewrite the ending.

"Savannah hasn't come back for a few months. I think her work might be done in this neighborhood," said Thuy. Everyone let out a sigh of relief. "But I think she might be back. There are rumors they're opening another location in Toronto. I think they're looking at a new space uptown." Thuy paused. "But you can't tell anyone I told you that!"

"Jeez! Another one?" said Phil.

"Good for them," Debbie murmured while rolling her eyes. "Good for them."

There was a knock on the door. Jessica walked in with an apple-cheeked brunette.

"Do you all have a minute?" Jessica asked. "My friend Gigi has something to tell you all."

They turned their attention to her friend. It took a moment for Debbie to realize this was the same girl Jessica went to grade school with, except she'd traded in her loose pigtails for a chic low bun.

"First of all," said Gigi, looking directly at Debbie and Phil, "I'm very sorry to hear you're closing. From everything Jessica has told me, I know how important this salon is to you."

Debbie gave a quizzical look to her daughter, who shrugged in return.

"But I think I might have a way you guys can stay open."

Debbie was intrigued, but then remembered why they were doing this in the first place. "It's too late," said Debbie. "The salon is closing in a few days. The business registration is going to be officially expired."

"You might want to hold off on that," Gigi responded.

Debbie waited for her to say more.

"I know a place. A fitness studio, a client of mine. They're closing in a few months. It's got tall ceilings, hardwood floors, brand-new track lighting. They're relocating and I think the space could be perfect for you. You might need to give it a new coat of paint, tear down all those mirrors, install new plumbing. I can take you to see it tonight if you're interested."

Debbie wasn't sure what to say. All she could think about was how expensive it all sounded. "I don't know. Money has been tight for us."

"That's the thing. The rent is really affordable right now. The studio owner's stepdad owns the building and he only charged them less than two thousand a month. If you take over the lease, he's willing to keep it the same. It's a steal!"

"I don't know . . ." Debbie repeated.

"There's no catch. I swear. You'll have to commute a bit farther and the neighborhood is still developing but I swear to you this is a legitimately good deal."

A cold quiet settled across the room. Somehow the silence felt louder than the music and chattering throngs outside.

"So, what do you think?" asked Gigi. "Can I take you guys to see it?"

Debbie scratched her itchy hands, stopping only when she noticed Phil's disapproval. They exchanged a look. The answer was no.

"Are you serious?" Jessica cried out. "You're not going to at least check it out? This is a chance at a fresh start. You can keep the salon going like you always wanted. This opportunity is practically being handed to you! Who knows when you'll get one like it again?"

Debbie was taken aback by that outburst. Then it hit her. How could she have not seen it before? The things Jessica did. The sham marriage she was willing to get into. All to save the salon. It was so obvious to Debbie now. Jessica needed the salon more than they did.

"Child, do you know what khi vui khi buồn means?"

Jessica shook her head.

"That's how we feel about closing the salon. We are sad to say goodbye to it, but we are happy at the same time. We've been working so hard all our lives and now it is time for rest. It's been a long time since we have been able to truly rest."

"That's it? You're just giving up because you're *tired*? I'm so . . . confused. I thought this was what you wanted. This is your whole life!"

Debbie inched a bit closer to squeeze her daughter's arm. "You should not be worrying about us. We are the parents. It is our job to be worrying about you."

Jessica dropped her head and let out a long breath. "But what will you guys do for money?"

"We will find work. We always do."

Gigi interrupted. "So is that a no then?"

There was a pause. "Wait," Jessica said. "I'll go check it out with you."

Everyone turned to her, confusion plastered on their faces.

"You mean, just you?" replied Gigi.

Jessica hesitated, then spoke with conviction. "Yes, I'm gonna do it. I'm gonna open my own salon." She turned to look at Debbie and Phil. "I know this sounds crazy, but I can do it. I know I can. You won't have to work ever again. I mean it. I'm going to take care of you both from now on."

Debbie didn't know what to say. Her heart was pounding and her legs felt wobbly. "Oh, you silly child. We don't need to be taken care of. You go live your life however way you want. Don't let us be a burden."

Jessica raised her voice. "I mean it. I want to do this. You've done so much for us and I just, I don't know, I want to do the same for you." She stared at them with that impossibly doe-eyed hope in her face. "Please."

Debbie's eyes filled up with tears. She spent her whole life wondering what the point of all her suffering and sacrifice was. As her daughter stood before her with that longing to bring peace to their lives and a promise to look after them until the day they died, Debbie finally found the answer she was looking for. Everything she did, everything she endured, had always been for her children. It was so simple, yet she'd lost sight of it so many times.

Phil walked up to Jessica and embraced her as tight as he could. "We've seen you work very hard, child. You took care of this salon like it was your own. And to hear you say all these things a parent dreams of hearing . . ." A tear fell from his eyes when he said these next words, "I've never been more proud of you than I am now."

Now Jessica was sobbing. "Thanks, Ba. To be honest, I have no idea what I'm doing. I just know it's what I want to do."

"You'll know what to do," Debbie said, stating it like it was a fact.

"Why are you so sure of that?"

Debbie walked over to the shelf and reached up to grab the laughing Buddha. Every time she looked at it, it seemed as if there was a new expression on his face. His lips were unnaturally red as if tinged by too many goblets of wine. His mouth was so wide it seemed his skin might crack under the pressure. As a kid, she used to believe that if you rubbed his round protruding belly, it would bring you good luck. She laid her thumb on the indented belly button and stroked it a few times.

"I want you to have this. It'll give you the luck and courage you need."

Jessica held the statue in both of her hands like it was a baby chick just hatched. "Thuy gave this to you though."

Thuy looked at Jessica and smiled, mouthing the words *it's okay*.

Gigi, standing impatiently by the door, asked again, "So, what's the answer?"

There was a pause. "I'll do it," Jessica said. "Oh my god, I'm doing it!"

Everyone stepped in for one large group hug. Debbie did not want to let go.

———

The Trans devoted the next several hours to mingling with their customers. Debbie spoke at length with Eliza (short, natural, French tips always) and Heather (long, gels, the more glitter the better). Several customers asked if they could come to the Trans' house to get their nails done. When Debbie laughed and said no, they insisted on giving her money. For what? she'd say. Just because, they'd reply. These kind gestures made Debbie misty. It was

starting to get to her, the emotional toll of saying goodbye to a community of
people who had her back.

"Picture! Picture!" someone was shouting. It was Mackenzie, swinging
around a camera as she herded the Trans together for a photo. Squeezed between her two children, Debbie stared out at the sea of people gushing at
them like they were saints. When the camera flashed, a tear streamed down
her face.

———

After the last person left, Debbie locked the door. It was just after eight and
she was finally alone. Jessica left with Gigi to see the studio. Thuy was back at
work. Phil and Dustin drove the garbage bags and empty bottles to the depot.
The silence was overwhelming, so she turned on the television and let the first
thing that came on fill the salon.

As an infomercial peddling antiaging creams roared from the speakers,
she swept the floors. She scrubbed the tables. She packed a few more supplies.
Standing before the wall of nail polish, she didn't know where to start. This
wall had paralyzed many a customer in the past as they vacillated between the
reds and the pinks and the purples. Debbie finally understood why now. There
were just too many possible versions of oneself to choose from.

Someone knocked on the door. A woman with curly brown hair peered
through the glass and made eye contact. Debbie shook her head and pointed
to the closed sign. The woman continued to knock, a desperate look spreading
across her face.

Debbie unlocked the door and opened it just a crack. The woman flashed
her hands to show her overgrown cuticles, raised ridges, and chipped black
polish. "Please, I'm desperate. I've got an important event tomorrow. It won't
take long. I promise!"

Debbie hesitated. It was late. She should be at home right now, resting on
the couch with her feet inside a pulsating massager.

But the woman's eyes were glued to hers, pleading as if she'd been
stranded for months and hadn't had a single sip of water. Debbie turned
around to scan the salon. Half their supplies were packed up in boxes, but

there was still a table, a chair, and a few tools lying around. How could she deny this woman?

"Come inside then," she said, waving the customer in.

As Debbie locked the door, she saw a couple walking down the street. They looked so in love, arm in arm like elks whose horns were permanently locked together. "Go ahead and pick a polish. I just need to take care of something."

Debbie walked a block over to the mailbox. She reached into her pocket and unfolded the envelope that she'd been carrying around for weeks. Inside was the photo. Savannah might have deleted it, but Debbie printed it out long before anyone else knew she had it. It was a gut instinct, a natural compulsion to save, passed down from ancestors who tenaciously held on to everything that reminded them of the past.

She scribbled down an address and a name: Lionel Shaw. The thought of the photo ending up in the hands of Savannah's husband lent a soft contentment in Debbie's heart. It was incredibly easy to find someone's address on the internet. All you had to do was want it bad enough. They could take away her salon, but they could never take away the power she wielded in the flick of her fingertip.

She dropped in the envelope and hurried back to the salon.

"So, have you picked a color yet?"

Acknowledgments

I was eight when my parents opened a nail salon in Halifax, Nova Scotia. When I got older, I learned there were thousands of nail salons all over North America run by Vietnamese immigrants who wanted to paint a new life for themselves after the Vietnam War. That's why I wrote *Sunshine Nails*. For all the immigrant nail techs out there. I hope you enjoyed being the main characters for once.

I am so grateful for my wonderful agent, Carly Watters, for loving the Trans as much as I do. From the moment you said yes, you made my dreams come true. Thank you to my incredible editor, Loan Le, for championing Vietnamese stories like this one. From day one, you got the story and made it more luminous than I could ever hope.

Thank you to the Atria team and everyone who helped make this book a book. Thank you to Simon & Schuster Canada, particularly Sarah St. Pierre and Janie Yoon, for bringing the Trans home to Canada.

Thank you to my writing group for reading so many rough drafts during your precious free time: Kyoko Sato, Rylan Daly, Samantha Burton, Sharon Hanson, and Louella D'Souza. I treasure those café critique sessions more than you know.

Thank you to Ann Y.K. Choi, the first person to read my novel in full, and to Diaspora Dialogues for connecting us. Ann, I wouldn't have written *Sunshine Nails* if you hadn't written *Kay's Lucky Coin Variety*. That book sparked something in me and showed me all that was possible.

I couldn't have done it without funding from the Canada Council for the Arts, Ontario Arts Council, and Toronto Arts Council. These grants helped me pay my bills and allowed me to write without financial worry.

To the editors at *Worn Fashion Journal*, for letting me write about the history of Vietnamese nail salons and catapulting my desire to write more on the topic. To my teacher Ibi Kaslik, for taking me aside and telling me I could be an author one day. Back then, you saw what I could not.

To all the friends who have cheered me on for the past five years and asked me, "How's your book going?" You have no idea how much your relentless check-ins propelled me to finish. I especially want to thank Yasmein Oweida for coming up with the name of the salon, which eventually became the title of this book. As soon as you said it, I knew it was the one.

To my siblings, Tony, Michael, and Amy, for filling our family with so much laughter. The reason there is any humor in this book is because of you.

To my love, Chris, for encouraging me to finish this novel even when all I wanted to do was give up and cry. You make everything lighter and brighter and better.

To Gemma, my perfect little beautiful darling. You will always live in my heart, where it will beat for you until the end of time.

Lastly, there would be no *Sunshine Nails* without my parents, Lan and Phai. Thank you for taking me to the library. Thank you for letting me read at the dinner table. Thank you for sharing your stories, even the ones that hurt to tell. Cảm ơn, cảm ơn, cảm ơn.

About the Author

M ai Nguyen is a National Magazine Award–nominated journalist and copywriter who has written for *Wired*, the *Washington Post*, the *Toronto Star*, and more. Raised in Halifax, Nova Scotia, she now lives in Toronto. *Sunshine Nails* is her first novel.

@bymainguyen